MW01716859

Lovecraft in the 21st Century

Lovecraft in the 21st Century assembles reflections from a wide range of perspectives on the significance of Lovecraft's influence in contemporary times. Building on a focus centered on the Anthropocene, adaptation, and visual media, the chapters in this collection focus on the following topics:

- Adaptation of Lovecraft's legacy in theater, television, film, graphic narratives, video games, and game artwork
- The connection between the writer's legacy and his life
- Reading Lovecraft in light of contemporary criticism about capitalism, the posthuman, and the Anthropocene
- How contemporary authors have worked through the implicit racial and sexual politics in Lovecraft's fiction
- Reading Lovecraft's fiction in light of contemporary approaches to gender and sexuality

Antonio Alcala Gonzalez is founder of the *International Gothic Literature Congress* and chair of the Humanities Department at Tecnologico de Monterrey, Mexico City.

Carl H. Sederholm is professor of Interdisciplinary Humanities at Brigham Young University and chair of the Department of Comparative Arts and Letters.

Routledge Studies in Speculative Fiction

Speculative Satire in Contemporary Literature and Film
Rant Against the Regime
Kirk Combe

The Biopolitics of Gender in Science Fiction
Feminism and Female Machines
Emily Cox-Palmer-White

Character and the Supernatural in Shakespeare and Achebe
Kenneth Usongo

Human Evolution and Fantastic Victorian Fiction
Anna Neill

Genre and Reception in the Gothic Parody
Framing the Subversive Heroine
Kerstin-Anja Münderlein

Lovecraft in the 21st Century
Dead, But Still Dreaming
Edited by Antonio Alcala Gonzalez and Carl H. Sederholm

For more information about this series, please visit:
https://www.routledge.com/Routledge-Studies-in-Speculative-Fiction/book-series/RSSF

Lovecraft in the 21st Century

Dead, But Still Dreaming

Edited by
Antonio Alcala Gonzalez and
Carl H. Sederholm

Routledge
Taylor & Francis Group
NEW YORK AND LONDON

First published 2022
by Routledge
605 Third Avenue, New York, NY 10158

and by Routledge
2 Park Square, Milton Park, Abingdon, Oxon, OX14 4RN

Routledge is an imprint of the Taylor & Francis Group, an informa business

© 2022 selection and editorial matter, Antonio Alcala Gonzalez and Carl H. Sederholm; individual chapters, the contributors

The right of Antonio Alcala Gonzalez and Carl H. Sederholm to be identified as the authors of the editorial material, and of the authors for their individual chapters, has been asserted in accordance with sections 77 and 78 of the Copyright, Designs and Patents Act 1988.

All rights reserved. No part of this book may be reprinted or reproduced or utilised in any form or by any electronic, mechanical, or other means, now known or hereafter invented, including photocopying and recording, or in any information storage or retrieval system, without permission in writing from the publishers.

Trademark notice: Product or corporate names may be trademarks or registered trademarks, and are used only for identification and explanation without intent to infringe.

Library of Congress Cataloging-in-Publication Data
A catalog record for this title has been requested

ISBN: 978-0-367-71304-1 (hbk)
ISBN: 978-0-367-71308-9 (pbk)
ISBN: 978-0-367-71306-5 (ebk)

DOI: 10.4324/9780367713065

Typeset in Sabon
by SPi Technologies India Pvt Ltd (Straive)

Life is a hideous thing, and from the background behind what we know of it peer daemoniacal hints of truth which make it sometimes a thousandfold more hideous. Science, already oppressive with its shocking revelations, will perhaps be the ultimate exterminator of our human species—if separate species we be—for its reserve of unguessed horrors could never be borne by mortal brains if loosed upon the world.

"Facts Concerning the Late Arthur Jermyn and His Family"

I have frequently wondered if the majority of mankind ever pause to reflect upon the occasionally titanic significance of dreams, and of the obscure world to which they belong.

"Beyond the Wall of Sleep"

Contents

Acknowledgments x
List of Contributors xi

Introduction 1
ANTONIO ALCALA GONZALEZ AND CARL H. SEDERHOLM

1 Lovecraft and the Stage: A Recent (Re)Discovery 12
KEVIN J. WETMORE, JR.

2 Lovecraftian Landscapes and Cosmic Horror in HBO's *True Detective* (2014) 28
ELISABETE LOPES

3 An Uncanny Absence: Lovecraft in Brazilian Cinema, 1975–2016 43
LÚCIO REIS FILHO AND SHEILA SCHVARZMAN

4 The Masks of E'ch-Pi-El: Interpreting the Life and Work of H.P. Lovecraft 57
JOHN GLOVER

5 "It's like a maze you can't see": Comics Cryptomimesis of Lovecraft and the Lovecraftian in Alan Moore's *Neonomicon* (2004–2005) and *Providence* (2015–2017) 71
STUART L. LINDSAY

6 Man or Cartoon: H.P. Lovecraft as a Comics Character 90
TOM SHAPIRA

7 Drawing the Unknowable – Lovecraft's Cosmic Horror in *Magic: The Gathering* and *Hearthstone* 103
SUZANNE ALBARY AND RICHARD ALBARY

8 Nuclear Inhumanities: H.P. Lovecraft's "The Colour Out of Space" and the Dread of Contamination 118
IAN FETTERS

9 An Eldritch Crisis: Capitalist Paradigms in the Cthulhu Mythos 132
DANIEL DONCEL

10 Lovecraft's Viral Networks: A Contaminated Ethics for the Chthulucene 143
NATASHA REBRY COULTHARD

11 "It Was the Vegetation": Ecophobia and Monstrous Wilderness in the Fiction of H.P. Lovecraft 158
FREDRIK BLANC

12 Nautical Horror and the Anthropocene: Lovecraftian Monsters in William Eubank's *Underwater* 172
ANTONIO ALCALA GONZALEZ

13 Racial (In)Visibility, Cosmic Indifference: Reimagining H.P. Lovecraft's Legacy in Victor LaValle's *The Ballad of Black Tom* (2016) 186
KATHLEEN HUDSON

14 Finding "Something and Not Nothing": Women of Color Repurposing Lovecraft in the Posthuman 21st Century 201
LOREN BARBOUR

15 The Crawling Chaos: H.P. Lovecraft, Closed Gothic Spaces and "Dungeon Crawler" Videogames 213
KEVIN CORSTORPHINE AND MATTHEW CROFTS

16 Dreaming in Layers: Lovecraftian Storyworlds in Interactive Media 227
EOIN MURRAY

17 "Bringing … Uncertain Geographies Under … Control"? Exploring the Lovecraftian 'Walking Simulator' 241
DAVID SIMMONS

18 Queering Cthulhu: Reclaiming Lovecraft's Monstrous Others 253
NOWELL MARSHALL

19 Weird Bedfellows: H.P. Lovecraft, m/m Romance, and the New Queer Families of Jordan L. Hawk's *Whyborne & Griffin* Series 268
BRIAN JOHNSON

20 Lovecraft, Hauntology, and the Rhetoric of Unthinkability 284
MICHAEL CERLIANO

21 Falling into the Void: "Nyarlathotep" 295
CARL H. SEDERHOLM

Index 308

Acknowledgments

The editors would like to thank Harmony Gailey for her help in organizing the manuscript and Jeffrey A. Weinstock for having the idea that we would make a good team for this project.

Carl would like to thank Cyndi for running the zoo and the asylum. Thanks, also, to Nathanael, Janelle, Chester, and Tabby for keeping life interesting and fun.

Tony would like to thank Miriarwen for being the black candle supporting him in all horror-related projects. *Ph'nglui mglw'nafh Cthulhu R'lyeh wgah'nagl fhtagn*. Pochia, thanks to you and all your bunch for being around us at all times.

Contributors

Suzanne Albary has a PhD in Art History and Theory from the University of Essex, awarded in 2016. Her research interests center around aesthetics and identity with particular focus on dress and representation. She is currently a senior lecturer at the University of Suffolk.

Richard Albary has an MA in Continental Philosophy from the University of Essex, awarded in 2009, and an MSc in computer science from the University of Hertfordshire, awarded in 2017. His research interests focus on the philosophy of H.P. Lovecraft and the aesthetics of horror.

Antonio Alcala Gonzalez is founder of the *International Gothic Literature Congress* and chair of the Humanities Department at Tecnologico de Monterrey, Mexico City. He has co-edited both a *Gothic Studies* special issue on *Nautical Gothic* and the critical collection *Doubles and Hybrids in Latin American Gothic*. He is currently preparing a monographic study on Nautical Horror. He has published articles and book chapters on creators such as H.P. Lovecraft, Algernon Blackwood, William Hope Hodgson, J.R.R. Tolkien, Ivan Albright, Carlos Fuentes, and Juan Rulfo as well as the connection between the Gothic tradition and the lyrics of Underground Metal music bands.

Loren Barbour is an English PhD student at the University of California Riverside. Her interests include feminist and queer theories, Black studies, speculative fiction, Gothic studies, and horror. She writes about monsters and the creative ways we find to love them. She is especially focused on the ways women, queer people, and people of color are reimagining narratives of monstrosity, conventionally used against them.

Fredrik Blanc is a PhD student in English at the Manchester Metropolitan University where he is currently writing a thesis on Nautical Horror and the Body at Sea. He holds a BA in English and Linguistics from the University of Geneva as well as MAs in English and Gothic Studies from the University of Lausanne and Manchester Metropolitan University, respectively. His research interests include the Weird and the Gothic, Nautical and Tattoo Studies from decidedly eco-critical and new materialist frameworks.

Michael Cerliano is a graduate student in the doctoral program in rhetoric at Texas Woman's University. His work focuses on occult philosophy and esotericism, weird and gothic fiction, rhetoric, and film studies.

Dr. Kevin Corstorphine is lecturer in American Literature at the University of Hull, and Programme Director in American Studies. His research interests lie in horror and Gothic fiction, both literary and popular, and he is particularly interested in representation of space and place, the environment, and haunted locations. He has published widely on authors, including Bram Stoker, H.P. Lovecraft, Ambrose Bierce, Shirley Jackson, Stephen King, and Clive Barker. He was co-editor for The *Palgrave Handbook to Horror Literature*, published in 2018. He is currently working on several research projects, including US imperialism, haunted graveyards, and Ecology in nineteenth-century US literature. He is a member of the editorial board for the journal *Gothic Nature*.

Natasha Rebry Coulthard is a senior instructor in the Academic Writing and Cultural, Social, and Political Thought Programs at The University of Lethbridge, located on the unceded territory of the *Siksikaitsitapi*. Her interdisciplinary research combines Gothic studies with post-anthropocentric theory, rhetorical criticism, and critical discourse studies. She has published works on Richard Marsh's engagement with mesmerism, Arthur Machen's Gothic neurology, and the post-humanist nature of Victorian dietetic discourses.

Matthew Crofts was awarded his doctorate at the University of Hull, England, UK, for his research on the importance of tyranny to the Gothic mode, utilizing a range of Gothic novels and historical eras. Matthew's previous publications include chapters on historical figures in MacDonald Fraser's Flashman in *Neo-Victorian Biofictions* (2020), an article in the special "Alternative Dickens" issue of *Victoriographies* (8:1, 2018), a chapter on Dracula's multimedia legacy in the edited collection *Gothic Afterlives* (Lexington Books, 2019), and a joint-authored chapter on Gothic rats in the edited collection *Gothic Animals* (Palgrave, 2020).

Daniel Doncel graduated from the University of Salamanca with an English Studies degree, went on to earn a Masters in Education from Carthage College in Kenosha, Wisconsin, and is currently a PhD student in the Spanish, Italian and Portuguese Department of the University of Virginia. His areas of study include Marxism, Caribbean and Latin American Studies, as well as weird fiction. He has previously written about the subversion of the detective genre in Blade Runner 2049 and the antidetective traits of H.P. Lovecraft's fiction.

Ian Fetters is a researcher of the Weird and the Hauntological He is the 2017 recipient of the S. T. Joshi Endowed Research Fellowship for the project "Lovecraft's Dark Continent: *At the Mountains of Madness* and Antarctic fiction." He is also the first recipient of the Donald Sidney-Fryer Research Fellowship in 2018. His research on Lovecraft and Clark Ashton Smith has been published in the journals *Lovecraftian Proceedings* and *Penumbra*. In light of recent world events, his research interests have taken a grim turn toward "Extinction Romances" of the Anthropocene epoch. Ian works in an abandoned library that rots amidst the ruins of specter-haunted San Luis Obispo, California.

Lúcio Reis Filho is a PhD in media studies at University Anhembi Morumbi (São Paulo, Brazil), historian, and author specializing in the relations between cinema, history, and literature, focusing on the horror and science fiction genres. Among articles on horror cinema and related themes, he wrote the chapters "Lovecraft out of Space: Echoes of American Weird Fiction on Brazilian Literature and Cinema," in *Lovecraftian Proceedings No. 3* (2019), and "Demons to Some, Angels to Others: Eldritch Horrors and Hellbound Religion in the Hellraiser Films," in *Divine Horror: Essays on the Cinematic Battle Between the Sacred and the Diabolical* (2017). In his dissertation, he investigated Lovecraft's appropriations by American cinema.

John Glover is humanities research librarian and associate professor at Virginia Commonwealth University, where he supports students and faculty in their research, instruction, and related activities. His scholarship encompasses horror and weird fiction, research practices of creative writers, and academic librarianship. His nonfiction has appeared in *The Silent Garden*, *Thinking Horror*, and *New Directions in Supernatural Horror Literature: The Critical Influence of H. P. Lovecraft*, among other venues. As J.T. Glover, he has published fiction in *Best New Horror*, *Pseudopod*, *The Children of Old Leech*, and various journals and anthologies.

Kathleen Hudson earned her PhD in Gothic Literature from the University of Sheffield and is currently a course instructor at the United States Naval Academy and Anne Arundel Community College. She is the author of *Servants and the Gothic: 1764-1831, A half-told tale* and editor of the collection *Women's Authorship and the Early Gothic: Legacies and Innovations*.

Brian Johnson is an associate professor of English at Carleton University in Ottawa, Ontario, Canada, specializing in sexuality, gender, and genre. His articles on Lovecraft's influence and sexuality have appeared in *The Age of Lovecraft* (Minnesota, 2016), *The Lovecraftian Poe* (Lehigh, 2017), and *New Directions in Supernatural Horror Literature* (Palgrave, 2018). His essays on superheroes and sexuality have appeared in *Sexual Ideology in the Works of Alan Moore* (2012), *Superheroes and Masculinity* (Rowman & Littlefield, 2020), and *Supersex: Sexuality, Fantasy, and the Superhero* (Texas, 2020).

Stuart L. Lindsay is a PhD graduate and teaching assistant at the University of Stirling. His research and publications focus on Memory and Trauma studies and Gothic studies in graphic novels, gaming, Internet sub-culture, and contemporary nostalgia.

Elisabete Lopes is an English professor at the Polytechnic Institute of Setúbal, and a researcher at the ULICES (University of Lisbon Centre for English Studies) since November 2015. She holds a master's degree in English Studies and a PhD in the field of North-American Literature, with a particular emphasis on gothic, horror, and more recently, weird Fiction.

Nowell Marshall is the author of *Romanticism, Gender, and Violence: Blake to George Sodini* (Bucknell University Press, 2013) and essays on queer literature, transgothic, and speculative fiction and film. He teaches at the University of Wisconsin–Madison.

Dr. Eoin Murray is from Bangor and holds a PhD in Game Narratives from Bangor University. His current research includes creative fan responses to popular game narratives and gender in mainstream video games. His publications include a creative piece published in the 2017 Bangor School of Creative Studies and Media Anthology and a book review published in *The Journal of Gaming and Virtual Worlds*.

Sheila Schvarzman is a PhD in social history at the State University of Campinas and professor of the post-graduate program in media studies at University Anhembi Morumbi (São Paulo, Brazil). She has specialized in the history of cinema and the relations between cinema and history and edited with Fernão Ramos the book *Nova História do Cinema Brasileiro* [*New History of Brazilian Cinema*, 2018] in two volumes, contributing three chapters, one of them dedicated to highest-grossing films in Brazilian contemporary cinema, among other articles and publications.

Carl H. Sederholm is professor of Interdisciplinary Humanities at Brigham Young University and chair of the Department of Comparative Arts and Letters. He is the editor of *The Journal of American Culture* and co-editor (with Jeffrey Weinstock) of *The Age of Lovecraft*. His other work includes the co-edited volume *Adapting Poe: Re-Imaginings in Popular Culture* (with Dennis Perry) and the co-authored book (also with Dennis Perry) *Poe, the 'House of Usher,' and the American Gothic*. He has also published essays on authors such as Edgar Allan Poe, H.P. Lovecraft, Stephen King, Jonathan Edwards, Lydia Maria Child, and Nathaniel Hawthorne.

Tom Shapira is a PhD candidate at the Tel-Aviv University School of Cultural Studies.He is the author of *Curing the Postmodern Blues: Reading Grant Morrison and ChrisWeston's The Filth in the 21st Century* (Sequart, 2013) and *The Lawman* (PanelXPanel, 2020). His research appeared in *Utopia and Dystopia in the Age of Trump: Images from Literature and Visual Arts* and The *Ages of the Flash*. He writes about comics for such publications as *PanelXPanel*, *The Comics Journal*, *Haaretz*, and *Solrad*.

David Simmons is a senior lecturer in English and Film and Screen Studies at the University of Northampton. He has published widely on US horror and weird fiction, including the books, *American Horror Fiction and Class: From Poe to Twilight* (Palgrave, 2017) and *New Critical Essays on H.P. Lovecraft* (Palgrave, 2013). David is currently writing a monograph on giant monster movies for Liverpool University Press.

Kevin J. Wetmore, Jr. is a professor of Theater Arts at Loyola Marymount University in Los Angeles where he teaches horror theater and horror cinema, among other topics. He is the author of over a dozen books, including *Eaters of the Dead: A Cultural History of Cannibal Monsters*, *Devil's Advocates: The Conjuring*, and *Post-9/11 Horror in American Cinema*. He has also twice been nominated for the Bram Stoker Award for his editing volumes such as *The Streaming of Hill House* and *Uncovering Stranger Things*. In addition to being the author of over a hundred book chapters and academic articles on everything from Godzilla on stage to African zombie plays, he was also the director of the first ever public performance of Lovecraft's only play, *Alfredo*.

Introduction

Antonio Alcala Gonzalez and Carl H. Sederholm

In a letter to J. Vernon Shea, H.P. Lovecraft reflects on how often he felt like he belonged more to the eighteenth century than to the twentieth. "I have never felt quite right without a powdered periwig [and] small-clothes," he explains (182). Lovecraft's thoughts were largely brought on by his experience seeing the film *Berkeley Square* (1933) and how it not only captured his sense of the late eighteenth century but also told the story of a twentieth century man who successfully willed himself back to that time. In that same letter, Lovecraft goes on to express a long-standing discomfort with time and the way he never completely feels at home in his own day:

> I always have a damnable feeling of living in some *unreal world of the future*. When I see a railway or telephone or motor-car I always have a short of impression that it is a joke or dream; [and] one reason I can't take the contemporary world—or the Victorian world of my own physical youth—seriously is that I *unconsciously* assume that these worlds are nightmares *not yet born*.
>
> (183, emphasis in the original)

The author from Providence never imagined that, despite his personal longing for the past, his life and work would leave a lasting impact not only on the nightmarish twentieth century but that it would continue to grow even stronger in the twenty-first century.

The purpose of this collection is thus to assess Lovecraft's place in the present moment by gathering together several critical essays that can help us understand why he is so influential across such a wide variety of media. Lovecraft's impact on contemporary culture is so strong that it has become increasingly commonplace to read him in terms of contemporary concerns over what we can and cannot understand. Although horror has typically addressed fears that appear to belong to the world, scholars are increasingly exploring the prospect of fears that reach beyond the seemingly comfortable range of human experience. Mark Fisher, for instance, comments on the ways Lovecraft attempts to

DOI: 10.4324/9780367713065-1

pull apart "the hierarchical relationship between fiction and reality" (24). Similarly, Eugene Thacker draws directly on Lovecraft to underscore the prospect of horrors beyond human thought and experience, particularly as we think about the unknown and the unknowable (9). One assumption behind such readings is that Lovecraft makes more sense in a world that no longer appears to make sense or that is teetering on the brink of collapse. Through his view of humanity as something insignificant when contrasted with a cosmic background, Lovecraft anticipated the kinds of concerns over uncertainty proper to the twenty-first century.

Although we are not threatened by physical hyperobjects,[1] at least not those in the shape of Lovecraftian monsters, we struggle harder every year to accept that no matter how much we pretend to be in control of what happens on Earth, we cannot escape the destructive effects of mere natural events which we insist on calling catastrophes. We face the undeniable truth that things like earthquakes or hurricanes cannot be stopped; besides, we also have to consider that this book was produced within the context of a pandemic whose social and economic effects will be felt all around the world for years—maybe even decades—to come. Finally, there is also the fact that, even if our coexistence with Nature is removed from the equation, human societies of the twenty-first century live in constant turmoil as their own members struggle to coexist in the face of persistent racial and gender prejudices.

Anthropocene

As articulated by some of the contributors to this book, the growth of interest in Lovecraft's work over the first two decades of the twenty-first century coincides with the growth of interest in understanding what the Anthropocene is and to what extent we are both responsible for it and directly affected by it. In general critics agree on locating the beginning of the Anthropocene in the Industrial Revolution. However, what is most relevant for our purposes is to understand how much the Anthropocene affects the actor responsible for it: humanity. In this regard, we need to consider that "humans have become a telluric force, changing the functioning of the Earth as much as volcanism, tectonics, the cyclic fluctuations of solar activity or changes in the Earth's orbital movements around the Sun" (Hamilton et al 3). Our intrusion into the workings that planetary systems have followed for countless millennia triggers unprecedented reactions from nature.

In this context, Gry Ulstein proposes an interpretation of Cthulhu—as well as other Lovecraftian creatures, or those of more recent vintage, but definitely inspired by them—as an "Anthropocene monster" (50)[2]. However, the presence of Lovecraftian thought in the Anthropocene goes beyond illustrating concerns related to our devastation of the environment. His monstrous creatures come from distant pasts and futures while the ultimate monster in our own times is humanity itself. We have become a monstrous entity whose manipulation of the planet affects everything around us—including ourselves. The effects of our marks left on the planet are so vast that we can neither grasp nor escape from their devastating proportions: "The Anthropocene is an antianthropocentric concept because it enables us to think the human species not as an ontically given thing I can point to, but as a hyperobject that is real yet inaccessible" (Morton 2016, 25). This forces us to reconsider the Western view that has placed humanity on the top of all the organic and inorganic presences. This view has surrounded us since at least the second half of the eighteenth century. When we rethink our alteration of the environment and the drastic changes it has produced, it becomes necessary to recapture the option of considering ourselves as part of nature once more. When we take such a position, we can understand that the apparent counterattack from natural forces, which seems to be the response to our disruptive manipulation of air, land surface and underground, as well as the bodies of rivers and oceans, is but a mere process through which the Earth's systems readjust to the alterations performed by our actions. The answer to stop the devastation is to quit our human-centered perspective and understand that many other possible perspectives emerge from non-humans (2018 xli). Cthulhu and other Lovecraftian creatures force his protagonists to accept that an anthropocentric perspective is meaningless when pictured against the vastness of the universe. Similarly, contemporary adaptations of the writer's thought and monsters in our *Anthropocenic* times can make us remember that we are not alone on this planet, but surrounded by countless life forms who are affected by our actions and whose existence is directly related to ours.

Adaptation

In *The Age of Lovecraft* (2016), Jeffrey Weinstock and Carl Sederholm addressed several of the ways Lovecraft has been adapted into media such as heavy metal music, comics, movies, television shows, visual art, and other media. The point was not to be exhaustive but to suggest something of the ways Lovecraft continues to influence others decades after his passing. Since that book was published, Lovecraft has remained a viable source of inspiration for adaptations in a wide variety of media. Lovecraft is sometimes understood as a challenging source for would-be adapters because his work has very little direct dialogue and frequently includes descriptions not well suited for visual media. And yet, these apparent difficulties have not prevented a host of people from drawing on Lovecraftian themes, moods, and environments to evoke fear and uncertainty in their own work. They also draw on Lovecraft to challenge the seemingly fixed boundary between the earthly and the cosmic. As technology continues to expand and develop, it is likely that creative teams will continue to explore the possibilities Lovecraft offers. As Linda Hutcheon explains, technology is often a significant instigator of creative innovation:

> Technology, too, has probably always framed, not to mention driven, adaptation, in that new media have constantly opened the door for new possibilities for all three modes of engagement. Lately, new electronic technologies have made what we might call fidelity to the *imagination*—rather than a more obvious fidelity to *reality*—possible in new ways, well beyond earlier animation techniques and special effects.
>
> (Hutcheon 29)

Several of the chapters in this book demonstrate how Lovecraft's ideas or moods or atmospheres can be adapted successfully without even drawing on his language or his plots directly. According to Linda Hutcheon, "As in a play or film, in virtual reality or a videogame, language alone does not have to conjure up a world; that world is present before our eyes and ears" (25–26). What we see is a significant reconfiguration of Lovecraft's aesthetic proposals rather than mere repetitions of his plots and ideas. These days creators reshape and appropriate Lovecraft's creatures and the atmospheres they inhabit in order to express their anxieties about the cultural, social, and environmental concerns of our times.

Video Games

Lovecraft's general impact on video games is so strong that it hardly needs commentary. But it is worth noting that there is something uniquely appealing about Lovecraft and video games that we need to mention. There are two main reasons why we consider Lovecraft so attractive for videogame adaptation: to begin with, there is the challenge of visually reproducing what he suggests only in words. Secondly, and perhaps more important, there is Lovecraft's preference for lone protagonists with a final emphasis on the mental effects resulting from the encounter with weird horrors. Even if the game requires the player to interact with others, her/his experience is also an individual one that takes place without the usual narrative distance of genres like literature, drama, and film. The immediacy inherent to gaming provides an emotional involvement exclusive to this type of media. The player has a richer role beyond that of audiences in other media since she/he can decide what turns to take and doors to open: "Through the juxtaposition of being in and out of control, horror-based videogames facilitate the visceral and oscillating pleasures/unpleasures of anxiety and expectation. The interactive dimension heightens this fluctuating sense of anticipation, implicating the player in his or her fate" (Krzywinska 21). As a result, while a reader of Lovecraft is forced to remain an external witness of the protagonist's adventure, the player immersed in a Lovecraftian videogame can become the protagonist her/himself. One may claim that the reader, as well as the film and theater audiences, has the advantage of remaining at a safe distance on the other side of the page, screen, or stage; nevertheless, the player can always disconnect from the real-like sensation of horror experience by turning off a mere button.

Lovecraft Forever

Every aspect of Lovecraft's life and career is being reevaluated, especially since access to his stories, his letters, and aspects of his life is so widely available. Consequently, Lovecraft has increasingly become a figure to reckon with, whether as someone who symbolizes offensive or frightening ideas or as someone who inspires a host of new writers, artists, video game designers, and so forth. Lovecraft has become an idea, a memory, something that we permanently have but are not sure about. We are not sure what to do because Lovecraft's revival is so vibrant and so alive that his legacy is constantly being readapted and molded by writers, game developers, and other types of creators. There seems to be no imminent end to this revival since adapting and dialoguing with the aesthetics of his cosmic horror and the weirdness of his stories provide channels for many, including audiences, to express and try to understand our concerns about the uncertainties of our current times, in which the "terrifying vistas of reality, and of our frightful position therein" seem to evoke the "dark age" predicted by the author from Providence (Lovecraft "Cthulhu" 22). The emergence of domesticated reinterpretations of Cthulhu has also become recurrent over the last several years. Its appearances in the three-part arc in the TV series *South Park* in 2010, and the *C is for Cthulhu: The Lovecraft Alphabet Book* project—an illustrated children's book series published since 2014 which has other similar titles and plush toys as spin offs—are but reflections of the fact that we are living in times of such turmoil that even the darkest fears about our future seem laughable when contrasted with our oozy presence, in which any possible certainty about the human condition is neither permanent nor stable, but always in flux.

Outline of the Volume

We have organized this volume largely around the topics and themes addressed in this introduction. Although authors were not assigned specific topics, we asked all of them to consider how specific elements of Lovecraft's life, fiction, and monsters significantly influence or shape various new settings, problems, or adaptations over the last twenty years. As the collection took shape, it was evident that one of its dominant claims is that Lovecraft's work is more relevant now than ever before because it evokes feelings that are often just as overwhelming, intense, harried, and confused as much of contemporary life. Given that the authors developed their chapters during the expansive shutdowns connected to the COVID-19 pandemic and the civil unrest following the murder of George Floyd, some of their discussions took on even greater urgency, especially as they also attempted to make sense of Lovecraft's challenging and sometimes controversial place in contemporary culture. The chapters included here do not shy away from addressing problems associated with Lovecraft's racism and sexism, but they also demonstrate new ways of approaching the Weird that resist racism, tradition, and prejudice.

The first four chapters explore the ways Lovecraft or Lovecraftian thought has been taken up in places such as theater, television, film, or literary criticism. Each chapter provides strong reasons for wanting to discover the impact Lovecraft may continue to have on stage and screen over the next several decades. The volume opens with Kevin J. Wetmore, Jr.'s "Lovecraft and the Stage: A Recent (Re)Discovery," a discussion that focuses not only on Lovecraft's personal interest in theater but also on the ways playwrights have attempted to bring various aspects of his life and work to the stage. Central to Wetmore's argument is a focus on the marked increase in Lovecraft-inspired stage adaptations since the turn of the new millennium and on how these adaptations wrestle with the constant challenge of representing the unknowable or the unspeakable. Elisabete Lopes next discusses how the critically acclaimed first season of the HBO television series *True Detective* (2014) develops a distinctively Lovecraftian sense of nihilism in both setting and atmosphere while it also establishes a powerful thematic means of reflecting on the prospect of impending global catastrophe. Although Lovecraft's influence on American horror film and television is fairly well established, his impact outside of the United States has yet to be as fully explored as it should be. In "An Uncanny Absence: Lovecraft in Brazilian Cinema, 1975–2016," Lúcio Reis Filho and Sheila Schvarzman take up the question of Lovecraft's significance within contemporary Brazilian culture and discuss the ways his work has been addressed, adapted, or appropriated within specific Brazilian cultural and cinematic contexts. John Glover then focuses on the critical challenges associated with approaching H.P. Lovecraft and his life, his prejudices, and his larger persona. Glover discusses, in particular, the various ways Lovecraft shaped his own larger reputation and considers the scholarly possibilities and setbacks associated with drawing on Lovecraft's massive correspondence, particularly in the heavily edited compilation, *Selected Letters*.

The next three chapters expand on the previous chapters by exploring the ways Lovecraft's life and ideas have been adapted into comics and other visual media. Lovecraft had a strong interest in the visual arts and frequently commented on art and artists in his letters. In his fiction, Lovecraft also drew on the visual arts as powerful means of evoking cosmic fear. Stuart L. Lindsay addresses not only the specific challenges that come from adapting Lovecraft's work into comics but also how comics themselves might be understood as a medium for the Weird generally. Lindsay's discussion largely focuses on the ways two comics series, Alan Moore's and Jacen Burrows' *Neonomicon* (2010–2011) and *Providence* (2015–2017), develop significant Lovecraftian themes, as well as shed light on the challenges of representing Lovecraft himself in graphic narratives. Lindsay also draws on the concept of cryptomimesis to examine the ways graphic novels address the problem of the unknowable. Next, Tom Shapira focuses on the challenges that stem from appropriating elements of Lovecraft's life and popular persona into graphic narratives, especially when that persona bears little resemblance to the man himself. Shapira discusses comics series such as *Providence*, The *Strange Adventures of H. P. Lovecraft* (2010) and *Howard Lovecraft and the Three Kingdoms* (2014) to show how easily complex lives can be transformed into stereotypes, convenient fictions, or just meaningless placeholders. Suzanne and Richard Albary next explore the problem of how well the visual arts can convey a sense of cosmic horror. Their chapter opens with a discussion of the ways Lovecraft draws on art in stories such as "Pickman's Model" (1927), "The Call of Cthulhu" (1926), and *At the Mountains of Madness* (1936). The authors then focus on the ways the artwork for popular games such as *Magic: The Gathering* (1993), *Hearthstone* (2014), and their various expansions, draw on Lovecraftian themes and components to provide players with a sense of the otherworldly, the horrific, and the weird.

Echoing what we mentioned above, many of our contributors observe that reading Lovecraft in the first two decades of the new millennium resonates in ways that it never has before. As Morton and others have also pointed out, elements of Lovecraftian thought may even shed light on the direct threat of climate change, pollution, nuclear waste, and other associated problems. As Ian Fetters argues in "Nuclear Inhumanities: H.P. Lovecraft's 'The Colour Out of Space' and the Dread of Contamination," Lovecraft's famous tale about a strange meteor and its terrible impact on a local community can also spark discussion about the ways inhuman agents like nuclear waste and radioactivity—things without clear motivation or purpose—can likewise spread long-term consequences on human communities and lives. Fetters also develops his original concept of the *nuclear weird* to suggest that nuclear materials collectively create a hyperobject with the kinds of destructive powers that Lovecraft could only imagine. Daniel Doncel, in "An Eldritch Crisis: Capitalist Paradigms in the Cthulhu Mythos," also reads Lovecraft from the perspective of all-too-real contemporary crises. But his approach is to explore the ways a looming capitalist crisis can also take on a distinctively Lovecraftian aspect. Doncel focuses on the ways Lovecraft dismantles commonsense notions of ontology and epistemology and then suggests some of the ways Lovecraft can be understood as a crisis author, someone who can help make sense of a late-capitalist crisis in a world seemingly on the verge of collapse. Natasha Rebry Coulthard also explores the themes of cosmicism and human insignificance, but she does so, not by looking outside but by looking at the seemingly vast world of microbes and viruses to which human beings routinely play host. Like Fetters, Rebry primarily focuses on "The Colour Out of Space" (1927), but her post-anthropocentric reading points to Lovecraft's potential relevance within larger debates within posthumanism, new materialism, and corporeal feminism. Fredrik Blanc's chapter focuses on the correspondence between contemporary interest in Lovecraft's fiction and the effects of climate change. Blanc applies an ecophobic perspective to "The Lurking Fear" (1923), "The Colour Out of Space," and "The Shunned House" (1924) which he reads as examples of monstrous manifestations of vegatation and the natural surroundings within Lovecraft's stories, both of which, in the end, prove the absurdity behind humanity's self-claimed superiority over nature. Antonio Alcala Gonzalez focuses on William Eubank's film, *Underwater* (2020), which relies on Lovecraftian aquatic monsters to address concerns about the exploitation of nature in the Anthropocene. From a Nautical Horror lens, Eubank's appropriation of said grotesque monsters is analyzed as the way through which the director shares his view of humanity as a species with a very limited role, not only in maritime depths but on the whole planet as well.

One of the ways Lovecraft is being reevaluated in the last twenty years comes from thinking through his legacy while pushing against the biases he sometimes brought to his themes, tropes, and ideas. The next two chapters discuss how contemporary authors have successfully challenged or worked through the implicit racial and sexual politics in Lovecraft's fiction. Kathleen Hudson's "Racial (In)visibility, Cosmic Indifference: Reimagining H.P. Lovecraft's Legacy in Victor LaValle's *The Ballad of Black Tom* (2016)" scrutinizes LaValle's novel as a conversation with "The Horror at Red Hook," one of Lovecraft's most explicitly racist narratives. Hudson locates in both texts a weirding of reality that pushes individual bodies into the realm of the abcanny where they are othered in a process that confirms race as an arbitrarily imposed concept. In her chapter, Loren Barbour looks at the ways short stories by women of color take up familiar Lovecraftian elements and rework them in ways that actively resist misogyny, racism, and heteronormativity. Barbour focuses primarily on two short stories, Gabriela Santiago's "None of This Ever Happened" (2016) and Valerie Valdes's "Shub-Niggurath's Witnesses" (2015) to show how vibrant Lovecraftian elements can be when they are repurposed by historically marginalized groups. The result is a new and much broader understanding of the possibilities of cosmic horror.

As indicated before, Lovecraft inspired video games have become so commonplace over the last twenty years that they increasingly risk becoming overly familiar or clichéd. The next three chapters provide strong reasons to look more deeply at Lovecraft's impact on video games and why it might even go beyond adapting specific stories or situations. Kevin Corstorphine and Matt Crofts take up that problem by showing that Lovecraft's influence runs much deeper than just adapting a few easily recognized themes or tropes. Through exploring Lovecraftian elements in "dungeon crawler" video games such as *Darkest Dungeon* (2016) and *Crawl* (2017), the authors demonstrate just how effective video games can be in developing Lovecraftian dread based on a combination of claustrophobia, loss of control, mental anguish, terror, and despair. Eoin Murray then explores the complexities of adapting Lovecraft's tales into the heavily visual and interactive world of video games. He focuses primarily on the ways *Bloodborne* (2015) draws on distinctively Lovecraftian components in both its themes and gameplay to create an experience that is frightening and strange. Though *Bloodborne* does not adapt any specific Lovecraft text, it allows players the opportunity to explore an environment that is clearly indebted to Lovecraft in the ways it establishes atmosphere, creates tension, and evokes Eldritch horrors. David Simmons next focuses on the paradoxical appropriation of Lovecraftian themes in several 'walking simulator' video games produced over the last twenty years. Given that walking simulators typically require players to develop a sense of mastery by exploring as much territory as possible, they do not appear particularly well suited to establishing Lovecraftian environments that rely on ontological uncertainty and cosmic dread. But as Simmons demonstrates, Lovecraftian 'walking simulators' work against expected gaming conventions to give players a keen sense of the Lovecraftian weird. Though some games are more successful at this than others, there is no denying that Lovecraft's influence is still a significant and viable part of the video game experience.

The next two chapters focus on the ways Lovecraft's fiction can be read in light of contemporary approaches to gender and sexuality. Nowell Marshall's chapter reminds readers that sexuality is a major, though often unaddressed, component of Lovecraft's fiction. Central to Marshall's discussion is a focus on how queer and trans theorists actively draw on themes of monstrosity to develop a broader means of negotiating identity. Marshall then turns to a careful and detailed reading of "The Call of Cthulhu" to demonstrate how Lovecraft's most famous story explicitly positions its male protagonists against the "queer monstrosity" represented by Cthulhu. Marshall's queer reading of Cthulhu sheds new light on the ways the story addresses secrets, spaces, masculinity, and monstrosity. Brian Johnson next addresses the ways Lovecraft's fiction has been readily appropriated by queer readers and writers in ways that not only confront Lovecraft's own homophobia but also point to the kinds of narrative possibilities that come from seeing Lovecraft and his Mythos through an explicitly queer perspective. Johnson primarily focuses on the ways Jordan L. Hawk's *Whyborne and Griffin* Series (2012–2019) effectively blends Lovecraft's interest in family secrets, forbidden knowledge, and male adventure with the popular subgenre of male/male romance and the possibility of finding one's happily ever after. Johnson concludes that Hawk's series is significant because it rewrites Lovecraft's Mythos as a sustained engagement with Lovecraft's own uncertainty surrounding questions of gender, voice, and sexuality.

The final two chapters approach Lovecraft, the fate of the world, and the problem of limited human perception. Michael Cerliano focuses on the increased ease in which human beings imagine the end of the world, especially during a time when COVID-19, climate change, increased natural disasters, and a host of other problems suggest that human existence is never completely stable. Cerliano argues that Lovecraft's increasing popularity is directly connected to the ways his fiction anticipates contemporary culture, especially in its suggestion of both impending doom and a decentering of human significance. By drawing on critical concepts such as hauntology, contemporary nihilism, and neo-pessimism, Cerliano develops insightful readings of "The Call of Cthulhu" and *At the Mountains of Madness* (1931) to demonstrate just how effectively Lovecraft captures our contemporary fears of mattering far less than we think. Similarly, Carl Sederholm argues that Lovecraft's prose poem "Nyarlathotep" (1920) may be read in light of contemporary concerns about just how difficult it is to make sense of an unknowable and overwhelming world. For Sederholm, the final paragraph of "Nyarlathotep" suggests that the once-confident first-person narrator has somehow disappeared in his own text and that he no longer has the capacity to represent his own experience. Faced with this sense of loss, the narrator can only open himself up to the strange displacement that comes from encountering what we might understand as a broader Lovecraftian eschatology.

Taken together, these chapters confirm that Lovecraft's growing popularity should not surprise us. He wrote with a keen sense of wonder, atmosphere, dread, and purpose; he also created a dynamic and flexible set of literary possibilities, any number of which can be adapted or appropriated into new settings and new media. But most importantly, he challenged readers to consider that they were perhaps too complacent or too caught up with "the spell of the daily routine" to remember, let alone acknowledge, that fear and pain and uncertainty are part of normal life (Lovecraft *Supernatural* 12). Rather than attempt to look past all that, Lovecraft suggested, human beings should embrace the dynamic or imaginative possibilities they represent. As he explained in *Supernatural Horror in Literature*,

> When to this sense of fear and evil the inevitable fascination of wonder and curiosity is superadded, there is born a composite body of keen emotion and imaginative provocation whose vitality must of necessity endure as long as the human race itself.
>
> (14)

Lovecraft's weird tales and the works they have inspired evoke imaginative possibilities that reach beyond the creatures and circumstances they can just barely describe, and it is in those possibilities that we begin to take on that "subtle attitude of awed listening, as if for the beating of black wings or the scratching of outside shapes and entitles on the known universe's utmost rim" (16).

Notes

1 Timothy Morton defines hyperobjects as "things that are massively distributed in time and space relative to humans." (*Hyperobjects*, 1) They challenge and distort human perception and, in doing so, they remind us of the impossibility of completely apprehending the contents of nature. Given their excessive dimensions, Morton compares hyperobjects to "Cthulhu-like entities" that intrude "into social, physic and philosophical space" (64).

2 Gry Ulstein indicates that, although contemporary weird monsters are different to Lovecraft's ones in that the horror they produce is based on the environment around them rather than in their bodies, "the cosmic specters of Lovecraft still haunt the cultural imagination in the confronting context of the Anthropocene" (62). She proposes that Anthopocene monsters "are figures conjured by the cultural imagination to give shape to many sources of anxiety brought on by the urgency of surfacing environmental issues such as plastic pollution, oil spill, deforestation, extreme weather, and forest fires" (50).

Works Cited

Fisher, Mark. *The Weird and the Eerie*. London: Repeater, 2017.

Hamilton, Clive, et al "Thinking the Anthropocene." *The Anthropocene and the Global Environmental Crisis: Rethinking Modernity in a New Epoch*. London: Routledge, 2015, pp. 1–14.

Hutcheon, Linda, with Siobhan O'Flynn. *A Theory of Adaptation*, 2nd ed. London: Routledge, 2013.

Krzywinska, Tanya. "Hands-On Horror." In *ScreenPlay: Cinema / Videogames / Interfaces*, edited by Geoff King and Tanya Krzywinska. London: Wallflower, 2002, pp. 206–223.

Lovecraft, H. P. *Letters to J. Vernon Shea, Carl F. Strauch, and Lee McBride White*, edited by S. T. Joshi and David E. Schultz. New York: Hippocampus Press, 2016.

———. "The Call of Cthulhu." *H. P. Lovecraft Collected Fiction, A Variorum Edition, Volume 2: 1926–1930*, ed. S. T. Joshi. New York: Hippocampus Press, 2017, pp. 21–55.

———. *Supernatural Horror in Literature. Collected Essays Volume 2: Literary Criticism*, edited by S.T. Joshi. New York: Hippocampus Press, 2005, pp. 82–135.

Morton, Timothy. *Being Ecological*. Penguin Books, 2018.

———. *Dark Ecology*. Columbia: Columbia University Press, 2016.

———. *Hyperobjects: Philosophy and Ecology After the End of the World*. Minneapolis, MN: University of Minnesota Press, 2013.

Sederholm, Carl H. and Jeffrey Andrew Weinstock, eds. *The Age of Lovecraft*. Minneapolis: University of Minnesota Press, 2016.

Ulstein, Gry. "'Age of Lovecraft?'—Antrhropocene Monsters in (New) Weird Narrative." *Nordlit 42: Manufacturing Monsters*, edited by Christian Beyer, Juliane C. Bockwoldt, Emil Lundeal Hammar, Holger Pötzsch, 2019, pp. 47–65.

1 Lovecraft and the Stage

A Recent (Re)Discovery

Kevin J. Wetmore, Jr.

Much has been written on Lovecraft and cinema, including his own interest (or disinterest) in film as well as analyses of films based on his work. Likewise, his engagement with literature is well documented in a number of scholarly surveys and analyses. Underrepresented in the study of Lovecraft and culture is his engagement with the stage. While cinema adapted his tales of cosmic horror within a few decades of his death, the stage long ignored him. It is only in the past two decades that the theatrical potential of Lovecraft's work has been discovered. The increasing presence of adaptations of his work on world stages can be accounted for by a number of factors: the increasing popularity and presence of Lovecraft in all popular cultures (film, graphic novels and comics, television, games and video games, and music)[1], the rise of a generation of theatre artists who were raised on tales of the fantastic and a steady diet of horror, science fiction, dystopia and magic, and the unique challenge of bringing Lovecraft to the stage. The RPG *Call of Cthulhu* and the number of current writers who introduce readers to Lovecraft through their own use of his work are surely responsible for some of the uptick in his presence in theatres.

Though a life-long fan of dramatics, Lovecraft's own approach to theatre was primarily as dramatic literature, and his own stories appear to resist dramatization (due to lack of dialogue, the narrative mostly being internalized, and the use of descriptors such as "indescribable"), and yet in the twenty-first century, we find a number of contemporary theatre artists adapting his work for the stage, finding challenges in doing so that Lovecraft himself foresaw, and yet also finding unique solutions to create horror, fear, the weird, and the supernatural on stage.

Lovecraft's Experience of Theatre and Drama

Although an early aficionado of the stage, Lovecraft's own experience of the theatre was primarily through dramatic literature. He claims he "saw my first play at 6, and my first Shakespearean play at 7" (Lovecraft *Lord* 20). The Shakespeare play he saw was *Cymbeline*, one of the bard's late

DOI: 10.4324/9780367713065-2

romances. In a letter to Reinhart Kleiner he reports that he first attended theatre in 1896, "which has furnished my life with the only real relaxation it has ever had…" (Lovecraft *Selected Letters 1*, 36). Lovecraft was enraptured by the production:

> The play – the first I ever beheld – was one of Denman Thompson's minor efforts – *The Sunshine of Paradise Alley* & had a slum setting, which rather enraptured me, since I had never beheld real slums. My memory of that play is yet more vivid than any of last season's offerings.
>
> (Lovecraft *Selected Letters 1*, 36)

The play Lovecraft had seen was a melodrama with songs that had opened on Broadway on May 11, 1896 and subsequently toured the nation. We should note the adult Lovecraft's claim that the stage was "the only real relaxation" he has ever had. As opposed to literature, which strikes him as work (both reading and writing), theatre proved relaxing – an adult Lovecraft continued to value the potential for "play" in every sense of the word. One might also note that Lovecraft remained an avid theatre-goer on and off throughout his life, regardless of his residence. In childhood he clearly valued the stage as a maker and consumer and continued to value it as an adult as a consumer, often unimpressed with what was offered. Lovecraft might have walked out of the movies, but he stayed to watch plays in the legitimate theatre his entire life.

Lovecraft frames much of his early childhood play as a form of theatre, staging scenes with his toys, "making up events of a highly melodramatic cast" (Lovecraft *Lord* 19). "I also had a toy theatre," he reports, "for in those days I took an interest in the drama," until about the age of 11 or 12 (Lovecraft *Lord* 20). Indeed, the week after seeing *Cymbeline* at the Providence Opera House, he "played nothing but *Cymbeline*. I still have the set of pasteboard performers, in faithful costume, which I drew and cut out for this miniature production" (Lovecraft *Selected Letters 1* 37). No doubt these juvenile performances later shaped his creative output as a horror writer – let us remember, the "Mad Arab," Abdul Alhazred, was first created as part of Lovecraft's youthful role-playing after reading *1001 Arabian Nights*. His favorite playwrights were eighteenth-century Anglo-Irish comedian Richard Brinsley Sheridan (known for his comedies of manners) and Shakespeare. He quoted Shakespeare not infrequently in later writings, citing *Hamlet*, *Richard II*, and *Merchant of Venice*, among others, in various essays (Lovecraft, *Collected Essays Vol. 5* 31, 49, 75, 194). A neighbor reported that Lovecraft and his mother loved to read Shakespeare aloud, and with particular bombast. "The more cruel the part, the better he liked it," the neighbor reported, "and would shout it out to be heard by the neighbors. I have had neighbors tell me of his quarrels but I know that it was only Shakespeare being read" (Cannon 29). In addition to the home dramatics designed to annoy the neighbors, Lovecraft studied a number of classical plays and playwrights. He quotes elsewhere from a number of playwrights, from the classical (Terence) to the almost-contemporary (Shaw). His proclivity for theatrics waned in his youth as his interest in astronomy and the sciences grew. He would, however, return to the theatre as an enthusiastic audience member in adulthood. One might also note that Lovecraft's humor, often eclipsed by his devotion to the weird and uncanny in his own work, shines through in his theatrical preferences and childhood performances.

Lovecraft's devotion to Lord Dunsany's work extended to that author's dramas as well, telling Elizabeth Toldridge in a letter dated February 21, 1929 that while he preferred Dunsany's fiction, his plays "are quite famous" and worth the read (Lovecraft in *Selected Letters 2* 277). He went to see Dunsany speak in Boston in 1919, sitting in the front row while Dunsany read his play aloud. Lovecraft critiqued Dunsany, not for his writing, but for his performance, observing:

> The only trouble with Dunsany as a public speaker is that he makes no pretense of *stage presence*. As a successful dramatist, one expects him to have a bit of the actor about him, but he is essentially of a non-dramatic type. His striving for dramatic effect is an intellectual one – exercised when he *writes*, not when he *reads* his plays. He addresses his audience not as a performer declaiming to a crowded pit, but as a gentleman entertaining friends in his own drawing room...He makes no effort at bodily pose – he is merely himself. [emphasis in original]
>
> (Lovecraft in *Selected Letters 1* 103)

It is fascinating that Lovecraft's rare reproach of one of his literary heroes was for his acting. Lovecraft here displays a knowing analysis of stage performance, shaped by his early love of the theatre. He recognizes the difference between public and private performance, and the very idea that he critiques Dunsany for being intellectual instead of emotional is fascinating, a glimpse into Lovecraft's own theatrical preferences.

In adulthood, dramatic literature served as his primary means of encountering plays, despite attending theatre irregularly in New York and Providence when he lived in each, respectively. In a letter to James F. Morton dated November 27, 1927, Lovecraft states that Manhattan would "seem more important to me if I continued to take interest in dramatick representations; but somehow with the years I've lost all power of imbibing illusion from the stage or from oral sources generally" (sic) (Lovecraft *Selected Letters 2*

198). When he lived in New York between 1924 and 1926 he did occasionally take in shows, often with his wife, but almost always criticized what he saw as being marred in some way or merely "tolerable." Similarly, in Providence, he would occasionally take in a play, either a touring show or one of the local productions.

He also seemed less interested in contemporary theatre and to prefer the writers of a previous generation: Oscar Wilde, Henrik Ibsen, and George Bernard Shaw were as recent as he was willing to go in advice on what to read. Only O'Neill was singled out for praise to his friends, particularly after Lovecraft saw his work on stage in New York, asserting O'Neill was "America's greatest living dramatist" and "the only American dramatist of note now living," based on what he had heard and seen in the theatre (Lovecraft, "Letter to Anne Tillery Renshaw" in *Selected Letters Volume 1* 187; Lovecraft, "Letter to F.C. Clark" in *Selected Letters Volume* 1 349). In September 1924, Lovecraft and his wife went to see *All God's Chillun Got Wings*, and despite the racially oriented subject matter, Lovecraft thoroughly enjoyed the production. But even O'Neill had lost his luster by 1931, Lovecraft referring to his Pulitzer Prize-winning play *Strange Interlude* as "five or so hours of unrelieved tedium" (Lovecraft, "Letter to Maurice W. Moe," in *Selected Letters: Volume III* 266). In short, with few exceptions, Lovecraft preferred his plays on the page, not the stage.

In his 1936 essay "Suggestions for a Reading Guide," he begins with the classics, recommending reading Aeschylus, Sophocles, Euripides, and Aristophanes (Lovecraft, *Collected Essays Vol 2* 185).[2] It is perhaps interesting given his own literary proclivities that Lovecraft does not mention the bloody tragedies of Seneca but instead leaps straight to Shakespeare from the Greeks. "Other books feed different parts of the mind," he states, "Shakespeare feeds the entire brain" (Lovecraft, *Collected Essays Vol 2* 187). We should note that Lovecraft here regards the plays of Shakespeare not as blueprints for performance but rather literature in its own right. He recommends reading the plays daily in fifteen minute doses. Lovecraft also recommends the plays of Shakespeare's contemporaries Christopher Marlowe, Ben Johnson, John Webster, Francis Beaumont and John Fletcher. This would also have been a literary recommendation, as few plays by those authors (other than Marlowe's *Doctor Faustus*, famously mounted by Orson Welles on Broadway in 1937, scant months before Lovecraft's death) were produced in the United States during this period.

He recommends a few Restoration comedies and then skips a century and a half to Goethe's *Faust* and from him to Henrik Ibsen, arguably the most significant late nineteenth century playwright (Lovecraft, *Collected Essays Vol 2* 189). "[August] Strindberg is another powerful dramatist," he states, but does not list any of his works (Lovecraft, *Collected Essays Vol 2* 189). In his list of contemporary writers, he will include the occasional title of a play, but never notes that it is a drama, simply listing it in a series of other titles, for example, including *The Lower Depths* in a list of novels and stories by Maxim Gorki (Lovecraft, *Collected Essays Vol 2* 190). In a section on good anthologies of different types of writing, he includes a paragraph on drama collections, the only place where contemporary American drama is mentioned. He notes the well-read person should read Quinn's *The American Drama* (1934–1937), Dickinson's *Contemporary Drama in England* (1933), *Mantle's Best Plays of 1919 to Date*, and George Pierce Baker's *Modern American Plays* (1920). Given that Lovecraft neither here nor in any of his other writings mentions a single play found in these volumes makes one wonder if he himself had actually read them or simply included them on a list in order to be complete.

Despite his obvious, deep, life-long love of the theatre and of drama present in his letters and essays, in his own fiction Lovecraft avoids the theatre. Lovecraft himself confessed to Harold S. Farnese in 1932 that he had no interest in writing drama:

> Probably the reason is that in the sort of work I am trying to do human characters matter very little. They are only incidental details, & can well be left in the puppet stage – since the real protagonists of my tales are not organic beings at all but simply *phenomena*. I doubt if I have the ability to handle human characters in a lifelike way, for they impress my imagination so much less than do the more impersonal forces of nature. This being so; it is clear that dialogue has never been much use to me… To create the living figures necessary to vitalize a music-drama of any ordinary sort, therefore, would seem to be a task definitely beyond me. [emphasis in original]
>
> (Lovecraft, "Letter to Harold S. Farnese," in *Selected Letters: Volume IV* 72)

Furthermore, he opposed the dramatization of his own work. In a letter to Farnsworth Wright dated February 16, 1933, Lovecraft expressed his distaste for the idea of a dramatization of "Dreams in the Witch House," or indeed, any weird tale:

> Indeed, it is not likely that *any* really finely wrought weird story – where so much depends on mood and on nuances of description – could be changed to a drama without irreparable cheapening and the loss of all that gave it power. Of course weird drama *can* be written -when the author starts out from the first to utilise the dramatic form… As a thorough soporific, I recommend the average popularly "horrible" play or cinema or radio dialogue. They are all the same – flat, hackneyed, synthetic, essentially atmosphereless jumbles of conventional shrieks and mutterings and superficial, mechanical situations.
>
> (Lovecraft, "Letter to Farnsworth Wright," *Selected Letters: Volume IV* 154)

He included no references to theatre in his own fiction, either. Randolph Carter, Inspector Legrasse, Robert Olmstead, Dr. Henry Armitage, Albert Wilmarth, or various unnamed narrators never go to see a play. Lovecraft's characters engage with neither drama nor theatre.

Lovecraft did, however, praise Robert W. Chambers' short story collection *The King in Yellow* in *Supernatural Horror in Literature*, observing, "very genuine…is the strain of horror in the early work of Robert W. Chambers," although he only refers to the eponymous play as "a monstrous and suppressed book whose perusal brings fright, madness, and spectral tragedy," only the final word hinting that the forbidden tome is actually a play (71). Chambers' collection includes numerous quotations supposedly from the anonymous play, which has at least two acts and three named characters: Cassilda, Camilla, and "The Stranger." Lovecraft appropriated Hastur and Carcosa from Chambers, but *The King in Yellow* remained a book, not a play, for him, just as the works of Shakespeare did.

The only drama Lovecraft himself wrote was never meant to be performed. Lovecraft's only "play," was a Jacobean pastiche written to mock his young associate Alfred Galpin's high school romances: *Alfredo: A Tragedy*, dated September 14, 1918 and attributed to the aforementioned Beaumont and Fletcher (Lovecraft, *The Ancient Track* 447–464). Many of the characters are based on people in Lovecraft and Galpin's social circle within the United Amateur Press Association (UAPA): Alfredo is obviously Galpin; Margarita, his beloved, is fellow student Margaret Abraham; King Rintaro, his father, is Rheinhart Kleiner; Teobaldo, the counselor and Alfredo's tutor, is H.P.L. himself; and Cardinal Mauricio is Galpin's teacher and UAPA member Maurice Moe. Romantic intrigues at court result in the majority of characters being poisoned, stabbed, or otherwise done in during the final scene. The piece was circulated among Galpin's friends for fun and published first in *The Dark Brotherhood and Other Pieces* (1966), but never performed publicly until 2018, when an all-horror author cast performed the piece as a staged reading in Providence, Rhode Island at StokerCon 2018. Lovecraft acolyte Ramsey Campbell played the role of King Rintaro.[3]

Dramatizing H.P.L. Himself

While Lovecraft paradoxically loved and admired theatre yet also had nothing to do with creating drama himself, in the late twentieth and early twenty-first centuries a number of dramatists have attempted to bring Lovecraft to the stage. The remainder of this chapter will concern itself with the two kinds of Lovecraftian dramatization: putting the man himself onstage and adapting his work for dramatic performance.

Two dramas in the second half of the twentieth century took somewhat similar approaches to dramatizing Lovecraft by integrating him into his own fiction and combining dramatization of his life with dramatization of his fiction. The first did not so much adapt specific stories as construct Lovecraft as a prophet of twentieth-century science gone mad. Trinity Square Repertory Company in Providence commissioned playwright and professor of English at Brown University, James Schevill, to write *Lovecraft's Follies*, which premiered in 1970 and was subsequently published in 1971 (Schevill). The play is a postmodern, ritualistic circus of sorts with Hitler, Tarzan, J. Robert Oppenheimer, Werner von Braun and "Black Lovecraft" (an African-American prisoner who prophesies a "Black Revolution") as characters, among dozens of others. Lovecraft's letters and stories are quoted, gods make appearances, and the world devolves as characters with names such as "Scientist," "Lawyer," "Physicist," and "Housewife" debate reality and the military–industrial complex. The play uses Lovecraft to celebrate what Buzz Aldrin called the "Magnificent Desolation" of the moon, according to Schevill (88).

More recently, playwright Brett Rutherford wrote *Night Gaunts: An Entertainment Based on the Life and Work of H.P. Lovecraft* for the fiftieth anniversary of Lovecraft's death, although not performed until 1988, a one-act version premiering at the Providence Athenaeum. Local actor and Lovecraft aficionado Carl Johnson played H.P.L. A two-act expanded play was then performed at the 1990 Lovecraft Centennial. Rutherford relied upon the letters of Lovecraft to develop much of the play's dialogue, which also contains excerpts from Lovecraft's stories. Set a few months before the writer's death in 1937, the play is structured around Lovecraft writing and remembering his life and work, particularly his relationships with his mother and his wife. The stories Rutherford includes are "The Shunned House," "The Colour Out of Space," "The Outsider," "Herbert West: Reanimator," "The Thing on the Doorstep," "The Dunwich Horror," "Pickman's Model," "The Rats in the Walls," and the poem "Astrophobos" (Rutherford 33–35, 40–43, 52–53, 62–70, 29–30).

The play blends Lovecraft's own sense of horror at the world, the cosmos, and his own life with his own fiction, finding resonances between the two. The drama ends with his death and assertion of his own immortality, telling a priest in the hospital who says he will pray for Lovecraft, "To whom? To WHAT? I am a priest, too. I MAKE GODS. Gods that would eat yours as a cat eats a mouse…" (Rutherford 74). Lovecraft is the high priest of the cult of his own making, the cult of Lovecraft. His stories and his life intertwine.

Newly Discovered: Lovecraft's Work Adapted for the Stage

While little of Lovecraft was adapted for the stage proper before the millennium, an explosion of stage adaptations of his fiction has spread in the first two decades of the twenty-first century. We now seem to be in a boom period for presenting Lovecraft's works adapted for live performance, as noted above. It is not an easy task, not least of which for the reasons Lovecraft himself gives below – above all, drama requires dialogue, characterization, at least a hint of plot and must be done within the confines of a physical stage. How does one bring incomprehensible, enormous, dread Cthulhu into a 99-seat theatre space? How does one stage a color out of space? Of increasing importance in American theatre culture, how does one bring performers of color or female characters into narratives that are almost exclusively white and male (not to mention racist)?

As noted in his letter to Harold S. Farnese, Lovecraft accurately captures the challenge of putting his work on stage. Dialogue, character, audience empathy with and for the human characters are not strengths of his work. It becomes the task of the adapter to create human characters that matter more than "very little," that speak in recognizable ways, and to dramatize in an at least semi-believable manner the "phenomena" and "impersonal forces of nature" that serve the live performance of Lovecraft. As we will see, using the audience's imagination as sparked through sound and suggestion is often more powerful than attempting to put Cthulhu, Yog Sothoth, or Deep Ones on stage. What follows is a survey of some of the more significant and inventive productions and companies adapting Lovecraft for the contemporary stage, each of which demonstrates the unique challenges of attempting to dramatize what Lovecraft himself thought unadaptable.

The Atlanta Radio Theatre Company, the H.P. Lovecraft Historical Society, and the Radiotheatre of New York City

A number of groups present adaptations of Lovecraft as live or recorded audio drama. The only special effects for these groups are sound effects. Performers stand in front of microphones and oftentimes work from a script in front of them. The Atlanta Radio Theatre Company was founded in 1984 in Atlanta, Georgia, for the purposes of producing and distributing original audio dramas. They have performed *At the Mountains of Madness* and "The Rats in the Walls" live, as well as recorded a number of adaptations of Lovecraft for distribution via CD and podcast.[4]

The H.P. Lovecraft Historical Society has also recorded a number of dramatizations of their namesake's canon under the title Dark Adventure Radio Theatre (DART). They have also performed live versions of Lovecraft at places such as the Huntington Library in San Marino, California, offering a live adaptation of "The Dunwich Horror" for Halloween 2018.[5]

The Radiotheatre Series in New York City has adapted and performed over fifty of Lovecraft's stories for the stage. As their name suggests, they present these stories live on stage, but as if for radio broadcast. Thus, for example, four actors will stand in solitary spotlights with a microphone in front of each. No attempt is made to visually represent the horrors of

Lovecraft, but rather sound effects allow the audience's imagination to create dread Cthulhu, Wilbur Whately's twin or a group of Deep Ones. Adapted by Dan Bianchi, Radio Theatre's founder and Artistic Director, the stories often demonstrate the challenge of adapting Lovecraft, let alone for the stage. Given that many of the stories reflect the narrator's slow loss of sanity, Bianchi often employs a narrator to tell the story first hand, with dialogue exchanges and events occurring in flashbacks.

Lovecraft "works" as live audio drama, utilizing narrators and sound effects, relying upon mood and atmosphere. As Bianchi himself writes,

> Unless such tales are adapted into musicals and dance or farce, the traditional Theatre world doesn't know how to adapt and succeed with serious, horrific works for the stage, especially if the production tries to emulate expensive motion picture reality.[6]
>
> (Bianchi *Lovecraft on Stage Volume 1* 6)

Bianchi argues the strength of theatre is its liveness – the fact that performer and audience are in the same space live at the same time, which can make for very effective creation of dread and fear.

Innsmouth in Chicago: Wildclaw Theatre

Wildclaw Theatre, a Chicago-based theatre company dedicated to bringing horror to the stage, has twice put Lovecraft on stage. In 2008, they presented "The Dreams in the Witch House" at the Athenaeum Theatre, adapted and directed by Charley Sherman. Lillith and Gilman, two young students at Miskatonic, explore the strange geometries of the old Witch House and journey through space and time in a well-reviewed production.

The company subsequently mounted Scott T. Barsotti's adaptation of "The Shadow over Innsmouth" in 2013. Barsoti interestingly creates a female protagonist from Ohio (Oberlin, not Miskatonic, is her alma mater, in keeping with Wildclaw's own location in the "second city" and heart of the Midwest) who visits Lovecraft's doomed seaside city. This is one of many changes from the original narrative. As with some of the other adaptations discussed here, Lovecraft serves as a jumping-off point. Individual incidents, characters and themes from the stories may be preserved, but all are sacrificed on the altar of what frightens contemporary audiences.[7] The interiority-based horror in Lovecraft's fiction must be made exterior through dialogue, characterization, action, and effect.

Open Circle Theatre

The Open Circle Theatre in Seattle was a theatre collective dedicated to performing works based on fantasy and myth from 1992 through

October, 2011. For many years their annual Halloween production was an adaptation of one or more of Lovecraft's tales, often with other dark authors such as Poe or Edward Gorey adapted as well. Beginning in 2002 with Zack Lenihan's adaptation of "Herbert West: Reanimator," which had initially been presented at the Seattle Fringe Festival, annual presentations of Lovecraft followed. October 2003 brought about *The Horror in the Theater: An H.P. Lovecraft Triptych of Terror*, with Lyam White and Ron Sandahl adapting "The Dunwich Horror," "From Beyond," and "The Haunter of the Dark" in a production that was neither the first nor the last to use puppets and lighting to realize the monsters of Lovecraft ("Brief Encounters"). *Theatre of Horrors* followed in 2004, featuring stage versions of *Nyarlathotep* adapted by Josh Knisely, "The Doom that Came to Sarnath" adapted by Ron Sandahl, and "Dreams in the Witch House" adapted by John McKenna and Lyam White.

October 2005 brought another anthology show to the stage. *Arkham* consisted of "The Shunned House" adapted by Josh Knisely, *Cool Air* adapted by Ron Sandahl,[8] and "The Shadow over Innsmouth" adapted by John McKenna. A well-reviewed adaptation of "The Colour out of Space" was performed in 2006, alongside a homoerotic adaptation of "The Thing on the Doorstep" (Constant). In 2007, two old and two new plays were presented: "The Picture in the House," "Nyarlathotep," "The Cats of Ulthar," and "Dreams in the Witch House". Most notable was the show that opened their new space in October 2008, *The Necronomicon*, an original work inspired by Lovecraft's stories (Berson). The following year, *The Madness out of Time*, a very loose adaptation of *The Case of Charles Dexter Ward* premiered. An adaptation of "Pickman's Model" in October 2010 was the company's final Lovecraft production before the company went out of business. Open Circle Theatre might be the only rival of Radiotheatre NYC in terms of sheer number of stories adapted for live performance.[9]

Visceral Lovecraft in Los Angeles

In terms of sheer numbers of performance, Los Angeles is the city to be in to experience Lovecraft on stage. The H.P. Lovecraft Historical Society, Visceral Theatre Company, Zombie Joe's Underground, and Unbound Productions/Wicked Lit are all regular purveyors of theatrical Lovecraft. It is also the city that gave us *Reanimator: The Musical*.

The Visceral Theatre Company of Los Angeles produced two major stage Lovecraft events. The first, *Lovecraft: Nightmare Suite*, was a compendium of six short stories adapted for the stage by Visceral Artistic Director Dan Spurgeon, which originally ran in New York in 2003, remounted in Los Angeles in 2013, and then produced by the Molotov Theatre in Washington, D.C. in 2015. The play consists of six separate stories: "The Statement of Randolph Carter," "The Cats of Ulthar," "The Outsider," "The Picture in the House," "Cool Air," and "Nyarlathotep" adapted in a variety of styles and using different techniques with a run time of less than seventy minutes. For example, "The Cats of Ulthar" was a monologue, a young woman in Egyptian-inspired wear on a throne (at least in the Los Angeles version), delivering the story as a spoken-word narrative. "The Statement of Randolph Carter," on the other hand, was presented realistically as it unfolds in the Lovecraft original. *Cool Air* also sees a female protagonist, who befriends Dr. Munoz next door. One aspect of Lovecraftian adaptation is the recurring change of character gender in many of these plays. Lovecraft's stories are predominantly male, so adapters often switch genders, sometimes intentionally to make a point (as T.L. Wiswell does, below), sometimes simply to ensure the female company members have roles to play as well, in which case the gender switch seems less thematically relevant.

Visceral followed *Nightmare Suite* with 2014's adaptation of "The Call of Cthulhu" as a one-man show. Adapted and performed by Frank Blocker, the play follows the Lovecraftian original rather closely, in which the solo performer plays the narrator in each of the sections of the story. Beginning the play as Francis Wayland Thurston, Blocker sifts through his uncle's papers and finds disturbingly similar narratives. He then becomes artist Henry Anthony Wilcox, describing his dreams, Gustaf Johansen, who describes what happened to the Emma and the Alert, and John Raymond Legrasse, who discovers the Cthulhu cult in Louisiana and Castro, a member of the cult. Cthulhu manifests at the end in the form of puppets by John Burton. The production was acclaimed, with Blocker being singled out for praise for his use of dialect, the creation of a half-dozen different characters, and for how effectively he conveyed the horror at the heart of Lovecraft's story (Dumars; Lower).

"The Call of Cthulhu" was subsequently adapted in Los Angeles again in 2018 by Zombie Joe's Underground, a theatre company best known for their ongoing *Urban Death* series – a performance consisting of several dozen vignettes designed to provoke fear at the macabre. Entitled *Lovecraft's Cthulhu*, the production devised by the cast of ten and directed by Denise Devin, follows a singular narrator with the rest of the cast playing all the other characters. Rather than an adaptation, the cast simply recited the entirety of Lovecraft's story, re-enacting moments as they were described in the story in another acclaimed production (McGrew; Becker).

Wicked Lit

Unbound Productions, a company dedicated to presenting classical gothic literature in alternative performance spaces, has been performing "Wicked Lit" – a site-specific set of plays that changes yearly – every fall since 2010, performing at Mountain View Mausoleum and Cemetery in Altadena, California, just north of Los Angeles. They present multiple, simultaneously staged plays in which the audience is split into thirds and each group attends the shows in a different order. The plays are adapted from literature and allow for the use of the site-specific nature of the pieces to create effective stage horror. Imagine seeing "The Cast of Amontillado" or "The Fall of the House of Usher" in an actual crypt or "The Legend of Sleepy Hollow" in an actual cemetery in a forest.

To date Wicked Lit has offered three of Lovecraft's stories: "The Lurking Fear," "The Unnamable," and "From Beyond." As with all adaptations, elements are changed or deleted and others added in order for the story to be told in the new medium. "The Unnamable" was the company's first foray into adapting Lovecraft, and dramatist Jeff G. Rack also incorporated elements of H.P. Lovecraft's "The Hound" as well (Josephson, Millet and Rack 175–196). It was performed in Mountain View Cemetery, the audience entering the main gates and approaching two characters looking for a tombstone. The ghost of Odessa arose out of an open grave, but the production wisely kept "the unnamable" offspring invisible, created through sound and visible only to characters holding an ancient amulet. It was surprisingly effective horror theatre, if not entirely Lovecraft's story. "The Lurking Fear," presented in 2013, adapted by Jonathan Josephson and Jeff G. Rack and directed by Paul Millet, featured a tour through the art gallery and chapel into the cemetery as the characters hunted down the monsters pursuing them.

In 2016, Wicked Lit produced "From Beyond" within the mausoleum itself, adapted by Trey Nichols and directed by Jeff G. Rack. The challenge of adaptation, of course, is to move from one medium to another while still retaining the essence of the original.[10] "From Beyond" concerns entities that can only be seen when Tillinghast's resonator is functioning. The darkness and size of the mausoleum itself lent the performance an atmosphere of dread, which allowed large puppets illuminated with UV light to appear at a distance from the characters (and audience) and grow closer without losing the utter sense of alienness. In order to tell the story, which is mostly conversation between Tillinghast and the unnamed narrator, Nichols adapted the story as a flashback, with the narrator, "Dr. Howard Phillips," explaining to the police the incidents that led to the disappearance of Tillinghast. The play begins with the police interrogation, moves back in time to a lecture by Phillips that Tillinghast attends, inviting his former classmate to his laboratory. The rest of the play is set in the lab as the entities that the resonator make visible grow closer and closer. It is, overall, an effective adaptation if one can get past the humor and inside jokes (Josephson, Millet, Myrvold, Nichold and Rack 107–131).

Lovecraft in London

The London Horror Festival, a celebration of horror in the performing arts, has featured several adaptations of Lovecraft during its decade-long existence, including "The Dunwich Horror" adapted by David Dawkins of

Ororo Productions in 2011. A two-hander adaptation of "The Shadow over Innsmouth" by Hidden Basement Productions was featured at the 2017 festival. 2018 saw an adaptation of "Pickman's Model" and Turnpike Productions' "Providence: The Shadow over Lovecraft," a production similar to *Night Gaunts*, in that it explored Lovecraft's life parallel to his fiction, and the remounting of T.L. Wiswell's adaptation of "The Thing on the Doorstep," discussed below.

T.L. Wiswell, an American playwright now based in London, specializes in gender-reversed adaptations of Lovecraft. In 2016 she adapted and directed a gender-reversed adaptation of *At the Mountains of Madness*. Wiswell had lived in Seattle before London and was influenced by the Open Circle Theatre adaptations of Lovecraft (Ball). For *Mountains*, while the character surnames remained the same (Dyer, Peabodie, Danforth, etc.), the characters were female scientists and explorers, recounting the fateful journey to the transantarctic mountains. Using projections of the actual Shackleton and Scott expeditions, and having the actors in monochromatic makeup (to approximate the black-and-white newsreel footage of the era), the play remained fairly close to the source material.

Wiswell followed this up with *The Thing on the Doorstep: Asenath's Tale* for the new London Lovecraft Festival in 2018, a two-hander in which Asenath Waite and her childhood friend Viola Danforth tell the tale of Asenath's slow possession by Ephraim Waite. The 2019 London Lovecraft Festival features Wiswell's *Albertina West: Reanimator*, a gender-reversed "Herbert West: Reanimator" in which the eponymous character and her roommate and fellow medical student Carla Milburn revive dead bodies to ill ends.[11] She has stated she hopes to adapt *The Dreamquest of Unknown Kadath* for the stage soon (Ball).

Reanimator: The Musical

Arguably the best-known example of Lovecraft on stage is the least Lovecraftian: Dennis Paoli and Stuart Gordon's *Reanimator: The Musical*, which is more of an adaptation of the 1985 film than the Lovecraft short story "Herbert West: Reanimator." First performed in Los Angeles at the Steve Allen Theatre in 2011, with remountings in New York and Edinburgh in 2012, the play tells the story of Dan Cain, a student at Miskatonic Medical School whose new roommate, Herbert West, drags him into experiments in reanimating the dead, resulting in the death of Dr. Carl Hill of the medical school, his subsequent resurrection, and the kidnaping and rape of Cain's fiancée, the daughter of the dean, who also dies. Gordon himself says *Sweeney Todd* and *Little Shop of Horrors* were the inspiration behind the production, but that he envisions the piece as more like opera than musical theater (Gordon). Indeed, the characters sing more than speak. Gordon concedes that the play is not Lovecraft: "This really was about taking the movie and turning it into a musical.

What surprised me was that I found many in the audience had never seen the movie," and therefore the focus was more on the comedy and entertainment than in horror or Lovecraft's themes (Gordon).

Conclusion

Given that Lovecraft did not care for horror theatre in his own day and certainly not for adaptations of his own work, no doubt he would find the feminist takes of T.L. Wiswell or the campiness of *Reanimator: The Musical* to be heresy and not at all representative of his own work or ethos. However, despite the truth of his concerns for much horror dramatization in many media, Lovecraft adapted for the stage has actually achieved some level of success in the twenty-first century. As often as not, the adapters have used the device of a narrator to capture the voice of "the Old Gent," allowing for those "nuances of description" and mood that he finds so vital. Similarly, as with his fiction, these adaptations use the imagination of the recipient to create the necessary dread and horror. They also see his work as a springboard – faithfulness to Lovecraft's original story itself is less important that taking his ideas to explore contemporary cosmic and weird horror. And they often work. And when the adaptations do not, the result is as Lovecraft feared. There is no power of horror in *Reanimator: The Musical*, for example, only camp and the "horror" of the gross-out. Yet when done well, as in a number of the adaptations surveyed here, the effect is one that perhaps even the Old Gent would have found satisfactory, if not praiseworthy. At the very least we, the contemporary audience, should respect any performer who attempts to say "Ph'nglui mglw'nafh Cthulhu R'lyeh wgah'nagl fhtagn" aloud on a stage in public.

Notes

1 See, for example, Don G. Smith, *H.P. Lovecraft in Popular Culture*; Gary Hill, *The Strange Sound of Cthulhu*; and W. Scott Poole, *In the Mountains of Madness*, pp. 103–269.

2 We may take some of these recommendations with a grain of salt; for as S.T. Joshi observes in his note to the essay, it was written to order for Anne Tilley Renshaw's *Well Bred Speech*, using mostly books in his own library, and not all of which he himself has read (202–203).

3 The play was read by an all-horror author cast at 11:00 pm on March 1, 2018 and featured Ramsey Campbell (Rintaro), Grady Hendrix (Alfredo), Ricky Grove (Teobaldo), Jeff Strand (Mauricio), James Chambers (Olero), Marcello (Marc Abbott), Teel James Glenn (Gonzago), Amanda Trujillo (Margarita), Lynne Hansen (all the ladies of the court), Lisa Morton (Hypatia), Elizabeth Massie (Hecatissa), and Kevin Wetmore (director and stage directions).

4 See their website: https://artc.org/ for details.

5 See their website: http:www.hplhs.org for details.

6 The table of contents for the two volumes of *H.P. Lovecraft on Stage* indicates that Radiotheatre adapts every kind of Lovecraft story from every period of his career – short or long, juvenilia or final stories, epic and small horrors alike.

7 See Wildclaw's website: http://www.wildclawtheatre.com/.
8 Sendahl's adaptation of *Cool Air* was subsequently used for a staged reading at the 2019 London Lovecraft Festival in February.
9 Company shows and seasons can be found at the Open Circle Theatre Archive: http://octheater.com/.
10 See Linda Hutcheon, *A Theory of Parody* for the challenges of the shift in medium.
11 See http://londonlovecraft.com/whats-on/in-2019/albertina-west-reanimator/.

Works Cited

Ball, Simon. "Climbing the Mountains of Madness: Bringing Lovecraft to the London Stage." *Diabolique Magazine* (March 18, 2018), https://diaboliquemagazine.com/climbing-mountains-madness-bringing-lovecraft-london-stage/.

Becker, Richard. "'LOVECRAFT'S CTHULHU' is a Lovingly Crafted Adaptation of 'The Call of Cthulhu.'" *CreepyLA* (March 9, 2018), http://creepyla.com/2018/03/09/lovecrafts-cthulhu-is-a-lovingly-crafted-adaptation-of-the-call-of-cthulhu.

Berson, Misha. "Open Circle Theater carved its own niche." *Seattle Times* (October 5, 2011), https://www.seattletimes.com/entertainment/open-circle-theater-carved-its-own-niche/.

Bianchi, Dan. *H.P. Lovecraft on Stage Volume 1*. House of Fear, 2015a.

———. *H.P. Lovecraft on Stage Volume 2*. House of Fear, 2015b.

"Brief Encounters." *Seattle Weekly* (October 9, 2006). http://www.seattleweekly.com/arts/brief-encounters-2/.

Cannon, Peter, ed. *Lovecraft Remembered*. Sauk City, WI, Arkham House, 1998.

Constant, Paul. "All Predictable, Some Fun." *The Stranger* (October 12, 2006), https://www.thestranger.com/seattle/Content?oid=86854>.

Dumars, Denise. "Stage Adaptation of 'The Call of Cthulhu.'" *Lovecraft E-Zine* (October 15, 2014), https://lovecraftzine.com/2014/10/15/stage-adaptation-of-the-call-of-cthulhu.

Gordon, Stuart. Personal interview. July 14, 2016.

Hill, Gary. *The Strange Sound of Cthulhu: Music Inspired by The Writings of H.P. Lovecraft*. Music Street, 2006.

Hutcheon, Linda. *A Theory of Parody: The Teachings of Twentieth-Century Art Forms*. Champaign, IL: University of Illinois Press, 1985.

Josephson, Jonathan, Paul Millet, Susannah Myrvold, Trey Nichold and Jeff G. Rack. *Wicked Lit: Volume II*. Stage Rights, 2017.

Josephson, Jonathan, Paul Millet and Jeff G. Rack. *Wicked Lit*, Stage Rights, 2017.

Lovecraft, H.P. *The Ancient Track: The Complete Poetical Works of H.P. Lovecraft*, edited by S.T. Joshi. San Francisco, CA: Night Shade Books 2001.

———. *Collected Essays Volume 2: Literary Criticism*, edited by S.T. Joshi. New York: Hippocampus Press, 2005.

———. *Collected Essays Volume 5: Philosophy, Autobiography & Miscellany*, edited by S.T. Joshi. New York: Hippocampus Press, 2006.

———. *Lord of a Visible World: An Autobiography in Letters*, edited by S.T. Joshi and David E. Schultz. Ohio University Press, 2000.

———. *Selected Letters Volume 1: 1911–1924*, edited by August Derleth and Donald Wandrei. Sauk City, WI: Arkham House, 1965a.

———. *Selected Letters: Volume 2: 1925–1929*, edited by August Derleth and Donald Wandrei. Sauk City, WI: Arkham House, 1965b.

———. *Selected Letters: Volume III: 1929–1931*, edited by August Derleth and Donald Wandrei. Sauk City, WI: Arkham House, 1971.

———. *Selected Letters: Volume IV: 1932–1934*, edited by August Derleth and Donald Wandrei. Sauk City, WI: Arkham House, 1976.

———. *Supernatural Horror in Literature*. New York, Dover, 1973.

Lower, Jenny. "The Stage Adaptation of H.P. Lovecraft's 'The Call of Cthulhu' Will Scare You, Maybe." *L.A.Weekly* (October 7, 2014), 47.

McGrew, Shannon, "Immersive Theatre: Zombie Joe's Underground Presents LOVECRAFT'S CTHULHU." *Nightmarish Conjurings* (March 6, 2018), http://www.nightmarishcojurings.com/immersive-experience/2018/3/6/immersive-theater-zombie-joes-underground-presents-lovecrafts-cthulhu.

Poole, W. Scott. *In the Mountains of Madness: The Life and Extraordinary Afterlife of H.P. Lovecraft*. New York: Soft Skull Press, 2016.

Rutherford, Brett, *Night Gaunts: An Entertainment Based on the Life and Work of H.P. Lovecraft*. Grim Reaper Books, 2005.

Schevill, James. *Lovecraft's Follies*, Swallow Press, 1971.

Smith, Don G. *H.P. Lovecraft in Popular Culture: The Works and Their Adaptations in Film, Television, Comics, Music and Games*. Jefferson, NC: McFarland & Company, 2005.

2 Lovecraftian Landscapes and Cosmic Horror in HBO's *True Detective* (2014)

Elisabete Lopes

> There are twists of time and space, of vision and reality, which only a dreamer can divine.
>
> (Lovecraft "The Silver Key" 86)

Despite the fact that H.P. Lovecraft only experienced a fair amount of literary success during his lifetime, he has become increasingly popular since at least the turn of the millennium. His tales are a significant inspiration for the so-called New Weird fiction and cinema; several recent TV shows have also contributed to a reigniting of interest in his literary legacy. In academia, Lovecraft's influence resonates with ongoing reflections in the areas of posthumanism, new materialism, speculative realism, object-oriented philosophy, and environmental humanities. So, how can we account for this enduring interest in Lovecraft that is responsible for his popularity nowadays? Jeffrey Andrew Weinstock and Carl H. Sederholm argue that we are, in fact, in the "Age of Lovecraft" (Weinstock and Sederholm 3) because the author's presence has now become pervasive in ways that align with the kinds of circumstances that characterize the current historical and cultural conditions in the world. Weinstock and Sederholm underline that a fascination for Lovecraft's literary works has been rekindled because he, being a man ahead of his time, "addresses questions, anxieties and desires that have become increasingly insistent since the start of the twenty-first century" (Weinstock and Sederholm 3). In the fiction of H.P. Lovecraft, we find a world which is highly seeped in external influences and phenomena that originated in other dimensions, whose frontiers are not stable, but fluid. In this sense, the author can be said to have envisioned our planet as a kind of "shunned house," a frail home that not only works as a shelter but, paradoxically, also possesses the potential of annihilating humanity.

Drawing on this atmosphere permeated by impending cosmic horror, Eugene Thacker argues that "The world is increasingly unthinkable—a world of planetary disasters, emerging pandemics, tectonic shifts, strange weather, oil-drenched seascapes, and the furtive, always looming threat

DOI: 10.4324/9780367713065-3

of extinction" (Thacker 1). In fact, the world has become overwhelmed by so many "unthinkable" things that the Lovecraftian term "weird" would seem appropriate to describe its constantly changing nature. In truth, the world is being haunted by global specters, such as the scarcity of resources, environmental disasters, overpopulation, racism and intolerance, and devastating pandemics. These specters are no longer regional concerns, but they are now global catastrophes that show no sign of slowing down. This is a world in commotion, one that requires a global and collective reflection on the impact of human actions upon it. Thus, because humanity is increasingly haunted by the shadow of cosmic horror, the growing popularity of H.P. Lovecraft in contemporary times does not seem so strange after all.

In light of all this complexity, Donna J. Haraway claims that the term Anthropocene[1] is no longer accurate enough to describe the period humanity is witnessing at the moment. Thus, the author contends that we are living in the Chthulucene, a historical moment that she describes as tentacular and permeable. Haraway observes, "The Chthulucene does not close in on itself; it does not round off; its contact zones are ubiquitous and continuously spin out loopy tendrils" (Haraway 32). Along similar lines, Timothy Morton alleges that it is not possible to think of the world via the simple dichotomy that pits human culture and technology against nature. Instead, the author contends that there is a "mesh," or an openness and a weirdness in the way things interact, which dates back to a primordial era. According to the author, we are living a period characterized by a "dark ecology," a new aesthetical category which enables the emergence of a comprehensive ecological way of thinking about the world "that includes negativity and irony, ugliness and horror" (17). Therefore, in order to attain greater ecological awareness, humanity needs to understand the interconnectedness that is implicit in what he deems the "mesh." Like Haraway's concept of tentacularity, Morton's concept points to an inclusive view regarding ecology and nature since all living and non-living things are linked together and their interaction is all-pervasive. Sometimes it is especially difficult to define where one thing ends and the other begins, and this interwovenness between living and non-living things lends ecology a certain complexity that the human brain has difficulty coming to grips with. Within this logic, we can say that the networks prevalent in nature are somehow enveloped by a semantic code that sometimes is not within the grasp of the human mind. This unknown dimension of ecology and nature lay the foundations for the resurgence of H.P. Lovecraft's cosmic horror in popular culture. It is, then, on the verge of this tentacular mesh that *True Detective* emerges, dragging with its *noir*-like narrative questions that haunt the twenty-first century and that extend themselves way beyond the tale it was meant to tell. Deeply ingrained in the Southern Gothic tradition, the criminal show overshadows the Louisiana landscape with fictional elements that plunge its roots in cosmic horror. Actually, Nic Pizzolatto (writer and executive producer of *True Detective*) confessed in an interview given to *The Arkham Digest* that, when writing *True Detective*, he noticed that the Southern Gothic style was slowly paving the way for the emergence of cosmic horror. When the two finally melded, he stated that "a kind of secondary language began to form in the scripts, where the notion of cosmic horror became a very real part of the environment" (Pizzolatto *The Arkham Digest*). This secondary language, as Pizzolatto also suggests, allows for the emergence of the underlying narrative impregnated by cosmic horror references, the one that, although latent under the grassy swamps of Louisiana, will ultimately come to the surface, informing a true "police mythography" (Arntfield 115). Therefore, apart from reflecting upon Lovecraft's legacy in *True Detective*, this chapter aims at examining the implications of this underlying mythographic narrative in Pizzolatto's visual work. In truth, this alternate narrative endows the criminal narrative with an aura of cosmic horror, and this intrusion of the weird into the real is precisely the aspect that lends the literal story its symbolic counterpart. It is specifically this subtextual narrative that brings to surface the Anthropocenic concerns which have rekindled interest in Lovecraft's *oeuvre*. By interspersing reality with cosmic horror, *True Detective* tackles the environmental imbalance and consequent deterioration that results from man's imponderable actions upon the devastated state of Louisiana, thus contributing to turn it into a ghostly and monstrous geographic location, haunted by the *Cthulean* tentacles of the petrochemical industrial complex.

In *True Detective*, the fear not only comes from the knowledge that there is a serial killer on the loose, but there is also this lingering shadow of dread and unknown forces that Detective Cohle is able to perceive and whose clues will prove decisive in solving the case. In this way, hand in hand with the main narrative that tells the story of a gruesome murder, this text aims at exploring this secondary narrative, whose mythic words infiltrate the landscape where the two detectives join efforts to find the individual(s) responsible for Dora Lange's death. In effect, this secondary language or underlying narrative that Pizzolatto alludes to, and that can be translated into the intrusion of cosmic horror within the diegesis, surfaces both in the portrayal of the landscape and through detective Rustin Cohle's (Mathew McConaughey) particular worldview. As Pizzolatto himself discloses, "If your character conveys a vision of cosmic horror, it felt appropriate for me to dramatize the Lovecraftian sense of madness, of a carnivorous universe in which you're food" (Pizzolatto *TheArkhamDigest*.com). Actually, within the visual narrative of *True Detective*, Detective Cohle is the character whose beliefs and worldview converge with Lovecraft's cosmic indifferentism in ways that cause him to become afflicted by the cosmic horrors that erupt from the universe to haunt him and his colleague, Marty Hart (Woody Harrelson).

Resorting to a creative recipe that mixes criminal investigation with literary references, Pizzolatto's Southern Gothic[2] visual narrative draws on postmodern *noir* aesthetics and tropes that are artfully combined with H.P. Lovecraft's framework of cosmic horror to create a unique narrative imbued with an original imagery that, apart from refueling the popularity of H.P. Lovecraft among the spectators, also brings about an ecocritical point of view that, once merged with the Southern Gothic genre, evokes the "return of the repressed" that appears shaped under the form of a dark and decayed ecology.

Lovecraft's cosmic horror suggests that human beings cannot fully apprehend all the dimensions that lie within our reality. Therefore, they become afflicted by the unknown forces of cosmic horror when they come across something that they are unable to define or explain. Reiterating this reasoning, David Oakes remarks, "The tales of H. P. Lovecraft rely on the frightening revelations that may result from the constant quest for knowledge and the inability of science to explain all the mysteries of an infinitely complex cosmos" (Oakes 34). Graham Harman, in *Weird Realism: Lovecraft and Philosophy* (2012) contends that Lovecraft was a "writer of gaps" (4), adding that, "No other writer is so perplexed between objects and the power of language to describe them" (3). Mimicking the characters in Lovecraft's tales, Harman claims that we live in a world full of gaps that occur when we do not have access to objects that lurk beyond our perception. According to Harman, Lovecraft knew how to fabricate these gaps, thus producing that dread of the unknown that is implicit in cosmic terror. It is in this vein that human beings can be considered meaningless before the vastness of the universe. That is why cosmic horror fiction generally features an encounter with some unexplainable phenomenon, something alien, beyond human understanding. H.P. Lovecraft reinforced his views on the inferiority of humankind when compared to the vastness of the universe, when he described the true essence of his fiction this way: "all my tales are based on the fundamental premise that common human laws and interests and emotions have no validity or significance in the vast cosmos-at-large" (*The Annotated H.P. Lovecraft* 337). In this respect, William F. Touponce remarks, Lovecraft "came to formulate a philosophical worldview… which he called cosmic or scientific indifferentism. Its central tenet was the notion that nothing in life really mattered from a cosmic point of view" (62).

By professing this point of view, Detective Cohle introduces Lovecraftian Cosmicism into *True Detective*. To a large extent, he resembles Henry Wilcox, a secondary character from "The Call of Cthulhu" (1928) who is described as intelligent, but also afflicted with "odd dreams" (25). Wilcox also describes himself as "psychically hypersensitive" (25), a profile that fits Rustin Cohle like a glove. In truth, Henry Wilcox and Cohle appear to share a mythic connection to the Old Gods. It is no coincidence that, in the episode "Form and Void," Cohle confesses to Hart, "I don't sleep,

I just dream."[3] In this regard, Bob Curran highlights that Lovecraft created "the Dreamlands, an alternate dimension that lay just beyond the real, tangible world (...) only accessible to individuals through dreams." (Curran 265) In *True Detective*, it is subtly hinted that Cohle has some kind of access to these dreamlands by means of his sleepless nights, and, like Wilcox, he is prone to "receive weird impressions ("Call of Cthulhu" 42) that likely originate from another dimension and that manifest themselves as hallucinations or waking dreams.

One of these hallucinations clearly evokes a passage from "The Call of Cthulhu." While in the car with Hart, Cohle has a vision of a thickening and threatening reddish cloud approaching, something that is highly suggestive of the red glare that Inspector Legrasse glimpses through the woods when seeking the individuals responsible for the strange rituals that occur in the Louisiana swamplands, as described in Lovecraft's story.[4] This hallucination and its connection to the plot of "The Call of Cthulhu" are reminiscent of the title of the first episode, "The Long Bright Dark," as they evoke the red glow of torches illuminating the dark woods.

By means of his hallucinogenic crisis, Cohle manages to have a glimpse of the other undisclosed dimensions that overlap with human reality. He is able to discern hidden messages and codified visions within the environment. The act of undressing the world and seeking its hidden places ties in with some premises present in Lovecraft's fiction.[5] This quality can be translated into the gift of understanding reality beyond what is visible. Cohle glimpses strange motions and tones in the sky; he sees a murder of crows forming a spiral similar to the one which is displayed on Lange's corpse; he loses his gaze upon the ghostly children that he sees wandering about the dismal Louisiana town.

The fact that Cohle carries around a black ledger in which he sketches and registers every important detail almost mirrors H.P. Lovecraft's legendary *Necronomicon*, a fictional grimoire containing magic and spells. The eagerness to write down every detail dovetails with the detective's statement in which he sees himself as essentially a witness of events, "I tell myself I bear witness" ("The Long Bright Dark"). By witnessing events and taking note of every minute detail in his own *Necronomicon*, Cohle can be considered a sort of Lovecraftian prophet, endowed with an aura of mysticism.

In truth, while at Dora Lange's crime scene, the detectives come across ritualistic symbols that call to mind voodoo practices and Santeria.[6] The body of the young woman is found in a sacrificial position: she seems to be silently praying, kneeling on the ground, her wounded body bent against a tree. She is wearing a crown of antlers and, on her back, a black spiral is drawn. Hanging from the trees, sculptures made out of branches, the so-called devil nets, impregnate the atmosphere with an eerie feeling. Among the plethora of symbols that both detectives come across, a wreath of twisted branches lying against a tree stands out, suggesting a portal to another unknown dimension and the consequent intrusion of cosmic horror into the real. When Cohle and Hart leave Dora Lange's crime scene, Cohle remarks, "I get a bad taste in my mouth out here. Aluminum, ash, like you can smell the psychosphere" ("The Long Bright Dark"). The psychosphere that Cohle senses encompasses the physical space and the psychic aura that envelopes Erath. This psychosphere is a byproduct of the toxic deserted landscape and of the violence inherent in the crime scene they witnessed. Therefore, the paraphilic lovemap that Cohle recognizes in the ritualistic staging of the crime scene seems to be interwoven with the damaged psychosphere, turning that place into a resemblance of the "Babylon of Elder daemons" described by Lovecraft in "The Call of Cthulhu" (51).[7]

Cohle's tormented soul (affected by the trauma related to the precocious death of his daughter), his hallucinations (that can be explained by virtue of his drug consumption while he worked as an undercover agent), alongside his synesthesia, make him a man who has one foot in the real and the other in the supernatural. These characteristics aptly lend him the qualities of an unreliable narrator, a type of character that pervades horror fiction and who often figures in the tales of H.P. Lovecraft. The author's cosmic point of view likewise reverberates throughout the corrosiveness of Cohle's pessimistic philosophy since he believes that self-awareness and "human consciousness is a tragic misstep in evolution" ("The Long Bright Dark"). He also argues that the notion of "personhood" is illusory, and humans are nothing than mere puppets being controlled by cosmic forces beyond their knowledge,[8] a vision which is in tandem with the aura of cosmic indifference that permeates Lovecraft's fiction and that is transferred to the visual narrative of Pizzolatto's show.

Cthulhu, the mythical creature that haunts Lovecraft's tale, shares this indifference toward mankind. Amidst these southern landscapes plagued by rituals, the viewers are introduced to a character whose outward appearance clearly alludes to Cthulhu. Errol Childress (Glenn Fleshler), the serial killer responsible for the death of Dora Lange, is described by witnesses as "the spaghetti-face man" due to the scars he has on his face. This spaghetti-like portrait vividly recalls the tentacles of the mythic Lovecraftian Old God, described "as a monster of vaguely anthropoid outline, but an octopus-like head whose face was a mass of feelers, a scaly, rubbery-looking body, prodigious claws in hind and fore feet" ("Call of Cthulhu" 31). In a similar fashion, Childress's accomplice, Reggie Ledoux, can also be said to evoke Cthulhu when he is seen by both Hart and Cohle, wandering through the woods in his underwear, mumbling while wearing a gas mask, an accessory whose filter is reminiscent of Cthulhu's tentacles.

The intricate mystery that surrounds the death of Dora Lange also draws on Cthulhu-inspired imagery in the way its manifold ramifications can be compared to the tentacles that form part of the monster's head. The powerful religious elite behind the ritualistic murderers of women and children in Louisiana, the Tuttles, also appear depicted as Cthulhu's descendants. Employing an ironic tone, Errol Childress (who is later revealed as an illegitimate Tuttle descendant) tells an officer, "My family has been here a long, long time" ("After You're Gone"), suggesting that his ancestors share a bond with Lovecraft's fictional Old Gods. This bond carries a metaphoric connotation, since it is implied that the Tuttles are the elite chosen to carry out rituals and deeds that pay homage to these deities, who, according to Lovecraft lay waiting for the right time to awake and reclaim their power. Thus, within the plot of *True Detective*, the Tuttles appear as the privileged family whose tentacles spread from religious to economic and political influence. Disguised as benefactors who build schools, and allegedly help the poorest members of the community, this old Louisiana family are also part of an organized ring of pedophiles that engage in murderous ritualist practices. Throughout the series, the camera focuses multiple times upon a lonely tree; its roots deeply ingrained in the soil; its long and intricate branches stretching against the horizon; an image that also highly resembles Cthulhu's tentacles. This tree operates as a strong iconographic symbol for the family tree of the powerful Louisiana elite, reminding the viewers of the timeless cosmic connection that is forged via ritualistic homicide rituals, a fact that explains the frequent disappearance of children around that area. In fact, the presence of Cthulhu seems to be ominously looming in the southern landscape. Detective Cohle observes, at one point, that Louisiana might be flooded within some years, and this observation speaks volumes as regard to the natural habitat of Cthulhu – R'lyeh, – a city that is located under the sea.[9] The pervasiveness of Cthulhu and its influence both in the surrounding atmosphere and in the narrative resonates with Haraway's conception of the Chthulucene and its intrinsic tentacled interconnectedness. Evil, pollution, and degradation thus seem to form part of a huge monstrous creature that appears to be insidiously encroaching itself in the southern landscape. In this vein, Cohle's observation aptly ties up the landscape of the South with the cosmic horror inherent in H.P. Lovecraft's narratives.

The sheer influence of the landscape upon its inhabitants is primarily visible in *True Detective*'s opening credits, in which the characters are depicted as vanishing due to the imposition of the oil industry that operates as a huge metallic Cthulhu-like monster; they appear erased, mangled, and violated by its heavy and massive presence. Marian St. Laurent, in her article "America as an Afterimage," points out that

> Immersive aerial views of sugar cane fields, cypress groves, and lush jungle are presented from above or in tracking shots and transitions that draw visceral connections between the physical degradation and disappearance of the bayou communities and the ubiquitous presence of oil refineries.
>
> (St. Laurent, Sensitiveskinmagazine.com)

As the passage above illustrates, the perception of swampy terrains of Louisiana can be infiltrated by cosmic indifferentism given their having been ravaged by the refineries and by successive natural disasters, that gradually have transformed it into a "giant gutter out of space" ("The Long Bright Dark"). Throughout *True Detective*'s visual diegesis, the landscape is afforded special relevance. In an interview, Pizzolatto remarks,

> The landscape is literally the third lead in the show. Very detailed, prosaic descriptions of setting were a large part of the script: taking these opportunities to witness the contradictions of place and people, to feel a sense of a corrupted, degrading Eden.
>
> (Pizzolatto TheArkhamDigest.com)

Attesting to this vision, Rachel Franks also notes that the landscape is depicted in the TV series "as a character as vibrant as the heroes and monsters that dominate the Gothic canon. Characters that destabilize, disturb and haunt us" (Franks 23).

Being a hybrid series that conjoins both criminal investigation and the Gothic genre, the landscape of Louisiana is also conveyed through a double lens. If on the one hand, we are offered the contemplation of a desolated South, pervaded by physical and moral decay, on the other, we are left with the sensation that there is something supernatural haunting the Southern landscape. This intrusion of the supernatural occurs precisely by virtue of the influence of Lovecraft. Permeated by cosmic horror, the series displays a well-crafted twofold space, one that blends a Lovecraftian type of landscape that constantly overlaps with the real geography of the Deep South.

This crossbreed between a real factual and historical landscape and the cosmic eerie setting that produces its haunting, consequently results in an amazing visual narrative that, once anchored by ambiguity, clears the way for a double interpretation. Much like the paradoxical landscape of Louisiana, the dead body of Dora Lange can be said to configure a landscape carved with the symbols of a hidden predator, the monster that Detective Cohle claims to await us at the end of a dream ("The Locked Room"). The physical geography of the American South, its scarred bayous and decayed buildings (the burnt church, the trashy trailer park, the derelict houses), work as a mirror for the brutalized female corpse. This detail unveils the lingering connection between femininity, motherhood, and the land. If one equates nature with the female dead body, we come across a landscape that is sterile. Metaphorically, then, the land becomes orphaned.

Assaulted by the intrusion of cosmic horror, reality becomes identical to the one perceived by Rustin Cohle, hence being turned into a weird kind of reality, rife with symbols for him to decipher. The solitary police officer displays a unique and comprehensive view of the surrounding environment because he understands the landscape as both being natural and supernatural. Cohle's double reading means that the South comprises not only the bayous, the abandoned plantations, and the derelict buildings but also its doppelgänger, or, in this case, a landscape filled with the ghosts of lost children and permeated by occult symbols, hidden messages, and voodoo-like cults. As Teresa Goddu has argued,

> Identified with gothic gloom and doom, the American South serves as the nation's 'other,' becoming the repository for everything from which the nation wants to disassociate itself. The benighted South is able to support the irrational impulses of the gothic that the nation as a whole, born of Enlightenment ideals, cannot.
>
> (4)

Encroached in the deep "benighted" South, Erath, Louisiana can be said to vividly illustrate what Martin Procházka terms "the ghost town syndrome" because it is a land that still "keep[s] the semblance of material existence, or, it could be said, display that spectrality" (Procházka 31). These ghostly remote places are spaces that are liable to generate feelings such as the suspension of real time or the summoning of ghosts and specters that problematize the relationship between past, present, and future (31). Detective Cohle senses the ghostly atmosphere that envelops the environment, as he notes, "This place is like somebody's memory and the memory is fading" ("The Long Bright Dark"). That is why, in *True Detective* the landscape gives off an uncanny feeling. It is as if there is an underlying curse that appears to infiltrate the whole place. As James Kneale remarks, H.P. Lovecraft also played with reality, destabilizing it with the introduction of the uncanny: "Realistically described settings become uncanny as Lovecraft introduces elements 'from beyond'" (112). This haunting kind of feeling that the landscape elicits in Cohle clearly points toward a return of the repressed, a recurrent trope in Gothic and horror fiction. In fact, reminiscences of the war, slavery, racism,[10] and environmental catastrophes are the specters that haunt an old and decayed Louisiana and that strongly contribute to turn Erath (an anagram for Earth) into a perfect crime setting.

Against this background, Louisiana can be said to be transformed into a variation of Lovecraft's "The Colour out of Space" (1927). As the southern American landscape featured in *True Detective*, the portrayal of the rural area where the tale takes place is ravaged by ruin, decay, and abandonment. As the narrator observes, "Weeds and briers reigned, and furtive wild things rustled in the undergrowth" ("Colour out of Space" 369). The inhospitable lands of West Arkham featured in "The Colour out of Space," are likewise overshadowed by a sick kind of psychosphere, similar to the one that looms over *True Detective*, as the narrator informs: "Upon everything was a trace of restlessness and oppression; a touch of the unreal and the grotesque, as if some vital element of perspective or chiaroscuro were awry" (369). This unusual psychosphere took root in Arkham due to the impact of a meteor that fell from space. As a result, the surrounding environment and the inhabitants were affected, both on a physical and psychological level: the dwellers not only seem to be driven to madness, but they also end up sick. As the oil refineries belonging to the petrochemical industry threaten to absorb the swampy lands around it, the meteor that caused "the blasted heath" (368), also seems to vampirize the surroundings as it progressively drains the lives of cattle and people. Like a disease, the lands become tainted with strange undefinable hues and nature assumes an abnormal and unruled aspect.[11] In the last paragraph of "The Colour Out of Space," the narrator observes in relation to the construction of the reservoir, "I shall be glad to see the water come" (Lovecraft 399), a wish that brings back the image of Cthulhu's underwater world and hints at the potential catastrophic fate that Cohle sees lurking in the Louisiana's landscape.[12]

When Hart and Cohle discover the serial killer's haven, they become face to face with a very literal infiltration of cosmic horror into the real. They come up with an underworld, whose passageway is filled with twisted branches, an image that resembles twisted bodies in pain, thus evoking a kind of unruly and sick type of nature as the one portrayed in "The Colour out of Space." Once there, Hart and Cohle come across the altar of the King in Yellow,[13] a sinister sculpture made from the mortal remains of the serial killer's victims. Mimicking the worshippers of the Cthulhu cult, Childress also has his own "morbid statue" ("Call of Cthulhu" 42).

In the end, there is a revelation, when the team of detectives discover Childress's own private kingdom, the monster's lair, the wound that affects the landscape and its psychosphere becomes finally visible. This revelation of the monster signifies "the disruption of categories, the destruction of boundaries, and the presence of impurities" (Halberstam 27). These impurities mentioned by Halberstam are in tandem with the doomed environment of Louisiana that Cohle perceives infested with "aluminum and ash," forming a negative type of "psychosphere," a kind of atmosphere where human decay aptly conflates with environmental desolation.

The show also hints that there are primal forces at stake, that nature is somehow sided with the killer in its rebellion to overcome the growing industrialization that imposes itself upon the natural landscape. Some clues are provided, as Marian St Laurent suggests,

> Wilderness is a constant threat to order in *True Detective*. Neglected weeds grow between the cracks, along deserted freeways and in the broken pavement of abandoned parking lots. (…) As if to flaunt the victory of chaos over order, the weeds show America as a forgotten afterimage of itself and reveals it for the "jungle" it has become and was before.
>
> (St Laurent Sensitiveskinmagazine.com)

Hiding in his own private Carcosa,[14] located "Far from every Road,"[15] the killer seems to successfully evade the detectives, thus symbolizing this unruly natural force. As Delia Byrnes remarks, "The detectives' investigative skills are predicated on the modernizing logic of roads, freeways and maps, while the criminal cabal's occult knowledges of the ever-shifting bayous elude the detectives cartographies" (Byrnes 101). In fact, the wilderness, and the imposing refineries contrast with each other. The monstrous petrochemical industry emerges as alien amidst the natural environment, which is scarred by roads and electrical power lines. In this perspective, technological progress is depicted as a kind of Cthulhean monster trying to engulf the geography. The return of the repressed seems to operate as violent reply to this situation. If these elements mean progress, the rituals associated with paganism and the occult signal, in turn, a return to the old ways, a regressive trip to the past. Reginald Ledoux and Childress recoil in the wilderness, symbolically operating as oppositional symbols to progress. This image of jungle interspaced with industrial complexes form a symbiotic weird environment, a variation of Morton's "mesh," that proves especially nefarious as it extends its tentacles over the South, negatively impacting the dwellers' lives. In *True Detective*'s arena we have industry, on the one hand, and wilderness, on the other, both incarnating Cthulhean powers competing and distorting the geographies of a desolated Louisiana.

True Detective, with its cosmic horror vibe and Lovecraftian references interwoven with a sense of the real make us wonder "what it feels like to live in the early twentieth-first century" (Shaviro 2). Although the denouement of the show proves that everything was rooted in reality, the cosmic horror that permeates the episodes is nevertheless the factor that gives the show its substance. The fact that *True Detective* ends up privileging the real over the fictional ultimately endows its narrative with pungency and rawness. It reveals that reality is far more dangerous than any fictional narrative, and therefore the issues related to pollution, including growing desertification and environmental deterioration, appear as flesh and bone specters in the show. Nevertheless, it is the cosmic dimension that highlights the show's true essence, since the allusion to very earthly subjects is magically turned into preternatural phenomena, coded clues infused with symbolic meaning. Deprived of that deeper cosmic point of view, *True Detective* would be just another criminal show and not a cult TV series solid enough to give rise to a true criminal and cosmological mythology.

Christopher Mountenai comments, with regard to Lovecraftian characters, that "All too often, ...heroes learn that the horrors they face are not only very real but also deeply woven into their own identity" (13). This implicates that the monster that Cohle alleges to be waiting for us at the end of a dream is liable to work as a mirror-image. In this way, *True Detective* opens a portal to a dimension where we can think opposites within a web of interconnectedness: good and evil, light and dark, man and nature, thus engendering a new cosmic conscience that truly embodies the essence of postmodernity present in the current century. In the epilogue of *True Detective*, a changed Rustin Cohle turns to his colleague Martin Hart telling him that, after all, light is triumphing over darkness. In metaphorical terms, the detective seems to be setting aside his pessimistic view so as to adopt a more positive conception toward life. Surprisingly, it is his partner, Hart, who re-establishes the premises of Lovecraftian cosmic horror in the show, replying that the dark has a lot more territory than the light. In fact, the "monster at the end of the dream" was caught, but the powerful religious elite related to the Tuttle family, responsible for the abuse and ritualistic murder of women and children, remained unscathed. Time proves to be a flat circle, and, in a land ravaged by "petrochemical aesthetics" (Byrnes 88), "Cthulhu and his hordes" ("Call of Cthulhu" 50) await the right time to awake again.

Notes

1 This is a term coined by Paul J. Cutzen, an atmospheric chemist, and Eugene F. Stoermer, a limnologist, in 2002, to describe the period in which human activities started to have a real impact on the Earth's environment.

2 Southern Gothic is a subgenre that comports features and tropes of the traditional Gothic combined with specific concerns and traits of the American South. The return of a repressed past: the depiction of ruined and decayed landscapes; racism; poverty and promiscuity; and grotesque representations figure among its recurrent motifs.

3 It is implied in "The Call of Cthulhu" that these mythical Old Gods communicate with certain individuals through dreams (Lovecraft 2017 24–25).

4 Another allusion to the "red glare" is introduced in the opening credits, when various images appear in flames.

5 Evoking Cohle's inquisitive personality, Lovecraft's characters are endowed with a curiosity that usually leads them to investigate the nature of the mysterious events that cross their path. In "The Outsider" the curiosity of a lonely young man leads to the exploration of a castle, where he discovers a mirror that ultimately discloses his real ghoulish identity. Another example can be found in "Pickman's Model," a tale in which a painter ends up discovering that the inspiration for his friend's paintings comes directly from hell.

6 Voodoo and Santeria are religious practices, brought by the slaves to Louisiana. As these involve rituals, Cohle believes that the killer has resorted to them to stage his crime scene.

7 Curiously, the name Rustin Cohle comprises two elements rust and coal, which are potentially toxic and evoke decay. In 2012, Cohle's life has taken a turn for the worse, as he seems to have been affected by the sick "psychosphere." Although he continues to investigate Lange's crime and other disappearances of women and children in the region, he has by now left the police and owns a bar. Cohle's situation brings to mind another H.P. Lovecraft's "The Shadow over Innsmouth" (1930), a tale in which the narrator must come to terms with his true identity and his origins, and ultimately has to accept that he is a descendant from the "Deep Ones" (hybrid creatures that live underwater).

8 In fact, the 2012 crime scene displayed in the show ties in with this vision, since the body of another young woman appears naked, suspended by strings from a wood structure, as if she were, indeed, a puppet.

9 Cohle's observation links the natural disasters that occurred in Louisiana with the aquatic environment where R'lyegh is located (since it is a submerged city).

10 *True Detective*, taking place in the South, also talks back at Lovecraft's racist beliefs. As Wes House remarks,

> So long as modern stories of white genocide, superpredators, and the alleged master race find fertile ground on American soil, the contemporary relevance of Lovecraft will extend beyond what some fans care to admit. His bigotry and race-inflected narratives can't be wished away, cherry-picked, or swept under the rug in favor of his more widely known literary techniques and accomplishments—especially as hell-bent right-wing insurgents proudly claim him as a true elaborator of reactionary horrors. His stories and politics are still breathing, even the most defiled and rotten among them.
>
> (House, lithub.com)

11 Echoing the logics of *True Detective*, "The Colour out of Space" bears a message according to which nature is not compatible with technological progress, as the landscape of West Arkham seems to rebel itself against the building of the new reservoir, a fact that is illustrated by the constant display of abnormalities in the landscape.

12 Contrasting with Cohle's dismal perspective, the narrator of "The Colour out of Space" sees water as a potential purifying element, something that could eventually wash away the evil traces left by the fall of the meteor.

13 The Yellow King is a sinister character associated with death who appears in Richard W. Chambers' *The King in Yellow* (1895). It forms part of the Cthulhu mythos, and it is a constant reference in Pizzolatto's show.

14 Carcosa is the mysterious city that appears in Ambrose Bierce's tale "An Inhabitant of Carcosa" (1886). It integrates the Cthulhu mythos explored in *True Detective*.

15 Title of the song of *True Detective*'s opening credits.

Works cited

Arntfield, Michael. *Gothic Forensics: Criminal Investigative Procedure in Victorian Horror and Mystery*. New York: Palgrave, 2016.

Byrnes, Delia. "'I get a bad taste in my mouth out here': Oil's Intimate Ecologies in HBO's *True Detective*." *The Global South*, No. 1, 2016.

Curran, B. *Inside the Dark, Twisted World of H.P. Lovecraft: A Haunted Mind*. Pompton Plains: The Career Press, 2012.

Franks, Rachel. "A Fear of the Dark: Landscape as Gothic Monster in HBO's *True Detective* (2014)." *No Escape: Excavating the Multidimensional Phenomenon of Fear*, edited by Dean Caivano, Oxford: Interdisciplinary Press, 2016, pp. 19–30.

Goddu, Teresa. *Gothic America: Narrative, History and Nation*. New York: Columbia University Press, 1997.

Halberstam, Judith. *Skin Shows: Gothic Horror and the Technologies of Monsters*. Durham, NC: Duke University Press, 1995.

Haraway, Donna J. *Staying with the Trouble: Making Kin in the Chthulucene*. Durham, NC: Duke University Press, 2016.

Harman, Graham. *Weird Realism: Lovecraft and Philosophy*. Winchester: Zero Books, 2012.

Haubrich, Wess. "A Great Film Demonstrates a Profound Sense of Place or Character… A Great Film is One that I Want to Dissect." *Meet author Laird Barron*. May 27 2018, https://medium.com/@HaubrichNoir/a-great-film-demonstrates-a-profound-sense-of-place-or-character-a-great-film-is-one-that-i-want-8a96bf2646ba Accessed June 8 2020.

House, Wes. "We Can't Ignore Lovecraft's White Supremacy." September 26 2017, https://lithub.com/we-cant-ignore-h-p-lovecrafts-white-supremacy/. Accessed June 8 2020.

"Interview: Nic Pizzolatto, creator/writer of HBO's *True Detective*." *The Arkham Digest*. January 21 2014, http://www.arkhamdigest.com/2014/01/interview-nic-pizzolatto-creatorwriter.html. Accessed June 8 2020.

Kelly, Casey Ryan. "The Toxic Screen: Visions of Petrochemical America in HBO's *True Detective*." *Communication, Culture and Critique*, vol. 10, no 1, 2017, pp. 39–57.

Kneale, James. "From Beyond: H. P. Lovecraft and the Place of Horror." *Cultural Geographies*, vol. 13, 2006, pp. 106–126.

Lovecraft, H.P. "The Call of Cthulhu." *H. P. Lovecraft Collected Fiction, A Variorum Edition, Volume 2: 1926–1930*, edited by S. T. Joshi. New York: Hippocampus Press, 2017, pp. 21–55.

———. "The Colour out of Space." *H. P. Lovecraft Collected Fiction, A Variorum Edition, Volume 2: 1926–1930*, edited by S. T. Joshi. New York: Hippocampus Press, 2017, pp. 367–399.

———. "The Silver Key." *H. P. Lovecraft Collected Fiction, A Variorum Edition, Volume 2: 1926–1930*, edited by S. T. Joshi. New York: Hippocampus Press, 2017, pp. 73–86.

———. *The Annotated H.P. Lovecraft*. edited by S. T. Joshi. New York: Dell Publishing, 1997.

Oakes, David A. *Science and Destabilization in the Modern American Gothic: Lovecraft, Matheson and King*. Westport: Greenwood Press, 2000.

Morton, Timothy. *The Ecological Thought*. Cambridge and London: Harvard University Press, 2010.

Procházka, Martin. "American Ruins and the Ghost Town Syndrome." *A Companion to American Gothic*, edited by Charles L. Crow, Chichester: John Wiley & Sons, 2014, pp. 29–40.

Sederholm, Carl H. and Jeffrey Andrew Weinstock, eds. *The Age of Lovecraft*. Minneapolis, MN: University of Minnesota Press, 2016.

Shaviro, Steven. *Post-cinematic Affect*. Winchester: Zero Books, 2010.

St Laurent, Marian. "America as an Afterimage in *True Detective*." Sensitiveskinmagazine.com, https://sensitiveskinmagazine.com/america-as-afterimage-in-true-detective/. Accessed November 18 2019.

Thacker, Eugene. *In the Dust of This Planet*. Winchester: Zero Books, 2011.

Touponce, William F. *Lord Dunsany, H.P. Lovecraft, and Ray Bradbury: Spectral Journeys*. Lanham, MD: The Scarecrow Press, Inc., 2013.

Filmography

"After You've Gone." *True Detective*, season1, episode 7, HBO, March 2, 2014.
"Form and Void." *True Detective*, season1, episode 8, HBO, March 9, 2014.
"Seeing Things." *True Detective*, season1, episode 2, HBO, January 19, 2014.
"The Long Bright Dark." *True Detective*, season 1, episode 1, HBO, January 12, 2014.
"The Locked Room." *True Detective*, season1, episode 3, HBO, January 26, 2014.
"The Secret Fate of all Life." *True Detective*, season 1, episode 5, HBO, February 16, 2014.

3 An Uncanny Absence

Lovecraft in Brazilian Cinema, 1975–2016

Lúcio Reis Filho and Sheila Schvarzman

Acknowledged worldwide for his horror fiction, Lovecraft has also significantly influenced cinema at least since the 1960s, when his writings inspired a new generation of filmmakers in the United States and planted the seed for an even larger fan base. In Brazil, foreign editions of his work—notably French translations, American pocketbooks, and the first versions in Portuguese—have also influenced writers, poets, and literary critics since the 1960s, with some echoes beginning to reverberate in Brazilian cinema. Since the mid-1970s, Lovecraftian themes and motifs have also inspired Brazilian horror films. However, even though Lovecraft's popularity has been traced in several ways, his increasing popularity in Brazil has not yet been discussed.

This study focuses on how Brazilian cinema engaged with, adapted, and appropriated Lovecraft, from the scarcity of local films inspired by his work in the last decades of the twentieth century to the new breadth of independent Brazilian filmmaking in the new millennium. In recent years, at least five productions connect both with his stories and with horror cinema made outside Brazil: the low-budget feature films *Nervo Craniano Zero* [*Cranial Nerve Zero*, 2012] and *Mar Negro* [*Dark Sea*, 2013], and the short films *Estrela Radiante* [*Shining Star*, 2013], *Nua por Dentro do Couro* [*Naked Under the Leather*, 2014] and *A Cor que Caiu do Espaço* [*The Colour out of Space*, 2016]. The discussion centered on these five pieces will demonstrate how Brazilian filmmakers rely on Lovecraftian themes and horror tropes to express anxieties related to violence, racism, and the naturalized inequalities in their country. There is also a Brazilian spin on these adaptations, characterized not only by the presence of specific social issues, but also by drawing on important local traits and customs. That is why it is necessary to pay more attention to these films, and why the Brazilian spin on them is so important. By entering this field, we intend to shed light on this heretofore uncharted territory.

Lovecraft's recognition was not immediate in Brazil. Although there have been readers of his work there since at least the 1960s, Lovecraft would only become a celebrity in the country in the twenty-first century. In the 2010s and the early 2020s, a growing interest in Lovecraft's

DOI: 10.4324/9780367713065-4

work has led to the mass publication of his stories which also coincides with the growth of Brazilian horror film productions. However, a broad understanding of Lovecraft's influence on Brazilian cinema requires an introduction to the history of the Brazilian editions of his work, and an examination of the first Lovecraft-inspired Brazilian films of the 1970s.

Lovecraft Editions in Brazil

In 1937, the year Lovecraft died, the writers August Derleth (1909–1971) and Donald Wandrei (1908–1987) founded Arkham House with the essential purpose of preserving the legacy of their friend, who was still relatively unknown at the time. Two years later, they published *The Outsider and Others*, the first collection of Lovecraft stories, which would be followed by others. Lovecraft, who used to sell his stories to *Weird Tales* and other pulp magazines for low prices, and who never had a book published during his lifetime, would eventually become a highly influential name in several countries, thanks to those Arkham House editions.

The first Brazilian edition of Lovecraft's selected works was published in 1966 by Edições GRD (GRD Editions). Translated into Portuguese by George Gurjan from *The Dunwich Horror and Others*, the collection *O que Sussurava nas Trevas* introduced Lovecraft to Brazilian audiences with three stories: "The Call of Cthulhu" (1926), "The Colour out of Space" (1927), and "The Whisperer in Darkness" (1930)—the story that lends this collection its name. The volume was part of an ambitious plan to revolutionize Brazilian publishing by promoting interest in fantastic[1] literature. Edições GRD had the support of the United States Information Agency (USIS), the official branch of a program intended to stimulate the publication and circulation of books "in tune with the US political interests" during the Cold War (Oliveira 105). The publishing house released many works of Brazilian literature and some reprints of world classics (Christofoletti 213; 215). A foreword by editor Gumercindo Rocha Dórea opens the volume as follows:

> Howard Phillips Lovecraft (1890–1937) é, indiscutivelmente, um dos maiores autores, de todos os tempos, no gênero do fantástico, seja ele representado pela ficção científica, pelo macabro, pelo terrorístico. Aqui [...] as histórias [...] bem demonstram o nível de sua capacidade criadora e a altitude de sua imaginação, garantindo a sua colocação, na história universal da literatura, ao lado de um Poe, um Bierce, um Potocki. H.P. Lovecraft, ao morrer, há quase trinta anos passados, era desconhecido na sua própria terra natal. Também o mundo o desconhecia, ressaltando-se, evidentemente, o círculo de seus admiradores, mas círculo diminuto. Hoje o mundo — inclusive os Estados Unidos da América do Norte lhe tributa as devidas honrarias, colocando-o no lugar que é seu desde as primeiras

> histórias que publicou. O Brasil, lógico e natural—com o atraso em que vivemos no tocante à cultura—desconhece H.P. Lovecraft.
>
> [Howard Phillips Lovecraft (1890–1937) is arguably one of the greatest authors of all time in the fantastic genre, whether represented by science fiction, macabre, or horror. Here [...] the stories [...] show the grandeur of his creative capacity and the scope of his imagination, ensuring his place in the universal history of literature next to a Poe, a Bierce, a Potocki. When H.P. Lovecraft died, almost thirty years ago, he was unknown in his own homeland. The world did not know him, except for the small circle of his admirers. Today, the world—including the United States of America—honors him, placing him in his rightful place, where he belongs since he published his first stories. Brazil, logically and naturally—considering the delay in which we live regarding culture—does not know H. P. Lovecraft].[2]

According to Dórea, Lovecraft was not known in Brazil before the mid-1960s because of what he describes as the "delay in which we live regarding culture." The editor's point refers to the way that Brazilian readership engaged with foreign literature. Some well-informed readers had privileged access to it, not having to wait for the translations. But that was a small circle of readers, a mostly refined group of middle- and upper-class people who obtained the products of "high culture" from France. One of these readers was the Brazilian poet and essayist Claudio Willer.[3] Close to the surrealists and beatniks, Willer discovered Lovecraft in 1963/64 through French editions.

The alleged delay also coincides with the sudden growth of Lovecraft's worldwide popularity. As Gary Lachman also points out, Lovecraft became one of the best-selling authors in the United States in the 1960s and was mentioned in the same breath as better-known writers such as Borges, Kafka, and Beckett (39). His writings had already crossed the borders of the Anglo-Saxon world at that time, first reaching France in the 1950s, then Brazil in the 1960s. Interest in Lovecraft may have been delayed in Brazil because of class-related issues, but that changed as soon as the market changed.

After GRD's initiative, the writer and literary critic Fausto Cunha would edit some of Lovecraft's stories in the 1980s for the series *Mestres do Horror e da Fantasia* [*Masters of Horror and Fantasy*]. The series was an endeavor of Francisco Alves, one of the oldest and most respected publishing houses in the country, a sign of Lovecraft's growing importance. Other ventures did the same in the 1990s, but Lovecraft's boom in popularity would only occur in the new millennium,[4] especially in 2015. Since then, Brazil lives and breathes the so-called "Lovecraft revival."[5] In the final part of this chapter, we will observe how this revival also manifested in contemporary cinema.

Lovecraftian Cinema in Brazil

Despite the positive reception of Roger Corman's films, in particular the cycle inspired by Edgar Allan Poe, Brazilian cinema did not embrace horror generally as a valid form of cultural expression. However, there was an amalgamation of local forms with the ubiquitous vernacular of American cinema, as defined by David Bordwell (1985). The most successful genre in Brazil was parody, a crowd-pleasing genre that was closely related to the comedies coming out of Hollywood. Beyond commercial films, a new expression would emerge in the 1960s with Cinema Novo, a movement that brought to light the urgencies of social reality, represented by the "Aesthetics of Hunger."[6] The search for a singular expression built bridges with neorealism, nouvelle vague, and Latin American cinema, making the economic and technical limitations a strength. On the other hand, filmmakers like Walter Hugo Khouri expressed a more universalist dimension. Relying on its own resources and sociocultural processes, modern Brazilian cinema incorporated narrative techniques and stylistic protocols from established genres such as horror, which adapted to Brazilian social and cultural realities.

In her doctoral dissertation (2008), Laura Cánepa cataloged the vast filmography of Brazilian horror cinema, analyzing the thematic diversity of these films. Her work suggests that there were no Lovecraft's adaptations up to that point. In fact, most of the Brazilian productions inspired by Lovecraft would emerge only after the 2010s. Before that development, however, there were two films that could be said to fit within the Lovecraftian mold: Carlos Hugo Christensen's *A Mulher do Desejo—A Casa das Sombras* [*The Woman of Desire—The House of Shadows*, 1975] and Jean Garret's *A Força dos Sentidos* [*Force of the Senses*, 1978].

Cánepa refers to *The Case of Charles Dexter Ward* (1927) as an "unconfessed inspiration" on *The Woman of Desire* (*Medo de Quê?* 235), a proposition later developed by Lúcio Reis Filho in the article "Lovecraft Out of Space: Echoes of the American Weird Fiction on Brazilian Literature and Cinema."[7] As suggested, Christensen grabs motifs from *Charles Dexter Ward* and "The Thing on the Doorstep" (1933), coming closer to Lovecraft's more "Gothic" vein (Joshi *I Am Providence* 458). A literary discourse created in the second half of the eighteenth century by English novelists (Cánepa 26), the Gothic evokes the imagery of the feudal past as a type of Dark Age. In America, the Gothic mode was adapted by Edgar Allan Poe into a means of exploring the possibilities of this literary genre. Later, Lovecraft "modernized and refined" its main features (Joshi *I Am Providence* 458). Christensen's film derives from this tradition and is quite similar to Corman's *The Haunted Palace* (1963), Lovecraft's first screen adaptation.

In *The Woman of Desire*, Marcelo (Jose Mayer) and his wife Sonia (Vera Fajardo) inherit from the man's late uncle (also played by Mayer) a "palace" in Ouro Preto, in the state of Minas Gerais, whose colonial architecture emulates the atmosphere of an ancient town. After arriving at the new residence, they meet the sinister butler (José Luiz Nunes) who persuades them to stay. Townspeople fear the old house, as they believe its former owner made a deal with the Devil. Later, Marcelo discovers the portrait of a mysterious young lady who bears a striking resemblance to Sonia. While diving into his uncle's past, Marcelo is ultimately possessed by him. Although there are possible Lovecraftian themes in this film, it is likely that the director was drawing on *The Haunted Palace*. Released ten years earlier, Corman's film received a positive response from Brazilian critics[8] and was broadcasted regularly on TV in the 1970s.[9] Argentine filmmaker living in Brazil at the time, Christensen could have watched the film without ever having read Lovecraft. *The Woman of Desire* deserves to be remembered, since it is a significant piece of Brazilian horror cinema and the filmmaker's work has been revisited in recent years.

For Eugenio Puppo (2015), the power of Christensen's films lies in their ability to assimilate different genres, since his auteurism and technical mastery have reshaped the classic genres by adding a transgressive ethos to them. In contrast, Afrânio Catani points to the apparent conservatism in the filmmaker's work: "(...) although [his] cinema was considered transgressive [...], it paradoxically ends up reasserting the traditional morals" (cited by Cánepa 230). This may be related to the Brazilian spin on Lovecraft's adaptations. *The Woman of Desire* combines Gothic tropes (the curse, the old house, the ghost) with larger idiosyncrasies of Brazilian culture: the patriarchy, the authority of rural oligarchs, the submission of its dependents, and the grasp of Catholic religion.

Jean Garret's *Force of the Senses* (1978) tells the story of a writer (Paulo Ramos) who moves to a secluded beach house to work on his new book and gets involved with his odd new neighbors. Interested in the history of Praia do Remanso [Blackwater Beach], he ends up being affected by its strange atmosphere: "como se a praia e o mar me amarrassem em suas entranhas...como se este lugar, objeto de tantos sonhos e fantasias, quisesse agora me prender para sempre" [as if the beach and the sea had me tied in their entrails...as if this place, the object of so many dreams and fantasies, wanted to imprison me forever (0:07:18–0:07:30)]. Night after night, the sea returns to the shore the same corpse of a mysteriously dead man, and the women next door can never remember their nocturnal sexual habits. There is no explanation for such events.

Force of the Senses evokes Gothic dream worlds in order to create a narrative that owes a great deal to the larger tradition of the fantastic. The disturbed character, the sinister coastal location, and the strange people who live there can be interpreted as Lovecraftian tropes, particularly in a story like "The Shadow over Innsmouth" (1931). The narrator in the film is also a traveler interested in antiques. The film ends with a translated quote from "The Call of Cthulhu": "Não está morto aquele que eternamente pode jazer, e após eternidades até mesmo a morte pode morrer" [That is not dead which can eternal lie / And with strange aeons even death may die (1:40:50–1:41:00)]. Thus, it also suggests something of the larger cosmic indifference that informs Lovecraft's fiction. Rachmaninoff's music and the literary source bring Garret closer to his major influence, the Brazilian director with Lebanese and Italian descent, Walter Hugo Khouri.

Given that elements of Lovecraft are scattered in Khouri's work, it seems likely that the writer did influence the filmmaker. An avid reader of horror and fantastic literature, Khouri once revealed to the journalist Jairo Ferreira[10] that by adding multiple references in his work he hoped to disorient and delight his viewers:

> My fascination with the fantastic, the unreal and the uncanny comes from my childhood readings...From a very early age I became familiar and fell in love with authors such as Edgar Allan Poe, Henry James... Sheridan Le Fanu, and Lovecraft....
>
> (qtd. in Cánepa *Tecnologias da comunicação* 232)

Christensen, Garret and Khouri appropriated Lovecraft and other authors in the "golden age" (1963–1983) of Brazilian horror cinema, when public policies fostered film production. After that, as Cánepa states (*Medo de Quê?* 115), the 1980s became generally unfriendly toward horror cinema in the country. In the broader picture, economic crisis raised production costs, the VCR reshaped the consumer market, and TV became the preferred source of entertainment. Brazilian cinema entered the 1990s in decline, with production plummeting almost to zero. A recovery process started in 1994, with thematic and stylistic diversity; some degree of concern with social issues; and adherence to a Hollywood-like standard. For these and other reasons, no Lovecraft adaptations would emerge before the new millennium.

Although horror was not ostensibly explored in the country during the late twentieth century, a "new wave"[11] of Brazilian horror cinema would occur in the 2000s, with new generations of filmmakers and aspiring artists gradually embracing the genre. Beyond the advantages of new technologies for making and sharing films, this recent boom relates to the fact that horror opens up new ways of exposing naturalized social inequalities. In fact, class-related issues have become effective horror tropes in Brazilian cinema. Racism, intolerance, patriarchy, and the oppression of women in gender relations also appear as horrific elements. The ironic titles of *As Boas Maneiras* (*Good Manners*, 2017) or *O Animal Cordial* (*Friendly Beast*, 2017) reveal the contradictions of a society organized under the guise of *cordiality*. In other words, the hierarchy of social relations is characterized by obedience tinged as "docility," when, in fact, the favor made men and women vassals of their masters—the powerful protect the weak in exchange for their services, so the weak consent and perpetuate their position as a seemingly natural destiny.

Starting in 2008, public policies and social programs were put in place to reduce inequality, including the expanding of minimum wage and granting much greater access to higher education. However, since 2016, these policies have been withdrawn and neoliberalism deepened the gulf between classes. As a result, a new generation of filmmakers entered the scene with critical and dissonant worldviews, sometimes exploring the ongoing social malaise. Brazilian horror cinema has grown in this context, with the appearance of big budget films like *Good Manners* and *Friendly Beast* as well as *Trabalhar Cansa* (*Hard Labor*, 2011) and *Morto Não Fala* (*The Nightshifter*, 2018). Independent production also grew during this time. Paradoxically, many of the horrors in recent indie films were suggested by the conservative skepticism that Lovecraft had. The analysis of five contemporary films will allow us to draw connections with his writings and its appropriation by Brazilian cinema. This discussion will show us the range of Lovecraft's influence and how it has been developed in Brazilian film.

Three Lovecraftian Short Films and Two Feature Films

Lovecraft has become a "twenty-first-century star" (Sederholm and Weinstock I), and cinema has certainly played an essential role in the popularization of his work. In the United States, the "call of Lovecraft"[12] was spreading since the 1950s, but it would not sound widely until the 1960s, when his writings influenced the works of Roger Corman, and subsequently Ridley Scott, John Carpenter, Stuart Gordon, and others. Besides "direct" adaptations such as *The Haunted Palace* (1963), Lovecraft emerged onscreen in ways "sometimes so indirect that one can never be sure whether the filmmaker was actually influenced by Lovecraft or merely thinking along parallel channels" (Joshi "Preface" 7–8). His themes, motifs, and characters would be recurring in popular culture, as they evoke latent fears in the American imagination through the ages.

According to Bernadette Lyra, contemporary Brazilian low-budget films deal with a refined, diverse repertoire that, in certain cases, appropriates the horror fiction of Lovecraft and other writers (132, 138). This is the case with three short films in recent years: Fabiana Servilha's *Estrela Radiante* [*Shining Star*, 2013], Lucas Sá's *Nua por Dentro do Couro* [*Naked Under the Leather*, 2014], and Petter Baiestorf's *A Cor que Caiu do Espaço* [*The Colour Out of Space*, 2016].

An uncredited adaptation of "The Colour out of Space" (1927), *Shining Star* begins with the arrival of a young black man in a rural town. A poor, wandering outsider, he is subject to the judging eyes of the locals, all white. Later, he joins a feeble man covered with a blanket to drink cachaça (a distilled spirit made from fermented sugarcane juice).

Terribly disfigured, the man explains in a flashback sequence what happened before he fell victim to a strange disease. One night, when trying to tune his static-affected radio, he sees a trail of green light crossing the sky, then a meteorite crashes in the vicinity. Curious, the man delves into the woods only to find a strange electronic device at the crash site. He takes the object to his home, where he examines it, but touching it makes him badly ill, with slimy skin and pustules sprouting all over his body. "Esse troço só me trouxe desgraça" [This thing only brought me disgrace (13:26–13:30)], he later explains, certain that he was "tocado pelo Coisa Ruim" [touched by the Evil One (05:58–06:01)].

In search of a cure, both men walk to a clearing lit by the crimson flames of torches. There, a black cultist wearing tribal ornaments chants in a strange tongue, his voice altered. The sinister figure performs a "diabolic" blood ritual, analogous to the voodoo rites and the "harrowing screams, soul-chilling chants and dancing devil-flames" (Lovecraft 34) described in "The Call of Cthulhu" (1926) and other stories. By representing the rite as a kind of diabolism, the film revisits Lovecraft's racial views and evokes the Brazilian racism against African religions, which has existed since colonial times and reflects a society whose dominant religion is Catholicism.

The next day, the man's health gets worse as he suffers from hallucinations caused by the greenish color. Suddenly, soldiers wearing white chemical suits and gas masks invade his hut and abduct him. Similar to the government troops in George Romero's *The Crazies* (1973), they add a conspiratorial dimension typical of zombie films. If radioactivity and its effects can be inferred from Lovecraft's story, the man's fate should remind viewers of the accident with Cesium-137 in Goiânia, the capital city in the Brazilian Central-West region. In 1987, scavengers found a radiotherapy device not properly discarded in an abandoned clinic. Believing it was valuable, they stole the device and disassembled it, sharing its pieces with others. They all died. Ignorance about science, radiation sickness, and the tragedy of those involved, the poor and the outcast, are important similarities between the film and the real event.

The Colour Out of Space (2016) is an original take on the eponymous story. This seven-minute short by trash film veteran Petter Baiestorf is the only direct adaptation of Lovecraft's work ever made in Brazil, and the only one to credit the writer. The film begins with a strange messianic figure fighting a military man in the countryside. The first defeats and kills the latter with a baroque crucifix. After the title sequence, the character sees a meteor crash, the fields catch fire, and an alien in an aluminum suit suddenly appears. A parody of the science fiction films from the nuclear age, the monster with batrachian face hunts down the protagonist who tries to protect himself with the crucifix. Soon after, while hiding in a house where a massacre took place, he ends up being killed with the same religious symbol, and the monster devours his guts. A traditional amulet against vampires, the crucifix proves to be ineffective against a Lovecraftian monster. There is no sacred bond between God and the object, and the Catholic religion holds no power. Baiestorf subverts the clichés of horror, parodying films like *The Exorcist* (1973) in which the priest and the crucifix represent salvation from evil.

The score encompasses berimbau rhythms and dissonant sounds. A traditional percussion instrument from Africa, the berimbau is a musical bow incorporated into the practice of capoeira—Afro-Brazilian martial art created by enslaved people in Brazil—to set the pace for the melee fight between two men, usually black. Widely included in Brazilian film scores, typical string/buzz sound of the berimbau plays in the first 30 seconds of the film, as the protagonist fights the military man. When he attacks with the crucifix, the music turns into a traditional carnival drum beat song, a "tropicalizing" feature in the rhythm of tambourine and cuíca (Brazilian drum). By including traditional Brazilian elements such as the music style and the Afro-Brazilian martial art scene, Baiestorf opposes the nuclear to the physical, technology to culture. The filmmaker's intention here is to mock tradition, institutions, and horror film conventions. The clumsy alien in the aluminum suit resembles the one depicted in Daniel Haller's *Die, Monster, Die!* (1965), the first adaptation of the story. The black and white footage of nuclear explosions in the final credits alludes to the ending scene of *Dr. Strangelove* (1964), but again the music playing is the carnival beat. Here, the director ironically subverts the technological tropes of the Cold War imaginary.

Baiestorf's interest in adapting Lovecraft's story dates back to 2015, but he had no money at the time and a friend helped him raise funds. "We shot everything in the middle of the night with a tiny team. (…) I tried to mix experimental film, sci-fi and marginal cinema, three of my passions."[13] As stated above, *The Colour Out of Space* is the only direct adaptation of Lovecraft's work ever made in Brazil. The film is a parody, which is an ironic subset of adaptation or an "extended, deliberate, announced revisitation of a particular work of art" (Hutcheon 170). What matters here is the variety of references, the low-budget production, and how Baiestorf deals with the literary source. In a bold, irreverent move, the filmmaker credited Lovecraft as screenwriter of his film, showing no ceremony to the consecrated writer. The result is one of the most original adaptations of Lovecraft's story to date.

A Lovecraftian short film with an all-female cast, Lucas Sá's *Naked Under the Leather* (2014) was exhibited at the H.P. Lovecraft Film Festival and CthulhuCon in Portland, 2016. The plot follows the ordinary lives of the residents of a flat block, like the housewife who goes to the supermarket and sells homemade blue cupcakes. However, behind the facade of apparent normality, she feeds the grotesque monster in her bathtub and cleans the black fluid it leaves on the bathroom floor. One of its victims will be the girl next door, a young woman in her twenties. She wears an eye patch and spends the day at home with her lesbian friends. After eating one of the blue cupcakes she buys from the housewife, she passes out. Then, the housewife drags the girl to her flat, where she cuts her into pieces in the bathroom and serves her as food to the monster. Strangely, when the monster's tentacles grab the housewife from behind, she feels sexual arousal.

The film can be read as a metaphor of individualism and lack of community. There is a latent intergenerational clash between the girl and the older female characters, the housewife and the landlady. In turn, the tentacular horror stands for the macho, homophobic society which devours the bodies of women and members of the LGBTQIA+ community every day in Brazil. Not by chance, the monster is kept locked in the bathroom, hidden behind the curtain. Its image represents the hatred deeply enclosed in the heart of Brazilian conservatism. The acts of disrespect and intolerance of some, or mere consent, are feeding the monster in their daily routines. In the bathroom scenes, we can only see its silhouette and its gooey tentacles. The partial revelation of the monster, which is unseen and, therefore, unnamable, and the horror it suggests are cinematic equivalents of Lovecraft's prose and narrative techniques. There is also a connection with body horror, an essential subgenre of horror cinema.

Two feature films of the 2010s also display connections with Lovecraft's work. Paulo Biscaia Filho's *Cranial Nerve Zero* (2012) develops the premise of the unethical or immoral medical experiment. The main characters are the horror writer Bruna Bloch (Guenia Lemos), who draws her inspiration "do esgoto, dos lugares podres, não apenas da cidade, mas principalmente da mente humana" [from the sewer, from rotten spots, not only from the city, but mainly from the human mind (06:32–06:39)] and the neurobiologist Bartholomeu Bava (Leandro Daniel),[14] inventor of a chip capable of controlling all bodily functions in order to stimulate creativity. Inspired by Lovecraft's Herbert West, the narcissistic scientist is arrested after his wife dies in one of his controversial experiments. After leaving prison, Bava offers the cold-hearted Bloch the chance to achieve unlimited creativity by having the chip implanted in her cranial nerve. They choose as their guinea pig the naïve Cristi (Uyara Torrente), a poor girl who came from the South to earn a living in the big city. Humiliated at a singing competition on TV and currently unemployed, the girl accepts the offer to subject herself to the experience. The cruel Bloch is proud to subjugate others, and extracting the girl's heart is a visceral metaphor for this process. But the exploitation does not end with the surgery, for the girl will become Bloch's enslaved ghostwriter. This body horror echoes two significant related works: Stuart Gordon's *Re-Animator* (1985) and *From Beyond* (1986), both adaptations of Lovecraft's eponymous stories. The medical experiment gone wrong is a theme drawn from these films, with the glowing green reagent referencing the first. The musical score includes Bonnie Tyler's *Total Eclipse of the Heart* (1983) as a diegetic song, reinforcing the influence of 1980s pop culture.

Another significant piece is Rodrigo Aragão's *Dark Sea* (2013), from the creator of a series of horror films that includes *Mangue Negro* [*Mud Zombies*, 2008],[15] *As Fábulas Negras* [*The Black Fables*, 2015], and *A Mata Negra* [*The Black Forest*, 2018]. As the titles denote, everything in his films is Black. The blackness here is literal, since it refers to black men, slavery, and colonial logic. It evokes the past, the imagery of tiny dark-skinned monsters in Brazilian folklore, which to some extent is also racist. *Dark Sea* brings the horror to a poor coastal village—a Brazilian Innsmouth. In the dead of night, two fishermen capture a grotesque sea monster that bites one of them. Later, the injured man becomes ill, turning into a zombie and attacking other villagers, who are also transformed. Eating the fish also effects the transformation, since a strange black fluid contaminated the seawater. The climax of the film takes place in a whorehouse where the battle against the zombies ends in a bloody massacre. The dread atmosphere, the grotesque monsters, the character of the book collector—although he is looking for Saint Cyprian's book, not the Necronomicon—and the macabre conjuring ritual are Lovecraftian motifs used to denounce the rawness of lack of compassion, pure evil, and taste for death in vogue in the Brazilian society. These themes also criticize social issues in Brazil, such as the economic exploitation, racism, and the machismo endemic and even more pronounced in impoverished rural areas. The black fluid alludes to recent catastrophes on the Brazilian coast, when oil stains leaked from vessels and poisoned the water. References range from Romero's zombie films to the body horror of Sam Raimi and David Cronenberg. The sea monster is an extreme version of the "Creature from the Black Lagoon," a Brazilian specimen in Universal's menagerie. *Dark Sea* uncovers the primitivism, the savagery, and the crudeness in the heart of Brazilian society, represented in the grotesque, raw, and explicit style of performance the cast adopts. Doing so, Aragão portrays Brazil's most racist and destructive face, one that proudly revealed itself in the last years with the ultraconservative turn in the country's politics. Lovecraft's transcendental horror lives and breathes in the various layers of a monstrous hell, endowed with Brazilian regionalism.

Conclusion

Lovecraft's presence in Brazilian cinema goes from a nearly total absence in the last decades of the twentieth century to major popularity in the new millennium. The sociocultural appropriation of his work results in significant expressions of local culture and its historical processes, such as social exclusion, racism, and class struggle. Historically, Brazil has built national myths such as the joyful mixture of races, the idea of racial democracy, and the peaceful nature of Brazilian society. These myths of national identity and social cohesion have eroded in recent years, with the deepening of neoliberalism, economic exploitation, and social malaise. In fact, the inequality in the country's formation is so deep that horror becomes a way of expressing the ills of such naturalized condition, especially for the oppressed and marginalized groups.

As Brazilian horror cinema has had to adapt to social and cultural reality, the genre allows filmmakers to express fears and anxieties. The films here discussed reveal a primitivism hidden behind the facade of morality, docility, and political correctness. By undressing the social reality, Baiestorf, Aragão, and other filmmakers denounce the sacrifice of human lives on the altars of famine, disease, and death by the wealthy classes, who celebrate guns, genocide, and the remnants of a slaveholding mindset. In this sense, echoes of Lovecraft unleash the unspoken and the unnamable of a society that does not want to be aware of its horrors. Mirroring their time, short and feature films made in different regions of the country bring together the writer's motifs and the idiosyncrasies of Brazilian culture. This makes them unique pieces of Lovecraftian cinema. The possible future of Lovecraft's influence on Brazilian horror films is unknown, as it may be waiting for new developments and new interpretations of the Mythos.

Notes

1 Although the Brazilian editorial project was centered on fantastic literature, Lovecraft's texts considered for it belong to the horror tradition.
2 Translated by the authors.
3 Interviewed by the authors on April 2, 2020.
4 Branco, Marcello Simão. H.P. "Lovecraft em língua portuguesa" [Lovecraft in Portuguese]. Retrieved from: www.scarium.com.br/artigos/sombras/simao06.html.
5 Retrieved from: https://oglobo.globo.com/cultura/livros/ignorada-por-decadas-obra-de-hp-lovecraft-renasce-com-novas-edicoes-no-brasil-14955626.
6 Created by filmmaker Glauber Rocha, this movement depicts the ugliness and misery of the Third World aiming at European audiences.
7 Article presented at The Third Biennal Dr. Henry Armitage Memorial Scholarship Symposium of New Weird Fiction and Lovecraft-Related Research in 2017. Granted with the Research Merit Award in the field of Social Sciences at Anhembi Morumbi University the same year, it was published in *Lovecraftian Proceedings* 3 in 2019.
8 Exhibited in Brazilian cinemas in 1964, *The Haunted Palace* received positive response. Luiz C. de Oliveira defined the film as "obra de terror puro e medido, que em nenhum momento perde seu impacto" [a pure and measured work on terror that never loses its impact]. As observed by the critic, the film left behind the "grotesco surrealista" [the surreal grotesque] and the "tom de caricatura" [caricature tone] of its predecessors *Tales of Terror* (1962) and *The Raven* (1963). Retrieved from: Oliveira, Luiz C. de. "O Castelo Assombrado" [*The Haunted Palace*]. *Jornal do Brasil*, 14 December 1964.
9 In 1973 and 1974, the years before the release of *The Woman of Desire*, Corman's films aired on TV Globo. Retrieved from: "Os Filmes da TV" [TV films]. *Jornal do Brasil*, 4 March 1973; 2 August 1974.

10 Cánepa retrieved this citation from: Ferreira, Jairo. "Os Mundos paralelos de Khouri" [Khouri's Parallel Worlds], *Folha de S. Paulo*, 5 March 1979.
11 Definition by Rod Gudino, Canadian journalist and editor of *Rue Morgue Magazine*.
12 This phenomenon, which paraphrases the short story "The Call of Cthulhu" (1926), was proposed by Lúcio Reis Filho in his doctoral thesis. It refers to Lovecraft's popularization and to the influence he exerts in later twentieth century, notably from the 1960s on, when his writings start to be adapted for cinema or to inspire horror and science fiction films.
13 Retrieved from: https://canibuk.wordpress.com/tag/a-cor-que-caiu-do-espaco/.
14 The character's names resonate with the larger horror tradition. There are obvious connections with the writer Robert Bloch and the Italian director Mario Bava.
15 Literal translation. The film was released worldwide as *Mud Zombies*.

Works Cited

Branco, Marcello Simão. *H.P. Lovecraft em língua portuguesa* [H.P. Lovecraft in Portuguese]. Retrieved from: www.scarium.com.br/artigos/sombras/simao06.html. Accessed August 18, 2020.

Bordwell, David, Kristin Thompson, and Janet Staiger. *The Classical Hollywood Cinema: Film Style and Mode of Production to 1960*. New York: Columbia University Press, 1985.

Cánepa, Laura Loguercio. "Medo de Quê? Uma História do Horror nos Filmes Brasileiros" [Fear of what? A History of Horror in Brazilian Movies]. Doctoral thesis. *State University of Campinas*, 2008.

———. Tecnologias da comunicação, horror e ficção científica: o caso de três filmes brasileiros. *Contemporânea - Comunicação e Cultura*, v. 10, n. 1, january/april 2012, pp. 223–238.

Christofoletti, Rodrigo. "A controvertida trajetória das Edições GRD entre as publicações nacionalistas de direita e o pioneirismo da ficção científica no Brasil." *Miscelânea - Revista de Pós-Graduação em Letras*, v. 8. Assis, SP: Universidade Estadual Paulista July–December 2010, pp. 208–225.

Hutcheon, Linda. *A Theory of Adaptation*. New York: Routledge, 2013.

Joshi, S. T. *I Am Providence: The Life and Times of H. P. Lovecraft*. New York: Hippocampus Press, 2013.

———. "Preface" in Migliore, Andrew, and John Strysik, eds. *Lurker in the Lobby: A Guide to the Cinema of H. P. Lovecraft*. Portland: Night Shade Books, 2006, pp. 5–8.

Lachman, Gary. *Turn Off Your Mind: The Mystic Sixties and the Dark Side of the Age of Aquarius*. New York: Disinformation Books, 2001.

Lovecraft, H. P. *O que sussurrava nas trevas*. Rio de Janeiro: Edições GRD, 1966.

———. "The Call of Cthulhu." *H. P. Lovecraft Collected Fiction, A Variorum Edition, Volume 2: 1926–1930*, edited by S. T. Joshi, New York: Hippocampus Press, 2017, pp. 21–55.

Lyra, Bernardette. Horror, humor e sexo no cinema de bordas. *Ilha do Desterro A Journal of English Language, Literatures in English and Cultural Studies*, v. 51, 2006, pp. 131–146.

Migliore, Andrew, and John Strysik. eds. *Lurker in the Lobby: A Guide to the Cinema of H. P. Lovecraft*. Portland: Night Shade Books, 2006.

de Oliveira, Laura. *Guerra Fria e política editorial: a trajetória da Edições GRD e a campanha anticomunista dos Estados Unidos no Brasil (1956–1968)*. Maringá: Eduem, 2015.

Oliveira, Luiz C. de. "O Castelo Assombrado." *Jornal do Brasil*, 14 December 1964.

"Os Filmes da TV." *Jornal do Brasil*, 4 March 1973.

"Os Filmes da TV." *Jornal do Brasil*, 2 August 1974.

Puppo, Eugenio. "Apresentação". *Retrospectiva Carlos Hugo Christensen*, 2015. Retrieved from: http://www.portalbrasileirodecinema.com.br/christensen

Ramos, Fernão Pessoa, and Luiz Felipe Miranda, eds. *Enciclopédia do Cinema Brasileiro*. São Paulo: Edições Sesc São Paulo; Editora Senac São Paulo, 2012.

Reis-Filho, Lúcio. "O Chamado de Lovecraft: Visões da América Profunda no Cinema de Horror da Segunda Metade do Século XX" [The Call of Lovecraft: Visions of Deep America in Horror Cinema from the Second Half of the 20th Century]. Doctoral thesis. University Anhembi Morumbi, São Paulo, 2019a.

———. "Lovecraft out of Space: Echoes of American Weird Fiction on Brazilian Literature and Cinema." *Lovecraftian Proceedings 3: Selected Papers from the Dr. Henry Armitage Memorial Scholarship Symposium–NecronomiCon Providence, 2017*, edited by Dennis P. Quinn. New York: Hippocampus Press, 2019b.

Sederholm, Carl H., and Weinstock, Jeffrey Andrew. *The Age of Lovecraft*. Minneapolis, MN: University of Minnesota Press, 2016.

Spaulding, Todd David. "H.P. Lovecraft & The French Connection: Translation, Pulps and Literary History." Doctoral thesis. University of South Carolina, 2015.

Willer, Claudio. Interview. 2 April, 2020.

4 The Masks of E'ch-Pi-El

Interpreting the Life and Work of H.P. Lovecraft

John Glover

That is not dead which can eternal lie,and with strange eons, even death may die.

H.P. Lovecraft

For a field that has largely moved on from the need to discuss in earnest whether or not authors are dead, literary scholarship nevertheless still encounters notable biographical challenges in treating the works of Howard Phillips Lovecraft. While 20th century decenterings of the author-as-person by Barthes and others, coupled with the move to Foucauldian "author-functions," helped to elaborate the textual focus of New Criticism, many literary scholars have more or less gently swung the pendulum back toward approaches considering the actual role of an author or, at least, the cultural matrix from which a work emerged. Any of these would provide plenty of space for nuanced, contemporary readings of Lovecraft's work.

While scholars may have taken diverse approaches to his work, Lovecraft, the author-as-person, has remained an obdurate specter, haunting critical conversations almost regardless of any given paper, book, or article's topic—not to mention its theoretical approach, whether grounded in ecocriticism, new historicism, or otherwise. Far from being an obscure or minority approach, however, this configuration of Lovecraft Studies dominated the field up until the turn of the century. It remains significant, by number of publications, even if it appears to be decreasing by impact on the overall scholarly conversation.[1] It was and is propagated by Lovecraft's foremost living champion, S.T. Joshi, along with many scholars who have followed Joshi's approach. Whatever the approach, as often as not studies of Lovecraft's work court controversy. This tendency has accelerated in recent years, driven by both simultaneous shifts in our sociopolitical environment and the continued rise in interest in Lovecraft and his work.

Scholarly and popular debates about how best to consider Lovecraft, particularly in light of his well-known prejudices, are hardly unusual during an

DOI: 10.4324/9780367713065-5

age of reckoning with idols whose feet are clearly made of clay. From #MeToo to the toppling of Confederate monuments in the United States, the 21st century is seeing a new wave of very public wrestling with creators' or historical figures' unsavory or unacceptable legacies—not merely the kind of academic squabbling for which ivory towers are built. As approaches to Lovecraft have broadened, and as his works have attracted the interest of scholars not solely focused on Lovecraft (or weird fiction from Golden Age pulps), the man and his imago are ever-more-often considered in light of his influential fictions. The rise of the Web, evolutions in literary discourse since landmarks like 1980s *Four Decades of Criticism* or 1991s *An Epicure in the Terrible*, and the spread of Lovecraft's influence have led increasing numbers of readers to encounter his work. In the current moment, Lovecraft is less a subject of study than a gift. Of enduring interest to scholarly and popular audiences, his work is continually elaborated, countered, remediated, and evolved by contemporary authors writing in many genres, popular and otherwise.

The biographical aspect of Lovecraft's study is no inexplicable accident of scholarly evolution. It is a direct result of Lovecraft's authorial self-fashioning, both in quality and quantity, and of the posthumous propagation of Lovecraft's imago, most notably by champions August Derleth and Donald Wandrei via their foundation of Arkham House. Being dead, despite this chapter's epigraph, Lovecraft cannot readily discourse on the intentions underpinning his rhetorical self-fashioning. That has not, however, restrained some of his defenders from repeated recitation of well-known views of Lovecraft as kindly "Uncle Theobald," reclusive aesthete, or avuncular mentor to young writers, all of which can be easily drawn from many textual sources, whether Lovecraft's letters or memoirs by his friends and acquaintances.[2] And yet, Lovecraft was well aware of the factors that go into the making of authorial careers (Mariconda 20). Even as we are not yet done with Lovecraft, it is long past time to begin serious consideration of Lovecraft's role in actively shaping his own legacy. Given what seems clear from the vantage point of the 21st century—persistent money troubles, comparative obscurity in his lifetime, and deliberate pose as gentleman of letters—it seems inevitable that we should ask what actions Lovecraft took that saved him from literary historical oblivion.

Some part of the survival of Lovecraft's work must also be attributed to the pains he took as a writer. Samuel R. Delany, in his essay "Emblems of Talent" points to characteristics of good writing as he perceives it to have existed in recent centuries. From Romantic *Begeisterung* to technical ambition, the traits that he describes could easily be applied to Lovecraft in his most active phases as a writer (Delany 9–14). While it may be tautological to describe a genre-defining author as a "talented writer," Lovecraft could no more see the future than he could happily live in New York City. His efforts in writing, whatever his paraliterary activities, were necessarily made in the hopes shared by all writers: readership.

This chapter explores hitherto largely unexplored aspects of the reception of Lovecraft's work, correspondence, and literary legacy that have only intermittently been held up to critical scrutiny. In particular, it explores the coherence of the Lovecraft Circle, the constitution of the posthumously published *Selected Letters* (*SL*), how controversy dogs and helps Lovecraft's reputation, and the hand Lovecraft himself took in shaping his own legacy. These are among many factors worth considering in a preliminary investigation of the peculiarities of how Lovecraft scholarship evolved, and how it has or has not grappled with the influence of Lovecraft's biography on the reception of his work.

Useful Constructs

While interest in Lovecraft's life has not actually eclipsed interest in his work, the frequency with which his doings or opinions appear in scholarly articles or the popular press is remarkable. The extent to which this occurs is evident, among other ways, by comparison with his pulp contemporaries. It would serve little purpose to set Lovecraft against the more-popular-in-his-time Seabury Quinn, who appears in vanishingly small scholarly or popular writing (Connors 51). Some of Lovecraft's fellow *Weird Tales* writers have attained something approaching a lasting prominence, however, or at least their works have. By comparison, Robert E. Howard rarely comes in for the same level of biographical interest that Lovecraft does, regularly going unmentioned in popular articles about his most famous creation, Conan the Cimmerian.

Lovecraft is hardly the first author to become a pop figure, but the extent to which his person intersects with publication, discussion, and remediation of his work has been noted before (Jones 234–235). While contemporary authors like Stephen King or Neil Gaiman have become widely known to the public, their prominence in this regard can at least to some extent be attributed to mass media permeation, along with their own active role in fostering their personal presences online. While "classic" authors like Austen or Shakespeare have become widely known, a large part of their prominence in this regard can be attributed to their cultural omnipresence and substantial role in Anglo-American (to say nothing of worldwide) literature curricula. There are no similarly popular authors from the pulps, or even in the history of early 20th century genres like fantasy or horror.[3] Lovecraft has now repeatedly appeared as a character in fiction, comics, and on screen, as well as being embodied as a playable character in multiple games. The omnipresence of the author-as-person in the fuzzy set of fields in which Lovecraft Studies resides could not but influence the scholarship; it also helps to account for his repeated presence in works where biography might otherwise have no remit. Among recent scholarship, one can point to such diverse works as James Kneale's "'Ghoulish Dialogues': H. P. Lovecraft's Weird Geographies," Gina Wisker's "Speaking the Unspeakable: Women, Sex, and the Dismorphmythic in Lovecraft, Angela Carter, Caitlín R. Kiernan, and Beyond," or Fiona Price's "Prosthetic Pasts: H. P. Lovecraft and the

Weird Politics of History" as making use of Lovecraft's personal writing to illuminate their sundry topics (44, 212–215, 141–143). This is in no way intended as criticism of these fine studies, merely an observation that Lovecraft-the-person insinuates himself into everything.

Regardless of how popular they were in their time, pulp authors generally receive scant biographical attention. Not so for Lovecraft. While perhaps the greatest attention has been paid over time to Willis Conover's *Lovecraft at Last*, de Camp's *Lovecraft: A Biography* (not least for purposes of refutation), and Joshi's *I Am Providence*, Lovecraft is the subject of over a dozen biographies or memoirs. Many of these works are of ongoing interest and continue to be cited in contemporary Lovecraft scholarship. What is less clear is how useful Lovecraft's life is in reading his work, and whether such readings still bear new fruit—or whether they *should* bear new fruit, if based on questionable premises. Articles explicitly *about* Lovecraft, of course, are another matter entirely. What is more interesting is the extent to which events from or aspects of Lovecraft's life are deployed in discussions about Lovecraft within the worlds of fandom or scholarship.

On the less-serious side of this, and to find sources for the new fruit previously mentioned, consider the beans. As attested by Lovecraft in many letters, his eating habits often reflected his impoverished status. In particular, during a particularly lean period in 1925, he wrote in detail about a diet heavily featuring beans, possibly unheated, from a can (Joshi "Providence" 576–577). Improbably, this regrettable episode has come to be more than a little known by Lovecraft readers. The story is occasionally deployed metonymously as a stand-in for greater descriptions of poverty. While episodes from many authors' lives have become known to the public over time (Hemingway's drinking, Highsmith's snails, etc.), and not necessarily attractive episodes, the references to Lovecraft's diet in popular discourse are at times perplexingly affectionate, up to and including fan-made art of Lovecraft and beans (Deranged Cultist).

Are minor aspects of an author's diet *really* worth considering in the context of the overall reception of their work? Perhaps not in the case of a minor author with little readership, but in the case of Lovecraft, "the beans" stand as a squib of implied narrative about the condition of the life of the author. What does it say about the relationship between work and reader, particularly either longtime or first-time readers, that their encounters with Lovecraft's work may be mediated through such a prominent biography? Interested readers have, after all, always ferreted out biographical information about all but the most reclusive authors. When it comes to Lovecraft, however, I submit that it may actually be impossible to have any sort of enduring relationship with the work without knowing about the life.[4]

More strongly related to criticism, among other commonly deployed constructs associated with Lovecraft, the Lovecraft Circle is perhaps the most well known. It is a useful shorthand for talking about Lovecraft's influence on and relationships with various of his literary contemporaries, and less commonly in talking about his correspondents generally. The Circle is a strange, unstable construct that has been propagated by Lovecraft's partisans and fans, often being used simultaneously as a signifier for "Lovecraftian things" and a reservoir of feelings about Lovecraft as a kindly person, inherently disarming criticism of Lovecraft's work and views. It is, in short, difficult to speak clearly about an author's literary or personal failings when participants in critical discussions, whether popular or academic, repeatedly imply or baldly state that "he was a nice guy," which—true or not—is beside the point.

The prominence and durability of the "Lovecraft Circle" is demonstrated by its use as a theme for the first World Fantasy Convention held in 1975 in Providence, Rhode Island. Despite the Convention's struggle with Lovecraft's influence in recent years, the event was founded in celebration of both then-contemporary authors and the greats of the Pulp Era (Wilson 15–16). The roster of honorees included many who knew Lovecraft at the first or second remove, or had at the time or since had much to do with the propagation of his legacy. Thirty-eight years after his death, the theme of the Circle was thought viable enough to draw attendees from far and wide, and it did. 1975 was an important year for Lovecraft Studies for many reasons, not least the publication of L. Sprague de Camp's biography, and the flood of reactions and counterarguments it produced (Joshi "Providence" 1037–1038). De Camp's portrayal of Lovecraft was neither resolutely hostile, nor deeply sympathetic, and it dwelled at length in psychological analysis offered without any training on the biographer's part, though the often negative judgment of posterity tends to ignore the book's role in spurring further work, and some reactions at the time were favorable (Black 247–248).

De Camp's was the first major biography of Lovecraft. What prompted its writing? As de Camp noted, he had previously written about Lovecraft, and August Derleth's 1971 passing had left Lovecraft's first great champion's biography unwritten (de Camp xii). De Camp considered himself a more objective biographer than Derleth, and he had obtained access to or personally collected many of Lovecraft's letters. What is not always evident from de Camp's notes is the extent to which he relied on *SL*, a useful, interesting work that has not been as thoroughly explored as it should.

An Odd Selection

Published from 1965 to 1976, *SL* is a five-volume set of letters written by Lovecraft, culled from his vast correspondence, the volumes variously edited by August Derleth, James Turner, and Donald Wandrei. The set was published by Arkham House, the publishing house founded by Derleth and Wandrei with the explicit intent of making available their friend's work in hardback. These volumes would make a fascinating study in editorial practice, as has been previously noted (Joshi "Index," 5–6). Some would appear from the published text many pages long, some a mere paragraph.

While the typography as a rule reflects when excerpting has taken place, it conveys nothing of the length of the original letters excerpted.

Critics, editors, anthologists, and others who have treated Lovecraft's correspondence have focused on such topics as the Cthulhu Mythos, subsequently notable authors like Ramsey Campbell or Robert Bloch, Lovecraft's racial or political views, or authors with whom Lovecraft is often perceived to have connections, whether Lord Dunsany or Lovecraft's fellow *Weird Tales* authors. Trying to understand how the creator of Yog-Sothoth and kin connected with his literary and personal correspondents, as well as figuring out exactly how those correspondents fit together, seems particularly important for an author whose social life was frequently lived through letters. What impact, for instance, did Lovecraft's association with Rheinhart Kleiner or James F. Morton have on him as an author? To judge by the depth and quality of critical bibliography, the common perception is "very little." Apart from explicitly autobiographical work, whether de Camp's, Joshi's, or otherwise, neither Kleiner nor Morton come in for much critical attention, though Lovecraft's correspondence with each was substantial, certainly compared to his comparatively brief correspondence with Robert E. Howard, although the latter has attracted far more scholarly notice.

While one can get a sense of Lovecraft's correspondents included within *SL* by looking at tables of contents, other methods exist that may be more illustrative, figuratively and literally. Network analysis and visualization are often used to understand large data sets, involving hundreds or thousands of relationships. *SL*, by contrast, is smaller: 930 letters to 73 different correspondents. The set is problematic in various regards, from transcription errors to radical editorial choices, but overlarge it is not. Here is a close-up of a simple model of the network, based purely on addressees, without reference to contents, post dates, locations, etc.[5]

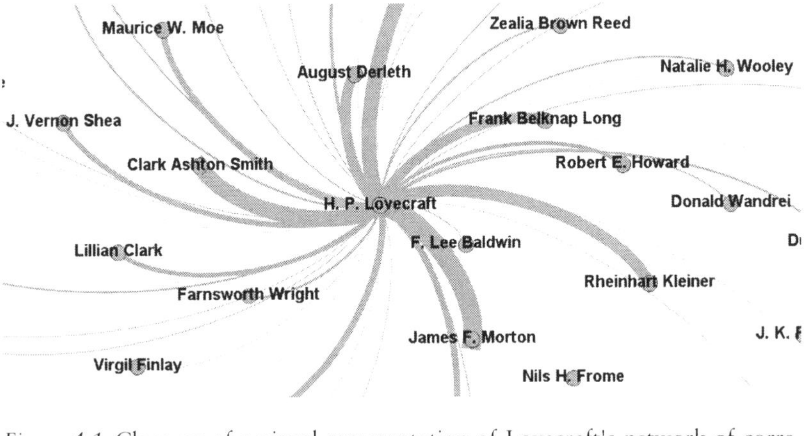

Figure 4.1 Close-up of a visual representation of Lovecraft's network of correspondents as represented in *SL*, illustrating frequency of appearance of different correspondents.

Lovecraft is at the center, as he sent all the letters in the set, and close to the center lie the names of correspondents who most commonly appear in *SL*. Some of these names clearly belong to the Lovecraft Circle, however vaguely one defines it; but others, less so: family members or revision clients, for instance. While Derleth and Wandrei surely would have encountered challenges in securing letters that might serve as a statistically proportionate representation of Lovecraft's overall correspondence—whether in toto or in the "Circle"—it seems strange in retrospect and from a thematic perspective that *SL* is not centered on either, and it speaks to the set's construction as a work for aficionados rather than scholars. Given the many years that stand between some of Lovecraft's correspondences, it seems that the roster of names is ahistorically compressed, combining notable and beloved authors with whom Lovecraft was in contact at various times in his life, sometimes decades apart.[6]

While the Circle could be a useful way to discuss an environment of literary production, or even a moment within the history of weird fiction, it overlooks the years or decades between some of the individual correspondences. If the Lovecraft Circle is achronic, and its value comes in considering how certain authors relate to Lovecraft, perhaps it is more helpful, in the 21st century, to talk about Lovecraft *Circles*. On the one hand, this would allow for more meaningful biographical consideration, and some have done this. Should we speak of a "Cthulhu Circle," or something to this effect? Composed of authors who have addressed Lovecraft directly, as correspondent or otherwise, whether Caitlín R. Kiernan or W.H. Pugmire? Many scholars have written about the perpetuation of the Lovecraft Mythos (or the Derleth Mythos, or Cthulhu Mythos, depending on the scholar), of course, but what attractive factors bring an author into the "Lovecraft Circle?" To this, there is no firm answer, other than that it has typically had something to do with association with Lovecraft in his lifetime, and some relationship with literary production, most commonly authorship.

Now, to return to *SL*, to describe its particular model as the simplest one could craft of Lovecraft's correspondence would be ludicrous. Is a model simpler if it is purely based on the numerical frequency of letters in *SL*? That says nothing about the fact that only one paragraph of some letters was reprinted, whereas in other cases many pages of a letter were reprinted. If digital editions of *SL* were available, one could perhaps use word count or other metrics to explore the work's composition.[7] Past scholarship has generally treated the Lovecraft Circle as a given, without bothering to delimit it. At the other end of the spectrum, in Joshi's two-volume biography, it is treated in such depth and nuance that the Circle vanishes, amalgamated with all the other minutiae of Lovecraft's life, although it has been the subject of more or less focused interest in various articles and graduate-level studies. Though some scholars still rely on *SL*, newer critical essays and monographs tend to cite his letters less frequently, and few have the character of the scholarship commonly published under Joshi's aegis in the early decades of Lovecraft Studies, in the eponymous periodical or otherwise. Such work typically tended toward close reading and frequently, if not always, eschewed explicit theoretical frameworks.

The shift away from *SL*, and perhaps the letters generally, may be understandable, given the need for new scholars to make new marks. It does leave unanswered the question of just what we now make of Lovecraft's voluminous correspondence, even as the publication of single-correspondent editions of the letters marches forward apace. The editions published by Hippocampus Press, in particular, are making available conversations that readers and critics with an eye to biography have wanted for as long as *SL* made clear the scope of Lovecraft's correspondence. These editions remedy some of the defects of *SL*, and in some cases they provide that which readers of Lovecraft's letters have long sought: letters from each side of a given correspondence. These newer collections have made more broadly available otherwise unpublished content, but they are only part of the whole one would need to understand the literary network that Lovecraft actually inhabited.

While I agree with the assessment of virtually the whole of the field that *SL* was a landmark that ushered in an entirely new era, what is most needed at this point is quality digitization of as many of the letters as can be digitized, made available through one electronic portal. Single-correspondent editions of his letters are enjoyable to read, and have much to offer, but what they offer is not comparable in type to the advances that could be made electronically. Lovecraft Studies may be able to make a true Great Leap Forward if both this and good electronic editions are to be had, or, still better, a corpus of *all* Lovecraftiana, from the fiction to the letters to the poetry to the nonfiction.

At the end of the day, I do not advocate for or against the use of Lovecraft's letters in criticism. That said, the letters may be inescapably tempting, as shifts in the attitudes and constitution of his readership have rendered Lovecraft unpalatable in many eyes, leading some to seek corroboration of perspectives and prejudices portrayed in the fiction.

Controversial Figure

One can hardly imagine an author better-suited than Lovecraft to our current moment. As major cultural figures are called to account, their works reconsidered from newly visible positionalities, Lovecraft is there like a gift. The breadth of his fiction, nonfiction, and personal writing renders him a perfect subject for study, and for many reasons. Sources for myriad claims can be found within the exhaustively documented final quarter-century of Lovecraft's life. He is certainly good for "thinking with" when it comes to prejudice: the particulars of his views ribbon through his work, frequently complicating and strengthening the effects he sought to produce. As has often been observed, works Lovecraft wrote at the height of his powers, like "The Shadow over Innsmouth," are often predicated on and revel in a sublime fear of otherness (Bealer 45–46). This fear stands in eldritch, terrifying fictional counterpart to the eye-popping hatred of foreigners that runs like a veritable Mississippi through his letters. The specifics of his attitudes in this regard have been considered in depth in reams of academic and popular discourse. Leaving aside the easy targets, like his anti-Semitism or xenophobia, his views on women have come into play in many articles and online discussions, and the perceived lack of interest in/appeal to female readers itself spurred in reaction the publication of an anthology of women authors writing Mythos fiction, *She Walks in Shadows* (Wisker 218).

A common rejoinder to charges of prejudice against any historical figure is the ever-popular claim that the subject was of their time (as in "Lovecraft was a man of his time"). The nuances of such claims, along with their rhetorical elaborations and counters, should be unfamiliar to no reader of this chapter. What is important in Lovecraft's case is his exhaustive and long-lived self-documentation. Unlike many of his contemporaries, who tend to have, at most, a volume or two of letters published, Lovecraft has dozens. Whatever critical fire one may wish to stoke underneath Lovecraft's works, fuel can be found in his other writings, adding further invitations to biographical criticism. The letters run to such depth, expressing such fine variations in his thinking over time, using so many differing formulations, that I believe one can draw support from them for truly contrary interpretations, if not literally any word a given combatant might wish to put in Lovecraft's mouth.

To the exploration of problematic aspects of Lovecraft's fiction can be added the controversies that have to some extent overshadowed his legacy in recent years, foremost among them the decision to remove his likeness from the World Fantasy Awards (Glover 181; Jarvis 1135; Sederholm and Weinstock 27). These will persist, surely, given the continued rise in popularity of Lovecraft's Cthulhu Mythos that is happening even as America grapples with ever-more-visible social, economic, and class inequalities, coupled with the impact of broadening racial and ethnic diversity. His readership is no longer limited to the white, male aesthetes whom he viewed as the optimal readers of weird fiction. What new audiences and authors will make of his work is an ongoing project and open question.

While we may believe that we know the extent of Lovecraft's prejudices, this may not be true. The general tenor of his views and their elaboration over time are known, but when dealing with an author whose correspondence is so voluminous, it seems safe to say that there must exist letters, not yet widely read, that contain vitriol as shocking as anything else he ever wrote. What is rarely asked is whether these seas of words were intended for the eyes of later readers, and whether Lovecraft may have taken care in advance to provide a suitable body of work that might survive him and propagate his literary legacy.

Building the (Im)Perfect Author

Among the 20th century's many diligently self-mythologizing writers, the great Modernists have a special place. From Woolf to Hemingway, from Eliot to Fitzgerald, self-construction was a heady, urgent game, played via newspaper profiles, letters, memoirs, and romans-à-clef. Lovecraft's attention to weird fiction in all of its forms overshadowed his other readings, but given he was an autodidact who keenly felt his lack of academic credentials, it is unsurprising that he was familiar with the authors of his time. As a rule, he seemed to have little love for their works, but that is not to say that he paid no attention to how they wrote, or how they framed their writing practice in interviews or other sources. And, of course, Lovecraft himself has previously been considered in light of the dominant literary movement of his time, most recently in Jason Ray Carney's *Weird Tales of Modernity: The Ephemerality of the Ordinary in the Stories of Robert E. Howard, Clark Ashton Smith and H. P. Lovecraft.*

Lovecraft has, however, been characterized so often as a naïf in matters of business and orderly operation of literary activities that it has become an all-concealing mask. Unlike Lovecraft the aficionado of cats, Lovecraft the antiquarian and faux-Georgian, or Lovecraft the doughty consumer of ice cream, this imago of hapless gentility leads readers away from the possibility that Lovecraft knew what he was doing in pursuing a literary agenda, and that he took rational actions designed to further his literary career and ultimate influence. While I do not argue that Lovecraft was a master manipulator who somehow managed to put his hand on the lever of fate in order to bring about our current Cthulhu-Industrial Complex, I believe that he had more agency and savvy than is sometimes attributed to him.

Lovecraft constructed the conditions for the reception of his work, for instance, by the writing of *Supernatural Horror in Literature* (Glover 172–175). By surveying the field of weird fiction and highlighting as the best those pieces that passed a subjective test for quality, he established himself as both an authority by virtue of his deep knowledge and a connoisseur by virtue of his excellent taste, inviting the reader to commune with Lovecraft in a shared set of "keen special sensibilities" (96). Whatever its objective merits as an assessment of its stated topic, this lengthy essay is a textbook exercise in Bourdieusian cultural capital, within which the author embedded bright lures. These lures, while on the surface designed to articulate the nature of affinities between readers of weird fiction, dug deeper, issuing a call to commune that had the clear potential to build Lovecraft's social capital by drawing to him more devotees of supernatural horror, who might have seen and been moved by his descriptions of the appeal of the best of the genre. Objections to this include such hard facts as Lovecraft's well-documented poverty in life, as well as the apparently modest impression that he left on other weird fiction notables of the time.

What of Lovecraft's letters, discussed at length above? Estimates of how many he wrote reach very high, sometimes as far as 100,000, although no catalog or census exists. Leaving aside Lovecraft's legible delight in many of the letters he wrote, as well as the interpretive scholarly potential embedded in computational approaches, there exist easily hundreds of thousands of words' worth of letters. In all probability, even accounting for the disappearance or destruction of some of his letters over time, there exist *millions* of words' worth of letters written by Lovecraft. Among the contributing factors to the perpetuation of a literary reputation—republication, anthologizing, critical champions, and so on—the existence of personal writing that is read by fans and studied by scholars is almost universally a supporting factor. Per de Camp:

> It has been guessed that he wrote at least 100,000 letters, totaling at least ten million words. His letters to Clark Ashton Smith alone averaged about 40,000 words a year. He usually had fifty to a hundred correspondences going at once[.] ... He averaged eight to ten letters a day; when he fell behind, he raised the figure to fifteen. Most letters were four to eight pages long, but some ran to sixty or seventy pages.
>
> (112)

These are not the actions of an author trying simply to schmooze his way into a career, but it cannot have failed to occur to Lovecraft that he was leaving to posterity a tremendous amount of verbiage, which he well knew could be deployed for many purposes. By writing thousands of letters, notes, and postcards, Lovecraft left behind a rich deposit of material with which to interpret his work and to potentially know a version—or versions—of his person.

Beyond the letters, when assessing Lovecraft's authorial self-construction, we should look to his fiction. To assess an author's entire oeuvre in a sentence would be folly, but it seems not unreasonable to say that Lovecraft by and large put his heart into his work. That he endeavored to write lasting stories is clear from, among other things, his own accounts of the writing of his strongest work, scattered throughout *SL*.

In the final analysis, when aiming at a healthy literary afterlife, an author can do worse than to try to write excellent, spirited fiction.

Far from the average Anglo-American pulp author who wrote as many words as possible, as quickly as possible, to generate as much revenue as possible, given per-word compensation rates, Lovecraft appears to have endeavored by all accounts—notably including his own—to take the time he needed in order to meet his artistic goals. Excellence alone, though, as literary history has shown, is no guarantee of posthumous readership. Fortunately for Lovecraft's legacy, he wore more masks than that of the aesthete dedicated to art for art's sake.

Notes

1 S.T. Joshi's publication of Lovecraft's letters, primarily if not entirely with Hippocampus Press, continues at a formidable rate. These volumes contain both sides of multiple correspondences and are unquestionably a service to the field, making available in unabridged format a meaningful portion of Lovecraft's voluminous correspondence that might otherwise never be published. These volumes' near-complete absence from peer-reviewed or otherwise academic scholarship, however, along with their absence from most academic library collections, marks bibliographically the Great Divide of Lovecraft Studies.

2 These views are so widely known that they are almost without fail deployed in arguments about Lovecraft's racism, xenophobia, anti-Semitism, or other prejudices in order to counter criticism. While these characterizations may be accurate, their presence has repeatedly derailed attempts to address Lovecraft's failings head-on, not entirely unlike the tendency of staunch defenders of the Lost Cause of the Confederacy to trot out stories of Robert E. Lee's "kindly" behavior toward the human beings he enslaved. It should also be said, in light of his status as Lovecraftian advocate and editor, that S.T. Joshi has written repeatedly and at length about Lovecraft and prejudice. Joshi's critics have often ignored his rigor on this matter—distracted, perhaps, by his frequently pugnacious critical stance.

3 One might include in this group such figures as Agatha Christie or Dashiell Hammett, famous in their time and after. In my opinion, however, each has been eclipsed by the fame of their creations, in ways that Lovecraft, however popular Cthulhu and kin may be, has not. Likewise, the majority of figures from the early decades of fantasy or science fiction are neither well known nor much read, and with the exception of Mary Shelley, those whose works are still read are known as little more than a name and lack broader cultural caché.

4 In the 30+ years since I first read Lovecraft, I have never met a Lovecraft reader not at least slightly familiar with the author's life. More common is the reader familiar with broad strokes of his biography and prejudices.

5 I mapped this using the analysis/visualization program Gephi. The letters sent between Lovecraft and correspondent are treated as "edges," the term used to describe connections between "nodes" (people in this case) in the network.

6 Despite this, I myself still find it hard not to talk about the "Lovecraft Circle," so strong is its allure, not unlike the reflexive blasphemy of some atheists.

7 A better question, perhaps, is whether it is worth the effort to study *SL* in greater depth. After various continued work on it, I have concluded that it is not, at least for me, however strange and interesting a work *SL* may be.

In my experiments with further visualizations of Lovecraft's network as it appears in *SL*, I had to find a way to establish interconnections among the letters. I would have much less confidence in the quality of my work without the existence of S.T. Joshi's *Index to Selected Letters*, which served as both a check against my own data and as an invaluable source in indexing the letters. It is not a perfect tool, and he has discussed revising it, but short of constructing a new index or re-reading the letters from end to end and collecting data as one goes, it is the best index available for the print version of *SL* (Joshi "Index" 8).

Works Cited

Bastian, Mathieu, Heymann, Sebastien, and Jacomy M. "Gephi: an open source software for exploring and manipulating networks." *Proceedings of the Third International Conference on Weblogs and Social Media*. 2009.

Bealer, Tracy. "'The Innsmouth Look': H. P. Lovecraft's Ambivalent Modernism." *Journal of Philosophy: A Cross-Disciplinary Inquiry*, vol. 6, no. 14, Winter 2011, pp. 44–50.

Black, Stephen A. "Literary Biography and Psychological Criticism: In the Matter of H. P. Lovecraft." *Canadian Review of American Studies*, vol. 10 no. 2, 1979, pp. 243–250.

Carney, Jason Ray. *Weird Tales of Modernity: The Ephemerality of the Ordinary in the Stories of Robert E. Howard, Clark Ashton Smith and H. P. Lovecraft*. McFarland, 2019.

Connors, Scott. "The Most Popular Writer in Weird Tales." *Weird Fiction Review*, vol. 1, 2010, pp. 51–59.

de Camp, L. Sprague. *Lovecraft: A Biography*. Doubleday, 1975.

Delany, Samuel R. *About Writing: Seven Essays, Four Letters, and Five Interviews*. Wesleyan University Press, 2005.

Deranged Cultist. "Happy Birthday Howard, you bean loving weirdo. Thanks for everything." *Reddit*. 2019. https://www.reddit.com/r/Lovecraft/comments/ct55mr/happy_birthday_howard_you_bean_loving_weirdo/. Accessed June 2020.

Glover, John. "Reception Claims in *Supernatural Horror in Literature* and the Course of Weird Fiction." *New Directions in Supernatural Horror Literature*, edited by Sean Moreland, Palgrave Macmillan, 2018, pp. 171–187.

Jarvis, Timothy. "The weird, the posthuman, and the abjected world-in-itself: fidelity to the 'Lovecraft Event' in the work of Caitlín R. Kiernan and Laird Barron." *Textual Practice*. vol 31, no. 6, 2017, pp. 1133–1148.

Jones, Mark. "Tentacles and Teeth: The Lovecraftian Being in Popular Culture." *New Critical Essays on H.P. Lovecraft*, edited by David Simmons, Palgrave Macmillan, 2013, pp. 227–247.

Joshi, S. T. *I Am Providence: The Life and Times of H. P. Lovecraft*. New York: Hippocampus Press, 2010.

———. *An Index to the Selected Letters of H. P. Lovecraft*. 2nd Ed., Necronomicon Press, 1991.

Kneale, James. "'Ghoulish Dialogues': H. P. Lovecraft's Weird Geographies." *The Age of Lovecraft*, edited by Carl H. Sederholm and Jeffrey Andrew Weinstock, University of Minnesota Press, 2016, pp. 32–61.

Lovecraft, H. P. *The Annotated Supernatural Horror in Literature*. Commentary by S. T. Joshi, 2nd Ed., New York: Hippocampus Press, 2012.
Mariconda, Steven J. "H. P. Lovecraft: Reluctant American Modernist." *Lovecraft Studies*, vol. 42/43, 2001, pp. 20–32.
Price, Fiona. "Prosthetic Pasts: H. P. Lovecraft and the Weird Politics of History." *Genre: Forms of Discourse and Culture*, vol. 49, no. 2, July 2016, pp. 135–158.
Sederholm, Carl H., and Jeffrey Andrew Weinstock, eds. *The Age of Lovecraft*. Minneapolis, MN: University of Minnesota Press, 2016.
Wilson, Gahan, Ed. *First World Fantasy Awards: An Anthology of the Fantastic: Stories, Poems, Essays*. Doubleday, 1977.
Wisker, Gina. "Speaking the Unspeakable: Women, Sex, and the Dismorphmythic in Lovecraft, Angela Carter, Caitlín R. Kiernan, and Beyond." *New Directions in Supernatural Horror Literature*, edited by Sean Moreland, Palgrave Macmillan, 2018, pp. 209–234.

5 "It's like a maze you can't see"

Comics Cryptomimesis of Lovecraft and the Lovecraftian in Alan Moore's *Neonomicon* (2004–2005) and *Providence* (2015–2017)

Stuart L. Lindsay

The history of H.P. Lovecraft's literary uncategorizability, reflected in the ever-shifting forms of his monsters and the instability of their representation as either images or characters' verbal description, is an issue of narrative transmission at the heart of Comics Studies. Chris Murray and Kevin Corstorphine (2013) have investigated the ways in which the medium's combination of words and images transposes Lovecraftian inadequacies of speech and sight in adapting Lovecraft's stories, mythos and style (Murray and Corstorphine 159). Both back when the non-realistic literary genres of the 1920s and 1930s were "in the throes of internal fission" (Amis 36) and now, in comics' still somewhat unknown symmetries of geometry—to established critical studies, at least—Lovecraft and his Weird fiction present something of a two-stage problem, one which is technical yet also, I claim, biographical. That is to say, the legacy of Lovecraft's notorious xenophobia, which stemmed from his fear of hybridity and miscegenation, provides his stories with the descriptive content of contact with alien, elder races (Mayer 2016). Additionally, Lovecraft's tales are Weird in part because of their racial subtexts and overtones, especially after his New York period (1924–1926), whereupon his channeled, negative experiences of the city into a form of messianic, "racial neurosis" helped power the chanting cults of his Cthulhu cycle (Houellebecq 2005). Following Murray and Corstorphine's research, as well as that of other comics scholars, I use a formal comics analysis to explore two Lovecraft graphic novels' challenging engagements in this dual adaptive process: Writer Alan Moore and artist Jacen Burrows' *Neonomicon* and *Providence*, which ran from 2004 to 2005 and 2015 to 2017, respectively. Namely, I intend to explore how this pair of texts incorporate the inarticulable horror of the mythos and the author as "Real Person Fiction" (Simmons 2016) into the comics format—itself a fundamentally haunted (Round 2019) and Weird narrative medium.

The first of these two interrelated issues concerns successive uptakes of the Cthulhu mythos and its representation by Moore and Burrows' innovations in the extensively visual medium of comics, which is positioned alternative to the literary genres of poetry, the novel and the pulp

DOI: 10.4324/9780367713065-6

short story from which Lovecraft drew inspiration. The second revolves around Real Person Fiction (RPF) representations of Lovecraft employed to explore the legacy of his dubious racial-cultural politics in the current era. The turns to this effect in *Neonomicon* and *Providence*, also present in other modern Lovecraft comics,[1] represent "recent instances of Lovecraft as a character in light of changing contemporary opinions concerning the cultural status of the author" (Simmons 153). The *Providence* comics, set in 1919 at the outset of Lovecraft's creative output, feature appearances of the writer himself, who enjoys and entertains a "fannish adulation" (Ringel 276) from the serial's fictional protagonist, journalist-turned aspiring author Robert Black.[2] This chapter analyzes how, through the comics medium, Moore and Burrows address issues of graphic and biographical reconstruction of the Lovecraftian and of Lovecraft, respectively. It also considers the influence of Moore's status as a contemporary chaos magician on his Lovecraft graphic novels at the level of the comics medium and its significance for the titles' thematic Lovecraftian content of arcane cults and spellcasting. To address these issues, I argue that the creators' manipulation of blank and repeated spaces within the comics frame illustrates the interdimensional and metafictional fragmentation central to Lovecraftian horror. I also explore how Cryptomimesis, another analytic tool of Comics Studies (Round 2014, 2019; Green 2017), is employed to reinterpret the rising star of Lovecraft's cult of personality and cosmic indifference in light of his current fans and, finally, the ascendance of hitherto obscure cultural-political ideologies involving racism and xenophobia in the contemporary "neoreactionary" movement (Sandifer 2018). To reach this conclusion, the second half of my chapter traces Moore and Burrows' efforts to put (the authentic) Lovecraft back into Lovecraftian fiction, along with the racism, anti-Semitism, and sex that had hitherto been expressed obliquely (Gieben). By portraying Lovecraft's life in situ, *Providence* reorients the retrospective understandings of his fiction from which appreciation and scholarship emerged and examines the posthumous exhumation of his prejudices encrypted therein.

"Beyond the Wall": The Comics Frame Adaptation of the Cryptic and Interdimensional

In the history of psychoanalysis, the image of the crypt identifies a hermetically sealed, psychological dimension of consciousness, encysted between waking life and the inaccessible no-man's land of the unconscious. Most thoroughly developed by Nicholas Abraham and Maria Torok in their 1994 volume, *The Shell and the Kernel*, the theory of the crypt in psychoanalysis functions as "a monument that bespeaks a willfully disregarded event," and a mnemic trace of fantasy and perception, in which esoteric words, sounds, and actions refer cryptically to an inexpressible trauma

(Abraham and Torok 92). Jacques Derrida famously described the crypt in his essay "Fors: The Anglish Words of Abraham and Torok" as a psychic structure that "hides [meaning] as it holds" it (Derrida xiv).

Lovecraft's fiction is full of hermetic crypts, monuments, lore, and rituals—unintelligible signifiers of a world that existed before the advent of human history. In "The Rats in the Walls" (1923), the narrator, sole surviving descendant of the cursed de la Poer line, renovates the "shell-like ruin" of his inherited, ancestral home and discovers the kernel of his repressed family trauma in the primordial caverns beneath the building's Roman vaults (Lovecraft "Rats" 1). Near the story's conclusion, he and his employed party of men descend into the ancient crypt with "powerful electric searchlights and implements of excavation" (19) in search of the source of the scurrying sounds of numberless rats, an event that, not unlike the psychoanalytic investigation of a mental crypt, is analogous to an archaeological dig (Derrida 1986):

> It was the antechamber of hell, and poor Thornton fainted again when Trask [the anthropologist] told him that some of the skeleton things must have descended as quadrupeds through the last twenty or more generations.
>
> (Lovecraft "Rats" 14, 21)

The encountered scenes of rat-gnawed human, primate, and unidentifiable humanoid bones strewn about the crypt beneath Exham Priory, and the inscriptions of increasingly ancient languages encrypted on its subterranean walls, constitute fragmented remnants that betoken the de la Poers' contact with an eldritch, intergenerational trauma. The genealogical, historical, and (d)evolutionary layers of the family's crypt also engender a verbarium or collection of cryptonymic words "divested of metaphorical reach" (Derrida lviii). As the narrator breaks from his companions and runs through the pitch black depths of the cave toward "the earth's center where Nyarlathotep, the mad faceless god, howls blindly in darkness," (Lovecraft "Rats" 23) he is possessed by his crypt's ancestral phantom: a return of repressed family history in buried words and progressively archaic and unintelligible languages that "works like a ventriloquist, like a stranger within the subject's own neural topography" (Abraham and Torok 173):

> Curse you, Thornton, I'll teach you to faint at what my family do! … 'Sblood, thou stinkard, I'll learn ye how to gust … wolde ye swynk me thilke wys? … Magna Mater! Magna Mater! … Atys … Dia ad aghaidh's ad aodaun … agus bas dunarch ort! Dhonas's dholas ort, agus leat-sa! … Ungl unl … rrlh … chchch ….
>
> (Lovecraft "Rats" 24)

The narrative of the crypt, though poetic at times, belongs to the age of psychoanalysis; "'as fantastic as a fairy tale,' perhaps, but 'as rigorous as mathematics'" (Derrida xxxiii). Lovecraft's "The Dreams in the Witch House" (1932), a story through which horror is derived from a combination of mathematics and folklore, is another exemplary deployment of cryptomimesis and useful for an analysis of its uptake by Lovecraftian graphic novels into the comics medium. Keziah Mason, the titular witch of the tale, told the judge at her trial "of lines and curves that could be made to point out directions leading through the walls of space to other spaces beyond" (Lovecraft "Witch" 236–237).

The permeation of barriers between worlds and encystment of time in Lovecraft's stories appear ripe for adaptation into the comics format—a medium in which understanding also requires one's passage from one bordered and temporal space into another. As Julia Round notes, gutters, the areas between comics frames, often hide as they hold cryptic content: material outside the diegetic panel but that intrudes upon it from beyond its spatial or temporal limit, or is hidden within the frame itself but obscured by diegetic or non-diegetic objects (an example of the latter would be speech bubbles) (Round 2014: 113). In their *Neonomicon* prequel, "The Courtyard" (2003), Moore and Burrows make use of the medium's layout at points in the narrative to structure the world, where gutters between frames become literal dividing walls through which sound can be heard. This setup extends to physical permeability, as frames-within-frames suggest the merging of spatial and temporal dimensions. At a turning point in the story, protagonist Aldo Sax, a federal agent on the case of a series of obscurely connected murders, leaves a tenement building in Red Hook, Brooklyn, after receiving Aklo from a supposed dealer named Johnny Carcosa. Aklo is not a narcotic, but a language handed down by ancient cosmic beings to perceive and describe the interrelations between worlds, events and periods of time. Listening to the "terrible syllables" lisped by Johnny Carcosa enables Aldo to grasp the interdimensional effects of the language (Moore "Courtyard" 45). In Figure 5.1, each panel encrypts the one preceding it, nesting both space and time in a concertinaed compression and revealing the encrypting capabilities of the comics format.

The use of Aklo as a language unrepresentable to human ears, save as a series of phonetic and spelled approximations, renders its words cryptic. The panels subject language and imagery to a staging power akin to Abraham and Torok's psychoanalytic theory of cryptonyms: words deprived of personal or social meaning but which, in their significant deployment, identify the site of totally unknown activities and traumas. Like obscure graffiti daubed on walls, pronunciations in Aklo gesture toward, yet hold, hidden knowledge. Moore and Burrows' uptake of the Lovecraftian mythos unpeels the crypt walls that their narratives encase it within, using the contextual framework of English speech: "The

Figure 5.1 Alan Moore and Jacen Burrows. "The Courtyard Chapter 2." 2003.
Source: Alan Moore's Neonomicon Collected, Rantoul, IL: Avatar Press, 2011, p.49. Print.

Wza-Y'ei of this" and the "much larger Y'R Nhhngr" (Moore "Courtyard" 49). Additionally, the artists disperse cryptic knowledge throughout their Lovecraft comics via metatextual fragments of short story titles and scenes written by Lovecraft that are recognizable to readers of his fiction.

"The Dreams in the Witch House": From Parallel Dimension to Panel Dimensions

Issue 5 of *Providence* (August 2015) adapts into the comics medium the mathematical and magical encryption of interdimensionality in Lovecraft's story, "The Dreams in the Witch House." In the original tale, protagonist Walter Gilman, a college student studying mathematics at Miskatonic

University, realizes the awful, palimpsestic relations between dimensional realms ciphered in the architecture and geography of Arkham. His obsession with the unsettling measurements of space in the city and witch house induce oneiric trauma and hint at geometrical requirements for navigating alternate realities accessible only in dreams. Walter uses non-Euclidean calculus and quantum physics mixed with folklore in his attempts to trace this strange background of multidimensional reality. Compelled to lodge in the house to seek the same unprecedented insight into mathematics that it had provided to its seventeenth-century occupant, Keziah Mason, "[h]e studied the timber and plaster walls for traces of cryptic designs at every accessible spot where the paper had peeled" (Lovecraft "Witch" 237).

Robert Black, *Providence*'s own amateur investigator, takes a room in a similar house at Goffs Falls in Manchester, New Hampshire, while seeking out local books and history to help him write his novel about ancient beliefs in modern America. The scene signals its metafictional relations with Lovecraft's Weird fiction, but in a manner beyond the intertextual propagations that characterize the literary circle. *Providence #5* utilizes characters akin to those in "The Dreams in the Witch House," with Robert's landlady Mrs. Macy an equivalent to Keziah Mason in possession of a Brown Jenkin of her own. However, the issue, and the entire serial, acquire the status as "ultimate Lovecraft fiction" (Méalóid) through their use of the comics format to depict and structure Lovecraftian elements as visual cryptonyms. They incorporate the oneiric properties of Lovecraft's stories, not only in the straightforward sense but also the psychoanalytic one coined by Abraham and Torok: the fantasy revealing a gap that points to missing content (Abraham and Torok 127). The dream in Robert's witch house does not lead him to the world of the elder god Azathoth as Walter's dreams do—the "boundless jungle of outlandish, incredible peaks, balanced planes, domes, minarets, horizontal disks poised on pinnacles, and numberless forms of still greater wildness" (Lovecraft "Witch" 253). They instead offer oneiroi at a structural level, inducing repetitions or "Yr Nhhngr" in the narrative—"a tense denoting nested time" (Moore *Providence #5* 3). Falling asleep in his rented room, Robert Black "blacks out," indicated by a panel of opaque darkness in which only a speech bubble containing the sentence: "Hee. It looks… Hee hee… It looks like you're dozin' off, there" appears (Moore *Providence* 17). Here, drifting into sleep and waking up are synonymous, as Robert finds himself apparently returned to his passenger seat in a red Buick roadster at an earlier point in the *Providence* narrative: being driven to Manchester by Mr. Jenkins, Mrs. Macy's Brown Jenkin in human disguise. After apologizing and explaining to Mr. Jenkins the vivacity of what Robert thus believed was the dream—the securement of lodgings, the pursuit of his research in Manchester—the duplicitous driver replies: "Hee hee hee. It's like a maze you can't see, ain't it?" (Moore *Providence* 17) This maze, in contrast to the outwardly exotic landscapes rendered in Lovecraft's prose, is constructed by the formal properties of the comics medium. The misconstruing of experience as dreams does not establish a split in the protagonist's consciousness or identity, as in "The Dreams in the Witch House" or an earlier story, "Beyond the Wall of Sleep" (1919), but instead folds experience back in on itself invisibly. Robert's dreams constitute a cryptic layer of time and space that can only be accessed from certain magical points, and which place a toll on his sanity. This crypt is not the dynamic unconscious of a parallel dimension, but an enclave of strange beings in the corporeal world, "a kind of artificial unconsciousness, lodged in the very midst of the ego" (Abraham et al. 65). In one of the panels sequencing the conversation between Robert and Mr. Jenkins, the latter's rat tail appears. Witnessing this traumatic sight thrusts Robert into another fragmentary experience, of waking up in his rented room to see the naked figure of Mrs. Mason, suckling a rat-like creature which has the head of Mr. Jenkins.

The coalescence of diegetic action and panel structure illustrates, as Round has argued, the haunted and dreamlike properties of the comics medium (Round 2019). While *Providence* offers a different sort of dreaming to that of Lovecraft's original stories, it is nonetheless possible to use this source material to analyze the narrative techniques of the maze which, though the characters cannot see it, is visible to readers. Visual equivalents of Walter Gilman's dreamlike experiences are expressed by the shape and contents of comics frames. In "The Dreams in the Witch House," the narration relates:

> Of his own condition he could not well judge, for sight of his arms, legs, and torso seemed always cut off by some odd disarrangement of perspective; [...] Gilman sometimes compared the inorganic matter to prisms, labyrinths, clusters of cubes and planes, [...] In time he observed a further mystery – the tendency of certain entities to appear suddenly out of empty space, or to disappear totally with equal suddenness.
>
> (Lovecraft "Witch" 241, 242)

Just as Mr. Jenkin's rat tail appears suddenly out of the "non-space" of the comics gutter between panels (Round 2014, 2019), so too are other objects and entities in the comics subject to "a kind of ophidian animation" between and within frames (Lovecraft "Witch" 241).

At the conclusion of *Providence* Issue 10, a shattered Robert Black, traumatized by his cumulative encounters with the arcane knowledge and practices of New England's stranger inhabitants, writes a letter to his friend and would-be lover, Tom Malloy, in New York. His room in Providence looks out onto the city and the distant church of St. Johns, in which a deadly meteorite fragment is housed. The panels that depict Robert from behind, sitting at his desk and writing his letter, are framed by a window through which the church is visible. Each successive panel details the progressing paragraphs of his letter across discrete captions and the seemingly impossible forward movement of the church, until the glowing window beneath its spire merges with the window of Robert's room. This imperceptible advance, which occurs in the gutters between frames, can only be tracked retrospectively at stationary points constructed by panels (Round 428). In keeping with Lovecraftian geography, time and navigation—the part-voluntary, seemingly non-physical movement though a surreal landscape of vague visual changes that evokes a simultaneity of the spatial and temporal (Lovecraft "Witch" 241, 242)—the sudden amalgamation of space is realized through conventionally opposing directions: a progression determined by the comics reader's "backward-looking thoughts" (Davenport-Hines 385).

Lovecraftian animation also occurs within frames. Upon noticing the spatial merge taking place between his room and the one in the church steeple containing the asteroid fragment, Robert is thrown from his chair by shock. A panel illustrating the two spaces coming together also depicts his fall in three distinct phases. Here, the comics format represents oneiric travel through this simultaneous blurring of space and movement, and heralds the return of Johnny Carcosa, in truth an avatar of Lovecraft's outer god, Nyarlathotep. In his peculiar lisp, he tells Robert: "We are wordth on a papyruth, a thouthand yearth ago" (Moore *Providence #10* 19). Johnny Carcosa is at once the uncanny embodiment of comics' hybridity of word and image (Round 419) and of Lovecraftian interdimensional movement—the scene in which he confronts Robert to congratulate him for his inadvertent role in the Great Old Ones' triumphant return depicts him as a collection of flat images stacked one in front of the other, each layer following the movements and gestures of the one preceding it. These intra-panel actions adapt Lovecraft's descriptions of the properties of alternate dimensions, the "obscure, relentlessly inevitable fluctuations" and "nebulous blur" of figures and objects (Lovecraft 242, 243). In *Providence*, the comics realm is contradictory in that it contains both self and other, human and god, past, present and future, and dimensions both terrestrial and alien. Johnny Carcosa's literal flat dimensions (in "The Courtyard" he escapes a police raid on his apartment by merging into a wall mural) represent the comics' intentional purposing of Nyarlathotep as representative of the magical properties of the medium: its ability to compress space and time, and render a figure messianic through their visual duplication. As Johnny Carcosa informs Robert: "Now is before," "Thith world thyall be Yuggoth; thyall have alwayth been Yuggoth," and "You are dreamth that we were exthpienthing. You are part of uth" (Moore *Providence #10* 19, 23).

The Magic Circle: Geometric Conjurations in *Providence*

Alan Moore's creative development as a magician since the early 1990s has influenced his work in comics significantly and provided fruitful material for critical understandings of his authorship. This relationship has been especially apparent in Moore's frequent returns to, and rereadings of, the corpus of H.P. Lovecraft (Green 253). Moore's exploration of the magical properties of oral invocations in his Lovecraftian writings, and its contribution to the perception of Lovecraft's fiction as having genuine magical insight (Grant, qtd. in Green "darker magic" 255), have been subjects of recent scholarship.

Lovecraft's mythos developed a cryptic etymology that is at once verbal, linguistic and symbolic. Beyond the distal utterances and runic inscriptions of otherwise forgotten elder languages lies a psychogeography of architectural arrangement that focuses magical power. As Moore and others contend, despite his hatred of the movement Lovecraft was a Modernist betrayed by his literary experimentations in narrative obscurity, temporal nonlinearity, and stream of consciousness technique (Carlin and Allen 2013; Higgs). Lovecraft's emphases on geometric configurations furthered the Modernist function of unseating the rational, historicist, humanist consciousness in the aftermath of Western, Imperial collapse. Indeed, one can read the geometric biology of his ancient, alien creatures—the barrel-shaped, star-headed Old Ones in *At the Mountains of Madness* (1931) or the conical forms of the Yithian Great Race in *The Shadow Out of Time* (1934)—as profound shatterings of the deistic proportions of Vitruvian Man.

The five-pointed star in *At the Mountains of Madness* which originates in the Old Ones' physiology and tells of humanity's genesis is imbued with terrible, reality-warping power—a geometric equivalent of the Aklo spoken by Johnny Carcosa to Aldo Sax in "The Courtyard." In both texts, the act of narrative address involves a psychological violation (Green 266) of the witness. The comics panel depicting Aldo's mind in receipt of the first Aklo "hit" includes images of scarabs, jellyfish, and starfish pouring from a figure in white, silhouetted profile to represent the transformative language that is at once image and word, inspired perhaps by artist M.C. Escher's *Metamorphoses* lithograph series (Moore "The Courtyard" 2011 42–43).

Providence #11 connects the serial explicitly to Moore and Burrow's earlier produced (but later set) miniseries, "The Courtyard" and *Neonomicon*. Their entire Lovecraft arc has as its central premise the idea that Lovecraft's stories realize the events contained therein. His plots, which refer to characters such as Thomas F. Malone, protagonist of "The Horror at Red Hook" (1925) or the monstrously formed Willard Whateley from "The Dunwich Horror" (1929) are prophesied by Robert's earlier encounters with their real-life variants in the *Providence* world. These people set in motion, either wittingly or otherwise, the plan of a loosely connected conspiratorial group called the Stella Sapient to redeem the elder home planet of Yuggoth to the terrestrial plane. Johnny Carcosa's statement to Robert at the end of Issue 10, "You have thurrendered our thtorieth to *Providenth*" (Moore *Providence #10*, 21, emphasis added) signals not only the comic world's submission before a stronger fiction through recognition of original character names' rearrangement. Johnny Carcosa's double meaning of the word Providence also identifies the comics' ability to shape their readers' mental world through use of the medium's geometric formatting in a way that echoes Moore's "Shamanic" views on magic and art (Babcock; Green 2017).

Matthew Green (2017) has analyzed how the regular rhythm of *Providence*'s four horizontal panel pages is altered by format changes corresponding to ontic changes in the diegetic narrative, between different realities or states of consciousness. This visual modulation of the plot's rhythmic chanting is accompanied by geometric alterations within frames, unacknowledged or at odds with certain characters' limited perceptions of a teleology that is partially representable only to the reader.[3] Following his traumatic encounters in New England, Robert returns to his native New York, haunted by visions of the strange people whom he encountered and recorded in his commonplace book; the figures described therein inspire the characters and plots of tales written by Lovecraft, who borrows it. After mailing this commonplace book to Thomas Malloy, Robert makes the decision to commit suicide by the same method as his former, jilted lover, Jonathan Lillian Russell, depicted in *Providence #1*. He chooses to die by gas in an "Exit Garden" chamber in Bryant Park while listening to the gramophone record, "You Made Me Love You" (1913), sung by Al Jolson. This end evokes the temporal circularity that is central to Moore and Burrows' notion of time in their Lovecraft comics and of Lovecraft's original tales, in which the narrator's overwhelming fears or mental situation at once anticipates and succeeds his traumatic experience. For example, the narrator of *The Whisperer in Darkness* (1930) begins his account with the following conclusive statement: "Bear in mind that I did not see any actual visual horror at the end" (Lovecraft *Whisperer* 154). Robert's demise also links his outsider status as a Jew to Robert Chambers' 1895 short story "The Repairer of Reputations," in which legalized suicide becomes an authoritative means through which an immigrant, primarily Jewish population might be subdued, as well as to the future history of Jewish trauma in the twentieth century.

In this sequence, Moore and Burrows utilize the geometric symbol of the circle to alert the reader to the interrelatedness of Robert's suicide, the Stella Sapient conspiracy, and the collapse of twentieth and twenty-first century Western civilization. As Robert travels back to New York by rail, a panel depicting a train wheel is matched by a close-up of the Jolson record in the following one, connecting Jonathan and Robert's suicides at the outset and close of *Providence* respectively (Moore *Providence #11* 3). The narrative implications of the circle are reinforced by the image of the record, both before and after Robert's suicide, and by a birds-eye view of a dessert cake and close-up of one of Robert's eyes after he sees Mr. Jenkin's red Buick roadster parked outside the post office (Moore *Providence #11* 6, 8). The panel of the record emerges repeatedly in subsequent action, of Lovecraft's gradual restoration to literary recognition by the inheritors of his Weird fiction and the realization of the prophetic plots therein. The record's continual return renders it as a symbol in the apocalyptic dirge of history which guides doom through the flow of time. Moore has articulated his thesis on magic as an act of creation which, though founded on written language systems, is conveyed through curiously spatial allusions that echo the first cave paintings produced by archaic humans. In an interview with journalist Bill Baker (2005), Moore says:

> I think that storytelling and creation are very close to the center of what magic is about. I think not just for me, but for most of the cultures that have had a concept of magic, then the manipulation of language, and words, and thus of stories and fictions, has been very close to the center of it all.
>
> (Baker 7)

For Moore, magic revolves around the social act of creation and the merging of fiction with contemporary culture. The circle is a primary descriptor of this process in Moore's comics' worlds. The blending of literature and culture in *Providence* operates at a fundamental level of the text's mise en scène. The comic's repetition of circular imagery establishes a series of visual incantations that shape readers' perception and understanding of the world. These circles not only enact the Stella Sapient's mantra of "the end is the beginning," but also narrate a traumatic return of latent power structures that resonate with liberal humanist experiences of contemporary socio-political upheaval derived from events such as the inauguration of President Trump in the US and the Brexit referendum in the UK. The following sections of my chapter will now explore this topic.

Named Cults: Moore's Interpretation of the Cultural Uptake of Lovecraft's Mythos

Whether they are aware of it or not, avid readers of Lovecraft's fiction form a quasi-cultish membership who are able to foretell narrative events in his stories from combinations of images and words therein. Such signals run through the intertextuality of his tales, most notably in the recurring episteme of the Aklo language and dreaded tomes that contain it, such as the Necronomicon and Cultes des Goules. "The Courtyard" and *Neonomicon* offer Postmodern simulacra of the mythos's transformative magic through depictions of the contemporary, popular, and largely benign cult that surrounds Lovecraft's work. "The Courtyard" introduces a Goth band called The Ulthar Cats who play songs called "Leng" and "Zann Variations," providing their audience with a trancelike experience through the crowd's recognition of lyricized Aklo fragments made famous by the Cthulhu literary cycle.

A subcultural movement that spreads—even inadvertently—the forbidden knowledge and language of ancient beings has dire consequences if artistic creativity is conflated, as it is in Moore's narrative configuration, with the fundamental, perceptual shaping of reality. The issue of cultural reproduction, which the later issues of *Providence* explore in depth by establishing the fictional literary relationship between Lovecraft and Robert Black, might signal the social dangers of consuming Lovecraft's stories uncritically, without an awareness of their racial subtext.

Providence provides a nuanced, useful reading of Lovecraft to echo current anxieties about the equivocation of prejudiced views and social policies by today's governments and far-right movements. Lovecraft is still renowned for having held such views, and though he had little interest in sharing them with contemporary racist polities, much scholarly attention has been paid to the influence and infiltration of fascism in his stories (Poole 2016). Moore and Burrows use the comics format to encrypt biographical aspects of Lovecraft's life—details of which may also be recognizable to habitual readers of his stories. However, by returning to 1919, a period prior to the realization of Lovecraft's extensive literary output and fame, *Providence* "hides as it holds" (Derrida xiv) his prejudices within the cryptic comics frame. Moore and Burrows' graphic novel creates a discourse from its medium's formal structures and potential as a cultural, historicist document on the burial and cryptography of xenophobic, anti-Semitic and traumatic genealogies that haunt the twentieth and twenty-first centuries.

"The Terrible Old Man": Cryptomimesis of Lovecraft's Prejudice in *Providence*

Providence Issue 8, in which Robert Black is first introduced to H.P. Lovecraft, appears superficially to whitewash the latter's character. Meeting by chance after Lord Dunsany's public recital of a selection of his stories, the conversations between Robert and Lovecraft, focusing on a shared appreciation of Weird fiction, seem mutually benign and enthusiastic. While these conferences between the two aficionados betray evidence of the Stella Sapient's conspiracy to bring them together, the final section of this chapter will focus on *Providence*'s construction of the pair's interactions, namely its cryptic registration of details that develop an account of Lovecraft's racism and would not reveal themselves as such to an uninitiated reader.

By *Providence* Issue 9, the pair have struck up a keen literary friendship. After visiting Lovecraft at his Providence house on 598 Angell Street, Robert, accompanied by his new friend, goes to secure lodgings for himself on College Street. In the panel showing their departure from Lovecraft's house, a black cat is seen sitting on the lawn, framed between two trees. This seemingly innocuous detail recalls the presence of Lovecraft's beloved pet cat, whose name reveals his owner's casual racism.[4] By situating this wordless knowledge in the scene, *Providence* directs our attention to aspects of Lovecraft's character unknown to Robert or the general public in 1919. Lovecraft addresses those in his acquaintanceship through curious appellation. He refers to himself as Robert's "Grandfather Theoboldus," calls Robert "young Robertus," and his aunt Martha "my young granddaughter" (Moore *Providence* #9). Lovecraft's odd self-identification as an old man here is used in the cryptomimesis of his family traumas and personal prejudices. Like many of his stories, his social quirks as portrayed in *Providence* provide a rebus of psychological trauma only disclosed in his diaries and letters. The graphic novel uses the incorporation of a past to read the silence of his trauma within fiction by and about him. As Robert and Lovecraft walk to the boarding house in which Robert is to be accommodated during his visit to the city, they pass Lovecraft's previous home, 454 Angell Street. After his grandfather, Whipple Van Buren Philips, suffered a severe economic setback and subsequently passed away in 1904, the remaining Lovecraft family members who lived there, namely Howard and his mother Susan, were forced financially and for practical reasons to give up the house and downsize to a section of the cheaper, smaller 598 residence. This effected a reduction in the family's fortunes that the young writer was never able to reverse adequately through his publications. In his letter to J. Vernon Shea,[5] Lovecraft recalled that he received this twofold loss with a shame that affected him deeply (Lovecraft, *Letters* 221–222), but this trauma is entirely absent in the graphic novel's portrayal of the author's former home and only readable through specific knowledge of his genealogy. Reflecting Lovecraft's distaste for contemporary psychoanalysis and its absence throughout his stories except as an occasional subject of ridicule, such silence on the topic of personal trauma constitutes an early effect of the narrative's uncanny merge between fictional and historical realms. Though the loss of 454 Angell Street is mentioned, its wounding properties go entirely unacknowledged, displaced by a site of "fond boyhood Elysium" and nostalgia (Moore *Providence* #9 18).

As Derrida states, language in the form of defunct words takes up residence in the crypt, words removed of their communicative function (Derrida xxxv). Those around Lovecraft are puzzled by his addressals, but the graphic novel soon afterward opens the psychic tomb it has erected. In *Providence #10*, after Lovecraft has made his disparaging opinions about Jews and homosexuals known to Robert, remaining unaware that his new friend's identity includes these minority groups, the pair returns to Lovecraft's 598 Angell Street house. Here, Lovecraft

Figure 5.2 Alan Moore and Jacen Burrows.

Source: Providence #10. 2016, Rantoul, IL: Avatar Press, 2016, p. 12, panel 4. Print.

indulges in an account of his genealogical history. He says to Robert that his late father, Winfield Scott Lovecraft, due to his mannerisms, was supposed by many to be an Englishman, a protégé of Howard's maternal grandfather whose pronouncements he reads as circulating "the import of tradition," which "shaped many of my prevailing attitudes" (Moore *Providence #10* 10). Here, the heterocryptic return of the ghost is known, "according to what might be the law of *another generation*" (Derrida xxxi). Lovecraft then shows Robert an image of this grandfather, Whipple Van Buren Philips, whose death is readable at once as Lovecraft's dispossession from his fortunes and happiness, and as an ancestral possession via his incorporated loss. Van Buren Philips is encrypted in both Lovecraft's obscure identification and in the comics panel: the grandfather encysted within the grandfather, the frame encysted within the frame, which is emblematic of how the crypt "writes a text on and in a text" (Derrida xxviii).

Ultimately, this chapter's aim is not to provide a genealogy and thus possible justification of Lovecraft's personal prejudices. Rather, in showing how *Providence* adapts into the graphic novel format his own reading of his traumatic past without expressing it as such and places it within a wider cryptic conspiracy, I claim the comic serial provides a theoretical structure through which the cultural and political far right's infiltration of contemporary, popular society and communication can be understood.

A Conclusion: Neoreaction

Elizabeth Sandifer's recent essays on the so-called Alt-Right movement in *Neoreaction A Basilisk* (2018) identify the community as a fractious group of fellow travelers on a racist, white nationalist warpath of internet memes, online message board shitposting and the techno-social theorization of science fiction and horror literature. It is aimed ostensibly at achieving an apparently mathematically perfectible, anti-democratic, rational posthumanism. Key members' accelerationist extrapolation of Lovecraftian "thought experiments" into counter-theories of xenophobic social policy is worthy of future detailed study, as are the ways in which Moore's liberal humanist comic project opposes such techniques.

Two of these major figures covered in Sandifer's book are foundational in the Neoreactionary community's ideology: software engineer Curtis Yarvin, formerly known by his blog pseudonym Mencius Moldbug, and accelerationist thinker Nick Land, who lectured at Warwick University in continental philosophy between 1987 and 1998 and co-founded the institution's Cybernetic Culture Research Unit in 1995. In their theories of accelerationism—the nihilistic commitment to pushing technology, capitalism and the destruction of the natural environment toward an ultimate bionic horizon where we are no longer human (Sandifer 105)—both writers espouse a horror philosophy as Lovecraftian fanfic. The drive toward Singularity through what Land calls "The Great Filter" fundamentally transhumanizes us, "so that we become Lovecraftian Others compared to our current nature" (Riggio 39). Moldbug established in his blog posts the critical image of a "Cathedral" of hypnotic democratic values under the sway of a Cthulhu which, in his words, "only swims [to the political] left" (qtd. in Sandifer 21). Land and Moldbug propose reactions against this current by retreating to their respective ideological bunkers. Moldbug's (only partially) rhetorical argument is to reinstate absolute monarchy and slavery, while Land's is the inauguration of a heavily armed tribal society operating on a brutal, racial basis.

It is beyond the scope and length of this chapter to examine what Moore's take on all this might be, or whether *Neonomicon* and *Providence* are part of an accelerationist cycle or not. For now, it is plain to see that Moore lets his Lovecraftian apocalypse happen. Lovecraft's genealogically based traditions in the comics do not offer an escape from impending doom like Moldbug and Land's do but rather constitute a key part of the Stella Sapient conspiracy. In *Providence* #9, Robert learns of the seemingly innocuous, consensual, arranged marriage of Winfield Scott Lovecraft and Susan Phillips for reasons of succession. Henry Annesley, the Stella Sapient member who reveals this information to him, comments on the practice, saying that "European monarchs do it all the time." Robert's response is that it seems almost dull (Moore *Providence* #9 6); he only realizes the significance of tradition in the revival of ancient horror belatedly, in the following issue.

Sandifer begins *Neoreaction A Basilisk* with the following premise: "let us assume we are fucked" (Sandifer 5). The protagonists throughout "The Courtyard," *Neonomicon*, and *Providence* are equally fucked, yet do not possess the foreknowledge to understand this until it is too late. Yet at the finale, Moore leaves his surviving characters' interpretative faculties intact, even as the cloud of the outer god Shub-Niggurath looms over them. He maintains a commitment to humanist philosophy amid the ruins of the human society that have been engulfed by the alien plant life of Yuggoth. At the conclusion of *Providence #12*, the comic's RPF representation of S.T. Joshi and another, entirely fictional character, FBI agent Merril Brears, discuss "Lovecraft's ideal state of Ataraxia: a freedom from anxiety or discomfort" (Moore *Providence #12* 29) and what new place humans, with their potential knowledge of this emerging, deterministic world, might occupy. The final four frames depict the destruction of human writing, with Brears' boss, Carl Perlman, tearing Robert Black's commonplace book in two. This scene echoes one at the beginning of *Providence #1*: Robert's bisecting of his unsent letter to his former lover Jonathan after the latter's suicide. This symbolic linkage suggests to the reader a chronological confluence or loop that takes place not in the gutters of the comics format but entirely beyond the limits of the comic as a narrative structure. Moore reinterprets the Lovecraftian cyclical condition of life on the planet that is a core function of Lovecraft's horror fiction, in which the human race is wiped out by eldritch beings so that the earth can be dragged off to some nameless place for some nameless purpose (Lovecraft "Dunwhich" 153). In Moore's reworking, this nameless place lies outside the confines of the comic where narration dissolves completely. Here, the end is the beginning in a maze that, finally, we cannot see.

Notes

1 David Simmons analyzes three Lovecraft comics in substantiating this claim: Hans Rodianoff's *Lovecraft* (2004), Mac Carter's *The Strange Adventures of H.P. Lovecraft* (2010) and Bruce Brown's *Howard Lovecraft* series of children's graphic novels (2009–2013). Unofficial Lovecraftian webcomics incorporate representations of Lovecraft in their narratives too, such as Larry Latham's series, "Lovecraft is Missing" (2008–present). Most of these titles however, as Murray and Corstorphine note, function as parody or in other ways that are rarely faithful to biographical understandings of the writer's life. See Murray and Corstorphine 180–181

2 Robert Black is *Providence*'s stand-in for Weird author Robert Bloch, who, in demonstrating the fan aspects of RPF writing, wrote one of the early instances of Real Person Fiction involving an approximate representation Lovecraft in "The Shambler from the Stars" (1935). See Simmons 149–150.

3 A popular theory suggests the relative power of the reader's narrative understanding to that of characters' is represented by Lovecraft's Great Old One, Azathoth, who, without fully knowing it, dreams the universe and all in it. The theory applied would be as follows: the reader of *Providence* is positioned as a Blind Idiot God (one of the epithets Lovecraft invented for his fictional master god), establishing an understanding of the narrative without the ability to see its full progress, which is partially obscured in comics gutters. See Lovecraft's story *The Haunter of the Dark* (1935) for details of this Outer God's basis.

4 Niggerman's "jetty form" can be identified through Lovecraft's use of Real Cat Fiction (?) in "The Rats in the Walls" ("Rats" 10). But his apparent return in *Providence* is a phantasmic image that speaks more to Moore's social program of encrypting Lovecraft's racism than one of reproducing history. As S.T. Joshi notes in his 2001 biography of Lovecraft, *A Visionary and a Dreamer: H.P.*

Lovecraft in his Time, the cat disappeared sometime in 1904, the same year the Lovecraft family moved from 454 to 598 Angell Street (Joshi 47).

5 This letter reveals some of the peculiar language which Moore sourced for his reconstruction of Lovecraft's dialogues with Robert Black in *Providence #10* and *#11*. In his letter, Lovecraft reflects on his loss of economic and (self-imagined) social status: "How could an old man of 14 (& I surely felt that way!) readjust his existence to a skimpy flat [...]?" (Lovecraft *Letters* 221). This is a humorous introjection in an otherwise serious tone, one that invokes the self-conscious performance of an earlier period in which adults were the adolescent Lovecraft's predominant social peers. See Joshi 47.

Works Cited

Abraham, Nicholas, et al. "The Topography of Reality: Sketching a Metapsychology of Secrets." *Psychoanalysis and Literature*, vol. 12, no. 1/2, 1990, pp. 63–68.

Abraham, Nicholas, and Maria Torok. *The Shell and the Kernel, Volume 1*. Edited and translated by Nicholas Rand. Chicago, IL: University of Chicago Press, 1994.

Amis, Kingsley. *New Maps of Hell: A Survey of Science Fiction*. London: New English Library, 1969.

Babcock, Jay. "Magic is Afoot: A Conversation with Alan Moore about the Arts and the Occult." *Arthur*, 10 May 2007, https://arthurmag.com/2007/05/10/1815/. Accessed May 7 2020.

Baker, Bill. *Alan Moore Spells it Out*. Milford, CT: Airwave Publishing, 2005.

Carlin, Gerry, and Nicola Allen. "Slime and the Western Man: H.P. Lovecraft in the Time of Modernism." *New Critical Essays on H.P. Lovecraft*, edited by David Simmons. New York: Palgrave, 2013, pp. 73–90.

Davenport-Hines, Richard. *Gothic: Four Hundred Years of Excess, Horror, Evil and Ruin*. Albany, CA: North Point Press, 1998.

Derrida, Jacques. "Foreword: Fors: The Anglish Words of Nicholas Abraham and Maria Torok." *The Wolf Man's Magic Word: A Cryptonomy*, edited by Nicholas Abraham and Maria Torok, translated by Nicholas Rand. Minneapolis, MI: University of Minnesota Press, 1986, pp. xi–xlviii.

Gieben, Bram. "Choose Your Reality: Alan Moore Unearthed." *The Skinny*, 1 September 2010, https://www.theskinny.co.uk/music/interviews/choose-your-reality-alan-moore-unearthed. Accessed May 7 2020.

Grant, Kenneth. *The Magic Revival*. Muller, 1972.

Green, Matthew J. A. "A darker magic: Heterocosms and bricolage in Moore's recent reworkings of Lovecraft." *Alan Moore and the Gothic Tradition*, edited by Matthew J.A. Green. Manchester: Manchester University Press, 2016, pp. 253–275.

———. "'An altered view regarding the relationship between dreams and reality': Magic, politics and the comics medium in Alan Moore and Jacen Burrow's Providence." *Studies in Comics*, vol. 8 no. 2, 2017, pp. 135–155.

Higgs, John. "Alan Moore talks to John Higgs about the 20th century." *Youtube*, 1 November 2015, https://www.youtube.com/watch?v=RpajFQECzAk. Accessed July 28 2020.

Houellebecq, Michel. *H.P. Lovecraft Against the World, Against Life*. Translated by Dorna Khazeni, Orion Publishing Group, 2005.

Joshi, S.T. *A Dreamer and a Visionary: H.P. Lovecraft in His Time*. Liverpool: Liverpool University Press, 2001.

Lovecraft, H.P. "The Rats in the Walls." *The Call of Cthulhu and Other Weird Tales*. Vintage, 2011, pp. 1–24.

———. "The Dunwich Horror." *The Call of Cthulhu and Other Weird Tales*. Vintage, 2011, pp. 99–153.

———. "The Whisperer in Darkness." *The Call of Cthulhu and Other Weird Tales*. Vintage, 2011, pp. 154–234.

———. *At the Mountains of Madness. The Call of Cthulhu and Other Weird Tales. Vintage*, 2011, pp. 362–490.

———. "The Dreams in the Witch House." *The Call of Cthulhu and Other Weird Tales*. Vintage, 2011, pp. 235–280.

———. "The Haunter of the Dark." *The Call of Cthulhu and Other Weird Tales*. Vintage, 2011, pp. 491–519.

Lovecraft, H. P. *Letters to J. Vernon Shea, Carl F. Strauch, and Lee McBride White*, edited by S. T. Joshi and David E. Schultz, Hippocampus Press, 2016.

Mayer, Jed. "Race, Species, and Others: H.P. Lovecraft and the Animal." *The Age of Lovecraft*, edited by Carl H. Sederholm and Jeffrey Andrew Weinstock, Minneapolis, MI: Minnesota University Press, 2016, pp. 117–132.

Méalóid, Pádraig Ó. "Interview: Alan Moore on Providence, Jerusalem, League and more – Part 1." *The Beat: The Blog of Comics Culture*, 16 April 2013, https://www.comicsbeat.com/interview-with-alan-moore-part-1/. Accessed May 7 2020.

Moore, Alan, and Jacen Burrows. "The Courtyard." *Alan Moore's Neonomicon Collected*, edited by Alan Moore and Jacen Burrows, Avatar Press, 2003/2011, pp. 1–54.

Moore, Alan. "*Neonomicon*." 2010–2011. *Alan Moore's Neonomicon Collected*, edited by Alan Moore and Jacen Burrows. Rantoul, IL: Avatar Press, 2011, pp. 55–159.

———. *Providence #5*. Rantoul, IL: Avatar Press, 2015.

———. *Providence #9*. Rantoul, IL: Avatar Press, 2016.

———. *Providence #10*. Rantoul, IL: Avatar Press, 2016.

———. *Providence #11*. Rantoul, IL: Avatar Press, 2016.

———. *Providence #12*. Rantoul, IL: Avatar Press, 2017.

Murray, Chris, and Kevin Corstorphine. "Co(s)mic Horror." *New Critical Essays on H.P. Lovecraft*, edited by David Simmons, Palgrave Macmillan, 2013, pp. 157–191.

Poole, Scott W. "Lovecraft, Witch Cults, and Philosophers." *The Age of Lovecraft*, edited by Carl H. Sederholm and Jeffrey Andrew Weinstock. Minneapolis, MI: Minnesota University Press, 2016, pp. 215–230.

Riggio, Adam. "The Violence of Pure Reason: *Neoreaction: A Basilisk*." *Social Epistemology Review and Reply Collective*, vol. 5, no. 9, 2016, pp. 34–41.

Ringel, Fay. "I Am Providence: H.P. Lovecraft." *A Companion to American Gothic*, edited by Charles Crow. Hoboken, NJ: John Wiley and Sons, 2014, pp. 267–278.

Round, Julia. *Gothic in Comics and Graphic Novels*. Jefferson, NC: McFarland, 2014.

———. "Gothic and Comics: From *The Haunt of Fear* to a Haunted Medium." *Gothic and the Arts*, edited by David Punter Edinburgh: Edinburgh University Press, 2019, pp. 418–433.

Sandifer, Elizabeth. *Neoreaction A Basilisk: Essays on and Around the Alt-Right*. CreateSpace, 2018.

Simmons, David. "H.P. Lovecraft and Real Person Fiction: The Pulp Author as Subcultural Avatar." *The Age of Lovecraft*, edited by Carl H. Sederholm and Jeffrey Andrew Weinstock. Minneapolis, MI: Minnesota University Press, 2016, pp. 149–165.

6 Man or Cartoon

H.P. Lovecraft as a Comics Character

Tom Shapira

> My fav'rite? Fie on printed information
> I'll frankly give myself the nomination
>
> "My Favorite Character," a poem by H.P. Lovecraft

In his novella *The Case of Charles Dexter Ward*, H.P. Lovecraft imagines the following horror scenario: a person is overwritten, and eventually erased. Ward's ancestor, Joseph Curwen, takes over his descendant's body. Noted horror writer Thomas Ligotti claims that this situation presents a fear that is fundamental to Lovecraft's stories: "And the worst possible thing we could know – worse than knowing our descent from a mass of microorganisms – is that we are nobodies not somebodies, puppets not people" (64). The horror in Lovecraft's tales is the horror of being a "nobody," a thing of lesser importance in the grand scheme of the cosmos.

This process also occurred to the writer himself, as Lovecraft the person was replaced by Lovecraft the character in public consciousness. While unknown during his lifetime, Lovecraft's name and popularity had only grown since his demise. This process of canonization goes hand in hand with a unique condition, in which the author had become a popular subject of fictionalization, particularly in the field of comics. As scholar David Simmons wrote: "Indeed, it is fair to say that the appropriation of Lovecraft as a fictional character in pseudo-biographical narratives has become one of the defining modes of recent Lovecraftian graphic fiction" (153). This chapter shall explore nine graphic texts, divided into three different categories (biographical, antagonistic, heroic), which follow an arc of changing public perception of H.P. Lovecraft. Simmons' article focuses on how comics presents these changing perceptions, while this essay grapples with the notion that comics *caused* these changes. The use of Lovecraft as a character helped to re-shape him in the public mind, not into a human being but to an amorphous symbol that could stand for different ideas. Lovecraft first appeared as a character in pulp stories, such as Frank Belknap Long's "The Space Eaters," (1928) or Robert Bloch's

DOI: 10.4324/9780367713065-7

"The Shambler from the Stars" (1935), but these tales were written by friends of Lovecraft, with his stated approval.[1] Pulps treated Lovecraft as a friend, while graphic fiction treats him as a public figure, one that is seen through the prism of his fiction.

While the trend of Lovecraft appearances in comic books goes back to the twentieth century, it has accelerated as we have entered the twenty-first century. As "Lovecraft," the writer becomes more popular, the number of fictionalized appearances grows. Yet, at the same time, these appearances owe less and less to the real individual. To transcend from reality into legend also means to lose control of yourself and your legacy. Just like poor Charles Dexter Ward, our protagonist now finds himself hijacked by alien powers – who will use his body and name for their own bidding.

Lovecraft Discovered

H.P. Lovecraft: He Who Wrote in the Darkness is a French graphic novel written by Alex Nikolavitch and drawn by the art team of Gersavio, Aon and Lee (translated to English by Ivanka Hahnenberger). The book seeks to describe the latter parts of the author's life (the narrative begins in 1925) with a specific focus on his relations with various professional acquaintances, including Frank Belknap Long, Robert E. Howard, Robert Bloch, and others. Thus, it combines two critical elements for this chapter: graphical representation of the author, which strives for realism, alongside an exploration of the peers that would be the first to fictionalize, and then canonize, Lovecraft.

Midway through the narrative Lovecraft sits for a meal with Harry Houdini to discuss a business opportunity – a combined effort in book form designed to take down "the cancer of superstition" (Nikolavitch et al. 48). This conversation is based on a real-life discussion between the two individuals following the success of the collaborative short story "Imprisoned with the Pharaohs." During the meal scene, the art team captures not just the image but the body-language of Lovecraft: Houdini is all forward movement and outstretched friendliness, as befitting a professional showman working for a crowd (even if it is a crowd of one). Lovecraft, meanwhile, is pressed into his chair, his hands crossed over his torso and staying away from his meager meal. Only when his interest is piqued by the mention of his hobbies, writing and astronomy, does his face alight.

Yet for all the labors of the art team, the writing shatters the effected realism with two simple words "Yeah okay" (Nikolavitch et al. 48). This casual English bears little similarity to the Lovecraft fans may recognize from the various biographies and the many volumes of published letters. Lovecraft, in his letters and articles, made a concerted effort to construct an image, a brand: an old-fashioned gentleman. As noted by biographer S.T. Joshi: "This passage [a letter by Andrew Francis Lockhart] itself reveals how Lovecraft is already fashioning a precise image of himself: the recluse buried in books: the man of frail health and therefore not suited to the turmoil of the outside world" (232). Lovecraft would do it throughout his life, not so much "lie" but exaggerate. Joshi cites a particular January 1915 letter to Maurice W. Moe as disingenuous on Lovecraft's part. In that letter the author claims: "In 1908 I should have entered Brown University, but the broken state of my health rendered the idea absurd." (Lovecraft, qtd. in *I Am Providence* 107). As noted by biographers, Lovecraft had never even properly graduated high school, so there was more preventing him continuing to higher studies than ill health (Klinger xxxiii–xxxiv).

This branding project, carried mostly among fellow writers, allowed Lovecraft to become a character. I refer here, with the word "character," both to the sense that he was easily recognizable, and to the notion that he was a person ready-made to appear in the type of fiction he was making. Indeed, as Maurice Levi noted, "In most of Lovecraft's tales, the main character – whether his name be Charles Dexter Ward, Edward Derby, Olncy, Malone, or simply 'I' – is the author" (118). Lovecraft's audience was small, but it was the right kind of audience to help spread his works further. Pulp scholar Bobbie Derie referred to this collection of colleagues as a "pulp writer grapevine" (Derie *Weird Talers* 79). Even if unconsciously, Lovecraft was cultivating just the right type of readership to make him famous.

He Wrote in the Darkness is not the singular graphic biography of Lovecraft's life. In 2017 Sam Gafford and Jason C. Echhardt created a different take called *Some Notes on a Nonentity: The Life of H.P. Lovecraft*. Named after an autobiographical essay by Lovecraft, this graphic novel attempts to be more straightforward in its presentation of Lovecraft's entire life. Despite the attempt at accuracy, the creative team still takes a rather theatrical approach to the of material. *Some Notes on a Nonentity* begins with a literal stage upon which H.P. Lovecraft stands to deliver another tale: "I have been asked to say a few words tonight about a subject of which I am an unintended expert: myself" (Gafford and Echhardt, 1). This harkens back to Levi's theory – Lovecraft's fist and last subject was himself. Already we see that the story of Lovecraft's life has little to do with some sense of absolute *objective* truth and more with the idea of performance.

Comparing the two biographical works, it is notable that *He Who Wrote in the Darkness* intentionally mixes reality and fiction. In every chapter there is an aside depicting one of Lovecraft stories. With this choice, the graphic novel implicitly connects the author's declining mental and physical state with the horrors in his fiction. *Some Notes on a Nonentity* is, comparatively, more straightforward in its presentation of the facts. The simple black and white art style, crafted without any varnish to distract one from the narrative is a testimonial to the intentions of the creators: here you will find no language out of place, no mixing of fact and fiction.

Yet, despite the insistence on realism, the book is not straightforward. A childhood scene of Lovecraft playing with his beloved cat is paused so the adult Lovecraft can address the readership from the stage upon which he tells his story: "I am being informed that my cat's name may be offensive to some, so I will refer to him simply as 'N'" (Gafford and Echhardt, 13). It's a curious choice. An admission by the authors that this detail, the writer infamously called his cat "Niggerman," is one which is essential to understand the life of Lovecraft (his love of felines, his inability to process sorrow, and his racism) yet cannot be fully addressed. The language Lovecraft used, the feelings it evoked, can no longer be used in polite society. It is therefore acknowledged without any additional consideration. Thus, even biographical Lovecraft is changed to fit the spirit of the time.

Another interesting work of semi-biography, one which both acknowledges and engages with the less-savory elements of the author's life, can be found in comic-book series *Providence* by writer Alan Moore and artist Jacen Burrows (Avatar Press, 2015–2017). The series is the third and final part of Lovecraft-inspired cycle of stories from the same team, following *The Courtyard* and *Neonomicon*. In *Providence* a New York writer called Robert Black travels across New England in 1919, chronicling occult phenomena in preparation to write the next Great American Novel. Robert Black is a reference to Robert Blake – the protagonist in Lovecraft's "The Haunter of the Dark." This character is meant to be the same unnamed protagonist from Robert Bloch's short story "The Shambler from the Stars."

Furthermore, the name and description of Robert Blake in Lovecraft's tale alludes (and is dedicated) to Bloch himself: "For after all, the victim was a writer and painter wholly devoted to the field of myth, dream, terror, and superstition, and avid in his quest for scenes and effects of a bizarre, spectral sort." (Lovecraft "Haunter" 452) Just as Lovecraft was being fictionalized so he was fictionalizing others. Yet Bloch never attained the level of publicity, or the many spots as fictionalized figure, that Lovecraft has.

In *Providence* Black doesn't believe in the supernatural and tends to assume all the monsters he encounters are the result of dreams and hypnosis. All the characters and beings encountered throughout the series are obvious analogues to Lovecraft's fiction (Herbert West becomes Hector North, Wilbur Whateley becomes Willard Wheatley). Most of the series concerns Lovecraft's creations rather than the man himself. However, things change in issue #8 in which Black meets Lovecraft during a lecture by Author Lord Dunsany. This is a real lecture that was delivered on September 20, 1919, and Lovecraft was indeed present.

Providence takes in to account the notion that fictionalizing, writing others and being himself written about, was part of Lovecraft's life. A biography of the man is therefore incomplete without considering his place within fiction. By mixing fact with fiction, Moore and Burrows attempt to present a more comprehensible view of Lovecraft, one that goes beyond the bare facts of his existence (as recounted in previous comics biographies) and into examining his place within the world.

In *Providence* Lovecraft is inspired to write many of his famous tales by reading Black's accounts of his travels throughout New England. Suggesting the sort of interdependency that existed between Lovecraft and his fellow authors: "I have even taken inspiration from your own work, young Robertus" (Moore and Burrows). Naturally, the real Lovecraft would change the names of the people involved while drawing inspiration for his own tales – explaining away the different names between *Providence's* protagonists and Lovecraft's own. For this reason, despite offering fictionalized reality *Providence* gives us a vision of Lovecraft that feels closer to the real-life individual than any before.

Moore captures Lovecraft's manner of speech, such as his quirk of adding classical suffixes to the names of people he knew, or his tendency to refer to himself as old man before the age of 30. Meanwhile, artist Jacen Burrows presents a near-replica of the time and place of the story. Thus, *Providence*'s fantastic reality of monsters and dream worlds is grounded in mundane reality of history. *Providence* #11 forgoes the slow rhythm of the previous issues, adopting instead a montage-mood as it moves fast forward from 1919 throughout the twentieth century, intermixing Lovecraft's actual life with the versions of his fictional creations shown previously in the series. The two flowing timelines become one as Lovecraft's creations and philosophy outlive him – becoming a dominant cultural force (Moore and Burrows).

It's important to understand this issue in the context of Moore's outlook on Lovecraft as a person. While most, including the man himself, would consider Lovecraft as an "outsider,"[2] Moore contends the opposite:

> Far from outlandish eccentricities, the fears that generated Lovecraft's stories and opinions were precisely those of the white, middle-class, heterosexual, Protestant descended males who were most threatened by the shifting power relationships and values of the modern world. Though he may have regarded himself, in accordance with the view held of him by his readership and even those that knew him personally, as an embodiment of his most emblematic fable, "The Outsider," in his frights and panics he reveals himself as that almost unheard-of fluke statistical phenomenon, the absolutely average man, an entrenched social insider unnerved by new and alien influences from without (Moore xiii).

The problem of Lovecraft's racism, which Moore acknowledges, is that while he might have been a "man of his time" his literature, and influences, prosper to this very day. Like old Joseph Curwen, reaching across the ages, spreading his malignancy to modern times.

Author Charles R. Saunders's essay "Die, Black Dog!" (written in 1975, revisited in 2011) notes that the influence of racist writers in the field of fantasy is felt to this day: "But in the world of today's fantasy, the racial atmosphere remains unchanged. Blacks are either ignored or are portrayed in the same hackneyed stereotypes that should have died with colonialism" (Saunders). Lovecraft was free to flaunt some social norms because he obeyed the most important ones: being white, being male. Bobbie Derie, commenting both on *Providence* in particular and on Moore's theories as a whole, notes: "The nuance of Black's position as an outsider echoes Lovecraft's own vision of himself, and colors his perception of the people that he meets" (Derie "American Dread"), we are discussing not the truth of Lovecraft but, rather, his "own vision of himself."

As issue #11 progress throughout the twentieth century we see it merge with the plotlines of *The Courtyard* and *Neonomicon*. *The Courtyard* presented a more obvious case of racism, the protagonist Aldo Sax makes several racist comments and is amused about being referred to as "a Nazi" rather than feeling appalled. At the time this seemed a simple case of meta-fiction, this story extrapolates from Lovecraft, who is a racist, and should engage with his racist attitudes as a commentary. However, when read together the Moore and Burrows cycle is suddenly charged with farther significance: the spirit of Lovecraft still prospers. His fears, these very common fears of a white man from anything different, are still a defining force in America. Despite his death, Lovecraft lives.

Lovecraft Defined

As we entered farther into the twenty-first century, comic books felt the need to confront Lovecraft's racism head on: "[Lovecraft's] elevation to provisional canonical status in the last decade has been beset with more asterisks, footnotes, and disclaimers than any other such recent rise" (Glover 171). Lovecraft's growing popularity as both a writer and fictionalized figure is problematized by the growing awareness of his racism. Thus, many who would still like to employ Lovecraft as a figure within their fiction turn him instead into an antagonist.

One can see this trend in *Planetary/The Authority: Ruling the World*, a one-shot crossover by writer Warren Ellis and artist Phil Jimenez between two ongoing superhero team books. The story opens with an attack by a gigantic tentacled monster in the present. One of the protagonists, the long-lived Elijah Snow, recalls the last time he encountered such a thing. A flashback takes us to the Rhode Island in early twentieth century, where Snow met a certain writer. The Author is not named, but the location, period, physical depiction and some small biographical details make it abundantly clear to all those in the know that this is H.P. Lovecraft. The Author is not a rounded character; he is an exaggeration of the real person's racist tendencies. When revealing the monstrous eggs he comes to the conclusion that those are "negro eggs" (Ellis and Jimenez). This writer believes that black people reproduce in some inhuman manner and that destroying the eggs is the only way to save "the white race."

The person of Lovecraft is not of great interest to Warren Ellis, but his influence on popular fiction is. The other villain figure in the story is the son of The Author's undertaker. The Author, he says, saw things "that he could only entrust to a man who understood death" (Ellis and Jimenez). There is no proper motivation for the villain's desire to unleash these monsters upon the world, nothing for him to gain nor any sense of the sublime in his actions, he simply wants to "murder the world." This choice actually echoes something Lovecraft once wrote in a letter criticizing a story: "I told my friend, he should conceive a man with a morbid, frantic, shuddering hatred of the life-principle itself, who wishes to extirpate from the planet every trace of biological organism, animal and vegetable alike, including himself" (Lovecraft qtd. in *Conspiracy* 36). In the world depicted in Lovecraft's fiction, death is the only proper release, either from the horror of Cthulhu's awakening or from the possession by some elder ancestry.

As an example of this view, we have Charles Dexter Ward, who is only free in death. As Doctor Willet tells his father, Mr. Ward, upon killing Joseph Curwen (who they believed to be Charles for quite a while): "When I call on you tomorrow Charles will have escaped. That is all which need remain in anyone's mind. He was mad, and he escaped" (Lovecraft *Charles Dexter Ward* 361). The cover story for the disappearance of Charles Dexter Ward from the institution is that he affected a miraculous escape. The truth is that he "escaped" from life, from the horror of being. Thomas Ligotti, whose *The Conspiracy Against the Human Race* quotes the above-mentioned letter, takes this philosophical notion from the fiction of Lovecraft into real life – self-annihilation is the only true free choice a person can make. The antagonist in *Planetary/The Authority: Ruling the World* is, therefore, a stand in for Ligotti. He is not merely quoting Lovecraft, but interpreting him in the most sinister way possible. Which is exactly what happened to Lovecraft himself once his fiction became popular enough.

Another extreme case can be found in *Atomic Robo and the Shadow from Beyond Time. Atomic Robo* is a series chronicling the life of a robot created by Nikolai Tesla in the early twentieth century (again, a semi-immortal protagonist) as he fights various monsters and menaces. In this story, Robo finds himself fighting a tentacled monster from a different dimension in four different time periods – 1926, 1957, 1971 and 2009. The 1926 encounter is our main of interest as it features Lovecraft. In these issues we discover that H.P. Lovecraft and Charles Fort worked together with Nikolai Tesla in the past – foiling an alien invasion in 1908. It was during that adventure that the Shadow contaminated the young Lovecraft (Clevinger and Wegener 21–22). The monster was slowly taking over his body, threatening the entire world as it finally emerged. Unlike the version from *Planetary/Authority* here Lovecraft is properly named and identified, and the creators made sure the dates are appropriate to the real-world history of the character. This story also takes Lovecraft noted attitudes toward race and amplifies them, creating a flattening effect.

Another case of flattened Lovecraft is in *Necronauts*, a horror story serialized in science fiction and fantasy anthology *2000AD* (issues #1223–1230). In *Necronauts*, Lovecraft teams up with fellow historical celebrities Charles Fort, Harry Houdini and Arthur Conan Doyle to fight cultists seeking to bring the end of the world. Lovecraft is presented here with the ability to enter the dream world, similar to that of his creation Randolph Carter, which the protagonists use to enter the domain of The Great Old Ones. Lovecraft is a coward who sells out his friends, the whole of humanity: "Y-you don't understand how powerful they are … they're everywhere, they see everything" (Rennie and Irving 37). The story frames his moral failings, this time focusing on his timidity and cowardice, in conjunction with his fiction.[3] It attempts to "justify" how he could become so. While *He Who Wrote in the Darkness* does it in a symbolic manner, here it is presented as a tangible connection.

Lovecraft the antagonist is, therefore, a continuation of Lovecraft the biography. An attempt by comics makers to engage with the public figure of the man and his influence on the world. There is a matter of choice, to focus one's attention on the less savory elements of Lovecraft's character. This focus brings about a flattening effect – everything that is not no relevant to the aspect in discussion is ignored. Lovecraft lives, but in a transformed manner – not what he was but what people want him to be.

Lovecraft Denied

The last sub-genre of Lovecraft appearances concerns the stories in which the character is a protagonist in the heroic sense of the term. In these stories, Lovecraft is largely, if not entirely, a positive figure that exists to evoke the audience's sympathy. The negative qualities evident in both his fiction and biography are either smoothed out or ignored entirely. This is philosophically opposite to Lovecraft's own fiction, which rejects the traditionally heroic:

> Traditionally, genre horror is concerned with the irruption of dreadful forces into a comforting status quo – one which the protagonists frantically scrabble to preserve. By contrast, Lovecraft's horror is not one of intrusion but of realization. The world has always been implacably bleak; the horror lies in our acknowledging that fact (Miéville xiii).

Casting Lovecraft as an outside observer or a malicious force works within the ethos of his own stories; casting him as a hero does not, because heroes do not exist in Lovecraft's world.

Out of all the roles Lovecraft may play, the least likely is that of the action hero; Lovecraft was both physically and mentally fragile. Action hero figures are not simply brave but also capable of dealing with threats by themselves. This notion goes against the grain not just of the person of Lovecraft, but also of the type of fiction he wrote – in which monsters could not be dispatched, and triumph came rarely if at all. Still, Lovecraft found himself several times drafted to play the role of a monster slayer, as if Cthulhu was nothing more than another vampire to stake.

Herald: Lovecraft & Tesla was a comic-book series written by John Reilly and drawn by Tom Rogers and Dexter Weeks. The series featured a team-up between the two historical figures, and some other notable individuals as guest stars. Already from the first issue we can tell there is little between the series' version of these people and history: Nikola Tesla is here engaged to famed aviator Amelia Earhart, whose sudden disappearance drives to meddle in occult affairs – which leads to a meeting with young Lovecraft (Reilly and Rogers). Lovecraft himself is reimagined as an active magician, his interest in occult book is translated in the comics into active knowledge of sorcery. In the second issue he sends powerful supernatural flame at an invading Mi-Go, boldly taking charge of the action.

There are flashes throughout the series in which Lovecraft becomes somewhat recognizable in his behavior: when he travels with Tesla in a bus, he gives a disgusted stare to a black traveler and makes to sit farther away from him, an act to which Tesla reacts with some visual concern. The creators of the series are aware of Lovecraft's racism, but do not wish to express it in a manner that is too obvious and would make him morally ambiguous to the modern reader. Thus, Lovecraft's racist beliefs are suppressed; his name and physical likeness are used, but the character is altered nearly beyond recognition.

A less extreme example of heroic transformation can be found in *The Strange Adventures of H.P. Lovecraft* which is a four-issue mini-series, later collected in a single volume, which works in the same manner. Once again, we have a Lovecraft who charges forward into the jaws of death, this time in attempt to save a love interest in peril. Among his first words to the reader in issue #1 are "this town is a pox on my life" (Carter and Salmons), spoken about his usually beloved Providence, Rhode Island. This hits a false note, as are many other small details throughout the series. By the time the plot reaches its climax, we see Lovecraft wielding a revolver against some unholy abomination in an attempt to save his beloved Sylvia; it is hard to worry about the small details when the whole picture is askew.

In chapter #3 Lovecraft stops to ponder about his place in history: "My name will never be linked to that writers pantheon, to those renowned conjurers of the uncanny – but my fame, or rather my infamy, is secured" (Carter and Salmons). One can almost read it as a meta-commentary: Lovecraft knowing he will become famous not as a writer but as a "character." This is, after all, a story whose subject is the merger of reality and fiction, with Lovecraft's nightmares hunting the people of Providence, just as his idea continued to hunt the world far beyond the readers of his actual fiction.

The final example to be considered is the *Howard Lovecraft and the Three Kingdoms* series. Written by Bruce Brown and illustrated by Renzo Podestá, it consists of three young-adult graphic novels centered around the young Lovecraft as he crosses into the dark dimension and befriends a Shoggoth, whom he calls "Spot" and treats like a dog. The series presents us Lovecraft that is both heroic and comedic in effect, affectively neutering any sense of danger associated with both the writer and the genre he helped to create. This is the final domestication of Lovecraft; his creations transformed into comforting fables for children; his tragic personal life into a happy-ending story in which his father lives to accompany the young boy and the creatures that hunted his nightmares become tame beasts.

The reference points of *Howard Lovecraft and the Three Kingdoms* appear to be other adaptations and continuations of Lovecraft's stories, as well as popular trends with young adult fiction of the early twenty-first century – including the broken family and the child hero as a chosen one. There are no chosen ones in Lovecraft's stories; the powers that do not care about the fate of humanity never mind that of a singular human. Yet in the first book in the series, *Howard Lovecraft and the Frozen Kingdom*, King Abdul refers to the young protagonist as a "deliverer" from the prophecy (Brown and Podestá). This is Lovecraft as *Harry Potter* or *Narnia*, a poor boy who suffers in "the real world," but gets to be the hero in a magical realm. This version of the author is shown in an entirely positive light, befriending giant beast and saving his family (and the world) from annihilation. While the Lovecraft's name is used, there is little one can learn about the writer or his fiction from reading *Howard Lovecraft and the Three Kingdoms*.

If *Providence* imagines a present in which Lovecraft's horrors "took over" reality through the unconventional means of pop-culture dominance, with Cthulhu plushies and video games starring Yog-Sototh filling the shelves, then *Howard Lovecraft and the Three Kingdoms* shows us the opposite end of the phenomenon – it is Lovecraft who ends up being dominated by pop culture. While in the story the Shoggoth is tamed it is actually Lovecraft himself who had been domesticated. Japanese manga artist Gou Tanabe, known for his adaptations of Lovecraft stories, had noted this modern approach: "In pop culture, I think the image of Lovecraft has changed completely. No one is scared of Cthulhu anymore. In fact, I wouldn't call what I do horror at all" (Tanabe 55). To work in Lovecraft is no longer considered to work in the field horror, it is to work in a genre of one man – the genre of "Lovecraft."

It is likely that Lovecraft, who saw writing-for-profit as a distasteful activity, would consider this almost as terrible a fate as any he imagined in his stories. The power of the capitalist mode of production, which commodifies and sands off the rough edges, has made its way to only to the works but to the man as well. Lovecraft the product, rather than Lovecraft the writer.

Lovecraft Unbound

Charles Dexter Ward, in his pride, thought he could call upon eldritch forces and control the knowledge they possess. Instead, he discovered he could not even control himself. Yet the end of *The Case of Charles Dexter Ward* shows us that even these same forces, the semi-immortal Joseph Curwen, can be swapped away by the tides of history. Reading through all these fictionalized depictions of Lovecraft, many of which are in conflict, it appears that Alan Moore depiction of a slow Lovecraftian takeover of reality in *Providence* #11 was both right and wrong. Right, for in his ascension from an unknown author into a fictional figure of icon Lovecraft had become a foundational part of culture. You cannot escape from Lovecraft's cultural presence in the twenty-first century. Even works which seek to refute his philosophy (*Planetary / The Authority*) or besmirch him personally (*Atomic Robo and the Shadow Out of Time*) must do so by first acknowledging his importance. Lovecraft's fictionalization is as important as the success of any of his texts; it is the proof the public cares not just for the art but for the artist as well. Yet Moore's theory is also wrong, because he did not fully take into account how Lovecraft's ascent was closely followed by the diffusion of his philosophy. Not a refutation, which demands certain care, but diffusion: The more Lovecraft appears in graphical fiction, the less said character resembles the real-life individual. "Lovecraft" is more known as a figure than as an artist, and that figure can be anything its creators want it to be – from an action hero to a precocious child.

David Simmons wrote about the wrapping of public perception of Lovecraft, and the way it is dependent upon fictional representations: "It is not too great a leap to believe that successive generations of readers and writers may have been more influenced by these fictional incarnations of the writer than by nonfictional texts" (151). Yet, we have seen in our examples that even incarnations that claim to be non-fictional (*He Who Wrote in the Darkness*, *Some Notes on a Nonentity*) present a version of the author that is based on the type of "story" they want to tell. By making Lovecraft a character in the first place his pulp contemporaries sealed his fate.

Twenty-first century graphic fiction is merely the zenith of that phenomenon; Lovecraft had become diluted in the cultural waters. He is omnipresent, existing in biography, superhero fiction, science fiction, adventure stories and even children's fiction; but at the same time, he is far less potent than he used to be. That both *Howard Lovecraft and the Frozen Kingdom* and *Providence* are each easily recognizable to the lay reader as "Lovecraft" tells you both how much and how little that name means; Lovecraft can be everything the writers of today want him to be, which also means that he is *nothing*. Each generation grows farther away from the source, until it is naught but a distant memory. Like the final fate of Joseph Curwen, Lovecraft had become the dust upon the winds of eternity – he is anywhere and everywhere, yet never quite the thing he had hoped to be.

Notes

1 The editors of *Weird Tales* magazine asked for Lovecraft's permission to publish a story with his likeness to which he replied: "This is to certify that Robert Bloch, Esq [...] is fully authorised [sic] to portray, murder, annihilate, disintegrate, transfigure, metamorphose, or otherwise manhandle the undersigned in the tale entitled THE SHAMBLER FROM THE STARS" (Johansen 308).

2 One of Lovecraft's seminal short stories is even named "The Outsider."

3 It is a recurring theme throughout these type of stories that Lovecraft is not so much malevolent as he is pathetic – a victim of his own racism and neurosis who spreads poison through the world unknowingly.

Works Cited

Belknap-Long, Frank. "The Space Eaters." *The Early Long*. Garden City, New York: Doubleday & Company, 1975, 22–49.

Brown, Bruce and Renzo Podestá. *Howard Lovecraft and the Frozen Kingdom* #2. British Columbia, Canada: Arcana Studio, 2009.

Carter, Marc and Tony Salmons. *The Strange Adventures of H.P. Lovecraft #1*. Berkeley, USA: Image Comics, April 2009a.

———. *The Strange Adventures of H.P. Lovecraft* #3. Berkeley, USA: Image Comics, June 2009b.

Clevinger, Brian and Scott Wegener. *Atomic Robo* vol. 3 #1. Calgary, Alberta, Canada: Red 5 Comics, April/May 2009.

Derie, Bobbie. *Weird Talers: Essays on Robert E. Howard and Others*. New York: Hippocampus Press, 2019.

———. "American Dread: Alan Moore and the Racism of H. P. Lovecraft." *Facts in the Case of Alan Moore's Providence*. 2015. https://factsprovidence.wordpress.com/moore-lovecraft-comics-annotation-index/american-dread-alan-moore-and-the-racism-of-h-p-lovecraft/ Visited May 2020.

Ellis, Warren and Phil Jimenez. *Planetary / The Authority: Ruling the World*. WildStorm Comics, June 2000.

Gafford, Sam and Jason Eckhardt. *Some Notes on a Nonentity: The Life of H.P. Lovecraft*. United Kingdom: PS Publishing, 2017.

Glover, John. "Reception and claim in supernatural Horror in Fiction and the course of Weird Fiction." *New Directions in Supernatural Horror Literature*, edited by Sean Moreland. New York: Palgrave, 2018, 171–187.

Johansen, Ib. *Walking Shadows: Reflections on the American Fantastic and the American Grotesque From Washington Irving to the Postmodern Era*. Leiden, Boston: Brill Rodopi, 2015.

Joshi, S.T. *I Am Providence: The Life and Times of H.P. Lovecraft*, Vol. 1. New York: Hippocampus Press, 2013.

Klinger, Leslie S. "Forward." *The New Annotated H.P. Lovecraft*, edited by Leslie S. Klinger, New York, London: Liveright, 2014. xv–lxiv.

Levi, Maurice. *Lovecraft: A Study in the Fantastic*. Detroit: Wayne State University Press, 1988.

Ligotti, Thomas. *The Conspiracy Against the Human Race*. New York: Hippocampus Press, 2010.

Lovecraft, H.P. *The Case of Charles Dexter Ward. H. P. Lovecraft, A Variorum Edition, Volume 2: 1926–1930*, edited by S. T. Joshi. New York: *Hippocampus Press*, 2017, pp. 214–366.

———. "The Haunter of the Dark." *H. P. Lovecraft, A Variorum Edition, Volume 3, 1931-1936*. New York: Hippocampus Press, 2017, pp. 451–477.

Miéville, China. "Introduction." *H.P. Lovecraft, At the Mountains of Madness: The Definitive Edition*. New York: The Modern Library, 2005, XI–XXV.

Moore, Alan. "Introduction." *The New Annotated H.P. Lovecraft*, edited by Leslie S. Klinger, New York: Liveright, 2014, xi–xiv.

Moore, Alan; Burrows, Jacen. "VIII: The Key." *Providence #8*. Rantoul, IL: Avatar Press, March 2016a.

———. "XI: The Unnamable." *Providence #11*. Rantoul. IL: Avatar Press, November 2016b.

Nikolavitch, Alex, Carlos Gersavio, and Lara Lee. *H.P. Lovecraft: He Who Wrote in the Darkness*. Translated by Ivanka Hahnenberger. New York: Pegasus Books, 2018.

Reilly, John and Tom Rogers. "History in the Making, Part 1" *Herald: Lovecraft & Tesla #1*. Pittsburgh, PA: Action Lab Entertainment, December 2014.

Rennie, Gordon and Frazer Irving. *Necronauts*. Oxford: Rebellion, 2003.

Saunders, Charles R. "Die, Black Dog! Revisited". *Charles R. Saunders Blog*, February 2011, http://reindeermotel.com/CHARLES/charles_blog42_die-blackdog.html. Visited April 2020.

Simmons, David. "H.P. Lovecraft and Real Person Fiction: The Pulp Author as Subcultural Avatar." *The Age of Lovecraft*, edited by Carl H. Sederholm and Jeffrey Andrew Weinstock. Minneapolis, MN: University of Minnesota Press, 2016, 149–164.

Tanabe, Gou. "Kindred Spirits: Zack Davisson Interviews Gou Tanabe." *Razorblades #2*, edited by Steve Fox. Tiny Onion Studios, October 2020, 50–57.

7 Drawing the Unknowable—Lovecraft's Cosmic Horror in *Magic The Gathering* and *Hearthstone*

Suzanne Albary and Richard Albary

H.P. Lovecraft's writings have provided rich source material for fantasy and horror artists since many of them first appeared, but that influence has only grown stronger since the 1970s. Lovecraft's influence can now be found in hundreds, if not thousands, of books, artworks, and games of all kinds, including both the digital and non-digital. Art frequently played a central role within Lovecraft's stories and serves as an important focal point in key stories such as "Pickman's Model," "The Call of Cthulhu," and *At the Mountains of Madness*. These three stories, along with Lovecraft's seminal essay *Supernatural Horror in Literature*, provide the starting point for our analysis of several Lovecraft-inspired artistic representations found in *Magic: The Gathering (MTG)* (Wizards of the Coast) and *Hearthstone: Heroes of Warcraft (*Blizzard Entertainment), two of the largest collectible card games of the last decade. This chapter will explore how the artworks for these games attempt to capture Lovecraft's cosmic horror; it will also discuss the kinds of challenges that come from drawing on the concept of the unknowable in visual media and in how that gets complicated when used in tactile and tangible games that require clearly defined mechanics.

Art and Cosmic Horror in Lovecraft's Works

In *Supernatural Horror in Literature*, Lovecraft writes that "[t]he oldest and strongest emotion of mankind is fear, and the oldest and strongest kind of fear is fear of the unknown" (82). Throughout the essay, Lovecraft argues that to create effective horror, the writer (or artist) must exploit this innate fear of the unknown while simultaneously giving readers a

> hint… "of that most terrible conception of the human brain—a malign and particular suspension or defeat of those fixed laws of Nature which are our only safeguard against the assaults of chaos and the daemons of unplumbed space.
>
> (84)

DOI: 10.4324/9780367713065-8

Though Lovecraft was capturing an ideal practice, he nevertheless strived to write with that principle in mind. In "Pickman's Model," he repeated the main idea when his narrator, Thurber, recalls that "only a suspension of Nature's laws could ever let a man [Pickman] paint a thing like that without a model—without some glimpse of the nether world which no mortal unsold to the Fiend has ever had" (69). This suspension of natural laws, the glimpse of possibilities that are otherwise unseen and unknown, creates a looming sense of horror and foreboding both for Thurber and his audience. Likewise, in "The Call of Cthulhu," the sculptures that Thurston inherits (as recounted by the narrator, Legrasse) "belonged to something horribly remote and distinct from mankind as we know it; something frightfully suggestive of old and unhallowed cycles of life in which our world and our conceptions have no part" (32). This story is particularly interesting for our purposes because it provides detailed descriptions of artworks representative of cosmic horror that Lovecraft explored, albeit through the limited scope of human understanding.

In the three stories considered for this chapter, Lovecraft uses the trope of the first-person "witness" to demonstrate this limited understanding and its potentially otherworldly implications: Thurber's unveiling Pickman's real artistic influences ("Pickman's Model"); Thurston's investigating cult activities ("The Call of Cthulhu"); and Dyer's gradual decipherment of the pictographic history of Antarctica (*At the Mountains of Madness*). Noël Carroll builds on this theme by arguing that character reactions to the "witness" show the reader what the witnesses see is not just monstrous, but is fundamentally unnatural, a "disturbance to the natural order" of things (52). Similarly, Roger Salomon outlines the problems these "witness" characters face in horror texts: they must somehow describe what it is they have witnessed, even though "what is witnessed has… no firm basis in empirical causality and rather invokes some dimension of supernature" (76). Salomon goes on to pose a question that Lovecraft himself grappled with: "how to naturalize [horror] narrative enough to make it credible without limiting the implications of issues raised and thus explaining away the horror" (76–77). There is a difficult balance between revealing enough to create fear without *explaining* too much and thereby make the horror mundane. This challenge is especially amplified in the visual arts, where an artist must represent some horror to their audience (the "witness") without giving away too much while also keeping the horrific thing "unknowable." These kinds of questions will be applied to the artworks discussed in this chapter. In particular, we are interested in exploring the question, how can artistic representation be both subtle enough to convey the unknown while also descriptive enough to be "cognitively threatening" (Carroll 56)?

As Timo Airaksinen argues (92), Lovecraft acknowledged that he sometimes failed to reach this important balance in his stories, especially when he falls back on descriptive prose to convey a sense of the monstrous.

Lovecraft is successful in living up to the standards of "art-horror" as laid out by Carroll some 50 years later. For Carroll, "art-horror" is that which contains within it not just monsters, but monsters that evoke horror *because* they challenge our understanding of the natural world (Carroll 52). These monsters not only create fear but also force observers to revulsion, nausea and disgust—monsters that are "so unwholesome that its very touch causes shudders" (Carroll 53). Importantly, the audience knows this not from the description of the creatures, but from the reactions and attitudes of the characters that the monsters happen upon. For "art-horror" to be effective, the audience responses to the horrors mirror those of the character responses to the horror within the story.

Lovecraft also attempts to elicit the reader's fear and disgust at the unwholesome nature of his monsters (see Luckhurst xviii). Rather than describing his monsters as one specific thing or another, he seeks to underscore their morphological nature (Maltolcsy 153). Because they are interstitial—neither one thing or another—they are more psychologically and cognitively frightening, perhaps even beyond description or beyond imagination (Carroll 56). In *At the Mountains of Madness*, the creatures dissected require the characters to rethink known science itself, as their anatomy is beyond understanding. To write successful horror, fear then should be created through the breaking of the laws of nature (Lovecraft *Supernatural*). It is this contrast between the real that we can know and the real that we cannot that creates such powerful feelings of fear.

Having discussed the characteristics of Lovecraft's notions of horror and the pertinent components of "art-horror," the following sections will introduce *Magic: The Gathering* and *Hearthstone* and their contextual narratives, in order to draw parallels with Lovecraft's fiction, especially in the three narratives discussed above. We then move onto a deeper analysis of several the artworks used within each game to explore the kinds of challenges artists face when they attempt to capture cosmic horror.

The Battle for Zendikar (MTG) and the Artwork of the Eldrazi

Released in October 2015, *Battle for Zendikar* is a 299-card expansion to *MTG*. Each *MTG* expansion is set against the backdrop of a fictional story which focuses on the main heroes and villains of the expansion. *Battle for Zendikar* is set on a plane of existence called Zendikar and chronicles the campaign to defeat the monstrous Eldrazi, a race of interdimensional titans who are accidentally released from their imprisonment and manifest physical bodies to devour life energy until the plane is destroyed.

The Eldrazi titans "do not dwell in physical space" (Wyatt et al. 2015) a detail that brings to mind Lovecraft would term a "particular suspension ... of those fixed laws of nature" (Lovecraft "Supernatural" 84). During the exposition of their true nature, it is revealed that their physical forms are simply projections into perceived reality, just as the fingers of a person putting their hand into a pond might appear as a five-headed monster to those beings that live in the pond (Wyatt et al.). This liminality and "otherworldliness" is often employed by Lovecraft. Cthulhu resides in R'lyeh, which rises from the bottom of the Pacific Ocean at the culmination of "The Call of Cthulhu." This transportation of the monster, from the unknowable (at the time) depths of the ocean to the surface, reawakening once again to its destructive nature, is echoed not only in the manifestation of the Eldrazi but also in their relation to the dark watery depths of the world they now inhabit.[1]

The influence of Lovecraft's horror is most obvious in the depictions and descriptions of the invading Eldrazi. A seemingly unstoppable tide of Eldrazi drones with "featureless, bony plates that passed for their heads" (Wyatt et al.) perpetrates the main onslaught against life on Zendikar. The crude anthropomorphization of these creatures made by the central characters in the story is due to a lack of understanding of the physiology of the drones. The creatures have bifurcated limbs, or "writhing masses of tentacles," which suggest a strong influence of Lovecraft's bestiary on the Eldrazi and evoke the concept of the horror in a morphing, indescribable monster in discussions by Maltolcsy (Wyatt et al.). The Eldrazi are clearly aligned to Lovecraft's Elder Things and Old Gods. The three great Eldrazi titans—Ulamog, Kozilek, and Emrakul—are discovered to have been the inspiration for the now "'forsaken gods"' of the Zendikar race of merfolk, Ula, Cosi, and Emeria. These three ancient deities are represented in the artwork of the MTG card "Shrine of the Forsaken Gods," where they have been given distinctly humanoid—and therefore knowable—physical traits. Despite this ancient worship, the Eldrazi are indifferent toward the native Zendikar races, much like Lovecraft's own forgotten Old Gods.

The story of the *Battle for Zendikar* inspires the artwork that appears on the playable cards in the set and makes clear references to the themes of Lovecraft's fiction and cosmic horror. The artworks for both *Incubator Drone* (Figure 7.1) and *Transgress the Mind* (Figure 7.2) show grisly close-up scenes of the monsters attacking helpless mortals in ways reminiscent of the artworks Thurber sees in Pickman's basement studio. *Incubator Drone* in particular looks eerily reminiscent of Thurber's "nameless blasphem[ies]" holding what "had been a man" while sitting in "a kind of crouch" but might "at any moment… drop its present prey and seek a juicier morsel." (Lovecraft "Pickman's Model" 69). The accompanying text to the artwork, "[t]he touch of an Eldrazi brings life and death in turn" (Wyatt et al.), creates a sense confusion for the audience by making them wonder if the creature has just killed someone or is attempting to create life (perhaps alluding to the kind of horror elicited by Mary Shelley's *Frankenstein*). *Incubator Drone* captures something

Figure 7.1 Incubator Drone.

Source: Artwork by Cynthia Sheppard.

inexplicable, a moment that defies explanation or rationalization in a way often seen in Lovecraft's stories.

"The Call of Cthulhu" is clearly referenced in several other artworks used for the set. *Breaker of Armies* resembles Cthulhu itself, which matches Lovecraft's description of a "pulpy, tentacled head surmounted [on] a grotesque" body (Lovecraft "The Call of Cthulhu" 127). One of the forsaken gods from Zendikar, *Ulamog, the Ceaseless Hunger* (Figure 7.3), also recalls Lovecraft's creature. So immense, *Ulamog* cannot be captured in one image and so its various appendages stray outside the frame, or just fade into the misty distance. Cthulhu is described as "a gigantic thing 'miles high'" (Lovecraft "The Call of Cthulhu" 27). The other depictions of *Ulamog* on cards, such as *Titan's Presence* and *Aligned Hedron Network*, also clearly emulate this. *Battle for Zendikar* is drawing on the same immensity Lovecraft used to elicit fear of Cthulhu. This combined with an extra-dimensional nature and seemingly indifferent destructive tendencies toward the plane's inhabitants shows clear connections to Lovecraft's creature.

Figure 7.2 Transgress the Mind.
Source: Artwork by Cynthia Sheppard.

Whispers of the Old Gods (Hearthstone) and the Artwork of the "Old Gods"

Whispers of the Old Gods, released in April 2016, is a 134-card expansion to *Hearthstone* and builds upon the ongoing story of Azeroth, the name of the world in which the majority of the *Warcraft* series is set. The creative setting of Azeroth has a long history of drawing on Lovecraft's world building for inspiration (e.g., see Hitchens and Ruch), as evident alone by the name, which is strikingly similar to Azathoth, one of the Outer Gods that appears in *The Dream-Quest of Unknown Kadath* and other tales. In *Whispers of the Old Gods*, we see clear references to Lovecraft's cosmic horror themes in the names of "characters" or cards: C'thun, N'Zoth, Soggoth, Yogg-Saron (the "Old Gods"), as well as cultists, horrors, disciples, and other squirming, infested, polluted aberrations. The naming of these cards is less subtle than those of *MTG*, as they directly recall creatures from Lovecraft's stories. For example, Yogg-Saron and Soggoth the Slitherer remind us of creatures like Yog-Sothoth and the numerous Shoggoths found in Lovecraft's fiction.

Figure 7.3 Ulamog the Ceaseless Hunger.

Other cards adopt conventions also employed by Lovecraft of creating names for monsters (e.g., Herald Volazj and Spawn of N.Zoth) that fall outside of human convention, not only in that they are difficult to pronounce, but they are also deliberately "confusing" and "unknowable."

Hearthstone's C'Thun bears a direct resemblance to Cthulhu (along with *Lord of the Rings* "Eye of Sauron"), because of its bulbous, tentacled head (Figure 7.4). *Master of Evolution* (Figure 7.5) and *Servant of Yogg-Saron* are similarly explicit in their reference to Lovecraft's monstrous Yog-Sothoth. Many of the other artworks show characteristics that bring to mind Lovecraft's cosmic horror. This set introduces a "forbidden" card for each playable class, in keeping with themes from Lovecraft about "forbidden" knowledge or images of "things which should not be." Other cards, such as *Forbidden Shaping*, are also notable for the creature being oozy or slimy in appearance, recalling once more Lovecraft's attempts to describe the indescribable horrors throughout his writings as having a "hideous slime-coating" or "ooz(ing) tightly onward" (*At the Mountains* 142, 150). Other features of the Elder Things can be seen within the artworks from this card set. *C'Thun*

Figure 7.4 C'Tun.

Source: Artwork by Michael Bell. Hearthstone®: Heroes of Warcraft™ © 2010–2021 Blizzard Entertainment

(Figure 7.4) and *Master of Evolution* (Figure 7.5), among other cards in the set, show creatures with many tentacles protruding from what might be described as a head, with the tentacles of the former ending in many eyes, once again influenced by the descriptions in Lake's autopsy report.

Whispers of the Old Gods, more than *Battle for Zendikar*, suggests a direct influence of Lovecraft. While the aesthetic themes of Lovecraft's creatures, descriptions, and ideas of cosmic horror appear in both sets of cards, *Whispers of the Old Gods* make the connections explicit in the naming conventions of the cards themselves, making direct comparisons with specific characters and monsters clearer. The creatures depicted in the artworks are more literal interpretations of Lovecraft's work than just being influenced by the principles of his horror.

Discussion

Having described some of the artwork from the cards in both *Battle for Zendikar* and *Whispers of the Old Gods* in relation to themes from

Figure 7.5 Master of Evolution.

Source: Artwork by Dan Scott. Hearthstone®: Heroes of Warcraft™ © 2010–2021 Blizzard Entertainment

Lovecraft's fiction, we can now turn to a discussion on whether these works of artistic representation are successful in fully embodying the ideas of cosmic horror that Lovecraft sought to convey in his texts. That the author himself acknowledged that he was not always successful (Airaksinen 92) poses a further challenge in analyzing specific works of art. In *At the Mountains of Madness*, the monster was a "thing that should not be… a terrible, *indescribable* thing" (Lovecraft 149–150). Something indescribable by very definition must defy representation, descriptively or artistically. Houellebecq notes that while Lovecraft's work stimulates the imagination, his writing "discourages any attempt at visual adaptation" (80). When Johansen finally glimpses Cthulhu in "The Call of Cthulhu" the description is simplistic, if unpleasant: a "gelatinous green immensity" with "flapping membranous wings" (52–53). When some*thing* is the embodiment of horror, then, perhaps it can only be so with its absence (Jackson 39). The manifestation of that horror is no longer to be feared. We return to the conundrum of "the witness," where the author of the horror must use language to produce the desired emotional response toward the horror, but not describe it in enough detail that the horror is made mundane. Lovecraft overcomes this, to some extent, by writing descriptions that are amorphous, talking of tentacles and size and slime without formulating a clear *picture* of the creatures in the mind of the reader. In Airaksinen words, we "get a picture which raises more questions than it answers" (191).

In Lovecraft's writings, we have the benefit of an intermediary, the narrator. We are hearing the accounts of these monsters second- or third-hand. In "Pickman's Model" we listen as Thurber recounts his experiences in exploring Pickman's studio to his audience, Eliot. In "The Call of Cthulhu," we read Thurston's first person account of his investigations. Being so removed, we cannot verify the descriptions we are given, thus coming to "know" the creatures for ourselves. In addition, we are subject to the narrator's reactions to the horrors before them. Their attitudes and observations serve to inform the audience of the "right" way to respond to such aberrations (Carroll 53) or cause the audience to have a sympathetic identification with the victim (Airaksinen 101). The horrors depicted in *Battle for Zendikar* and *Whispers of the Old Gods* are served to us as the initial witness in most cases, not through the lens of another character. We are forced to confront the monsters first-hand, and thus come to *know* them ourselves, removing much of the fear that we might feel if we were not familiar with them. Here, visual representations of horror are susceptible to the problem of the witness, as they are not something we experience through another's eyes. Instead, we see them as clearly as the characters do, allowing us to experience the horrors directly. Through this, they become more familiar and while they may appear to us grotesque or inhumane, they are not something to be feared due to their unknown nature.

As Hitchens & Ruch point out (6), it is very rare that Lovecraft's narrators glimpse the Old Gods themselves. Thurston never *sees* Cthulhu (although he does possess a crude statue supposed to represent the creature); instead, he walks readers through the embedded narrative that recounts Johansen's own encounter with the Old God. The fear of those monsters is made all the more focused when coming into contact with a mere servant of one of the Old Gods is "enough to destroy a human in both mind and body" (Hitchens and Ruch 2). The drones, servants, and cultists of Lovecraft are, themselves, things to be feared. In the *Battle for Zendikar* and *Whispers of the Old Gods* there is very little to distinguish them visually from the larger, older, more powerful monsters. This is done not in the artist's representation, but in the mechanics of the gameplay, once again removing the "unknown" quality required for true horror. *Incubator Drone* (Figure 7.1) is as otherworldly and disturbing to look at as *Ulamog* (Figure 7.3), an unfathomably large behemoth. *Incubator Drone*, however, is shown as only slightly larger than the victim it has imprisoned. It has a distinguishable head, arms, and body—human-like, but not, it is close enough to the known to be recognizable, but different enough to be abhorrent. It is, as Carroll might suggest, a sign of the natural order disrupted (52). *Incubator Drone* is similar to moments in "Pickman's Model," but, as Lovecraft himself details, a true representation of horror relies on challenging a fundamental understanding of reality, which leads to horrific implications based on a lack of the safety that was believed to be there (*Supernatural*). Simply portraying something as "otherworldly," or "other," is not enough to elicit true fear from the witness.

The concept of "otherworldly" is further complicated by the very purpose of these works of art. *Ulamog* (Figure 7.3) and *C'Thun* (Figure 7.4) are, indeed, terrible to behold. But they are quantified in statistics which fit into the gameplay. Ulamog, a devastating creature, is assigned 10/10 (attack power/defense); similarly, C'Thun is a 6/6 (attack power/defense) creature who has an additional ability whereby its attack damage is randomly assigned. The latter card's abilities perhaps best embody Lovecraft's principles of cosmic horror, albeit in a rudimentary way. The idea that the creature's damage could be dealt randomly embodies the "chaos" of worlds without the laws of nature, and the "assaults of chaos" that exist in the unknown spaces of the universe (Lovecraft "Supernatural" 84). Ulamog, on the other hand, has functional abilities which are designed not to elicit the psychological fear of the unknown, but the physical fear of the known force for which there is no answer: the mechanics of the card are so strong that they become almost impossible to deal with.

That these concepts and characters of cosmic horror—Old Gods, extraplanar beings, monsters of (im)measurable power—can be represented graphically and statistically belies the very nature of Lovecraft's intentions. As Hitchens and Ruch explore through Blizzard Entertainment's *World of Warcraft*, the very nature of gaming is to ensure that all creatures are precisely defined in name, statistics, and abilities. To do so removes the unknown quality which Lovecraft outlines as central to cosmic horror. Furthermore, the very nature of the settings makes true representation of cosmic horror nearly impossible. In his writings, Lovecraft reminds us that in order for cosmic horror to elicit fear, humanity must be "handled with unsparing realism," so that the "hideous unknown" (Lovecraft *Selected Letters II* 150) can have the greatest impact. The very nature of a fantastical setting, where there are heroes of power and nonhuman protagonists that fight—physically and magically—against the Old Gods and Elder Things, means that there is no "natural" order of things. One option we might look to subvert this natural order visually, rather than mechanically, would be to challenge the viewers' fundamental understanding of spatial occupancy using non-Euclidean geometry. This is lacking throughout the artworks for *Battle for Zendikar* and *Whispers of the Old Gods*.

From Lovecraft's own measures of cosmic horror, then, we are left with building an atmosphere of dread: "Atmosphere is the all-important thing, for the final criterion of authenticity is not the dovetailing of a plot but the creation of a given sensation" (*Supernatural* 84). The physical absence of the source of horror, evoking the hidden or unseen, could be used to elicit the sense of horror. *Transgress the Mind* (Figure 7.2), for example, reveals not only the monster, but the *act* that monster commits, but for the characters depicted on the card, only one is aware. The victim is set upon from behind, and thus feels not only the physical (and perhaps mental) agony of the attack, but the *fear* of not knowing where the attack comes from. The "flavor text" on the full *MTG* card, drawn from Wyatt et al.'s accompanying fictions, accompanies the artwork: "Fear of the unknown can be a wonderfully innocent thing, relatively speaking." That the character feels that sense of fear is portrayed through their agonized and horrified expression, thus letting the audience know what and how to feel about the scene. Unlike *Battle for Zendikar*, the cards from *Whispers of the Old Gods* display more simplistic representations. There are no "scenes" or vistas, and all cards represent single characters. Thus, the audience is denied the opportunity to see the "intended" and "correct" reaction to the horrors that are present, or fully realize the scale of the monsters themselves. While not all cards from the *Battle for Zendikar* set have that secondary narrator present, those that do reveal the horror and fear that the monstrous "others" evoke.

Creating an atmosphere of cosmic horror, not to mention a larger fear of the unknown, might also be presented through incomplete artwork, or through depictions of things with certain aspects hidden from the viewer. Artistic representation never tells the whole story and relies, instead, representing a specific moment within the narrative. Incomplete depictions of the monsters not only create the feeling of unease in the viewer that the worst is yet to be witnessed, but that the sheer immensity of the creatures is—as yet—unknown. In this way, a partially seen creature can still retain some sense of mystery, hiding its full nature. As Houllebecq (91–96) argues, the entities which Lovecraft wrote about remain shadowy, and he did not articulate their powers fully. They remain then, fundamentally unspeakable. We have only furtive glimpses of their eldritch powers; and humans who seek to know more will pay ineluctably in madness or in death. As representations of Lovecraft's horror in the *World of Warcraft* fall ultimately short of producing cosmic horror due to the requirement of them being fully formed creatures with finite statistics (Hitchens and Ruch 6), the card artworks for collectable card games are free of this restriction. While the cards themselves must be fundamentally mechanical for gameplay, the artwork itself does not need a complete representation, even if it relates to a specific "character."

Conclusion

Lovecraft uses written language to convey ambiguity around the weirdly horrible creatures in his stories. When attempts to describe the monsters render the creatures mundane, things no longer to be feared, he can fall back on calling them "indescribable" (*At the Mountains* 150). The visual arts have no such luxury. Visual representation can hint at a thing, create an atmosphere, or depict a horrified "witness," but cannot simply *ignore* the horror that is the subject of the work.

This chapter acknowledges that Lovecraft was not able to consistently apply his own framework of what constitutes high quality "weird horror," as he understands that "his direct descriptions of what is weird are not successful" (Airaksinen 92). The artwork on the cards from *Battle for Zendikar* and *Whispers of the Old Gods* are visual representations of this struggle, between wanting the audience to feel horror and disgust, but offering too much *description*. Instead, the audience is intrigued and disturbed, but not *horrified*. In the case of these particular representations, which form the aesthetic for a game, with its associated mechanics and rules of gameplay, the artists have instead fallen back on attempts to visually create creatures that violate the laws of nature within the *story*. This has created monsters that are physically threatening—both in terms of how they look and their strength within the game. By their very nature, they are not able to elicit the kind of fear that is born out of deeper consideration of the fundamental nature of the world that leads to terrible, and terrifying, conclusions—they have not created the psychologically threatening creatures of our nightmares but have instead domesticated them for popular consumption.

Perhaps the greatest challenge that artworks drawing on Lovecraft for inspiration have is to play on the human fear of the unknown. Our improved understanding of the universe, the spaces beyond our world, and those in the depths of the oceans have rendered that which is simply "otherworldly" less of a threat than it was. *Battle for Zendikar* and *Whispers of the Old Gods* are distinct, "otherworldly" settings that are not themselves constructed to be places of horror. The mechanics of the game create order to these otherworldly spaces, offering the audience an understanding of the rules of the natural order of things in these settings. The creatures fit within these settings mechanically, and while powerful and intimidating, do not break the rules.

Similarly, the narratives that surround the artwork are fantastical, whereas Lovecraft was writing "unrealistic things" in a "realistic setting" (Airaksinen 91). What these fantasy worlds do offer are "world(s) of peril and evil possibilities" (Lovecraft "Supernatural" 83) which the artists draw on to represent the strange and malevolent monsters that seek to destroy what came before. By drawing on Lovecraft as inspiration, the artists are allowing the audience to experience the horror as the "witness" would in Lovecraft's writings, albeit from a safe distance. This undermines the "weird horror" that may be experienced but offers a new perspective on the themes and creatures created by Lovecraft which is part of the natural evolution of his real-world setting. This evolution of the framework that Lovecraft sets out in his writings offers us fertile ground for further research on his influences on contemporary popular culture.

Note

1 Lovecraft uses this sense of liminality when describing the ocean-dwelling Deep Ones in "The Shadow over Innsmouth," although he argues the story is "defective," containing "hackneyed phrases & rhythms [that] have crept in despite all precautions" (H.P. Lovecraft, letter to August Derleth, December 10, 1931). The narrator recalls Zadok's description of the creatures rising from the water in "The Shadow over Innsmouth." This story influenced another *MTG* "block," *Shadows over Innistrad* (published April 2, 2016), in which Jace Beleren investigated a source of madness affecting the Innistrad denizens. The source is eventually revealed to be Emrakul, one of the Eldrazi Titans.

Works Cited

Airaksinen, Timo. *The Philosophy of H.P. Lovecraft: The Route to Horror. New Studies in Aesthetics vol 29*. Bern: Peter Lang Publishing, 1999.

Carroll, Noël. "The Nature of Horror." *The Journal of Aesthetics and Art Criticism*, vol. 46, no. 1, 1987, pp. 51–59. *JSTOR*, doi: 10.2307/431308.

Hitchens, Michael and Ruch, Adam. "Form over function: the use of Lovecraftian elements in World of Warcraft." *IE 2013 – Proceedings of the 9th Australasian Conference on Interactive Entertainment: Matters of Life and Death*, edited by Greuter, Association for Computing Machinery (ACM), 2013, pp. 1–8.

Houllebecq, Michel. *H.P. Lovecraft Against the World, Against Life*. Cernunnos, 2005.

Jackson, Rosemary. *Fantasy: The Literature of Subversion*. Routledge, 2008.

Joshi, S.T. *A Subtler Magick: The Writings and Philosophy of H.P. Lovecraft*. Wildside Press, 1999.

Lovecraft, H.P. *Supernatural Horror in Literature. Collected Essays Volume 2: Literary Criticism*, edited by S. T. Joshi. New York: Hippocampus Press, 2004, 82–135.

———. "Pickman's Model." *H. P. Lovecraft Collected Fiction, A Variorum Edition, Volume 2: 1926–1930*, edited by S. T. Joshi. New York: Hippocampus Press, 2017, pp. 56–72.

———. "The Call of Cthulhu." *H. P. Lovecraft Collected Fiction, A Variorum Edition, Volume 2: 1926–1930*, edited by S. T. Joshi. New York: Hippocampus Press, 2017, pp. 21–55.

———. *At the Mountains of Madness. H. P. Lovecraft Collected Fiction, A Variorum Edition, Volume 3: 1931–1936*, edited by S. T. Joshi. New York: Hippocampus Press, 2017, pp. 11–157.

———. *Selected Letters II (1925–1929)*, edited by August Derleth and Donald Wandrei. Sauk City, WI: Arkham House, 1964. https://archive.org/details/LovecraftH.P.SelectedLettersIIArkhamHouse1968/mode/2up (accessed 21/01/2020)

———. "The Shadow Over Innsmouth." *The new annotated H.P. Lovecraft*. WW Norton & Company, 1936b/2014, pp. 573–642.

Luckhurst, Roger. "Introduction." *The Classic Horror Stories, H.P. Lovecraft*, edited by Roger Luckhurst, Open University Press, 2013, pp. vii–xxviii.

Matolcsy, Kálmán. "The Monster-Text: Analogy and Metaphor in Lovecraft." *Hungarian Journal of English and American Studies (HJEAS)*, vol. 18 no. 1/2, 2012, pp. 151–159. *JSTOR*, doi: 10.2307/431308.

Salomon, Roger. *Mazes of the Serpent: An Anatomy of Horror Narrative*. Cornell: Cornell University Press, 2002.
Wyatt, James et al. "Battle for Zendikar." *Wizards of the Coast LLC*, 2015, https://magic.wizards.com/en/content/battle-zendikar-story (accessed 21/01/2020).

8 Nuclear Inhumanities

H.P. Lovecraft's "The Colour Out of Space" and the Dread of Contamination

Ian Fetters

In H.P. Lovecraft's 1927 story, "The Colour Out of Space," a meteorite crashes to earth near Nahum Gardner's farm located in a rural valley in western Arkham, Massachusetts. The meteorite arrives without apparent purpose or known cause, yet its presence in the ground, evidenced by the bizarre flowering of plants and the ruination of crops, signals the initial stages of the Gardner family's tragic demise. Unprovoked, unsummoned, and unknowable, the titular "colour" wreaks havoc on all organic life, including the bodies and minds of the Gardners themselves. By the end of the tale, the once stoic and proud Nahum Gardner is reduced to a gibbering, disintegrating heap, while the fates of his wife and children are left unspeakable. The malign, contaminating influence of the colour, once merely suspected as the culprit for the Gardner's misfortunes, is, in the end, the destructive force responsible for the five acres of grey desolation that was once the Gardner farm—known by locals in the decades afterwards as the "blasted heath" (Lovecraft 1927).

As modern readers coming to Lovecraft, the "killer meteorite" premise can seem blasé at first, especially in the wake of dozens of variations on the theme in science fiction literature and film since the publication of "The Colour Out of Space." However, it is in the realm of science fact that the story takes on a sinister new context. I propose a reading of the colour as an inhuman agency that lacks obvious motivation, but is nevertheless unparalleled in its destructive capabilities, comparable in regard to both the real-world phenomenon of radiation and radioactivity. This reading re-envisions the alien colour in the context of twentieth and twenty-first century experiences and accidents in the field of nuclear science as a means to better understanding the essential weirdness of radioactivity. Part one of my reading establishes a key aspect of the colour-radiation comparison: that both are motiveless inhuman agencies acting in similar ways, especially when acting upon organic bodies. This is demonstrated through the colour's degenerative effects on all members of the Gardner family, effects that mirror the aftermath of prolonged exposure to radionuclides on organic bodies. Both the colour and radiation are hazardous outsiders contaminating the inside, sensed through

DOI: 10.4324/9780367713065-9

the effects on the body; both are known to fluctuate their visible and invisible phenomenological aspects; and they are motiveless, destructive forces from the inside out.

Nevertheless, my reading does not rest simply on a phenomenological comparison between the colour and its real world, radioactive counterpart. Even though Lovecraft is obviously writing before the Nuclear Age, I address in the second part "The Colour Out of Space" with an expanded nuclear context—including the lived-in anxieties shaping domestic nuclear policy in the present. The human and environmental cost of nuclear disaster casts a long shadow over the United States. Issues of high-level radioactive waste, contamination, and the far-reaching consequences of past nuclear accidents continue to dominate the debate surrounding the nuclear energy industry in the present, showing no signs of abatement. Drawing on the past traumas and consequences of our tainted nuclear legacies reinforces my reading of radioactivity as a "weird message from [...] other realms of matter, force, and entity," likening it to the colour as a "real externality" which exceeds our capacity for representation (374).[1] Nuclear radioactivity is one of these real externalities, belonging to a hypernatural cosmos that we humans lack the capabilities to fully comprehend; yet, we exist in a constant state of contamination and interpolation by nuclear radiation into our lives. This phenomenon is herein termed the *nuclear weird*—a hyperobject-like assemblage of nuclear materials, wastes, and contaminations distributed massively across time and space that exists at the extreme limits of our scientific understanding of the cosmos and cannot be contained by human capacities for representation.[2] Thus, part two collates the fictional Gardner experience with the nuclear weird, bringing to the fore old and new concerns about the dread possibility of radioactive contamination into public and private life—the "real externality" of the cosmos coming in. This *weirding* of the nuclear relocates the sites of cosmic horror in the twenty-first century away from the void and into our own communities, and often our own backyards.

A Piece of the Great Outside

The 1896 discovery of invisible rays emanating from uranium initiated a radical shift in scientific inquiry across the fields of physics and chemistry. New experiments on the relationships between particles, atomic structure, thermodynamics, and perplexing new elements—like Uranium and Radium—upended traditional notions about matter, energy, and transmutation. In culture and society, particularly in Western Europe and the United States, these early radiological studies evoked a "romantic vision" of a radical, new science shrouded in mystery. Radioactivity's invisibility as well as its high potential for energy production appealed to ambitious scientists; additionally, early observations on possible health benefits associated with mild exposure attracted businessmen intent on commercialization, according to Marjorie Malley in her book, *Radioactivity* (209). Radiation, it seemed in the early days of the twentieth century, would be the cure-all, the philosopher's stone, the next opportunity to cash-in, and the miracle of modern science that would usher humanity into a new era of prosperity.

However, Malley contends, by the 1930s a very different view of the mysterious science was developing. As early as 1905, fatalities directly correlated to the handling of and exposure to radioactive substances in laboratories were documented. Famously, Marie Curie (1867–1934), the French scientist who spearheaded the most significant research on radium, died of blood diseases caused by prolonged exposure to the very substance she championed. Curie was plagued by chronic illness and near blindness in the last years of her life, now thought to have been caused by her reluctance to adopt early safety precautions when working with the deadly element. Her laboratory notebooks are still radioactive a century later (Malley 157–158).

Across the Atlantic, the incipient field of radiation and radioactivity studies transformed into nuclear physics. But in the mid-1930s, after several high-profile deaths and disfigurements in the United States related to the manufacture and consumption of radioactive goods purported to cure a range of common ailments, the nigh mystical romance of radiation vanished, and with it the nascent radiation health-and-well-being industry. The public's fervour for radioactivity cooled off once the undeniable hazards of the new science became clear: the phosphorescent glow of irritated materials no longer elicited fascination, but a wariness of radiation's deadly potential.

Given H.P. Lovecraft's well-documented interest in the new discoveries of the age and his commitment to scientific verisimilitude as a "preparation for the unreal element" to enter his stories, the notion that the colour's effects are comparable to radiation poisoning is not new; it has been observed before that the story is, in a sense, a parable on the dangers of scientific endeavour.[3] However, to say that Lovecraft's alien colour is simply a radioactive substance is not entirely faithful to its "unreal" qualities either: the colour acts more so as Lovecraft's weird rendering of the real scientific phenomenon rather than being an actual radioactive substance.

How, then, does the colour act as a radiation analogue, a monstrous evocation of the nuclear weird? The likeness between the two motiveless inhuman agencies is demonstrated by a shared ability to "invade" the local biosphere and organic bodies from within. According to Anthony Sciscione, in the aftermath of the disappearing meteorite, the colour acts as the "Outsider-turned-subversive-Insider," seen and sensed only through the inconsistencies that arise in the organic forms touched by—or contaminated by—the inhuman agency (137).[4] The colour's regime of contamination, Sciscione argues, is accomplished through "chthonic and molecular channels," resulting in a "de-familiarizing or *weirding*" of the local milieu. The meteorite and its alien cargo vanish into the ground (a chthonic channel), and the colour seeps invisibly into the biosphere, a network of molecular channels. We will see later how the colour subverts the flora and fauna of the Gardner farm by "mottling it with inconsistencies," but the primary molecular channel through which the colour acts is the human: the members of the Gardner family (137–139).

The Gardners remain helpless against the contaminating influence of the colour on their bodies just as radiation exposure can wreak havoc on a human subject—the Outsider subverting the Inside. For example, one of the ill effects of the colour's internal subversion is a persistent "burning" said to accompany the gradual disintegration of the body and mind. In his final moments, Nahum Gardner bursts forth with a hysterical declaration: "it burns… cold an' wet, but it burns […] burns ye up… in the well water […] an' it burns an' sucks" (Lovecraft 387–388). Here, the colour is encountered as an impression and perceived as a burning sensation, rather than an object or an entity; the way in which it subsumes into and becomes Nahum Gardner's phenomenological experience causes a rupture in humanity's "presumptuousness of self-contained closure to the outside" (Sciscione 134). In other words, the burning sensation signals a breakdown in the delineation between the human and the inhuman agency. What becomes of Nahum Gardner and his family after their prolonged contact with the colour is horrible to behold: a grotesque metamorphosis into something more than human—*weirder than human*.

This same boundary collapse is seen in cases of extreme radiation exposure. During the emergency response to the infamous 1986 Chernobyl nuclear disaster in Pripyat, Ukraine, firefighters were subjected to lethal doses of radiation within minutes of their arrival on scene. Most first responders suffered severe burns, caused not by the fire at the power plant but by the highly radioactive material on site. Lyudmilla Ignatenko remembers what the nurses told her at the Moscow hospital where her husband, firefighter Vasily Ignatenko, was being treated for his burns:

> I was staying with him at night in the bio-chamber. The nurses let me in. At first they pleaded with me, too: "You're young. Why are you doing this? That's not a person anymore, *that's a nuclear reactor. You'll just burn together* […] What did you expect? He got 1,600 roentgen. Four hundred is a lethal dose. You're sitting next to a nuclear reactor."
>
> (qtd. in Alexievich 16; emphasis added)

According to Lyudmilla's account, Vasily died days later, his body disintegrating from the radiation burns to such an extent that morgue workers could not dress him properly in his uniform for burial ("There wasn't a whole body to put it on").[5] Like the colour, the radiation burns indicate a catastrophic hybridization of the boundaries between the human and the inhuman. Given the intensity of the radiation still emanating from the firefighter's body, he is somehow *more than human*, exhibiting an excess of weirdness brimming from the inside out. The firefighter's crumbling form (a molecular channel) is weaponized by the Outsider-turned-subversive-Insider (radiation); its presence in the room is a threat to other humans, not unlike the Gardners' presence in Ammi Pierce's home conjuring up "a breath from regions unnamed and unnamable" (Lovecraft 383). Granted, the Chernobyl firefighters suffered from Acute Radiation Syndrome caused by brief but high intensity exposure; while the Gardners live with the colour for a year before the ill effect of the "burning" takes its final toll on their frail, poisoned bodies.[6] Yet, the burning sensation of the colour and the horrific result of extreme radiation burns remain alike in their functioning as the dreaded Outsider-turned-subversive-Insider.

Likewise, the fluctuating visibility and invisibility associated with the colour and its radioactive counterpart represent another phenomenological similarity between the two inhuman agencies. Almost a year after the arrival of the alien meteorite, the colour's presence in the biosphere surrounding the Gardner farm takes on a luminescent aspect. A passing salesman glimpses the highly unusual glow emanating from the farm one evening: "A dim though distinct luminosity seemed to inhere in all the vegetation, grass, leaves, and blossoms alike" (Lovecraft 379). The narrator speculates that the Gardners are mostly unaware of the eerie phosphorescence as its "familiarity had dulled them" (379). So it is that the Gardners' cattle are pastured on the same land near the barn, feeding on the grass that seemed to them untouched by the colour.

Soon thereafter the milk goes bad, indicating the meteorite's contamination of the grazing land. The luminescence that once cast the entire farm aglow then fades away. The lessening of the phosphorescent effect signals only a further degeneration of the biosphere, rather than a withdrawal of the inhuman agency. After the glow fades, the grass and leaves display a "highly singular quality of brittleness," a descriptor that appears time and again in the story's latter half; the brittleness comes to typify the final stages of colour's traumatic subversion of organic matter (379). The decay of luminosity followed by that grim transformation of the farm foreshadows the eventual fates of the Gardners, as they too are turned to brittle husks that crumble into the self-same grey dust that the narrator recalls from a visit to what was once the Gardner farm.

From an eerie phosphorescence to the brittle, grey moonscape of the blasted heath, the colour's phenomenological shift from visible to invisible, and in-between, signals an interior change in the organic bodies which the colour has subsumed. This visible shift can occur with radioactive substances as well, especially in the case of the element radium. As early as 1906, according to Majorie Malley, radium was touted for its particular ability to enhance the phosphorescent quality of certain paints. When radium is added to a phosphor-rich paint blend, the radioactive energy in the element would, theoretically, produce a glowing effect for thousands of years (168–169).

The US Radium Corporation capitalized on this quality and began manufacturing luminescent watch dials with radium-laced paint, initially for use in military applications. However, tragedy soon struck the new industry. Dial painters at US Radium's factories, who were mostly women, began exhibiting symptoms of bizarre and often fatal illnesses in the years after the watch manufacturing began. The so-called "Radium Girls" were exposed to dangerous levels of radiation as they practiced pointing brushes between their lips, ingesting the radium paint mixture on a daily basis (Malley 170). Malley explains how the ingested radium wreaked havoc on the women's bodies from the moment the paintbrushes touched their lips:

> The painters' bones readily assimilated the radium in the paint, since this element resembles calcium chemically and calcium forms part of bone structure. The embedded radium emitted alpha particles, which gradually destroyed the unfortunate workers' bodies from within. Many died gruesome and painful deaths, while others were disfigured or incapacitated.
>
> (170)

In addition, radium dust and small particles perpetually contaminated the workspace as well as the workers' clothing, hair, and skin. Like the Gardners, the Radium Girls grew accustomed to the luminous substance, thinking nothing of its unusual visual properties or its deadliness until it was too late. By the time the glow of the radium watch dials began to fade, most of the women who manufactured them would be permanently disfigured, internally damaged, or dead—recalling the graphic images of the Gardner family at the end of their ordeal with the colour.

We have seen how the colour operates as a motiveless inhuman agency, and how its degenerative effects are observed as a weird rendering of radiation's effects on organic bodies. The colour is not radioactive in any literal sense, nor is Lovecraft "predicting" future experiences with radiation exposure. However, the similarities are striking at times: the alien agency's fluctuating aspects of phosphorescence, invisibility, sensation, and molecular subversion all seem to echo in a warped sense the weirdness that is always-already associated with real-world radioactive substances, and the horrific tragedy that often follows in the wake of their exploitation. Radioactivity is thus likened to its weird cousin from another dimension as "a piece of the great outside; and as such dowered with outside properties and obedient to outside laws" (Lovecraft 374).

The Dread of Contamination

As humanity is posed to navigate its way through a second nuclear age in the twenty-first century, old and new concerns about radiation and its interminable presence in our lives arise once again. In part two, I explore the legacies of nuclear conflict and the future of nuclear energy coalesce around the narrative of the ill-fated Gardner family and the colour's inside-out regime of contamination and degeneration. The nuclear weird and its constitutive histories, narratives, injustices, and future challenges become productive sites of dread—inspired by the fear of contaminating outside influence that Lovecraft amplifies to a horrific degree in "The Colour Out of Space." By exploring the past, present, and future of nuclear industry in the United States, I demonstrate the ways in which the Gardner farm in the rural Arkham valley becomes a tainted "downwind" area, a repository of the weird, and above all, a site of dread evoking the intergenerational devastation that is as much an aspect of the fiction as it is the disturbing reality of nuclear progress.

A Lasting Disgust

From the dark woods of western Arkham, we move westwards: to the vast, dry deserts of the American southwest in search of the nuclear weird and our relationship to that strange phenomenon that exists at the extreme limits of our knowledge. In many ways, the Gardner family and their terrible fate anticipates the narratives of "downwinders" living in those areas affected by uranium mining and nuclear weapons testing during the Cold War, and who are still struggling to be recognized for their suffering generations after the fact.[7] Even after weapons testing moved underground, the radionuclides emitted by years of bomb denotations and the waste byproducts of their development still exist in the environment today. Sarah Fox records the narratives of surviving downwinders and their radiation-related sicknesses in her 2014 book, *Downwind*. She recalls the story of Claudia Peterson's family, suffering the life-long, intergenerational effects of exposure:

> Peterson's daughter Bethany was born in 1981, nearly two full decades after nuclear testing went underground [...] In 1987 Bethany Peterson died of acute monoblastic leukemia. Her case might have seemed an isolated tragedy were it not for the cancers that also had plagued her mother, both of her grandfathers, and her aunt.
>
> (14)

Unfortunately, Claudia's story is not unique. Her family's experience tends to reflect a more common downwinder narrative: whole families riddled with cancers and rare illnesses caused by their proximity to the testing sites. The Gardners' own experience with the colour lasts for little over a year, while downwinders often cite decades of illness and death as part of their contaminated living. In a sense, the degeneration of the colour is mercifully quick when compared to the longer-term outcomes of radiation contamination—the horrors of real life surpassing fictional creations.

The Gardners and the downwinders share in a sense of hopeless dread evoked by the similarities of their circumstances. For example, both sets of farmers—real and fictional—undergo economic difficulties and psychological trauma as a result of the contamination not only of their bodies but of their entire livelihoods. Harvest arrives for the Gardners in the months after the meteorite vanishes into the soil. All is as it should be: the fruits, vegetables, and crops appear normal and healthy—that is until they are tasted.

> Into the fine flavour of the pears and apples had crept a stealthy bitterness and sickishness, so that even the smallest of bites induced a lasting disgust. It was the same with the melons and tomatoes, and Nahum sadly saw that his entire crop was lost.
>
> (Lovecraft 375)

Nahum's anxiety grows, while the family stops attending church; poor health and a "feeling of vague disquiet" fall upon the Gardners, as is reported by Ammi Pierce (375–76). The complete loss of the crops (and any annual income to be made from them) drives the Gardner family into a spiral of dread—the invisible contaminator from beyond taking from them everything that once provided life.

The sense of "vague disquiet" is reflected in the downwinder accounts of animal deaths as well, which graduates to hopeless dread at the prospect of further contamination. After the Upshot-Knothole series of nuclear tests in 1953, Nevada and Utah ranchers began reporting massive die-offs of their cattle and sheep. They were quick to correlate events:

> Ranchers noticed the dust [radioactive fallout particles carried by wind] settling on the sage the sheep foraged on and the sores that appeared on the animals' faces soon after eating. In a business where success depended on thriving of healthy animals, the ranchers could ill afford to ignore what the sheep consumed.
>
> (Fox 73)

The agricultural workers of the downwind region grew more concerned as the typically rare event of a complete die-off became commonplace after the tests. Delayne Evans, a rancher from Cedar City, Utah, recalls the emotional impact of the persistent loss: "I was buying sheep all the time to replace them … it breaks you. It broke me" (Evans qtd. Fox 76).

Similarly, Nahum Gardner reaches "his wit's end" with the devastation wreaked on his animals, the livelihood of the farm: "Poultry turned greyish and died very quickly, their meat being found dry and noisome upon cutting. [...] When the harvest came there was not an animal surviving on the place" (Lovecraft 382).

But the downwind population most affected by the interminable presence of radiation in daily life were—and continue to be—the Navajo uranium miners, whose reservation bordered on vast underground reserves of the radioactive element needed to create atomic weaponry at the time. In the 1940s and 1950s, droves of Navajo workers signed up to mine the substance and make a paltry, but essential, living wage, often travelling with their families to different sites across the southwest. Every day the miners were exposed to high levels of radioactive dust, particles, and tailings (the solid waste byproducts created from processing), always without protection. Not even their homes were safe from the contamination. Earl Saltwater Jr., a former Navajo miner, recalls the contaminated homelife:

> These miners, they don't wear pajamas. Their working clothes were their pajamas. They touched their women like that. [...] Right from the beginning, they [mine administrators] should have told the families to live away from the mine site.
>
> (Fox 40)

The very homes that the miners constructed out of the solid tailings—the only "construction materials" available to the disenfranchised workers at the time—were highly irradiated and remain so today. A 1975 *Los Angeles Times* exposé revealed that because there were uranium tailings in the foundations, roofs, and walls of the worker's former homes, the occupants and their families were receiving triple the amount of radiation exposure per year as the average American simply by walking inside (45). Today, those homes sit abandoned in the desert. Their haunting silhouettes are still a source of dread for the generations of Navajo raised up in their shadows—a legacy of contamination manifested decades later in a horrifying array of diseases and defects that plague the survivors and their kin.

In "The Colour Out of Space," the alien agency is first detected in the soil but later makes its presence known in the Gardner home by way of an eerie luminescence that appears to taint every aspect of the home's structure. In the climactic middle sequence of the story, the narrator invokes the fear Ammi Pierce felt while inside that contaminated house: "What eldritch dream-world was this into which he had blundered? [...] the sense of dread expectancy, the darkness [...] and merciful heaven! ... the faint but unmistakable luminosity of all the woodwork in sight" (Lovecraft 386). Earlier, luminosity was said to be an advance indication of the colour's dangerous presence—but the Navajo miners had no such warning that their homes were the sites of radioactive contamination so profound that they are still dangerous decades after the fact. The walls of the Navajo homes did not glow; the water well did not shimmer with strange light. The true horror was not the revelation of the danger that their homes posed, but the fact that by the time it was known to them, it was far too late.

Ruined crops and livelihoods, hazardous homes, and intergenerational disease all caused by exposure to radioactive fallout and industrial nuclear waste: the reality of the nuclear wasteland of the American southwest is possibly more horrifying than the Weird Fiction invoked here. With radioactive contamination, the past and future become one hopeless reality, always-already contaminated by the inhuman—a reality which began in the 1940s for the ranchers, miners, and all the rural folk of the American southwest, and will never leave them.

"This is not a Place of Honor"

The fear evoked by images of vast mushroom clouds on the horizon has long since been replaced by enormous cooling towers and containment buildings in the post-Cold War nuclear landscape. Any discussion about the nuclear weird and the dread possibility of radioactive contamination into daily life is also a discussion about the present and future challenges of high-level waste management at these commercial sites. Yucca Mountain, in the Nevada desert bordering on both the Nellis Air Force Range and the Nevada Test Site, just over 80 miles from Las Vegas, is the nation's selected geologic repository for high-level waste produced by military and commercial nuclear sites. However, there is currently no waste stored inside the carved-out mountain, nor is there likely to be any stored in the near future. Yucca Mountain's status as the sole repository for all waste has been contested by scientists, politicians, Nevadans, Native Americans from the Western Shoshone and Southern Paiute tribes, environmental activists, and experts on radioactive waste since its selection in 1987 as part of the Nuclear Waste Policy Act Amendment (Ginsburg 29). The permanent storage of nuclear waste is considered one of the world's greatest techno-scientific challenges—and Yucca Mountain, in short, does not seem up to the task.

Time is of the essence when dealing with high-level waste accumulating from nuclear sites. According to Valerie Kuletz in her book, *The Tainted Desert*, waste containers stored locally at power plants across the United States are already showing signs of compromised integrity from years of sitting and cooling, some containers exhibiting leaks as long ago as 1998 (265–66). This desperate need for a repository solution highlights the risk involved with the whole venture; as we have seen, accidental or unknowing radiation exposure is a strange and dreadful thing to imagine, let alone experience. As such, the danger posed by high-level nuclear waste and the possibility of contamination into our own biosphere and bodies is a nightmarish scenario—not unlike the scenario Lovecraft devises in "The Colour Out of Space." The narrator of the tale muses about the coming reservoir, the entire expanse of the western Arkham hills covered by water: "Then the dark woods will be cut down and the blasted heath will slumber far below the blue waters"(Lovecraft 368–371). It is the narrator's hope at this point in the story that the reservoir will act as a kind of repository for the colour, a container of sorts—one that will, hopefully, bury "the secrets of the strange days" (368).

If the reservoir is indeed a repository for the horrible weirdness of the colour's radiation-like presence, then despite the narrator's self-assurances, the possibility for further contamination is a very real prospect. The story ends with a dreamed image of Ammi Pierce, the lone survivor of the colour incident still living in the Arkham valley, as a brittle, grey heap suffering from the same colour disease that annihilated the Gardners and created the acid-eaten moonscape of the blasted heath. This enduring image suggests an underlying dread to the conclusion of the tale—an implication that the reservoir brings not closure to the horror, but potentially more to come. The inhuman agency of colour is drawn to the Gardner water well as its primary ingress point into the biosphere and its human victims (via drinking water): what is to say that flooding the blasted heath will not exacerbate the colour's regime of contamination, allowing it to spread unchecked? If the "daemon hatchling" is still present in the ground, in the well, then the reservoir's coming does not present a safe prospect for the future, rather its arrival is a dreadful portent for the surrounding areas. The narrator even acknowledges his personal dread of future contamination, despite earlier statements to the contrary, saying, "nothing could bribe me to drink the new city water of Arkham" (371). Here, one sees the incongruities coexisting in the narrator's anxious state of mind: hope that the dam will submerge the blasted heath, allowing the world to forget the "strange days," and dread at the prospect of that same body of water spreading contamination beyond the Arkham valley. In the present, this same incongruity of thought is reflected in the debate between the nuclear industry's hope for a future of carbon-free, clean energy, and the dread that that promise is too good to be true, that the threat of contamination is teeming and ever-present.

At Yucca Mountain, one of the chief concerns about the site's suitability for permanent storage of nuclear waste is the possibility of water table contamination by leaking containers. According to Kuletz, Tritium (a radioactive isotope that is dangerous primarily when ingested) was discovered in a bore hole in a 1994 Department of Energy experiment at the repository site. The unsettling implication of this finding is that other, deadlier radioactive substances may find their way through the porous geological foundation of the mountain, and leak from cask containers into the massive water table below. The risk factor for this type of contamination to occur is increased greatly given that the repository must be able to contain high-level waste for upwards of 250,000 years without accident or container integrity collapse (275–276). As already demonstrated, leaks can occur within several years of cask storage, let alone hundreds of thousands of years.[8]

Indigenous opposition to the Yucca Mountain site comes from the Western Shoshone and Southern Paiute tribes. The Western Shoshone call it "Snake Mountain, a place with rock rings that transmit prayers to the Great Spirit and messages back to the people" ("Yucca Mountain"). To the Western Shoshone, the mountain is both conduit to and burial ground for their ancestors, the water running through the area having further religious significance for both tribal nations. The Western Shoshone worry that pollution of these sacred waters will bring contamination to "all living things," and will in turn awaken the Snake Mountain, causing it to split open to the sky and spew poison, as is foretold by traditional Western Shoshone folklore and holy men (Kuletz 277; "Yucca Mountain"). The suitability of the Yucca Mountain site is at this moment still contested by scientists and indigenous peoples alike, but as calls for a national repository continue and commercial nuclear waste accumulates further, I cannot help but see a parallel between it and the arrival of the Arkham reservoir acting as both a repository and a possible arch-contaminator, enabling otherworldly poisons to enter the biosphere at large. It must be pointed out that this comparison is not meant as an indictment of nuclear energy. Concerns ranging from the scientific to the political to the technological all intersect at Yucca Mountain, where the decades long debate about the eternal internment of strange and deadly waste reaches a fever pitch. Nevertheless, the dread of a future contaminated by the nuclear weird remains for those opposing Yucca Mountain and the downwinders who have lived and suffered through accident and exploitation.

Though the Gardners' story in "The Colour Out of Space" is a fictionalized account of an alien insurgency into the human itself and the biosphere at large, the dread at the core of the story evokes that same fear of the motiveless inhuman outsider that is seen in examples of the nuclear weird. Often the nuclear weird is found where accidents or exploitation occur—fecund ground for an inhuman agency to embed itself and carry out a regime of contamination. The Gardners' fates anticipating the real horror experienced by downwinders in the American southwest is testament to this. Additionally, exposure to high levels of radiation erases the boundaries between the human and inhuman; luminosity is a dreaded phenomenological experience as much as it is awe-inspiring. Lovecraft's invention of the extra-dimensional colour anticipates many of these aspects, which in turn *weirds* the nuclear both at the level of scientific phenomenon and socio-cultural legacy. In other words, radiation is itself a "piece of the great outside," a humbling reminder that our knowledge of the universe and its properties is still largely incomplete, frequently resulting in devastating consequences.[9] Lovecraft accentuates his brand of cosmic horror through this lens: the weirdness of the universe can come crashing down at any time—as demonstrated, in our communities, our backyards, and our homes—and humanity is mostly powerless against it. When the outside comes in, there is not much that can be done; in the twenty-first century, we are always-already contaminated by the nuclear weird.

Notes

1 In his book, *The Weird and The Eerie*, the late Mark Fisher borrows the phrase "*real externality*" from a 1927 correspondence from Lovecraft to *Weird Tales*. In Fisher's terms, real externality is represented by a "hyper-naturalism – an expanded sense of what the material cosmos contains" (18). Confronting the strangeness of nuclear radioactivity and its contaminations necessitates a realization that so much of the universe is a real externality—that is, external from human subjectivity.

2 The nuclear weird, as an "assemblage" of objects, time, and space, can be thought of in terms of Timothy Morton's concept of *hyperobjects*. Morton says a hyperobject (radiation could be one; or the "sum total of all nuclear materials on Earth" another) radically upsets human notions of situatedness in the cosmos. Thus, situatedness—an anthropocentric self-certainty of being in the universe—becomes "a very uncanny place to be," a *weird* place to be (Morton 1–5).

3 See Andy Troy's article in *Lovecraftian Proceedings, vol. I*, "'A Stalking Monster': The Influence of Radiation Poisoning on H.P. Lovecraft's 'The Colour Out of Space,'" and Dr. Fred S. Lubnow's posts on the *Lovecraftian Science* Blog ("The Human-Health Related impacts of The Colour Out of Space" and "The Ecological Impacts of the Colour Out of Space"); Letter correspondence from Lovecraft to Clark Ashton Smith in 1930: "The more I consider weird fiction, the more I am convinced that a solidly realistic framework is needed in order to build up a preparation for the unreal element" (*Lord of A Visible World* 210–211).

4 Sciscione on the colour as an "agency" rather than an "agent": "Conceptually, both [the colour] and its somatic vector of emergence are couched in pronominal obscurity, with passive constructions emphasizing the absence of a determinable or localizable agent" (139). For the purposes of this chapter, the colour shall be an inhuman agency of the type Scisione defines here.

5 "No one could look long at them [the Gardners], and even the medical examiner admitted that there was little to examine" (Lovecraft 389).

6 Acute Radiation Syndrome (ARS) is characterized by the following symptoms: the destruction of marrow, resulting in infection and haemorrhage, irreparable damage to the gastrointestinal tract, and the collapse of the circulatory system. ("Acute Radiation Syndrome").

7 "'Downwinders' are defined as individuals who can demonstrate having resided in certain counties in Utah, Nevada, and Arizona between January 21, 1951, and October 31, 1958, or between June 30, 1962, and July 31, 162 [...] and Arizona's Apache, Coconino, Gila, Navajo, Yavapai, and that part of Arizona that is north of the Grand Canyon" (Fox 202–203).

8 The metal casks designed for waste storage will begin to disintegrate anywhere from three hundred to one thousand years into the future, according to Sara Ginsburg's comprehensive 1995 assessment of the proposed geologic repository (102).

9 Once again, the nuclear weird is presented here as *hyperobject*-like, in that it forces us to reconcile the "immanence of thinking to the physical"—in this case, contamination, death, and destruction on a vast scale is the consequence of our meddling with real forces, objects, that exist outside of our subjectivity (Morton 2). The nuclear weird, like the colour, belongs to a universe of objects that is weirder than we humans can anticipate.

Works Cited

"Acute Radiation Syndrome: A Fact Sheet for Clinicians." *cdc.gov*, Centers for Disease Control and Prevention, 2018.

Alexievich, Svetlana. *Voices from Chernobyl.* Translated by Keith Gessen. Dalkey Archive Press, 2005.

Corbin, Amy. "Yucca Mountain." *Sacredland.org*, Sacred Land Film Project, 2010.

Fisher, Mark. *The Weird and The Eerie.* London: Repeater, 2017.

Fox, Sarah Alisabeth. *Downwind: A People's History of the Nuclear West.* Lincoln, NE: University of Nebraska Press, 2014.

Ginsburg, Sara. *Nuclear Waste Disposal: Gambling on Yucca Mountain.* Aegean Park Press, 1995.

"Key Issues: Disposal of High-Level Nuclear Waste." *gao.gov*, U. S. Government Accountability Office, 2020.

Kuletz, Valerie L. *The Tainted Desert: Environmental and Social Ruin in the American West.* London: Routledge. 1998.

Lovecraft, Howard Philips. "Chapter 5: Homecoming (1926–1930)."*Lord of a Visible World: An Autobiography in Letters* 1st ed., edited by S. T. Joshi and David Schultz. Ohio University Press, 2000, pp. 201–266.

Lovecraft, Howard Philips. "The Colour Out of Space." *H. P. Lovecraft, Collected Fiction: A Variorum Edition: Volume 2, 1926–1930*, ed. by S. T. Joshi. New York: Hippocampus Press, 2017, pp. 367–399.

Malley, Majorie. *Radioactivity.* Oxford: Oxford University Press, 2011.

Morton, Timothy. *Hyperobjects: Philosophy and Ecology after the End of the World.* Minneapolis: University of Minnesota Press, 2013.

Sciscione, Anthony. "Symptomatic Horror: Lovecraft's 'The Colour Out of Space'." *Leper Creativity: Cyclonopedia Symposium*, edited by Edward Keller et al. Punctum Books, 2012, pp. 131–146.

9 An Eldritch Crisis

Capitalist Paradigms in the Cthulhu Mythos

Daniel Doncel

Reading Lovecraft today feels weirdly familiar. Somehow, the doomscapes he so hysterically painted for us almost a century ago sound like an appropriate emotional expression of the mood of our time. And this is no wonder: the sensation of a world on the verge of collapse that Lovecraftian tales induce on us is very, very similar to the one we have here, in a capitalist world that cracks a bit more every day. The point of this chapter is to look closer at the ways these parallel emotional reactions are so alike: Lovecraftian weird tales are about terrible discoveries that shake the foundations of common-sensical knowledge, a situation with serious similarities to the ideological turmoil that comes with each crisis of capitalism. The starting point will be a reading of Lovecraft's "The Call of Cthulhu" as an antidetective fiction, that is, a subversion of the detective story in which some of the genre's central tenets, such as reason, logic, and science, are proven wrong by their own methods and resolutions. This process of self-refusal overlaps with that of the hegemonic, but slowly collapsing, capitalist system. Mark Fisher's books, *The Weird and the Eerie* and *Capitalist Realism* will help establish the weird story as crisis narratives with affective ties to the experience of living through economic and ideological crisis, as well as to point out capitalism's self-fulfilling prophecy that cannot even fulfill itself.

The collapse of a hegemonic ideology brought about by its own weight finds its parallel in the process of paradigm shift as explained by T.S. Kuhn in *The Structure of Scientific Revolutions*. Fisher's investigation on the Weird, understood as a feeling of being invaded by some external object that proves wrong an established worldview just by existing, is a good candidate for an application of Kuhn's theory to literature. As both of them deal with reconfigurations of humanity's ideas about the world, the connection with the moment of crisis central to the Lovecraftian tale is as natural for Fisher as it is for Kuhn: this moment comes with the realization of cracks in a firmly established paradigm such as the one Fisher himself tells us about in *Capitalist Realism*, a setup for a situation that could very well lead to a Lovecraftian twist if written into a tale. Connections will be drawn too between these ideas and Timothy

DOI: 10.4324/9780367713065-10

Morton's hyperobject, a concept that can be considered as Weird as defined by Fisher and as a catalyst for scientific revolutions as mapped by Kuhn. Thus, it serves as a common category for both Lovecraftian creatures and the effects of capital itself, as well as a common thread for the theoretical concepts discussed here. This reading of Lovecraft against a capitalist background should help establish the weird tale as a crisis genre, able to resonate easily with times of crisis like the twenty-first century.

The usefulness of reading "The Call of Cthulhu" through an antidetective lens is that it makes explicit its preoccupation with the reaction to new knowledge. An antidetective story, or metaphysical detective story, "is a text that parodies or subverts traditional detective-story conventions—such as narrative closure and the detective's role as surrogate reader—with the intention, or at least the effect, of asking questions about mysteries of being and knowing which transcend the mere machinations of the mystery plot" (Merivale and Sweeney 2). If detective fiction is a dramatization of the idea that reason can explain the world to humans, so that we can find fitting solutions for our problems by thoroughly knowing them, antidetective fiction is the subversion of this idea through the mechanisms of the same genre. Previously, I have looked at "The Call of Cthulhu" as a supernatural antidetective story, a subversion of the tenets of detective fiction – reason, logic, science – through their defeat against the opposing supernatural. There, I established that "[Lovecraft] also charges against logical thinking by picturing [the detective's] logic-directed detection not only as unable to reach useful conclusions, but also as leading to the event that will demonstrate reason's uselessness" (Doncel 5). In "The Call of Cthulhu," the application of logic by the narrator, Francis Wayland Thurston, only leads to the debunking of that logic, usually by having his mind break at the view of a conclusion it cannot withstand, much less explain. Furthermore, his involvement is only important for himself and has no consequence over the wider world: "The narrator is almost as much a reader of the story as the actual readers (…). The process of detection is completely contingent to the solution of the mystery, which is 'solved' by an unwilling part. Since detection stands for the application of reasoning to solve problems, both are revealed to be expendable" (Doncel 6). Lovecraft was not worried about writing compelling characters: his writing was focused on the world itself, with his narrators being more recorders of impressions than narrators. In "Notes on Writing Weird Fiction," he explains his choice of genre:

> I choose weird stories because they suit my inclination best—one of my strongest and most persistent wishes being to achieve, momentarily, the illusion of some strange suspension or violation of the galling limitations of time, space, and natural law which for ever

> imprison us and frustrate our curiosity about the infinite cosmic spaces beyond the radius of our sight and analysis.
>
> (175–176)

What Lovecraft was concerned about, then, was the limits of the world and the process of breaking them. He wrote narratives of crisis in which his characters' minds break at the sight of things that should not be. Given, for example, that the existence of Cthulhu is enough in itself to thwart the whole method used to find out about him, they conclude that human reason is powerless when facing a cosmos that contains *that* and react by fearing new knowledge. The very first paragraph of "The Call of Cthulhu" reads: "The most merciful thing in the world, I think, is the inability of the human mind to correlate all its contents. We live on a placid island of ignorance in the midst of black seas of infinity, and it was not meant that we should voyage far" (21). New data that does not fit any conceivable category is taken as proof that none of those categories really work. A crisis of knowledge is upon us: the universe is too big for humans to understand.

At least that is what Lovecraft regularly implies. And yet, the structure of "The Call of Cthulhu" only subverts science because it stops short of actual breakthroughs. Every antidetective story has an ending that attacks the detective genre by not having a satisfactory conclusion.[1] In the essay in which he coined the term, William V. Spanos defined the antidetective as having "the formal purpose of (…) evok[ing] the impulse to 'detect' and/or to psychoanalyze in order to violently frustrate it by refusing to solve the crime" (Spanos 154). Some of these stories directly oppose the method as useless, while others simply provide a non-solution, an ending that is not satisfactory. This is the case of the Lovecraftian weird tale, in which detection leads to new information about the problem at hand, but cannot process it in any meaningful way. "The Call of Cthulhu" can benefit from being read as a supernatural antidetective story, as it rightly disqualifies a certain way of reasoning as unable to explain its own findings. However, it can also be read not as a *failed* investigation, but as an *incomplete* one.

After piecing together the fragments that lead to a description of the finding of Cthulhu, the narrator writes the account that makes up the short story, in which he says: "… some day the piecing together of dissociated knowledge will open up such terrifying vistas of reality, and of our frightful position therein, that we shall either go mad from the revelation or flee from the deadly light into the peace and safety of a new dark age" (Lovecraft "Cthulhu" 21–22) In these lines we find a very pure example of Mark Fisher's definition of the Weird—about which I will discuss more below—that is, the reaching of the following conclusion: if the entity or object is here, then the categories which we have up until now used to make sense of the world cannot be valid. The weird thing is not wrong, after all: it is our conceptions that must be inadequate (Fisher 15). What the narrator calls "go[ing] mad from the revelation" is what Fisher theorizes as the invalidation of our categories. Cthulhu's mere existence, with the place's "wrong geometries" and its "angle[s] which [were] acute, but behaved as if [they] were obtuse" (Lovecraft "Cthulhu" 53) is enough for any witness to conclude that we do not understand the world after all. But where Lovecraft sees this realization as either a reason to "flee (...) into the peace and safety of a new dark age" (21) or as a one-way ticket to madness, T.S. Kuhn's essay *The Structure of Scientific Revolutions* can help us frame it as a normal part of the advancement of science.

Kuhn is better known as the creator of the notion of the scientific paradigm, "models from which spring particular coherent traditions of scientific research" (10). Far from Lovecraft's fatalism, Kuhn would call the discovery of the corpse city of R'lyeh an "anomaly," something the current paradigm cannot explain and that must wait for the apparition of a more adequate one to be solved. If the reigning theory of a given field is incapable of predicting an event, then we can say that this event is an anomaly—and at the same time we can call it "weird" in Fisher's definition, which he describes as being "constituted by a presence—the presence of that which does not belong" (61). In the same way that the many things that led to the Copernican heliocentric theory "did not belong" in the Ptolemaic astronomical paradigm, Cthulhu does not belong in Francis Wayland Thurston worldview—a worldview, to be fair, shared by every other human, fictitious or otherwise. However, while Kuhn indicates that anomalies are either put aside until they can be solved through another framework or provoke a crisis that stimulates the search for that new framework, the stories within the Cthulhu Mythos tend to have the crisis itself as their climax. No chance for a human revision of their old paradigms is given, no solutions but madness or purposeful overlooking of the new information is offered. The infamous *Necronomicon* is full of this kind of groundbreaking data that could mean a veritable scientific revolution, yet it is referred to as forbidden knowledge many times in many separated stories. So the question arises: why is it that Lovecraft is so keen to discourage his characters from following these trails to better, more comprehensive, paradigms?

What we find in Lovecraft is either a powerful terror of newly found knowledge, or a fatalist skepticism about the possibilities of getting the general public (even the scientific community) to take it seriously. "The Call of Cthulhu," along with other stories like "The Shadow Over Innsmouth," "The Colour Out of Space," and "The Shadow Out of Time," is a first-person account from characters that acquire new, terrible knowledge about the world. This knowledge is rarely developed, if at all: either the narrator tries to cover it up to keep others sane (as happens in "The Call of Cthulhu"), or someone else does (as is the case in "The Shadow Over Innsmouth," where it is the government that hides the truth from the public light). At one point or other, someone looks at these enormous things and assumes it is beyond their power, or anyone else's, to influence them. This new knowledge would disturb our world too much for us to keep living in it, they seem to think. Using it to reach more accurate ideas about the universe would destroy our world (view) just as much as letting Cthulhu destroy it at some later point in time, so we better settle for what we have now and forget how we are unable to solve this gargantuan problem that is the universe without changing how we behave now. The fear of advancing "too much," or the punishment for advancing too much, stops scientific progress in Lovecraft, effectively turning the stories into antidetective fictions. If the investigation was carried out to the end, the result would be madness.

The Lovecraftian crisis is not framed as a struggle between two scientific models. It is rather written as the shift from sanity to madness: for Lovecraft, finding out about the size and nature of the universe equals losing one's mind. Beyond his intentions, however, there is a deep distrust of any knowledge that could change the current paradigm, meaning that the problem is not so much that whatever is next will be bad but that changing how things work right now would be terrible. As quoted earlier, Lovecraft aimed to create in his stories an aesthetic impression of rupture of the fundamental laws of the world. Behind Lovecraft's cosmic horror and his trademark mind-shattering revelations lies an epistemological crisis: learning too much about the world would mean madness; therefore, we should turn our backs to that "forbidden knowledge," but at the same time, once we learn about it, it is impossible for us to forget.

An overwhelming presence that imposes itself on our consciousness turns into knowledge that we would rather not have. We are lucky enough to have a theoretical concept that can help us navigate this issue under the name of "hyperobjects." They are, in summary, objects that affect our world at so massive a scale, that are so extremely extensive, that no other neighboring objects can ignore them at all. In Morton's words, "There is no exit from this situation. Thus the time of hyperobjects is a time of sincerity: a time in which it is impossible to achieve a final distance toward the world" (130). This forceful realization of what the world is, as opposed to what we believed it to be, precisely the situation in which the characters of the Cthulhu Mythos usually find themselves. Thus considered, Lovecraft's eldritch abominations turn out to be a kind of hyperobject.

As Morton's argumentation goes, the idea of world is some kind of "stage" in which we humans perform our drama. The moment we realize the existence of a hyperobject (such as global warming, in Morton's example), it stops being a part of the stage/the background and it becomes a character/the foreground. This is the central moment of crisis for our current paradigm. When Nature[2] stops being a background, we supposedly gain "intimacy," equal grounds between humans and non-humans, "the prospect of forging new alliances between humans and non-humans alike, now that we have stepped out of the cocoon of world" (108); and then, "The specialness we granted ourselves as unravelers of cosmic meaning… falls apart since there is no meaningfulness possible in a world without a foreground–background distinction" (103). There is an important point of contact with Lovecraft in this nihilist conclusion: what makes Lovecraft so dear to Object-Oriented Ontologists is that his stories do as much as they can to take importance from humans to give it to the universe as a whole. But Morton's (and Lovecraft's) implication that there is only human meaning in a world in which we reign supreme over every other thing is dangerous. It takes as dogma the capitalist idea that assumes that Nature is some bottomless reserve of resources that we can mindlessly exploit, first, and then despairs when evidence of the contrary bursts out from the very Earth we mine. A capitalist economic system, based on the mindless exploitation of both human labor and natural resources, necessarily forces the idea that these are natural processes and that things just work like that. Of course, there is existential shock when we base our existence on foundations as flimsy as those!

The assumption that things "just work like that" is precisely what Mark Fisher looks into in his book *Capitalist Realism: Is There No Alternative?*, where he defines capitalist realism as "the widespread sense that not only is capitalism the only viable political and economic system, but also that it is now impossible even to imagine a coherent alternative to it" (2). Building on Margaret Thatcher's infamous claim that "there is no alternative," Fisher argues that

> the lack of alternatives to capitalism is no longer even an issue. Capitalism seamlessly occupies the horizons of the thinkable… [T]he fact that capitalism has colonized the dreaming life of the population is so taken for granted that it is no longer worthy of comment.
>
> (8)

What we are looking at here is the artificial protection of an outdated paradigm by making any other alternative seem impossible. Capitalism feeds on natural resources and exploited labor, blocks any attempt to stop those processes, and then takes the fact that these processes seem unstoppable as proof that such a state of things is the only conceivable one. It is easy for those of us who live under this impression to think about a different future as terrifying and uncertain. It is not so easy to reconcile this world that supposedly cannot be any other way with the very evident truth that it cannot stay this way either, given both the global warming that Morton describes as "the objects take revenge, terrifyingly huge, ancient, long-lived, threateningly minute, invading every cell in our body," (115) and the cyclical crises so long ago unveiled by Marx to be a necessary consequence of a capitalist economy. We end up with a world that cannot be different but cannot stay the same, with the need to face imminent crises and the conscious and subliminal efforts made to keep us from finding out too much about the kind of world that causes them.

If *Capitalist Realism* is useful for defining this sense of capitalism being all that appears to be visible, another one of Fisher's works can help us see more clearly what happens during these times of crisis; that is, if one book focuses on a worldview that makes itself so pervasive it is unthinkable to have a different one, the next one deals with literary works in which such worldviews are proven wrong and destroyed in the minds of those that never doubted them. In *The Weird and the Eerie*, he reflects on the two eponymous modes that, he argues, are preoccupied with the strange, the things that do not fit. According to Fisher, the stranging modes of the weird and the eerie appear throughout the works of creators among whom he lists H.P. Lovecraft. Fisher starts his analysis of those modes by differentiating them from the Freudian *unheimlich*, which he translates as "unhomely." Where the *unheimlich* deals with "two things that do not belong together," the weird and the eerie deal with the outside as opposed to the familiar. Equipped with these two concepts, Fisher points out their presence in several works and objects. We will be mostly working with two of them: Lovecraft's fiction, which Fisher identifies as weird; and capital itself, which he ascribes to the eerie.

According to Fisher's argument, Lovecraft is a writer of the weird due to his treatment of the fantastic genre's usual exploration of different worlds. The weird is preoccupied with *wrong* presences, things that are in a world to which they do not belong. Whereas fantasy literature writers like Dunsany and Tolkien set their stories in worlds that are not ours, he says, the weird, by contrast, is notable for the way in which it opens up an egress between this world and others. (…) With Lovecraft, there is an interplay, an exchange, a confrontation and indeed a conflict between this world and others (*Weird* 19). The invasion of our world by alien entities like Cthulhu means the invasion of our world by what seems like a world alien to ours (even though, as we will see later, this should not be taken as a literally different world), hence Lovecraft's weird. As opposed to the weirdness characteristic of the Lovecraftian tale, Fisher argues that "[c]apital is at every level an eerie entity: conjured out of nothing, capital nevertheless exerts more influence than any allegedly substantial entity" (Fisher 11). Fisher reaches this conclusion because he realizes that "the eerie is fundamentally tied up with questions of agency" and that questions like "What happened to produce these ruins, this disappearance? What kind of entity was involved? What kind of thing was it that emitted such an eerie cry? (…) also apply to the forces governing capitalist society" (11). Indeed, the eerie as he defines it is the sensation that "occurs either when there is something present where there should be nothing, or if there is nothing present when there should be something" (61). The reason capital is eerie is because it *seems* to have come out of nothing. The mystery of who made/makes capital makes capital itself eerie.

But as we have been implying, there are specific interests behind capital that would rather have it seem like "things just work like that" instead of a possible state of things out of many. This expression has not been chosen at random: it is important to use the much vaguer word *that* as opposed to *capitalism*, as non-conscious individuals do not know what capitalism is or how it works. They do know that it exists; they have heard the word, but in the absence of an alternative and a historical perspective; they cannot see its particular characteristics, the same way a blind person cannot define black without first seeing white. A blind man's world is not "black"; it is "just like that." But even when faced with a world identical to itself, with no obvious contrast with any other worlds, we cannot help but to ask "Why is it like that?" With that in mind, we should ask the question: In what kind of world is capital eerie? In what kind of world does capital have the quality of the unknown? To which the answer is: exclusively in a capitalist realist world, where the reasons behind the existence of capital(ism) are veiled. The problem with that approach—or maybe the solution to that issue—is that, since Marx, capitalist society has been going through an ideological conflict between a bourgeois worldview that needs to keep things as they are to thrive, and a proletarian one would be benefitted from a break with the current status quo. While Marxism seeks the emancipation of the proletariat by educating it about what society *really* looks like, capitalist ideology, as Fisher himself says, consciously fights for a cultural hegemony that takes the form of capitalist realism, that is, the illusion that we live in a world where "things just work like that."

I am insisting on the word "world" because I recognize three different uses of it as identical: First, Morton's critique of it as the illusion of a glorified stage for our puny human issues. Second, T.S. Kuhn's assertion that Paradigm changes do cause scientists to see the world of their research-engagement differently. In so far as their only recourse to that world is through what they see and do, we may want to say that after a revolution scientists are responding to a different world (111). Finally, when Fisher describes the weird, he says that "[it] is notable for the way in which it opens up an egress between this world and others" (*Weird* 19). In putting together these three instances of "world," I am obviously not talking about an empirical physical world, but neither was Lovecraft (nor Fisher on Lovecraft, for that matter). Fisher talks about a war of the worlds in terms of two different universes, but immediately clarifies that, at least in the case of Lovecraft, this difference is completely perceptual, as for Lovecraft there is no real separation between Cthulhu's world and our own:

> [In the Cthulhu Mythos] there is never any suggestion of the involvement of supernatural beings. Human attempts to transform the alien entities into gods are clearly regarded by Lovecraft as vain acts of anthropomorphism, perhaps noble but ultimately absurd efforts to impose meaning and sense on to the "real externality" of a cosmos in which human concerns, perspectives and concepts have only a local reference.
>
> (*Weird* 18)

Differently phrased, when the cultists in "The Call of Cthulhu" call Cthulhu a god, they are just ascribing the alien being to a different world with different rules, instead of admitting to themselves that the rules they had been using to make sense of their own world do not apply after all. The universes at war in Lovecraft are not the natural and the supernatural colliding. They look much more like two scientific paradigms used to interpret the same world. It is not that our world is literally invaded by another one; it is only that the picture of the world we built in our heads now needs to fit elements that contradict it, which in turn forces us to discard that outdated schema and start again. Lovecraft's narrators do not face supernatural threats; they only make contact with beings which their worldview cannot explain. The famous Lovecraftian mindblow is basically a failed attempt to adopt a new paradigm. If the separation between worlds is only ideological, we should not think of their limits as frontiers or walls, but as a veil before our eyes that can be "lifted" by adopting a more adequate framework. The weird conflict between worlds should be thought about as a conflict between world*views*, paradigms, and ideologies.

Let's not forget, however, that the Weird is not defined by the presence of something that has been overseen, but by the presence of something *external*. The thing that appears as weird might have objectively been there since the beginning, either potentially or just unrecognized; but the Weird mode requires that this thing is perceived as an invading force rather than a discovery. It is easy to see how this difference between reality and perception plays out in Lovecraft, where Cthulhu is thought of as either a foreign entity that came from the stars or as a god that occupies a plane different to ours. Lovecraft himself makes explicit the separation between perception and reality while describing his creative process, for which his first two steps are "(1) Prepare a synopsis or scenario of events in the order of their absolute *occurrence* —not the order of their narration" (in other words, what actually happened), and "(2) Prepare a second synopsis or scenario of events—this one in order of *narration* (not actual occurrence)" (in other words, what the narrators perceive is happening) ("Notes" 176). To understand the sense of externality in capitalism, we will need to dig a bit deeper than that by resorting to Marx's theory of alienation.

Alienation can be summarized as the separation between a worker's ability to act and their ability to direct those actions. If workers are forced to put their labor into a product without being able to decide whether to do it or not, to choose how to do it, to own the result of doing it, and to relate to other people (and to society in general) through labor, they are almost completely alienated from the consequences of their labor. "The object produced by labour, its product, now stands opposed to it as an *alien being*, as a *power independent* of the producer" (Marx 171). The workers and the product of their labor are now alien to each other, as are the workers and Nature: if the workers have no say in how they work, they have no say in what they work *on* either, which is the reason they also feel disconnected from Nature. Even worse than that, this disconnection is so deeply ingrained in explicit and implicit representations of society that it is not even realized: "Political economy conceals the alienation in the nature of labour in so far as it does not examine the direct relationship between the worker (work) and production" (Marx 124). As a result, the wielding of systemic power by the bourgeoisie through exploiting proletariat labor is hidden from sight, substituted instead by a mysterious agency-less (therefore, eerie) force that imposes its influence on the world. The workers that populate this world thus feel powerless before a power that they not only created but also keep creating every day. The fact that this power determines their lives seems as unavoidable as the fact that gravity keeps their feet on the ground. Given the assumption that the rules of capitalism are the rules of the world, it is an understandable shock to witness them crumble in front of phenomena like global warming and continuous economic crises. Given a capitalist realist world, it should come as no surprise that events that prove it wrong should be felt as Weird.

Reading Lovecraft in the twenty-first century requires an awareness of how our common-sensical worldviews are shattered by reality. Because at the end of the day he is a crisis author, it is reasonable to say that the reason his fiction is appealing to contemporary audiences is because it deals with the very same kinds of crises we deal with here and now, in a capitalist world growing more decadent every day. The themes and narrative structures of the Cthulhu Mythos resonate with our own existential issues in that they all consist of the contradiction between a collapsing worldview and its resistance to being substituted by a more accurate one. They resonate, in a word, with a capitalist worldview that is the only thing we have been taught to see, and that is also quickly proving to be a lie. Lovecraft portrays a universe over which humans have no power, but he writes whole pseudo-mythological cycles about how deeply connected we are to it. The presence of that which cannot be present in our world proves our world wrong, just as the presence of Cthulhu forces Lovecraft's characters to acknowledge a different state of things, and just as growing socio-economic turmoil forces us to acknowledge the need for a socialist world. A crisis of knowledge follows a crisis of existence, and its witnesses must find new paradigms for it. This is the real appeal of Lovecraft: that he writes about how "things just work like that" only until we are forced to see how fragile "that" is. The epistemological crises he writes are closely related to those of a capitalist society that cannot hold on for much longer under siege of its own consequences. Things do not just work like that anymore: things demand new paradigms that can actually make sense of them. Either that or we must go mad.

Notes

1 Some examples of this technique are Jorge Luis Borges' "Death and the Compass," where the whole investigation turns out to be an elaborated trap for the detective, who is murdered upon solving it; Thomas Pynchon's *The Crying of Lot 49*, where the protagonist ends up with four different explanations for the mystery, not being able to tell which of them (if any) is the right one; and Umberto Eco's *The Name of the Rose*, where the crime is in fact solved, but only through luck, effectively proving the uselessness of detective work.
2 Morton refers to the concepts of "the world," "Nature," and "the environment" as cognates of each other.

Works Cited

Doncel, Daniel. "An Eldritch Crime: Supernatural Antidetective Fiction in H.P. Lovecraft's 'The Call of Cthulhu.'" *Gredos USAL*, 7 June 2018, https://gredos.usal.es/bitstream/handle/10366/138878/TG_DoncelMart%c3%adnD_AnEldritchCrime.pdf?sequence=1&isAllowed=y

Fisher, Mark. *Capitalist Realism: Is There No Alternative?* London: Zero Books, 2009.

Fisher, Mark. *The Weird and the Eerie*. London: Repeater, 2017.

Kuhn, Thomas S. *The Structure of Scientific Revolutions*. Chicago: The University of Chicago Press, 1996.

Lovecraft, Howard Phillips. "The Call of Cthulhu." *H. P. Lovecraft Collected Fiction, A Variorum Edition, Volume 2: 1926–1930*, edited by S. T. Joshi. New York: Hippocampus Press, 2017, pp. 21–55.

Lovecraft, Howard Phillips. "Notes on Writing Weird Fiction." *Collected Essays Volume 2: Literary Criticism*, edited by S.T. Joshi. New York: Hippocampus Press, 2005, pp. 175–178.

Marx, Karl. *Economic and Philosophical Manuscripts*, in *Karl Marx: Early Writings*. New York: McGraw-Hill Book Company, 1964.

Merivale, Patricia, and Susan Elizabeth Sweeney. "The Game's Afott: on the Trail of the Metaphysical Detective Story." *Detecting Texts: The Metaphysical Detective Story from Poe to Postmodernism*, edited by Patricia Merivale and Susan Elizabeth Sweeney. Philadelphia: University of Pennsylvania Press, 1999, pp. 1–26.

Morton, Timothy. *Hyperobjects*. Minneapolis, MN: University of Minnesota Press, 2013.

Spanos, William V. "The Detective and the Boundary: Some Notes on the Postmodern Literary Imagination." *Boundary* 2, vol. 1, no. 1, 1972, pp. 147–168. *JSTOR*, www.jstor.org/stable/302058. Accessed July 27 2020.

10 Lovecraft's Viral Networks

A Contaminated Ethics for the Chthulucene

Natasha Rebry Coulthard

> But of all the space unoccupied by familiar material objects not one particle was vacant. Indescribable shapes both alive and otherwise were mixed in disgusting disarray, and close to every known thing were whole worlds of alien, unknown entities. It likewise seemed that all the known things entered into the composition of other unknown things, and vice versa
>
> —H.P. Lovecraft, "From Beyond"

> What's in here is out there. What's out there is in here now.
>
> —Richard Stanley, *Color Out of Space*

H.P. Lovecraft's cosmic horror, which diminishes human supremacy and undoes polarities between humans and nonhumans, resonates with contemporary understandings of human interdependencies and precarity. In a well-known letter to *Weird Tales* editor Farnsworth Wright, Lovecraft described "mankind" as a "negligible and temporary race" and explained that his stories "are based on the fundamental premise that common human laws and interests and emotions have no validity or significance in the vast cosmos-at-large" (qtd. in Joshi xiii). Based in this philosophy, his horrors depict humankind mentally and physically transformed by encounters with ancient, nonhuman forces. While Lovecraft framed human insignificance and impurity as horrific, his emphasis on human vulnerabilities and nonhuman influence evokes contemporary trends in biology, ecology, and post-anthropocentric theory.[1] New understandings of symbiosis and the networked nature of our world[2] belie human pretensions of sovereignty and security, exposing the interconnections of humans and their Others. The steadily-expanding body of posthumanist-oriented Lovecraft scholarship in recent years reveals his work as an important source of non-anthropocentric sentiment in line with current scientific and philosophical theories of human–nonhuman intimacies. Indeed, Lovecraft's fictive heterogeneous assemblages and infectious, parasitic relationships mirror twenty-first century theories of human being and the associated posthumanist call to develop multispecies kinships. Exploring the contemporary relevance of Lovecraft's diminishment of Man, this chapter shifts

DOI: 10.4324/9780367713065-11

our view from the "vast cosmos-at-large" to the infinitesimal microbial world and ultimately into the realm of viruses. In various forms, viruses infect, mutate, and multiply, and their transgressive, communicable traits make them apt models to outline the openness to transformation characteristic of both Lovecraft and post-anthropocentric ethics.

Applying a posthumanist reading, this chapter will explore how viruses and fellow microbes within Lovecraft's oeuvre along with the mutational nature of his Mythos contribute to a post-anthropocentric ethics tailored to the twenty-first century networked world and "the emergent, unexpected, and challenging interactions, engagements, and limits between the human and nonhuman" that define it (Blas 29). Lovecraft's non-anthropocentric fiction and generosity with his Mythos, which continues to grow as it is shaped by new authors, suggest the transformative potential of encounters with difference. In my reading, I blend posthumanist, new materialist, and corporeal feminist theory, treating posthumanism as a deconstructive (Wolfe) or "generative tool" (Braidotti 5) that helps us to interrogate and dismantle humanist ideology along with the restrictive subjectivities it promotes. My blended methodology combines posthumanism's challenge to binaristic models of self/other with new materialism's and corporeal feminism's emphasis on the interconnections between self and environment. These interrelated post-anthropocentric theories embrace the nonhuman nature of the human (Wolfe xxv); emphasize the mutable, open nature of bodies and identities; and stress the interdependence of humans, nonhumans, prosthetics, and environment. Ultimately, post-anthropocentric theory calls the human to responsibility "for the role we play in the differential constitution and differential positioning of the human among other creatures" (Barad 136), prompting us to recognize and act upon our obligations to fellow creatures.

A posthumanist-inflected reading of viruses and virality in and through Lovecraft's work out the nuances and possible ethical applications of the assemblages, networks, contaminations, mutations, and paradoxes defining Lovecraft and his oeuvre. Lovecraft's ability to paradoxically champion the outsider while subordinating the Other and to elevate nonhumans while denigrating non-whites has made him and his fiction a subject of controversy; at the same time, his ability to "vividly render" the nonhuman in "multifarious forms" (Mayer 117) and to "rethink life in an ecological mode of multiplicity and connectivity" (MacCormack "Lovecraft's" 201) has been linked to a posthuman ethos. Following the lead of critics like Patricia MacCormack and Jed Meyer, I argue that Lovecraft's infectious networks are important examples of the openness to nonhumans and the "radical" (199) or "absolute" alterity (Mayer 119) demanded of non-anthropocentric-oriented ethics. Lovecraft's openness to difference and mutation is further reflected in his generosity with his Mythos, inviting others to adapt and transform his creations. Associated with the "parasitic" (Wills) and "mutational" (Wolfe), posthumanism acts like a viral mode that promises to infect, exceed, and therefore rupture the tensions between "empathy and enmity" for nonhumans and Others informing Lovecraft's oeuvre (Mayer 119). With particular attention to "The Colour Out of Space"—a tale that centers on infection, mutation, and human–nonhuman networks—I argue that despite Lovecraft's emphasis on the horror of nonhuman contamination, his works outline the transformative potential of cross-species infection in ways akin to post-anthropocentric theorists like Anna Tsing, Donna Haraway, and Stacy Alaimo. By revealing the intimate connections between humans, nonhumans, and environment, Lovecraft helps "us to think about what lies 'beyond'" the human (Kneale 106), including the nonhumanity within. Ironically and against his xenophobia, Lovecraft was a generous host, and his stories model a posthuman ethical engagement based in the vulnerabilities, inevitable asymmetries, and transformative encounters of humans and their Others.

After briefly outlining Lovecraft's engagement with microbial entities and viral modalities, I turn more specifically to a post-anthropocentric reading of Lovecraft's "The Colour Out of Space." I end by arguing that Lovecraft's viral networks along with the virality[3] of the Mythos model a contaminated ethics for the Chthulucene—Haraway's term for the contemporary era of human–nonhuman-environment entanglements.

Lovecraft's Viral Modalities

Viruses metaphorize characteristic Lovecraftian themes of nonhuman infection and human mutation. Variously interpreted as poisons, life-forms, and biological chemicals, viruses are interstitial entities hovering "between living and nonliving" (Villarreal 101) and combining "'animate' (reproduction and the ensuing evolution) and 'inanimate' features (lack of autonomy, existence of an inert state)" (Koonin and Starokadomskyy 125). They are "everywhere in, on, and around living things" (Pradeu 86), but they also move between bodies and boundaries—"traversing species, genus, phylum, and kingdom" (Galloway and Thacker 86); infectiously breaking "through barriers or quarantines" (Blas 31); and resisting "any tidy division of the physical" into categories like organic/non-organic and self/other (Ansell-Pearson 133). Viral relationships are asymmetrical, with materials transferred transversally (between higher and lesser life-forms) (Ansell Pearson 133) and sometimes parasitically. Similar modalities define Lovecraft's oeuvre. Heterogeneity and "swarming *multiplicity*" characterize Lovecraftian monsters (Lévy 60, emphasis original), while "'transition' or 'mutation'" underlie Lovecraft's cosmic horror (MacCormack "Lovecraft Through"). Through fixations on "thresholds"; metaphors related to "contact," "transgression," "invasion," "contamination," and "transmission"; and themes like hybridity and miscegenation (Kneale 113–114), Lovecraft depicts the lines between self/other as fundamentally permeable.

In portrayals of unseen nonhuman entities surrounding and infesting humans, Lovecraft's fiction resembles discoveries in contemporary microbiology. The "loathsome profusion" of imperceptible beings in "From Beyond" (28) and the microscopic "intruder[s]" of "The Shunned House" (106), for instance, capture the essence of microbes. Although invisible, "the things that float and flop about you and through you every moment of your life. ... form what men call the pure air and the blue sky" ("From Beyond" 28). Not "actively hostile" but "dictated merely by blind motives of self-preservation," they "penetrate" and "completely [merge themselves]" into the "fabric" of other life-forms ("The Shunned House" 106). In similar ways, microbiology exposes a world populated by invisible and ubiquitous entities living alongside and inside us, contaminating, colonizing, consuming, and connecting us while driving our evolution. Studies of symbiosis highlight the prevalence of "interactive relationships among species" (Gilbert et al. 326), revealing that humans are multispecies collectives—heterogeneous hosts to colonies of infinitesimal species,[4] far more ancient, abundant, and resilient than Man. Biology teaches that human evolution is a story of "cell gorgings and aborted invasions" from which "merged beings that infected one another were reinvigorated by the incorporation of their permanent 'disease'" (Margulis and Sagan 194). Today, scientists proclaim that "We are not alone in our bodies" (Brody); with "trillions of microorganisms" (Brody) living inside us, we are "more microbial than human" (Robinson et al. 3). Microbiology thus contributes to the contemporary decentring of Man, challenging traditional notions of human purity, sovereignty, and exceptionality. That microbes corporealize us, bind us, guide us, and mutate us is both exciting and horrific, a tension between hope and horror that informs my reading of Lovecraft.

"The Colour Out of Space" illustrates the vulnerabilities of this networked or symbiotic being. In the tale, an alien entity comes to earth *in, on, and/or as* a meteorite, parasitically inflecting with humans, animals, and plants while spreading an ambiguous poison throughout the Gardner family farm, just outside of Arkham. The most striking feature of this "lone, weird [messenger] from other universes and other realms of matter, force, and entity" (176) is its unworldly luminosity, which under the spectroscope, "displayed shining bands unlike any known colors of the normal spectrum" (174). The "colour" endlessly spreads, voraciously consuming and infecting plants, animals, and humans alike until the Gardner farm and surrounding area are left a sprawling, grey desolate space, which the locals name "the blasted heath." Although at least *some* of this alien matter eventually returns to space, the story ends with the looming threat of the "demon hatchling" (197) infecting and "infesting" (Harmon 81) New England. With the pending Arkham reservoir, slow yet continuous spreading blight (197), and lingering affective (or *infective*) quality of the area, which is said to bring about disturbing nightmares and strange anxieties, it seems that the infectious alien parasite remains.

Through themes of alien infection and unworldly contamination, Lovecraft's "The Colour Out of Space" depicts the vulnerable connections between organisms and their environment. The swarming, agentic, imperceptible entities associated with the meteor and its "colour" cannot "be seen or heard or handled" (170) but invade, contaminate, and mutate host bodies and minds in an endless proliferation of itself. The colour's inimical effects are seen in the paradoxical harvest of spectacular yet inedible fruits and vegetables, "phenomenal [in] size and [of] unwonted gloss, and... abundance," but bitter and sickish so that the pears, apples, melons, and tomatoes "induced a lasting disgust" (176). Monstrous skunk cabbages and other flora that "ought never to sprout in a healthy world" sow, while unusual footprints and peculiar specimens reveal that "something [was] not quite right about [the] nature and arrangement" of the local woodchucks, foxes, rabbits, and squirrels (178). The Garners' hogs become bloated monstrosities before their snouts turn grey and collapse into themselves, while their cows, riddled with similar cancerous grey sores, produce tainted milk. By the end, the Gardners mutate into unknowable, unspeakable things and die in unspeakable ways. Degenerating into crawling, mad, "slightly luminous" (181), and eventually grey, brittle monstrosities like the livestock, Nabby and Nahum Gardner become a "blasphemous monstrosity" and a "distorted parody" of humanity that the stoic farmer Amni Pierce must destroy. The "strange," "insane," unwholesome and "hectic ... prismatic variants of some diseased, underlying primary tone" (179) uniformly imbuing all reveals the shared materialities and vulnerabilities connecting the Gardners, hogs, woodchucks, and skunk cabbages.

In what follows, I apply a post-anthropocentric reading of Lovecraft's "The Colour Out of Space" and related viral networks, drawing on elements of posthumanism, new materialism, and corporeal feminism. In doing so, I illustrate that Lovecraft narrativizes intimate human–nonhuman-environmental connections and asymmetrical relations in ways that decenter Man, reveal his vulnerable and porous nature, and thus help to theorize a post-anthropocentric ethics based in multispecies entanglements and transformative contamination.

Transformative Contamination

"The Colour Out of Space" reveals the vulnerable openness of humans to nonhumans and environment, which might inform a post-anthropocentric ethics. The once "rural idyll" embodied by the Gardner farmstead (Janicker 59)—with its "fertile gardens and orchards" (Lovecraft 173)—becomes a contaminated, barren space. With "no vegetation of any kind..., but only a fine grey dust or ash" and "sickly and stunted ... dead ...[and] rotting" trees (171), the lifeless area around the "blasted heath" reminds readers of the dangers of an overly voracious environmental consumption and/or unmitigated pollution. The barren landscape is characterized as "a great spot eaten by acid," with the "yawning black maw" of the Gardner well an appropriate home for the consuming, colonizing "monstrous constellation of unnatural light" that looks and acts "like a glutted swarm of corpse-fed fireflies" (193). According to Nahum, the alien matter "burns an' sucks ... the life out" of "everything alive ... [poisoning] the whole place" (188). Here, Lovecraft extends his typical concern with corruption to "the very earth itself" (Janicker 68) and emphasizes "humanity's inescapable imbrication in the nonhuman world" (Johnson 106). The affinities between Gardners, hogs, woodchucks, and skunk cabbages powerfully remind us of our ecological connections. As new materialists argue, understanding ourselves as "interconnected with the wider environment marks a profound shift in subjectivity" and with it, our ethics (Alaimo 20), for it forces us to recognize that our "very embodiment" and "very existence" are "integrally entangled" with the world around us (Barad 158).

Indeed, the viral entanglements of "The Colour Out of Space" demonstrate corporeal feminist and new materialist theories of porous embodiment and human/nonhuman interdependence. Corporeal feminists and new materialists collectively aim to counter humanist "fantasies" of individuality and sovereignty, of "human uniqueness in the eyes of God, of escape from materiality, or of mastery of nature" (Bennett ix). Concepts like Stacey Alaimo's trans-corporeality, Nancy Tuana's interactionism, or Karen Barad's intra-action emphasize that "the substance of the human is ultimately inseparable from 'the environment'" (Alaimo 2), that the "boundaries between our flesh and the flesh of the world we are of and in" are "porous" (Tuana 198), and that humans and nonhumans are "mutually constituted" as integral parts "*of* the world ... part of the world in its differential becomings" (Barad 185, emphasis in the original). In this Mobius-strip model of embodiment,[5] distinctions between self/other or inside/outside are arbitrary or constructed, and the nonhuman is an intimate part of the human. Borrowing heavily from microbiology, new materialists embrace the "filthy lesson" of symbiosis: because humans are multilayered microbial colonies and sites "of contamination and abduction by alien forces" (Ansell Pearson 124, 5), they "have never been individuals" (Gilbert et al. 336). For theorists like Karen Barad, it matters *how* we matter, and our mutuality with and dependence on nonhumans mean that "we" are "co-constituted and entangled" with our "others" (178–9), obliging us to become responsive to their needs.

Although horrific for Man, Lovecraft's infectious networks incorporate the individual human into an assemblage of self-other-environment in ways that challenge the self/other dynamic of humanist subjectivity. Much like the Gardners, who disintegrate into the spreading alien blight, Elihu Whipple of "The Shunned House" finds himself absorbed into a parasitic "anthropomorphic patch of mould" (104).[6] A "contagious" (95), monstrous mycelium haunts the fetid, damp "Shunned House" house, notorious for its unhealthy atmosphere and long line of anaemic, dead residents. Mycelium is "the fungi's underground network of filaments" (or subterranean "Internet") (Mershon 267) that forms a heterogenous web with adjacent life. The "fungous loathsomeness" (111) of "The Shunned House," a nebulous living-dead-fungal-vampire, "[spreads] itself through Whipple's body" (109) as it "[dissolves] and [mixes]" him into a "kaleidoscopic vortex" (109). While Whipple's loss of individuality and corporeality is horrific, the assemblage he becomes demonstrates the inherent interconnections and mutability of matter underpinning the post-anthropocentric decentring of Man. These "secrets of inner earth," although "not good for mankind" (113), reveal elements of matter, substance, and energy that humans, "for lack of a proper vantage-point, may never hope to understand" (112).

However, by shifting our vantage-point, these contagious exchanges can indeed help us to understand our porous, vulnerable embodiment and our intimate, uneven, and at times dangerous entanglements with the "'earth' others" (Braidotti 190) around us in ways that can generate sensitivity to our fellow creatures and respect for our environmental interconnections. Viruses both literalize and metaphorize these intimacies, for they cross between bodies and undo polarities between inside/outside and human/nonhuman. Tales like "The Shunned House" and "The Colour Out of Space" shift the perception of humans from individuals to collectives by focussing on the mutuality of humans, nonhumans, and environment. In "The Colour Out of Space," these interdependencies are amplified by the horrors of living in a contaminated landscape—an experience that resonates for contemporary readers. In the twenty-first century, an increasing awareness of "pollution, mass extinction, and climate change" has illuminated that "all our lives are precarious," as Anna Tsing puts it (3, 2). Precarity, or the recognition of the uncertain fate of the earth and our collective vulnerability to ruin, reveals that all species require "livable collaborations" to survive (Tsing 28). For Tsing, precarity prompts us to acknowledge that "survival always involves others" (29). Lovecraft's infectious exchanges crystalize this vulnerability and dependence through what Alaimo describes as "sinister trans-corporeality," whereby "unseen, unknown hazards" invade and contaminate bodies (45, 68). Sinister exchanges "between the human and more-than-human worlds" illustrate how "all creatures [exist] as part of their own corporeal crossroads of body and place, provoking an ethics of concern for a multitude of creatures and their habitats" (110–111). Lovecraft's depictions of shared decay and ruin steer us in this direction.

Shifting our perspective from individuals to symbionts also emphasizes that transformational encounters with difference are necessary for our continued existence. Symbiotic interactions require interspecies exchanges, "ugly or otherwise" (Tsing 31). According to Tsing, who explores the paradoxes and intricacies of multispecies relationships and ecological devastation, contamination can be a means of transformative collaboration. Contamination is "transformation through encounter" that "makes diversity" and facilitates "work across difference," including work "across species" (Tsing 28, 29). MacCormack's "perverse" feminist reading of Lovecraft illuminates the liberatory possibilities of opening ourselves up to diversity in this way. MacCormack posits that the "visceral connections with the unlike" common in Lovecraft reflect "the sticky, abject, but jubilant viscosity of jouissance that is premised on lack of demarcation between entities … [and] shared fluidities" ("Lovecraft's" 208). Through an "ethical erotics of alterity," Lovecraft models a feministic "voracious drive for proximity with alterity and … openness to creativity and newness found in the acknowledgement that the earth and life are nothing more than a mesh of unlike entities coexisting" ("Lovecraft's" 209, 211). Such contaminating, uneven exchanges can help us to navigate "ecologies [that] are open and messy, rife with relationships that are painful and asymmetrical, but also full of possibility" for modelling "a way out of bounded individualism and anthropocentric hubris" (Samyn 245). There are no stable "self-contained units" (Tsing 33) in symbiotic assemblages. Such "encounter-based collaborations" are relational and "ever-changing" (Tsing 34, 33). To work with and through extreme contemporary asymmetries (Samyn 261), we need to cultivate an openness to these transformative encounters our Others offer.

Post-anthropocentric ethics demand this radical openness to mutation and diversity. Breaking from humanist notions of progress or telos, posthumanism embraces "the complex and random processes of mutation," which can never be mastered by humans (Rutsky 111). Posthuman subjects remain open to "continuous construction and reconstruction" (Hayles 3), "inhabiting the boundary between the human and the almost-human" (Graham 221). Posthumanities exist "between-betweens," a type of "becoming" (Halbertam and Livingston 10, 14) in the Deleuze-Guattarian sense of "creative *involution*": an ongoing process of "transversal communications" and contagious, heterogeneous *involvements* with Others to create subjectivities based in multiplicities and assemblages (Deleuze and Guattari 238, 273). Through modalities of infection and mutation, then, post-anthropocentric subjects "becoming-with" others in "unexpected collaborations and combinations"—a process Donna Haraway describes as "making oddkin" (4). That "nothing is truly sterile" is simultaneously a "terrific danger, basic fact of life, and critter-making opportunity" (Haraway 64). Our "symbiotic assemblages," or oddkin relationships, are not always "mutually beneficial" (60); however, these cross-species "ethical and political obligations" can and should be "infectious" (115), transferring "meanings and materials across kinds in order to infect processes and practices" towards "multispecies recuperation and maybe even flourishing" on our damaged planet (Haraway 114).

Viral modalities are thus methods for infectious, mutational engagements that can transgress various boundaries and open up human hosts to transformational encounters, which makes them promising for critiquing and possibly exceeding Lovecraft's paradoxical attraction and repulsion to the Other (Simmons 19). As Mayer demonstrates, "Lovecraft's work is haunted by the prospect of kinship with other ethnic groups, even while he avidly explores connections with nonhuman beings both cosmic and earthly" (119). Turning again to Lovecraft, I maintain that counter to his infamous bigotry, his fictional oddkin relationships and openness to creative mutation not only contribute to his contemporary relevance, but, more importantly, model the contaminated transformations promoted by post anthropocentric theory.

Viral Lovecraft: Contaminated Ethics for the Chthulucene

Lovecraft's notorious racism and xenophobia certainly complicate any celebration of the post-anthropocentric ethical insights we might glean from his fiction. While "The Colour Out Space" does not link its nefarious nonhuman contaminants to nonwhites and foreigners, Lovecraft's fiction more generally frames "fears of infection and contamination" (Kneale 116) often in terms of racialized bodies (Kneale 115) and horror over swarming, swarthy "Orientals" and "mongrels" ("The Horror at Red Hook" 112, 136).[7] The irony, of course, is that while he offered poignant depictions of outsiders and Others, Lovecraft personally disavowed "the very insights within his fiction celebrated by posthumanist theorists" (Sederholm and Weinstock, *Age* 37). China Miéville has claimed that Lovecraft's racism can neither be ignored nor divorced from his fiction, leaving readers with the nauseating task of "metaboliz[ing]" his "toxic ideologies" (241). Although we can perhaps never truly digest this poisonous racism, we must find ways to incorporate it into our applications of his work, and perhaps we might even find ways to dilute its power through posthuman critique and continuous mutation of the Mythos.

With his influence spreading further and further into contemporary scholarship and culture, it seems fair to say that Lovecraft has *gone viral*. But as Carl Sederholm and Jeffrey Andrew Weinstock ask, "which Lovecraft?" ("Lovecraft Now" 446). Lovecraft and his dynamic, hyper-adaptable Cthulhu Mythos have been constantly transforming, mutating, "expanding and hybridizing" (Kneale 116) into an endless and at times paradoxical array of "Lovecrafts." Infectious, proliferating, yet multiple and mutating, this "viral" Lovecraft demonstrates the openness to asymmetries and hybridity required of present-day post-anthropocentric engagements. As Blas describes it, "To think the virus and the viral is to engage in their continuous states of flux [and] transformation" (30). Not merely destructive, viruses can be performative, exploratory, and disturbing (Galloway and Thacker 83), offering models for "creative openings"

(Blas 30) and "creative evolution" (Ansell Pearson 133). Because viroid networks tend to deprivilege hosts, they illustrate parasitic, asymmetrical, possibly dangerous, yet powerfully transformative encounters with "radical" (MacCormack) or "absolute" (Mayer) alterity. Lovecraft's viroid networks contaminate, mutate, and dissolve protagonists into "horrors beyond horrors" ("The Shunned House" 111), but MacCormack would ask, "horror for whom?" ("Lovecraft's" 202). What might be "horror for some" is "the very opening of the world to others" ("Lovecraft's" 213). The horror for Lovecraft's protagonists might be the "collapse, greying, and disintegration" ("The Colour" 188) or dissolution of the subject "to an abhorrent plasticity" ("The Shunned House" 111), but it is only a "very particular kind of subject" who finds the asymmetries, parasitic odd-couplings, and "Ancient One-infected universe uninhabitable" (MacCormack, "Lovecraft's" 212). As MacCormack explains, the "horror experienced by Lovecraft's protagonists need not close off the possibility that his readers would negotiate their own subjectivity and elements of alterity" ("Lovecraft Through") so as to inhabit *this* particular world. An openness to diversity calls for an "unconditional" hospitality that "opens the door to the inhospitable," inviting the "guest" to occupy and transform the host like "an invader" (Wills 18–19).[8]

Lovecraft, for all his racism and noxious views, was also an unconditional host who openly shared and invited others to inhabit and shape—indeed infect and mutate—his Mythos. Lovecraft's "Cthulhu Mythos has remained a living work," expanding by the creation of new stories and adaptations into new mediums (Mullis 514). The "open-ended and dynamic quality" of the Mythos (Evans 128) coupled with a hyper-adaptability that allows his narratives to "flourish in different environments" means that "Lovecraft-inspired texts will likely continue to proliferate within popular media, shaping"—and reshaping—"the ways people recognize and understand his work" (Sederholm 270). Such mutational (indeed, viral) possibilities offer "an aesthetic of creating new realities" (Evans 128) that results in "'Lovecraft'… in a process of endless transformation," including the occasional rejection (Kneale 116) or reconfiguration of his racism.[9] Justin Mullis speculates that Lovecraft is so popular today because his Mythos is complex, compelling, and heterodoxic, providing "the ideal platform for world building and social critique" as well as "a means of acting out a desired reality" (525, 516). Lovecraft—as "*the generator of dreams*" (Houellebecq, emphasis original 42) who helps "us to think about what lies 'beyond'" the human (Kneale 106) and reflect "on the vast, and sometimes frightening, nature of the universe and humankind's fragile place within it" (Sederholm 269)—provides contemporary readers with stories for navigating the asymmetries of the Chthulucene.

Contra Haraway, I suggest that Lovecraft, through his heterogeneous assemblages and viral networks, illustrates the multispecies flourishings she promotes in her theory of the Chthulucene, her term for the contemporary networked world of multispecies kinship and risk. Although her term might evoke Lovecraft, Haraway rejects these associations, explaining her term as a compound of the Greek roots *khthôn* and *kainos*, roughly meaning *earth* and *time* (2, 173n4). The Chthulucene is "[a] timeplace for learning to stay with the trouble of living and dying" with our oddkin "on a damaged earth" (2). Her dismissal of Lovecraft for his misogyny, racism, and nihilism is understandable; yet, her claim that "Lovecraft could not have imaged or embraced" the "myriad intra-active entities-in-assemblages—including the more-than human, other-than-human, inhuman, and human-as-humus" modalities she promotes (101) seems false. This is not to excuse Lovecraft's racism, which is, as Miéville claims, innately noxious. Rather, this is to suggest, as MacCormack does, that Lovecraft—as a writer of "becomings," rhizomatic collectives, and relations "that should not be"—"opens up the very possibilities of ethical alterity and encounters premised on the destruction of the privileged subject" and the feministic joy of "the vast connective tissue" entwining all "materiality, animality, life, and reality" ("Lovecraft's" 204, 206). Lovecraft's viral networks demonstrate the shared materialities, inhuman assemblages, and categorical breakdowns that underpin such a posthuman ethics. The alien "colour" of "The Colour Out of Space" can be read as "a source of destabilization" (Oakes 39) that ultimately undoes "categorical thinking" and with it any pretense to mastery (Burleson 108), humanist superiority (Nyikos), or human exceptionality.

There is a lingering, affective—perhaps *infective*—quality to reading Lovecraft. In a manner akin to his protagonists, whose ingestion of cosmic knowledge infects and forever alters them sometimes unto madness and death, Lovecraft's readers can experience "material effects in the post-structural sense of re-negotiating signifying systems and relations of difference and otherness in the world" (MacCormack "Lovecraft Through"). MacCormack's contention that the ways in which we read and make use of Lovecraft matter seems apt; thus, we might ask not only "what Lovecraft means," but also (and perhaps more importantly) "what reading Lovecraft might do" ("Lovecraft Through"). Although his characters "are too entangled in the web of ... cosmic horror to contemplate the vast expanses of nature" (Ralickas 297) to gain post-anthropocentric understanding, contemporary readers of Lovecraft—embroiled as they are in the everyday weird, dangerous, networked, nonhuman world of the twenty-first-century—are well poised for the ethical insights that might follow from our entanglements with the "more-than-human-world" (Abram)[10] or "the *world-without-us*" (Thacker 5). We should neither forget nor excuse the noxious elements of Lovecraft's philosophy and fiction; however, we can perhaps infect our host to transform their power, generating and proliferating a post-anthropocentric respect for impurities and difference.

Notes

1 Theories that challenge human exceptionality and humanist hierarchies, including posthumanism, new materialism, Critical Animal Studies, and Object Oriented Ontology.
2 See, for example, Galloway and Thacker's *The Exploit: A Theory of Networks*.
3 Viral marketing, viral media, and viral news are some examples of viral phenomenon, which get their name from the ways that ideas, videos, images, etc. seemingly reproduce themselves or mutate other objects into copies of themselves online.
4 Known formally as the human microbiome: the collection of bacteria, archaea, protozoans, viruses, and fungi living on and in humans.
5 See Elizabeth Grosz's *Volatile Bodies: Toward a Corporeal Feminism*. Indiana University Press, 1994.
6 Although they are rarely pathogenic, fungi have long evoked associations with infection and decay, making them symbolic harbingers of disease and death akin to thier viral relatives.
7 "The Shunned House" subtly illustrates this trend by locating the originary source of horror with the French immigrant Roulet family, associated with devil-worship, lycanthropy, and vampirism.
8 For a fulsome discussion of unconditional or "absolute" hospitality, see Jacques Derrida's *Of Hospitality*. Trans. Rachel Bowlby. Stanford University Press, 2000.
9 See, for example, Elizabeth Bear's "Shoggoths in Bloom" or Matt Ruff's *Lovecraft Country*, recently adapted for television by Jordan Peele.
10 See Abram's *The Spell of the Sensuous: Perception and Language in a More-Than-Human World*. Vintage Books, 1996.

Works Cited

Alaimo, Stacy. *Bodily Natures: Science, Environment, and the Material Self*. Bloomington, Indiana University Press, 2010.

Ansell, Pearson Keith. *Viroid Life: Perspectives on Nietzsche and the Transhuman Condition*. London: Routledge, 1997.

Barad, Karen. *Meeting the Universe Halfway: Quantum Physics and the Entanglement of Matter and Meaning*. Durham, Duke University Press, 2007.

Bennett, Jane. *Vibrant Matter: A Political Ecology of Things*. Durham, Duke University Press, 2010.

Blas, Zach. "Virus, Viral." *WSQ: Women's Studies Quarterly* vol. 40, no. 1 & 2, 2012, pp. 29–39. Accessed Nov. 29 2019.

Braidotti, Rosi. *The Posthuman*. Cambridge, Polity Press, 2013.

Brody, Herb. "The Gut Microbiome." *Nature*, 29 Jan. 2020 https://www.nature.com/articles/d41586-020-00194-2. Accessed Feb. 12 2020.

Burleson, Donald R. *Lovecraft: Disturbing the Universe*. Lexington, Kentucky, The University Press of Kentucky 2009.

Deleuze, Gilles and Félix Guattari. *A Thousand Plateaus: Capitalism and Schizophrenia*. Trans. Brian Massumi. Minneapolis, MN: University of Minnesota Press, 1987.

Evans, Timothy H. "A Last Defense against the Dark: Folklore, Horror, and the Uses of Tradition in the Works of H. P. Lovecraft." *Journal of Folklore Research*, vol. 42, no. 1, 2005, pp. 99–135. Accessed Mar. 6 2020.

Galloway, Alexander R., and Eugene Tacker. *The Exploit: A Theory of Networks.* Minneapolis, MN: University of Minnesota Press, 2007.

Gilbert, Scott F. et al. "A Symbiotic View of Life: We Have Never Been Individuals." *The Quarterly Review of Biology*, vol. 87, no. 4, 2012, pp. 325–341. Accessed Apr. 4 2019.

Graham, Elaine. *Representations of the Post/Human: Monsters, Aliens and Others in Popular Culture*. Manchester: Rutgers University Press, 2002.

Halberstam, Judith and Ira Livingston. "Introduction: Posthuman Bodies." *Posthuman Bodies*, edited by Judith Halberstam and Ira Livingston. Bloomington: Indiana University Press, 1995, pp. 1–20.

Haraway, Donna J. *Staying with the Trouble: Making Kin in the Chthulucene*. Durham, NC: Duke University Press, 2016.

Harmon, Graham. *Weird Realism: Lovecraft and Philosophy*. Winchester, UK; Washington, USA, Zero Books, 2012.

Hayles, N. Katherine. *How We Became Posthuman: Virtual Bodies in Cybernetics, Literature, and Informatics*. Chicago, IL: Chicago University Press, 1999.

Janicker, Rebecca. "New England Narratives: Space and Place in the Fiction of H.P. Lovecraft." *Extrapolation*, vol. 48, no. 1, 2006, pp. 56–72. Accessed May 25 2019.

Johnson, Brian. "Prehistories of Posthumanism: Cosmic Indifferentism, Alien Genesis, and Ecology from H. P. Lovecraft to Ridley Scott." *The Age of Lovecraft*, edited by Carl H. Sederholm and Jeffrey Andrew Weinstock, Minneapolis, MN: University of Minnesota Press, 2016, pp. 97–116.

Joshi, S. T. "Introduction."*Introduction to The Call of Cthulhu and Other Weird Stories*, edited by S. T. Joshi, New York, NY: Penguin Books, 1999, pp. v–xvii.

Kneale, James. "From Beyond: H. P. Lovecraft and the Place of Horror." *Cultural Geographies*, vol. 13, no. 1, 2006, pp. 106–126. Accessed June 12 2019.

Koonin, Eugene V. and Petro Starokadomskyy. "Are Viruses Alive? The Replicator Paradigm Sheds Decisive Light on an Old but Misguided Question." *Studies in History and Philosophy of Biological and Biomedical Sciences*, vol. 59, 2016, pp. 125–134. doi: 10.1016/j.shpsc.2016.02.016. Accessed May 15 2020.

Lévy, Maurice. *Lovecraft, a Study in the Fantastic*. Detroit, Wayne State University Press, 1988.

Lovecraft, Howard Phillips. "From Beyond." *The Dreams in the Witch House and Other Weird Stories*, edited by S. T. Joshi, New York, NY: Penguin Books, 2004a, pp. 23–29.

———. "The Colour Out of Space." *The Call of Cthulhu and Other Weird Stories*, edited by S. T. Joshi, New York, NY: Penguin Books, 1999, pp. 170–199.

———. "The Horror at Red Hook." *The Dreams in the Witch House and Other Weird Stories*, edited by S. T. Joshi, New York, NY: Penguin Books, 2004b, pp. 116–251.

———. "The Shunned House." *The Dreams in the Witch House and Other Weird Stories*, edited by S. T. Joshi, New York, NY: *Penguin Books*, 2004c, pp. 90–115.

MacCormack, Patricia. "Lovecraft's Cosmic Ethics." *The Age of Lovecraft*, edited by Carl H. Sederholm and Jeffrey Andrew Weinstock, Minneapolis, MN: University of Minnesota Press, 2016, pp. 199–214.

———. "Lovecraft Through the Deleuzio-Guattarian Gates." *Postmodern Culture*, vol. 20, no. 2, 2010. doi: 10.1353/pmc.2010.0008. Accessed Apr. 5 2019.

Margulis, Lynn and Dorian Sagan. *What is Life?* Berkeley, CA: California University Press, 1995.

Mayer, Jed. "Race, Species, and Others: H. P. Lovecraft and the Animal." *The Age of Lovecraft*, edited by Carl H. Sederholm and Jeffrey Andrew Weinstock, Minneapolis, MN: University of Minnesota Press, 2016, pp. 113–148.

Miéville, China. "Interview with China Miéville." Interview by Jeffrey Andrew Weinstock. *The Age of Lovecraft*, edited by Carl H. Sederholm and Jeffrey Andrew Weinstock, Minneapolis, MN: University of Minnesota Press, 2016, pp. 231–243.

Mershon, Ella. "Pulpy Fiction." *Victorian Literature and Culture*, vol. 48, no. 1, 2020, pp. 267–298. doi:10.1017/S1060150319000548. Accessed June 2 2020.

Mullis, Justin. "Playing Games with the Great Old Ones: Ritual, Play, and Joking within the Cthulhu Mythos Fandom." *Journal of the Fantastic in the Arts*, vol. 26, no. 3, 2015, pp. 512–530. Accessed May 11 2020.

Oakes, David A. *Science and Destabilization in the Modern American Gothic: Lovecraft, Matheson, and King*. Westport, CT: Greenwood Press, 2000.

Pradeu, Thomas. "Mutualistic Viruses and the Heteronomy of Life." *Studies in History and Philosophy of Biological and Biomedical Sciences*, vol. 59, 2016, pp. 80–88. doi: 10.1016/j.shpsc.2016.02.007. Accessed May 15 2020.

Ralickas, Vivian. "Art, Cosmic Horror, and the Fetishizing Gaze in the Fiction of H. P. Lovecraft." *Journal of the Fantastic in the Arts*, vol. 19, no. 3, 2008, pp. 297–316. Accessed June 5 2019.

Robinson, Jake M. et al. "Walking Ecosystems in Microbiome-Inspired Green Infrastructure: An Ecological Perspective on Enhancing Personal and Planetary Health." *Challenges*, vol. 9, no. 40, 2018, doi:10.3390/challe9020040. Accessed Feb. 12 2020.

Rutsky, R. L. "Mutation, History, and the Fantasy in the Posthuman." *Subject Matters: A Journal of Communication and the Self*, vol. 3, no. 2 – vol. 4, no. 1, 2007, pp. 99–112. Accessed Apr. 3 2020.

Samyn, Jeanette. "Intimate Ecologies: Symbioses in the Nineteenth Century." *Victorian Literature and Culture*, vol. 48, no. 1, 2020, pp. 243–265. doi:10.1017/S1060150319000561. Accessed June 2 2020.

Sederholm, Carl H. and Jeffrey Andrew Weinstock. "Introduction: Lovecraft Rising." *The Age of Lovecraft*, edited by Carl H. Sederholm and Jeffrey Andrew Weinstock, Minneapolis, MN: University of Minnesota Press, 2016, pp. 1–42.

———. "Introduction: Lovecraft Now." *Journal of the Fantastic in the Arts*, vol. 26, no. 3, 2015, pp. 444–449. Accessed May 5 2019.

Sederholm, Carl H. "H. P. Lovecraft, Heavy Metal, and Cosmicism." *Rock Music Studies*, vol. 3, no. 3, 2016, pp. 266–280. doi: 10.1080/19401159.2015.1121644. Accessed May 22 2020.

Simmons, David. "'A Certain Resemblance:' Abject Hybridity in H. P. Lovecraft's Short Fiction." *New Critical Essays on H. P. Lovecraft*, edited by David Simmons. New York: Palgrave, 2013, pp. 13–30.

Thacker, Eugene. *In the Dust of this Planet: Horror of Philosophy* Vol. 1. Winchester, UK; Washington, USA, Zero Books, 2011.

Tsing, Anna Lowenhaupt. *The Mushroom at the End of the World: On the Possibility of Life in Capitalist Ruins*. Princeton, Princeton University Press, 2015.

Tuana, Nancy. "Viscous Porosity: Witnessing Katrina." In *Material Feminisms*, edited by Stacy Alaimo and Susan Hekman. Bloomington: Indiana University Press, 2008, pp. 188–213.

Villarreal, Luis P. "Are Viruses Alive?" *Scientific American* vol. 291, no. 6, 2004, pp. 100–105. Accessed May 11 2020.

Wills, David. *Matchbook: Essays in Deconstruction*. Stanford, CA: Stanford University Press, 2005.

Wolfe, Cary. *What is Posthumanism?* Minneapolis, MN: University of Minnesota Press, 2010.

11 "It Was the Vegetation"

Ecophobia and Monstrous Wilderness in the Fiction of H.P. Lovecraft

Fredrik Blanc

The recent resurgence of interest in H.P. Lovecraft's weird fiction starkly coincides with the increasing consequences of climate change. The snowballing effects of industrialization, greenhouse emissions, and rising sea levels appear as veritable counterpoints to such concepts as the Anthropocene, which understands our current geological era as one largely influenced and determined by humanity's hold over its environment. While it is overwhelmingly clear that humanity has caused these environmental upheavals, it is also becoming increasingly clear that so-called nature seems to be retaliating, striking back in unprecedented and unnerving ways. If, as Carl H. Sederholm and Jeffrey Andrew Weinstock explain in *The Age of Lovecraft*, Lovecraft's "unprecedented growth in popularity" is due to the ways in which he "addresses questions, anxieties, and desires that have become increasingly insistent" in recent years, then one of these concerns is indubitably that of humanity's fraught relationship with the other agencies of nature (3). Material ecocritics such as Serpil Oppermann and Serenella Iovino argue that the "world's material phenomena are knots in a vast network of agencies," where apersonal agencies such as that of hurricanes, primeval forests, and the Gulf Stream all have a hand in shaping through their interplay the very environment of which humanity is a part (1).

Viewed through such lenses, the environmental agencies that appear so violently to assail humanity at the dawn of the twenty-first century reveal themselves in keeping with Lovecraft's weird fiction, or cosmic horror, in which an "atmosphere of breathless and unexplainable dread of outer, unknown forces" must overtake the inadequate and uncomprehending humans, characters, and readers alike (Lovecraft et al. 2004, "Supernatural Horror" 84). These agencies reflect not malignancy, but the consequences of forces beyond humanity's control and the cosmic indifference of an untamable universe.

Lovecraft's weird depictions of encroaching forests and dangerously active vegetation participate in the articulation of such agencies, presciently elaborating on "anthropocenic crises," which, according to Gry Ulstein, "muddle the preconceived role division between actor and

DOI: 10.4324/9780367713065-12

acted-upon" (49); that is, such traditional backdrops of horror as the woods are not content to remain mere settings, but they now come alive, their terrible agencies made clear, as they become enweirded, ecological monstrosities. This illustrates Timothy Morton's view of ecological awareness as taking a weird "twisted, looping form" which entangles together the human and other-than human (6).

H.P. Lovecraft's short stories "The Lurking Fear" (1923), "The Colour Out of Space" (1927), and "The Shunned House" (1937) strikingly illustrate the many ways in which the natural world can become monstrous, whether as the prime infector or as the later infected, within a given narrative. The purpose of this chapter is to investigate these narratives through an ecophobic lens, one which reveals how Lovecraft's weird fiction articulates the natural environment and its agencies as monstrous and unnerving in their wild fecundity. Roger Luckhurst importantly argued that "ecocriticism has been thoroughly weirded" (1042). In other words, contemporary views and discourses surrounding ecology and the natural world are now infused with the perturbed "sense of wrongness" which Mark Fisher defines as one of the core elements of the weird (13). This chapter offers a detailed textual analysis of the vegetal and environmental elements in some of Lovecraft's weird fiction, thus bringing to the fore the ecophobic motifs that underpin much of the author's cosmic horror. It participates in the contemporary critical re-evaluation of weird fiction and aims to provide a precise example of an ecocritical study of the weird, through the concept of ecophobia.

These narratives particularly lend themselves to ecocritical readings, especially within the framework of what Andrew Smith and William Hughes have termed the "ecoGothic," which Elizabeth Parker defined as "Gothic stories in which the natural environment, or the elements within it, are eerily ambient and arouse our anxieties" (Parker 2016, 218). All three narratives contain descriptions of grotesque and sometimes even monstrous vegetation and landscapes such as the "ancient lightning-scarred trees" in "The Lurking Fear," which "seemed unnaturally large and twisted" (Lovecraft 350); the house's overgrown garden in "The Shunned House," with its "barren, gnarled, and terrible old trees, long, queerly pale grass, and nightmarishly misshaped weeds" (Lovecraft 454); and the region around the *blasted heath* in "The Colour Out of Space," that "dark westward tangle of glens and slopes" where "trees grew too thickly, and their trunks were too big for any healthy New England wood" (Lovecraft 368). These narratives exemplify and adapt to the beginnings of the twentieth century what Smith and Hughes have argued in terms of the "Romantic Gothic" of the late eighteenth and early nineteenth century, which "illustrates how nature becomes constituted in the Gothic as a space of crisis which conceptually creates a point of contact with the ecological" (3). In other words, the arresting power of these descriptions of landscape and their constitutive vegetation draws attention not only to the horror and disquiet of these locales but also to the interrelationship between nature and the horror in their midst, as well as to the potential influence the former may have on the latter. The feelings of unease and unrest that these narratives evoke in their portrayal of nature further constitute what Simon C. Estok termed "Ecophobia," or the "irrational and groundless hatred of the natural world" (208). Lovecraft's short stories exhibit ecophobic tendencies inasmuch as they portray the monstrous possibilities of nature in ways that draw upon prior conceptions of dangerous landscapes, the wilderness, and the pastoral.

The strange, inhospitable, and often dangerous landscapes depicted in Lovecraft's fiction are, first and foremost, manifestations of ongoing tropes to an extent specific to North America and its colonial history, where the powerful motifs of the open frontier and the untamed wilderness are especially prevalent (Smith and Hughes). The wilderness, in particular, corresponds to the large swathes of land, seemingly empty and uninhabited, that the first American colonists encountered upon their arrival, evoking both new opportunities and toilsome hardship. For the early settlers, the wilderness was a new and scary environment, a space which escaped their control and conceptually became a battleground in which was actuated, as Bernice M. Murphy puts it, "the belief that the forest beyond the settlement is the place where the representatives of 'civilisation' are pitched against forces that embody 'savagery,' and order – moral, psychological, and geographical – is opposed to 'chaos'" (Murphy 16). The wilderness etymologically means "the place of wild beasts," the locus of the uncontrollable, of which the root "wild" came to "convey the idea of being lost, unruly, and confused" (Murphy 20). This landscape ultimately comes to function as the North American equivalent of the European Gothic tropes of old castles and foreboding crypts in narratives which, as Jerrold E. Hogle explains, characteristically "include … antiquated settings, often with obscured undergrounds harboring age-old texts, from moldering castles, graveyards, mansions/houses, and primitive wildernesses to urban and suburban underworlds" (4). This North American equivalent, moreover, seems to have critically preceded the latter, as Tom J. Hillard argues, in that the wilderness is "just an early version of what becomes the dark dungeon or haunted castle in later Gothic fictions—that fearful space inhabited by threatening characters, creatures or ideas marked by deep-seated secrets or past transgressions that threaten the status quo" (115). Lovecraft himself, in his *Supernatural Horror in Literature*, emphasizes the idiosyncratic nature of horror within a North American context, as he details that

> America, besides inheriting the usual dark folklore of Europe, had an additional fund of weird associations to draw upon … from the keen spiritual and theological interests of the first colonists, plus the strange and forbidding nature of the scene into which they were

> plunged. The vast and gloomy virgin forests in whose perpetual twilight all terrors might well lurk; the hordes of coppery Indians whose strange, saturnine visages and violent customs hinted strongly at traces of infernal origin.
>
> (Lovecraft 104)

The three short stories chosen for the present analysis reflect a keen awareness of the New England diminishing wilderness as a space of potential horror, where Lovecraft's attention to regional topography meets his careful consideration of the roots of primordial fear. It is no accident that in "The Lurking Fear," the reader's first encounter with a foreboding sense of the weird takes the form of a description of the New England hinterlands as the narrator describes how the "country bore an aspect more than usually sinister as we viewed it by night" on their way to the "deserted mansion atop Tempest Mountain" (Lovecraft 349–350). The first locus of horror in the narrative is thus the very nature surrounding the narrator. It is there that fear, here personified in the eponymous "Lurking Fear," pointedly resides. Lovecraft reminds us that "the oldest and strongest emotion of mankind is fear, and the oldest and strongest kind of fear is fear of the unknown" (*Supernatural Horror* 82). The fear here explored is thus the very fear of nature defined by Estok as ecophobia, that fear which as Hillard details "may lie at the heart of Western culture's long-held desire to alter, change and even destroy those aspects of our environments that (seem to) threaten us" (105). This anxiety toward the natural world, the need to reshape and control it, as well as protect oneself against it is a driving force within each narrative, one that is thus particularly salient within an ecophobic framework.

Nevertheless, the ecophobic dynamics are articulated differently and for different purposes within each narrative, for example, exemplifying the dangers of devolution in the face of colonial landscape in "The Lurking Fear." Here, the area around Tempest Mountain, that "remote, lonely elevation in that part of the Catskills where Dutch civilisation once feebly and transiently penetrated" (Lovecraft "Lurking" 350), becomes the hunting-ground of the cannibalistic and degenerate spawns of the Martense family, last remnants of the Dutch colonists that have terrorized the land for centuries. The land is a space of degeneracy and decay, corruption, and decadence, where the rest of the population are but "scared and witless shanty-dwellers" and "simple animals ... gently descending the evolutionary scale because of their unfortunate ancestry and stultifying isolation" (357). The blatant xenophobia and racism at work here highlight the central conceit of the narrative of the degenerative potential of non-English settlers in their encounter with the American wilderness. Indeed, the English Puritan settlers were, to an extent, successful in their subjugation of the land. They were able to win their battle over the wilderness, to conquer and tame an environment that for them had, as Garrard explains, an "almost sacramental value" as "it holds out the promise of a renewed, authentic relation of humanity and the earth, a post-Christian covenant, found in a space of purity" (59). The Dutch settlers in "The Lurking Fear," by contrast, were singularly unsuccessful in their efforts. On the contrary, they have found themselves transformed into that "filthy whitish gorilla thing with sharp yellow fangs and matted fur," into the "ultimate product of mammalian degeneration; the frightful outcome of isolated spawning, multiplication, and cannibal nutrition" (Lovecraft "Lurking" 373). The narrative thus clearly links both the landscape and the non-English origins of the settlers to the threat of devolution through inbreeding.

What is interesting, moreover, is the dynamics of agency at the core of such an interrelationship. Where at first glance, the narrative seems to articulate the ecophobic anxieties at work in such descriptions as "hoary grove," "wild-armed titan trees," and "morbidly overnourished forest" as the atmospheric consequences of the Martense wrongdoings and debasement, a closer reading actually seems to reveal the reverse (355, 357). Indeed, it is the thunder-ridden Tempest Mountain "liabl[e] to frequent thunderstorms" (351) which appears to have partly caused the Martense seclusion and subsequent inbreeding within their mansion. The original builder of the mansion, Mynheer Martense, apparently chose rather recklessly the new location of his family's seat and, after a while, "having found these storms injurious to his health, he fitted up a cellar into which he could retreat from their wildest pandemonium" (363). In other words, the narrative points at a correlation, however subtle, between the madness befalling the family and the sublime powers of a wild landscape, driven as they were to grotesque atavism because of incessant thunder and lightning. The wilderness seems to have a transformative power, an untamable capacity to shape its new inhabitants in otherwise unpredictable ways. It has, as Murphy points out, a "profound, and not always *positive* effect, upon those who reside there" (16). The agentic power of Tempest Mountain is thus made clear, as well as the network of interconnections that link settlers and environment. "The Lurking Fear" stands as the exemplification of the interrelationship between settlers and the land they have settled that Murphy further defines. According to her, while it has become clear that "the Puritans would irrevocably change the American landscape," what is less often contemplated and what "they did not take into consideration at first were the ways in which the land would change *them*. Adaptation is, after all, a two-way street ... you may possess the land, but you should never forget that it also possesses *you* [italics in the original]" (19). This interrelationship between the transformative wilderness and the conquering colonists is then mediated in the narrative through the weird, evoking this adaptive necessity as a grotesque devolution, where nature quite literally possesses the Martense and reduces them to debased animality. Brad Tabas, in his analysis of weird spaces, concurs as he details how "rather than becoming masters and possessors of nature, we slowly realize that we are possessed by nature, and that nature ... is possessed, ready to annihilate us" (10). The Catskills landscape is thus portrayed as infectious and dangerous, a space where seemingly weaker individuals, within the xenophobic conceit of such writers as Lovecraft, become transformed and monstrous.

Moreover, the transformative impact of the New World wilderness appears here to enact a process of contagion, where nature converts a human substratum into monstrous configurations not unlike itself. The countless members of the Martense tribe, as they appear to the narrator upon their exit from their underground abode, take the form of an oozing multitude:

> [A] loathsome night-spawned flood of organic corruption more devastatingly hideous than the blackest conjurations of mortal madness and morbidity. Seething, stewing, surging, bubbling like serpents' slime it rolled up and out of that yawning hole, spreading like a septic contagion and streaming from the cellar at every point of egress.
>
> (Lovecraft "Lurking" 371)

This remarkable and primal horde literally embodies Jack Morgan's argument that "horror monstrosities typically carry primarily the threat to pollute and infect, or they epitomize a repugnant and nauseating organicism, a fleshly stupidity" (101). Infected by the landscape, this creeping mass in turn represent this infectious organicity through their sheer fertility, they concentrate in their hybridity the accumulating properties of the human, the animal, and the vegetal, becoming one with their nightmarish landscape as the narrator further conflates them with their surroundings, picturing the whole as:

> [F]orests of monstrous overnourished oaks with serpent roots twisting and sucking unnamable juices from an earth verminous with millions of cannibal devils; mound-like tentacles groping from underground nuclei of polypous perversion ... insane lightning over malignant ivied walls and daemon arcades choked with fungous vegetation.
>
> (372)

This intricate and logorrheic description of the Martense horde thus marks the complete merging of the former with their environment. Beyond the grotesque imagery lies the ultimate notion that the Martenses ironically have achieved a union with the wilderness, populating the land with their spawn and surviving, even thriving within its terrifying limits, engaged in a material conversation between human and other-than human agencies which Opperman and Iovino would term a "hybrid, vibrant, and living world" (3). This ties in with the Bakhtinian notion of the grotesque body as "a body in the act of becoming. It is never finished, never completed; it is continually built, created, and builds and creates another body … the body swallows the world and is itself swallowed by the world" (Bakhtin 317). Indeed, this inundating mass, this over-abundant and overfecund multitude, seems to epitomize the grotesque body as it merges with the natural world, constantly devouring and being devoured by the nightmarish wilderness. According to James Kneale, such prototypical Lovecraftian horrors "represent life, just as Bakhtin's grotesque body represents fertility, change and resistance to closure," all the while being marred and configured as "corrupt and contaminated" forms of grotesque sublimity of the natural world (118).

The narrative further articulates the colonial impulse to dominate the wilderness in an almost parodic reversal of the pastoral imperatives within the North American context of colonization. Indeed, the initial failure of the Martense family to survive in the wilderness is counterbalanced by their success as atavistic cannibals in building their underground habitat. The "curious mounds and hummocks in the weedy, fulgurite-pitted earth" which "reminded [the narrator] of snakes and dead men's skulls swelled to gigantic proportions" turn out indeed to be the many doors to the Martense subterranean estate, its inside ultimately brimming with members of the secluded clan (Lovecraft "Lurking" 350). These "low snake-like mounds" can be seen everywhere around the desolate landscape of Tempest Mountain, even in the heart of the nightmarish forest full of "baleful primal trees of unholy size" and within the anti-pastoral "abandoned Dutch garden whose walks and beds were polluted by a white, fungous, foetid, overnourished vegetation" (359, 362). The narrator, in a flash of terrified lucidity, realizes that these mounds and their network of tunnels, connected to the old manor-house "as if the unwholesome Martense mansion had thrown visible tentacles of terror," are the very passageways of the *lurking fear*, this yet undiscovered manifestation of horrific nature, and are in effect "molehills" that the bestial Martense descendants inhabit (369–370).This final realization draws attention to the ultimate parody and reversal of the colonial impulse as these molehills stand as horrific and distorted mirror-images of the rustic farmsteads, pens and fences normally associated with the early settlers and colonists. The Martenses have indeed colonized and reshaped the landscape around them or, rather, under them, as the tunnels come to represent their own needs and a parodic form of debased civilization. This weird pastoral conceit can also be hinted at in the age-old murder of Jan Martense, his "skull crushed as if by savage blows" by his own "kinsm[e]n" (364) in an episode reminiscent of the murder of Abel by his brother Cain in the Bible and related to the Puritan idea of the wilderness as a "symbolic, 'cursed,' postlapsarian earth" (Hillard 110). "The Lurking Fear" thus reveals itself as an ecophobic and weird reframing of the colonial venture, articulating the wilderness' ultimate victory over the supposedly feeble and inadequate Dutch colonists, transforming them into monstrous parodies of the early settlers, fully fused with the frightening landscape that they finally enclose and fill with molehills and tunnels as grotesque equivalent to villages and farmsteads.

"The Colour Out of Space," on the contrary, articulates the conceptual colonization of a New England farmstead by an extra-terrestrial invader in the form of a curious meteorite. Whereas "The Lurking Fear" explores the impact of monstrous inbreeding upon the land, it is the very land here that becomes infected and, in turn, comes to destroy the Gardner farmstead and its inhabitants. The narrative reifies the extra-terrestrial's agentic mastery over nature and humans alike, where the complete transformation of the pastoral landscape by the fallen meteorite mirrors and surpasses any attempt by humans to subjugate the land. "The Colour Out of Space" clearly evokes pastoral ideals of the careful tilling of the land and rearing of livestock, with its description of the farmstead as the "trim white Nahum Gardner house amidst its fertile gardens and orchards" and Nahum's own toil as he "worked hard at his haying in the ten-acre pasture across Chapman's Brook; his rattling wain wearing deep ruts in the shadowy lain between" (Lovecraft 371, 375). Garrard, drawing on Terry Gifford's definition of the pastoral, outlines the trope as constitutive of narratives that present a dichotomy between the rural and the urban as well as the more "pejorative sense … imply[ing] an idealisation of rural life that obscures the realities of labour and hardship" (33). Lovecraft's short story clearly presents the initial circumstances of the Gardner family as a pastoral narrative, seemingly representing the strong and industrious Gardner family as an example of pastoral idealism. Even the first consequences of the fall of the meteorite seem to correlate with what Garrard explains forms the *idyllic* version of the pastoral trope, which corresponds to the "celebrat[ion] of a bountiful harvest" (Garrard 37), the narrative conforming with what Rebecca Janicker describes as a "kind of rural idyll" (257). Indeed, at first, the vegetables and fruits seemed indicative of a plentiful harvest, as "Nahum vowed that his orchards were prospering as never before. The fruit was growing to phenomenal size and unwonted gloss, and in such abundance that extra barrels were ordered to handle the future crop" (Lovecraft "Colour" 375). Idyllic pastoralism, however, quickly gives way to a Lovecraftian reversal that not only sees the crop fail, as "into the fine flavour of the pears and apples had crept a stealthy bitterness and sickishness, so that even the smallest of bites induced a lasting disgust," but the farm and family destroyed by the unnerving invasion of a natural world, both animal and vegetal, transmogrified by the strange and "cryptic vestige of the fathomless gulfs outside" (375, 374).

On the one hand, "The Colour Out of Space" functions as an anti-pastoral narrative, the exact opposite of the category of narratives that Garrard identifies as "remain[ing] significant for an American ecocriticism

... because it continues to supply the underlying narrative structure in which the protagonist leaves civilisation for an encounter with non-human nature, then returns having experienced epiphany and renewal" (49). There is indeed a confrontation between humanity and non-humanity, yet the point of contact in this case is with that of a natural world increasingly veering into the weird and the monstrous, with strange and uncanny "footprints in the snow" as well as a frightening woodchuck of which "the proportions of [the] body seemed slightly altered in a queer way impossible to describe" (Lovecraft "Colour" 376). The narrator, too, comes to a realization that correlates with Garrard's notion of an epiphany, but it is one of dread and fear at the great unknown, finding himself now privy to the story of the "blasted heath" "unwilling to have the stars come out above [him] in the open," nor would he ever "drink the new city water of Arkham," after the whole area had been flooded and turned into a reservoir (371). The narrative thus offers in the first instance an anti-pastoral account which reverses the typical uplifting narrative of a growing and thriving farmstead, instead presenting an encounter with an unknowable "beyond" which effectively destroys the farmstead and kills its inhabitants. The narrative serves as another example of "New England history of man's aversion to the land," Janicker argues, because it may be understood as "a regional tale directly tapping into old local fears about wild space" in much the same way as "The Lurking Fear" (64).

On the other hand, the anti-pastoral characteristics of "The Colour Out of Space" further exemplify the ecophobic underpinnings that go beyond the simple representation of a threatening wilderness. What Janicker observes as the "old fears of a savage nature repelling the human intruders vividly returning" (65) is indeed just that: a furious comeuppance perpetrated by a nature not so easily tamed and controlled, what Parker underlines in her definitions of ecoGothic and ecohorror as "a clear and immediate sense of nature's *revenge*" (217). Indeed, the subsequent transformation of nature and vegetation within the narrative highlights the monstrous and threatening possibilities of a natural world gone, as it were, *wild*:

> It was the vegetation. All the orchard trees blossomed forth in strange colours, and through the stony soil of the yard and adjacent pasturage there sprang up a bizarre growth which only a botanist could connect with the proper flora of the region. No sane wholesome colours were anywhere to be seen except in the green grass and leafage; but everywhere those hectic and prismatic variants of some diseased, underlying primary tone without a place among the known tints of earth. The Dutchman's breeches became a thing of sinister menace, and the bloodroots grew insolent in their chromatic perversion.
>
> (Lovecraft "Colour" 378)

The newly found strangeness of the plants and of the trees especially, which "swayed also when there was no wind" (377), takes hold of the narrative and exemplifies a vision of nature as the monstrous Other, suddenly unfamiliar and ultimately dangerous. The unnatural fecundity of the land draws attention to our ancient fears, our primal conception of the landscape. Dawn Keetley, in her detailing of what she has termed *Plant Horror*, analyses of the vegetal as monstrous, explains that "[a]t its most basic, plant horror marks humans' dread of the 'wildness' of vegetal nature—its untameability, its pointless excess, its uncontrollable growth. Plants embody an inscrutable silence, an implacable strangeness" (1). It is this last property that most vividly characterizes the farmstead's transformed vegetation. Its weirdness highlights its profound otherness, the implacable possibilities of a natural world suddenly different to our expectations. It is the example of this "absolute alterity" that staggers both characters and readers (Keetley 6). Infected by an otherworldly invader, the unnatural vegetation has become a prism through which we can imagine other worlds and other natures as we remember that the meteorite and its *colour* were "nothing of this earth, but a piece of the great outside; and as such dowered with outside properties and obedient to outside laws" (Lovecraft "Colour" 374). This ultimate otherness of plants, as it is starkly conveyed in the narrative, then results from both a fear of their powerful capacity for growth as well as their strangeness. They have become in "The Colour Out of Space" "thoroughly uncanny … familiar and yet deeply unfamiliar at the same time" (Keetley 7). Lovecraft's short story reveals itself as a vivid example of an ecophobic worldview, an exploration of the potential monstrosity of plants and the natural world, as it is infected—effectively colonized—by an entity which serves as the revealing catalyst of our fraught relationship with nature, so much so that the ultimate recourse is a literal welling up, a flooding of the entire area to better bury this uncanny example of humanity's powerlessness in the face of a natural world gone strange and wild.

In "The Shunned House," however, the relationship between the human and the natural world is deeply associated with ideas of pollution that, unlike "The Colour Out of Space," seem to be caused by supernatural possession rather than by visitors from outer space. The eponymous Shunned House represents a contaminated space, a place made "unhealthy, perhaps because of the dampness and fungous growth in the cellar" (Lovecraft "Shunned" 453), where strange, phosphorescent accumulations of "mould or nitre … amidst the sparse fungous growth" ultimately reveal themselves as products of an ancient evil occupying the house (455). It is from the overgrown fungal nature that the spirit—or vampire, as the narrative inconclusively implies—ultimately surges and possesses the narrator's uncle, as

> [O]ut of the fungus-ridden earth steamed up a vaporous corpse-light, yellow and diseased, which bubbled and lapped to a gigantic height in vague outlines half-human and half- monstrous … It was

> all eyes—wolfish and mocking—and the rugose insect-like head dissolved at the top to a thin stream of mist.
>
> (474–475)

This monstrous entity thus contaminates and inhabits a withering natural space within the urban, polluting the environment around it and correlating with what Allan Lloyd-Smith contends is

> [T]he distinctive theme and deepest insight of American Gothic, the sense that there is something *behind*, which may not be, as in European Gothic, the Past, but some perpetual and present Otherness, hidden with, behind, somehow below the apparently benign "natural" surface.
>
> (86)

In other words, the monstrous here occupies a space within and under the otherwise banal, urban setting.

What is interesting, however, from an ecophobic standpoint, is that the possessing evil here manifests itself through the natural world and impacts it thoroughly, twisting the plants and trees of the house's garden, feeding the growth of unholy fungi which "grotesquely like the vegetation in the yard outside, were truly horrible in their outlines; detestable parodies of toadstools and Indian pipes," as well as driving animals away so that "birds never lingered" in the garden (Lovecraft "Shunned" 455, 454). This links again to anxieties regarding contamination: nature becomes twisted and infected by an old secret, a return of the repressed here epitomized by the ancient spirit which may or may not be linked to the strange Roulets, French colonists who occupied the house centuries before and were associated with strange tales of magic and lycanthropy (469). Morgan further details this threat of contamination as he argues that in "Lovecraft, horror more often than not is connected with the threat of repulsive contact with anomalous, proliferating biological *stuff* that falls short even of thingness, or repulsive organic matter—molds, slime" (101). The fungal and the vegetal, infected by the spiritual, become revolting, a nauseating blight that requires cleansing. Indeed, the narrative concludes with the destruction of the spirit's remains, uncovered under the cellar floor. It is ironically and tellingly through the use of an industrial acid, a man-made compound, that the hold of the spirit on the natural world is finally broken, in what was later mistaken by locals as "the virulent and horrible fumes [which] arose from the factory waste dumped in the Providence River" (Lovecraft "Shunned" 478). The narrative thus once more pits "civilization" against the primordial forces of "nature," the acid ironically standing as a purifying element.

Furthermore, what is rather unlike other Lovecraftian narratives is that the nature is in the end unequivocally cleansed, and the human world victorious, as

> the next spring no more pale grass and strange weeds came up in the shunned house's terraced garden ... the barren old trees in the yard have begun to bear small, sweet apples, and last year the birds nested in their gnarled boughs.
>
> (479)

I suggest this uncharacteristically triumphant outcome is related to the more urban setting of "The Shunned House." The rural environments found in both "The Lurking Fear" and "The Colour Out of Space," being further removed from the epicenters of human civilization, are more susceptible to be overtaken and reclaimed by other-than-human agencies. By contrast, "The Shunned House" takes place in the city of Providence itself, a space perennially claimed and occupied by human agencies. The house itself is a "dingy, antiquated structure," which lies at the confluence of the human and the other-than-human with its "great unkempt yard dating from a time when the region was partly open country," and was "originally a farm or semi-farm building" (451–452). Its liminal position as a vestige of both the past and the pastoral alludes, within an ecophobic framework, to its capacity to be overcome by monstrous other-than-human agencies at the same time as it offers the possibility of its restoration. The Shunned House is thus, in part, the locus of struggle between the natural and the human and is only salvageable, to an extent, because it lies now so centrally within human confines.

In conclusion, all three narratives, read through an ecophobic lens, prove themselves intricate examples of the difficult relationship people cultivate with the natural world around them. In their portrayal of the monstrous potential of the animal and the vegetal, they exemplify through the prism of the weird, on the one hand, typical North American conceptions of the wilderness as a threatening space, where the landscape alters us as much as it is altered by us, prompting in such writers as Lovecraft a fear of devolution and degeneration; and, on the other hand, they epitomize the general fear of nature's ultimate otherness and agency, its strange alterity which we do not anymore recognize in ourselves and contradicts our pastoral desires. In our cultural divorce from the rest of the natural world, we find ourselves afraid of the overfecund qualities of nature, threatened by its blind capacity for growth where we do not wish it. As Garrard pointedly writes, "a 'weed' is not a kind of plant, only the wrong kind in the wrong place" (5–6). Likewise, as Mark Fisher notes of the "sensation of wrongness" at the heart of the weird that "the weird is not wrong, after all: it is our conception that must be inadequate" (15). Thus, what can be gleaned from such narratives through an ecophobic frame of reference is not, ultimately, that the natural world is a truly threatening place, but rather a place that frustrates our expectations and defies our will to subjugate it entirely.

Works Cited

Bakhtin, Mikhail. *Rabelais and his World*. Trans. Helene Iswolsky. Cambridge, MA: Massachusetts Institute of Technology Press, 1968.

Estok, Simon C. "Theorizing in a Space of Ambivalent Openness: Ecocriticism and Ecophobia." *Interdisciplinary Studies in Literature and Environment*, 16, 2, 2009, pp. 203–225.

Fisher, Mark. *The Weird And The Eerie*. London: Repeater, 2017.

Garrard, Greg. *Ecocriticism*. Routledge, 2004.

Iovino, Serenella, and Opperman, Serpil. "Introduction: Stories Come to Matter." *Material Ecocriticism*, edited by Serenella Iovino and Serpil Opperman. Bloomington, IN: Indiana University Press, 2014, pp. 1–17.

Hillard, Tom J. "'Deep Into That Darkness Peering': An Essay on Gothic Nature." *Interdisciplinary Studies in Literature and Environment*, 16, 4, 2009, pp. 685–695.

———. "From Salem Witch to Blair Witch: The Puritan Influence on American Gothic Nature." *Ecogothic*, edited by Andrew Smith and William Hugues. Manchester: Manchester University Press, 2013, pp. 103–119.

Hogle, Jerome E. "Introduction: Modernity and the Proliferation of the Gothic." *The Cambridge Companion to Modern Gothic*, edited by Jerome E. Hogle. Cambridge: Cambridge University Press, 2014, pp. 3–19.

Janicker, Rebecca. "New England Narratives: Space and Place in The Fiction of H.P. Lovecraft." *Extrapolation*, 48, 1, 2006, pp. 54–70.

Keetley, Dawn. "Introduction: Six Theses on Plant Horror; or, Why Are Plants Horrifying?" *Plant Horror: Approaches to the Monstrous Vegetal in Fiction and Film*, edited by Dawn Keetley and Angela Tenga. New York: Palgrave, 2016, pp. 1–30.

Kneale, James. "From Beyond: H.P. Lovecraft and the Place of Horror." *Cultural Geographies*, 13, 2016, pp. 106–126.

Lloyd-Smith, Allan. *American Gothic Fiction: An Introduction*. New York: Continuum, 2004, 65–132.

Lovecraft, Howard P. *Supernatural Horror in Literature*. *Collected Essays Volume 2: Literary Criticism*, edited by S. T. Joshi. New York: Hippocampus Press, 2004, pp. 82–135.

———. "The Colour Out of Space." *H. P. Lovecraft Collected Fiction, A Variorum Edition, Volume 2: 1926–1930*, edited by S. T. Joshi. New York: Hippocampus Press, 2017, pp. 367–399.

———. "The Lurking Fear." *H. P. Lovecraft Collected Fiction, A Variorum Edition, Volume 1: 1905–1925*, edited by S. T. Joshi. New York: Hippocampus Press, 2017, pp. 349–373.

———. "The Shunned House." *H. P. Lovecraft Collected Fiction, A Variorum Edition, Volume 1: 1905–1925*, edited by S. T. Joshi. New York: Hippocampus Press, 2017, pp. 451–479.

Luckhurst, Roger. "The Weird: A Dis/orientation." *Textual Practice*, 31, 6, 2017, pp. 1041–1061.

Morgan, Jack. *The Biology of Horror: Gothic Literature and Film*. Carbondale, IL: Southern Illinois University Press, 2002.

Morton, Timothy. *Dark Ecology*. Columbia: Columbia University Press, 2016.

Murphy, Bernice M. *The Rural Gothic in American Popular Culture: Backwoods Horror and Terror in the Wilderness*. New York: Palgrave, 2013.

Parker, Elizabeth. "'Just a Piece of Wood': Jan Švankmajer's Otesánek and the EcoGothic." *Plant Horror: Approaches to the Monstrous Vegetal in Fiction and Film*, edited by Dawn Keetley and Angela Tenga, New York: Palgrave, 2016, pp. 215–225.

Sederholm, Carl H. and Weinstock, Jeffrey Andrew. (2016). "Introduction: Lovecraft Rising." *The Age of Lovecraft*, edited by Carl E. Sederholm and Jeffrey Andrew Weinstock. Minneapolis, MI: University of Minnesota Press, 2016, pp. 1–42.

Smith, Andrew and William Hughes. "Introduction: Defining the EcoGothic." *Ecogothic*, edited by Andrew Smith and William Hugues, Manchester: Manchester University Press, 2013, pp. 1–14.

Tabas, B. "Dark Places: Ecology, Place, and the Metaphysics of Horror Fiction." *Miranda*, 11, 2015, pp. 1–21.

Ulstein, Gry. "'Age of Lovecraft?'—Anthropocene Monsters in (New) Weird Narrative." *Nordlit*, 42, 2019, pp. 47–65.

12 Nautical Horror and the Anthropocene

Lovecraftian Monsters in William Eubank's *Underwater*

Antonio Alcala Gonzalez

The drastic changes brought to our lives due to the presence of a virus, COVID-19, can prompt reflection on the fragility of our claimed position as rulers of the planet. However, even pre-COVID, parts of the globe resisted human encroachment. Though some technological advances have allowed us to reach corners at the bottom of the ocean in recent decades, we have found them to be dark areas under tons of water where it becomes rather complicated to leave permanent marks of our presence; thus, abyssal depths remain some of the ultimate frontiers for humanity to dominate. On this obscure maritime stage, William Eubank's film, *Underwater* (2020) relies on Lovecraftian aquatic monsters to address concerns about the exploitation of nature in the Anthropocene. Eubank's monsters are inspired by Cthulhu and the Deep Ones, Lovecraft's underwater entities that emerge from oceanic depths to bring impressions of absolute horror. The intention of this chapter is to approach Eubank's film as a Nautical Horror narrative and scrutinize the director's appropriation of Lovecraftian grotesque monsters to foreground humanity as a species with a very limited role not only in maritime depths but on the whole planet as well. The first step I consider necessary in order to analyze the connection between Eubank's film and Lovecraftian aquatic monsters is to focus on the similarities shared by film and literary languages. After that, I will focus on the relationship between the Anthropocene and the Nautical Horror perspective leading to a consideration of Lovecraft's aquatic monsters and their adaptation in Eubank's film.

Films in some respects have a close relation to literature. According to Brian McFarlane, their shared "capacity, via their separate semiotic systems, to evoke place and to move us from one to another with astonishing fluidity, is one that they indubitably share" (23). Although both can be approached as narrative codes, literary fiction does a better job with past tense—in the shape of memories of a narrator; film, in contrast, generally occurs in the present. Even when there is a flashback sequence, the experience lived by audiences is of immediate action. This occurs because literature relies on verb tenses to indicate time, but film relies on resources like camera transitions, sound effects, or voice-overs. Besides,

DOI: 10.4324/9780367713065-13

films follow their own grammar and language that, unlike literature, tend toward an economy that renders space, time, action together to motivate the immediate involvement of the viewer (22). These and other differences imply that the focalization of viewers and readers changes when moving from a literary narrative to a cinematic one. When literary elements are incorporated into cinema, we abandon "the realm of imagination" and instead face "an unrelenting, forward-driving story. We have moved from the imagination to the realm of direct perception—with its mix of both detail and broad focus" (Hutcheon 23). Instead of the call to our imaginative powers from the words on a page and the conceptual reading experience, cinematic resources allow the production of a depth sensation on a two-dimensional surface, which drags the viewer to a perceptual experience where they accompany characters and their stories as they move and develop inside the screen thorough multiple spaces and temporalities. Given these and other differences between film and literature, I will focus on the similarity shared by both codes as narrative discourses. My attention will center on the monster as a crucial element in each narrative considered in this study and will leave aside any reference to the differences between literature and film. In Hutcheon's terms, I propose to consider the connection between Eubank's 2020 film, *Underwater*, and Lovecraft's fiction as an "extended intertextual engagement with the adapted work" (8).[1]

Eubank is inspired by Lovecraft's "Dagon" (1919), "The Call of Cthulhu" (1928), and "The Shadow over Innsmouth" (1936). The monsters appearing in these texts evidence the writer's perspective of humanity as insignificantly microscopic when compared to the universe as a whole:

> Therefore we are able to comprehend that the human race is but a thing of the moment; that its existence on this planet is extremely recent, as infinity is reckoned; and that its possible existence in all the expanse of illimitable space is but a matter of yesterday. Space and time have always existed and always will exist... may not all mankind be a mistake—an abnormal growth—a disease in the system of Nature—an excrescence on the body of infinite progression like a wart on the human hand? Might not the total destruction of humanity, as well as of all animal creation, be a positive *boon* to Nature as a whole? How arrogant of us, creatures of the moment, whose very species is but an experiment of the *Deus Naturae*, to arrogate to ourselves an immortal future and considerable status! How do we know that we have a right to live?
>
> (Lovecraft, *Lord of a Visible World* 53–54)

The attitude from Lovecraft's monsters toward humans constantly confirms that they find us irrelevant. Their existence and corporeality transcend our capacity to understand space and time. Rather than retelling any of these stories or combining them, *Underwater* proposes a human encounter with the monstrous creatures described in such texts in a near twenty-first-century future. Hutcheon proposes that "stories travel to different cultures and different media. In short, stories adapt just as they are adapted" (31). In the case of *Underwater*, what is adapted to our contemporary moment are the monsters created by Lovecraft. They are revisited from an ecocritical perspective that uses their presence to remind us about our trivial position on the Earth, and question humanity's irruption into the dark corners of Nature for extractionist purposes.

In horror narratives, characters who confront monsters experience two related affective moments. First, they undergo the distressing irruption of the monstrous entity. Second comes a more devastating occurrence: they have no choice but to accept that the irrefutable existence of the monster proves that our surroundings contain more than we could possibly know. In *Underwater*, Emily Haversham (Jessica Henwick) illustrates through her experience the occurrence of these two moments in a nautical scenario. The horror she undergoes stems from the immediate threat to survive amidst the hostilities of unknown forces of wilderness located in the abysmal oceanic depths, and the resulting realization that we are neither alone nor in control. The film presents the viewer with a scenario in a close possible future where the Anthropocene has reached the bottom of the ocean in the form of the "World's Deepest Drill" (Eubank 01.32). *Kepler Station* is part of a network of new and abandoned drilling facilities at the bottom of the Mariana Trench at an average depth of nearly seven miles. The station is apparently hit by an earthquake that makes it urgent for survivors to leave the place. A mechanical engineer, Norah Price (Kristen Stewart), leads two other drill workers who manage their way through corridors partially blocked with debris; on their way, they meet with the station captain (Vincent Cassel), who stayed after he helped other survivors escape in pods. They are also joined in a control room by Emily, a biologist, and her boyfriend (John Gallagher Jr.); they confirm to the others that any attempt to contact the surface is impossible. Moreover, they listen to the last transmission from the drill site in which a desperate voice requesting help is suddenly cut off and replaced by a mysterious sound of unknown origin (22.00). At this point, as far as we know, a mere natural event has left an extremely expensive facility useless and out of reach. The survivors' uncertain and helpless condition confirms that even the most advanced human-made construction is prone to collapse when affected by an inescapable natural disaster. No matter what expertise the different crew members possess, when the technology providing the artificial conditions to survive at the bottom of the ocean fails, everyone faces a hopeless condition. We can relate this to our own experiences of tornadoes, hurricanes, earthquakes—and viral pandemics such as COVID-19, whose effects will be felt for years to come.

The first two decades of the twenty-first century show a stronger impact of the Anthropocene on Earth than the one witnessed in the two previous centuries.[2] The mark left by human activity on land, in the air, and under the water is more evident as time advances. Eubank's film scrutinizes possible implications of our manipulation of oceanic resources for our own benefit. *Tian Industries*, the corporation behind the drilling facility in the film, represents the fact that humanity has forgotten to think of itself and all other beings on the planet as what Timothy Morton calls a "mesh" (2010, 39), which extends to all living entities. Inside it, all creatures coexist in a complex network of interlaced shared relationships that emphasize their differences and bring them together. Morton's view is echoed in Donna Haraway's argument on "tentacular thinking" (33) which refers to the interconnectedness of life that rules all organic interactions on our planet. The artificial denial of our belonging to this network led to the end of the Holocene and the beginning of the Anthropocene. Actually, in *Underwater*, Emily alludes to the fact that we have turned the oceans into targets for our attempts to objectify and exploit our surroundings: "I used to love the ocean. It was like a giant petri dish" (Eubank 1-07.46). The result of this transformation is the end of all dialogue between humanity and Nature.

Although Nature is indifferent toward us unless affected by our presence, we behave toward it as if we were facing an opponent with selfish intentions similar to ours:

> *Humans are more powerful; nature is more powerful.* Taken together; there is more power at work on Earth. A power struggle between humankind and Earth is underway, a tug-of-war in which humans strain to drag the Earth into our sphere of influence while Earth attempts to pull us back into its domain.
>
> (Hamilton 40)

We misinterpret Nature's adaptation to the changes caused by our actions as if they were intended reactions and insist on claiming supremacy over anything nonhuman. The intense resulting activity endangers all lifeforms including our own existence. Paradoxically, the apparent control we hold over the planet in the Anthropocene is contested by our inability to react to the changes that result from our drastic transformation of our surroundings (see Hamilton et al. 10). In the film, as the opening credits are presented, the viewer is first shown excerpts from documents that emphasize the dangers to human well-being after long stays in *Tian Industries*' facilities. Besides, some "newly discovered deep sea species" (Eubank 02.36) as well as the dismissal of "Rumors of strange sightings at drill site" (01.52) are mentioned. It is not only that humans are encroaching on the habitat of nonhuman entities never before bothered by our presence but also that our own bodies and minds are put at risk by being forced into long stays of confinement in the abyssal depths. The first shot following the opening credits is a high angle. This emphasizes the sense of sublime depth as the camera quickly descends from an intermediate point in the ocean depths to the sea bottom where the drilling station is located. All the scenes until the last one occur at the oceanic floor either inside the human-made facilities or outside them with the characters wearing atmospheric diving suits for extreme depths. Despite the impressive sight of the station, throughout the film these special suits as well as pods easily prove prone to damage by unexpected natural events. This reinforces the feelings of hopelessness and horror when humans move into scenarios where recent technology becomes essential to guarantee our survival and the presence of monsters tests its reliability.

Part of the essence of horror is being confronted by creatures that annihilate our faculties and shatter all knowledge, perceptions, and convictions. Eugene Thacker's definition of horror reinforces this conceptualization of the term; for him, "horror is the always potential threat of the senses being overwhelmed, of something being sensed that is in excess of the sorting mechanism of the understanding, and the synthetic function of reason" (117–118). The term "ecohorror" has been used to describe the linking of horror with environmental concerns. Christy Tidwell, together with Stephen A. Rust and Carter Soles, has provided explanations of this genre that are helpful here. For Tidwell, ecohorror applies to "narratives in which the central narrative is frequently one of some elements of the natural world attacking humanity" (115). Rust and Soles locate ecohorror in texts "grappling with ecocritical matters" where "environmental disruption is haunting humanity's relationship to the non-human world" (510). These definitions propose ecohorror texts as those in which the damage made by humans to ecology is responsible for an attack on humanity from natural forces.

Building on these ideas, my intention is to discuss *Underwater* as pertaining to a significant subset of ecohorror: Nautical Horror. In it, the striking threat from Nature originates specifically in aquatic contexts, such as oceans and waterways, as well as more liminal spaces, including shores, islands, and ships. It incorporates a sublime maritime background from Nautical Gothic[3] and combines it with a monstrous encounter of horrifying proportions. Margaret Cohen (2013) identifies a persistent view of the sea as sublime from the eighteenth century to the present day: "Shaped by this Enlightenment view, the aesthetic of the sublime would yield the wild ocean, a terrific domain of uncontained nature, which remains the vision of the ocean that springs to mind when we think of this realm today" (116–117). Early resonances of the ocean as a sublime obscurity appear in Samuel Taylor Coleridge's "The Rhyme of the Ancient Mariner" (1798), where the mariner is punished by overwhelming supernatural forces for despising Nature's creatures. Later on, Edgar Allan Poe's *The Narrative of Arthur Gordon Pym* (1838), and "MS. Found in a Bottle"

(1833) become early manifestations of Nautical Horror, in which the immensity of the ocean causes frightening experiences. These texts precede contemporary narratives of Nautical Horror in that they illustrate the struggle for survival against horrifying maritime threats.

While the Nautical Gothic focuses on the relationship between the ocean and its depths with "the unknown, the uncanny, the secret and the secreted" (Packham and Punter 28), Nautical Horror centers on devastating encounters with the monstrous nonhuman to emphasize the arbitrariness behind the conception of human supremacy over the seas. The resulting encounters evidence our inferior position when we are threatened by creatures emerging from the depths and the vastness of the oceanic waters that challenge the ability of human minds to understand size and volume. In Nautical Horror, the attack from the ocean and its creatures against our presence on ships, islands, or the coast is labeled as a violent irruption of horrifying proportions. Nevertheless, we fail to acknowledge that, from the perspective located in the sea and its creatures, it is us, humans, who are the encroachers that have disturbed and polluted the place they inhabit. Nautical Horror narratives remind us about the dangers of our insatiable exploitation of aquatic resources as well as the absurdity behind the feeling of superiority over Nature.

Resonances of sublime oceanic obscurity are essential sources of horror in Lovecraft's "Dagon," "The Call of Cthulhu," and "The Shadow over Innsmouth."[4] These stories illustrate the fear aroused by the presence of menacing monsters from maritime abyssal environments that oppose human will and understanding. The undeniable existence of these creatures forces Lovecraft's protagonists to accept that the universe around them is vaster than the artificial limits we have imposed on it. Through the confrontation with aberrant nautical monsters, the narrators in these three stories unveil hideous knowledge that makes it impossible for them to consider the position of humanity on the planet as safe. To begin with, the anonymous narrator in "Dagon" cannot remove from his mind the hideous memory of the "Vast, Polyphemus-like, and loathsome" sea creature with "gigantic scaly arms, the while it bowed its hideous head and gave vent to certain measured sounds" (Lovecraft *The New Annotated* 8). He fears similar entities who crawl and flounder on the sea's "slimy bed… may rise above the billows to drag down in their reeking talons the remnants of puny, war-exhausted mankind—of a day when the land shall sink, and the dark ocean floor shall ascend amidst universal pandemonium" (8–9). In "The Call of Cthulhu," the narrator, Francis Wayland Thurston, fears a return of Cthulhu that "would teach them [humans] new ways to shout and kill and revel and enjoy themselves, and all the earth would flame with a holocaust of ecstasy and freedom" (142). He knows that the end will sooner or later come for humanity since "What has risen may sink, and what has sunk may rise. Loathsomeness waits and dreams in the deep, and decay spreads over the tottering cities of men" (157). Regarding "The Shadow over Innsmouth," the narrator, Robert Olmstead, recounts Zadock Allen's warning about the technical advance of the Deep Ones:

> They're a-bringin' things up aout o' whar they come from into the taown—ben doin' it fer years, an' slackenin' up lately. Them haouses north o' the river betwixt Water an' Main Streets is full of 'em—them devils *an' what they brung*—an' when they git ready.... I say, *when they git ready...*
>
> (612)

It is a combination of this fear and the repulsive memories of the grotesque bodies of the Innsmouthians that makes him urge the government to act and eradicate the abnormal beings populating Innsmouth.

Just like the three stories by Lovecraft, *Underwater* presents two elements that I suggest are essential for a text of Nautical Horror: first, of course, it must have an aquatic background—in this case, the Mariana Trench—and second, the presence of one or more monstrous creatures that awaken an annihilating fear in the human characters who encounter them. Horror fiction is recurrently based on an encounter of the human and the monstrous in liminal regions:

> Horror narrative involves thresholds—a narrative in which two worlds, settings, environments impinge, where crossing (and the resulting experience of horror) is the basic action. Movement (at least in many explicitly fictional contexts) can be in either direction in these mirror worlds. That is, some spook invades our commonplace reality, or our apparently sane and rational self enters a categorically malign environment.
>
> (Salomon 9)

The doorstep dividing our realm and an alien one is crossed in either or both ways, bringing menaces in the shape of monsters and incoming destruction. In the case of Nautical Horror, those two worlds are the civilized comfort afforded by the stability of the land or on board a vessel versus the unpredictable aquatic surfaces and depths, populated by creatures that can easily move in a watery environment into which humans cannot venture for long without artificial aids. The creature types confronted by the narrators in Lovecraft's stories emerge from the depths of the ocean and its "vast reach of black slime" (Lovecraft *The New Annotated* 5) where they thrive. The Deep Ones seem to live much longer lives than humans in that "Them things never died excep' they was kilt violent" (603). Likewise, Cthulhu "would never rally die" (142). Such entities, with longer life spans than humans, are monstrous only to the human eye: "Monstrosity is in the eye of the beholder. If there is anything monstrous in evolution, it's the uncertainty in the system as any and every point… All organisms are monsters insofar as they are *chimeras*, made from pieces of other creatures" (Morton 2010, 66). Their mere presence confirms that the human race is just another temporary inhabitant rather than master of the planet. In Eubank's film, the creatures threatening the well-being of Emily and her companions are also superior to humans in terms of their ability to move and thrive within the oceanic depths. In all four narratives, the creature that becomes grotesque to the rational human eye is an entity with better chances of survival on Earth than those in the hands of humanity.

The grotesque body, like the ones present in the four narratives referred above, results from a confluence of alien parts that "by combining disparate and even logically incompatible elements, undermines the myth of corporeal unity insistently promoted by Western thought" (Connelly 190). When the monster confronts us with its grotesque corporeality, it denounces the incompleteness of our categorizing systems: "The grotesque insults our need for order, for classification, matching and grouping; it violates a sense of appropriate categories." (Edwards and Graulund 29). Our ideals of order and normality categorize the grotesque body as a monstrous one that points at the limits of the permissible.[5] Through either its body that subverts limits and rejects any possibility of classification, or the actions that parallel such challenges, the presence of the monster celebrates the arbitrariness of limits. However, at the same time, it warns about the dangers that would ensue if similar bodies and actions were allowed outside the page or screen in the world of readers and viewers. The Deep Ones'[6] bodies as well as that of Cthulhu are aberrant combinations of characteristics belonging to many different species combined in the same anatomy; the former are perceived by the human eye as "monsters of abhorrent grotesqueness and malignity - half ichthyic and half batrachian in suggestion" (Lovecraft *The New Annotated* 582). This apparent combination of human traits and others of two different aquatic clades is less disturbing than the overlapping of elements from multiple species in Cthulhu's body; on a humanoid shape, cephalopod, reptile, and even bat-like elements combine: "A pulpy, tentacled head surmounted a grotesque and scaly body with rudimentary wings; but it was the general outline of the whole which made it most shockingly frightful" (127). Even before realizing the threat that Cthulhu represents for humankind, this grotesque combination is identified as abnormal by Thurston from the very first moment he sees it.

In "Dagon" and "The Call of Cthulhu," the creatures' bodies are not the only monstrously grotesque elements in the stories. The narrator from the first one is telling his narrative "under an appreciable mental strain" (Lovecraft *The New Annotated* 3). He "cannot bear the [mental] torture" (3) which has possessed him from the time he witnessed a living representative of the carvings on stone: "Grotesque beyond the imagination of a Poe or Bulwer, they were damnably human in general outline despite webbed hands and feet, shockingly wide and flabby lips, glassy, bulging eyes and other features less pleasant to recall" (7). Concerning Thurston, he collects different accounts connected with versions of the sculpture that depicts Cthulhu's body; all of them are linked to the presence of humans who behave aberrantly according to the standards of Western civilization. The Cthulhu worshipers in Greenland are described as "degenerate" followers of a religion that chilled "with its deliberate bloodthirstiness and repulsiveness" (136). Those in the dark swamps of Louisiana prove to be of a "mentally aberrant type" (140). Moreover, the crew of Cthulhu followers encountered on the Pacific by Johansen and the rest of his companions on the *Emma* show such a "peculiarly abominable quality about them which made their destruction seem almost a duty" (152). Similarly, in his first encounter with an Innsmouthian, Robert Olmstead experiences "a wave of spontaneous aversion" (584) after facing a being whose "oddities certainly did not look Asiatic, Polynesian, Levantine or negroid" (585). He later learns that the grotesque combination of humanoid, reptile, and frog characteristics in the bodies of Innsmouthians are the result of miscegenation between humans and the Deep Ones, "fish-like frogs or froglike fishes" (602) that populate the bottom of the ocean. In *Underwater*, there are no indications of pollution from the aquatic creatures affecting humanity; however, the contact between both groups has occurred for such a short time that some uncertainty remains about this possibility. In the end, these Lovecraftian monsters possess humanoid bodies just like the ones they have been adapted from and who were able to contaminate both human bodies and minds in Innsmouth and beyond.

In an interview available at the *Mr H Reviews* YouTube channel, Eubank confirms that the huge creature appearing in the final minutes of the film is inspired by Cthulhu and that the beings emerging from its body are inspired by Lovecraft as well. These latter anthropomorphic-aquatic creatures chase Emily and the other survivors throughout their attempts to escape. The similarities between them and the amphibians described in "Dagon" and "The Shadow over Innsmouth" are loose but obvious enough for a reader familiar with Lovecraft;[7] Eubank strikes his audience with hybrid beings of humanoid appearance but who also have traces of frogs and fish that resemble the "saraband" witnessed by Robert Olmstead at the end of his narrative.

> I think their predominant colour was a greyish-green, though they had white bellies. They were mostly shiny and slippery, but the ridges of their backs were scaly. Their forms vaguely suggested the anthropoid, while their heads were the heads of fish, with prodigious bulging eyes that never closed. At the sides of their necks were palpitating gills, and their long paws were webbed. They hopped irregularly,

> sometimes on two legs and sometimes on four. I was somehow glad that they had no more than four limbs. Their croaking, baying voices, clearly used for articulate speech, held all the dark shades of expression which their staring faces lacked.
>
> (Lovecraft *The New Annotated* 634)

As it occurs to Olmstead when he is chased by such monstrous hybrid beings during his escape from Innsmouth, Emily and the others are struck not only by the transgression of boundaries evidenced in the bodies of similar monsters but also by their relentless violence. It is also their attack on human presence what scares the group of survivors who find it extremely difficult to defend themselves. As for the giant Cthulhian leader, whose size challenges the magnitude of the drilling facilities, it seems to coordinate the whole attack on the human intruders in the abyss, just as in "The Shadow over Innsmouth" where Cthulhu's leadership is alluded to when the narrator foretells that the Deep Ones will "rise again for the tribute Great Cthulhu craved" (641).

Like the ocean where the Deep Ones inhabit, Cthulhu by itself fits into the category of *hyperobjects*[8] coined by Morton:

> By understanding hyperobjects, human thinking has summoned Cthulhu-like entities into social, psychic, and philosophical space. The contemporary philosophical obsession with the monstrous provides a refreshing exit from human-scale thoughts. It is extremely healthy to know not only that there are monstrous beings, but that there are beings that are not purely thinkable, whose being is not directly correlated with whatever.
>
> (2013, 64)

Hyperobjects emphasize the limitations of the human intellect to comprehend the immenseness, in terms of both space and time, that surrounds the ephemeral existence of humanity. When the structure produced by our technological advance can easily be destroyed by an incontrollable reaction from Nature to its presence, both the vastness of the ocean and the mammoth size of this Lovecraftian creature remind the viewer of the impotence of humanity to understand and therefore readapt to Nature. In addition, our insistence for resources has produced a hyperobject of our own creation in the shape of a gigantic network of consequences that falls beyond our comprehension. As part of a permanent circle created to satisfy our industrial needs, the technology that made possible the creation of the impressive drill stations in the film is also the one that demands the resources extracted there.

The intertextual engagement with Lovecraft's creatures in *Underwater* is not only visual but also auditory. The monsters prove to be the source of the mysterious sounds heard at the beginning of the film in the last transmission before the drill site collapsed. This resembles the fact that those apparently contacted by Cthulhu in their dreams mention: "a voice that was not a voice; a chaotic sensation which only fancy could transmute into sound, but which he attempted to render by the almost unpronounceable jumble of letters, "Cthulhu fhtagn" (Lovecraft *The New Annotated* 128). Regarding Olmstead, he refers to the voices of those trying to intrude into his hotel room as follows: "I felt less sure that the deeper sounds were voices, since the apparent hoarse barkings and loose-syllabled croakings bore so little resemblance to recognized human speech" (618). Both frightening sounds and images combine in Lovecraft's stories to reinforce the idea that his protagonists are facing horrors that challenge their understanding; the same combination is also used by Eubank to gradually increase the uncertainty and despair that surround his protagonists in their attempts to survive the horrors from the abyss.

In the three stories by Lovecraft, it is the unrestrainable curiosity of his narrators that leads them into discovering the existence of the grotesque monsters that challenge the idea of human supremacy on the planet. The castaway in "Dagon" examines the monolith emerged from oceanic depths with some "archaeologist's delight" (Lovecraft *The New Annotated* 7); Thurston cannot resist opening his uncle's "exceedingly puzzling" box, which he manages to unlock though the use of reason by associating the lock with the "the personal ring" (125) his uncle always carried in his pocket. As for Olmstead, his "antiquarian and genealogical" tour around New England is diverted to a mysterious town after he hears the dark rumors about "shadowed Innsmouth" (575). Likewise, scientific curiosity is responsible for having provided the technology that allowed the construction of the drilling station in *Underwater*. It combines with the human greed for mineral extraction to produce the activity that provokes a violent response from hideous creatures in the film. The demand for resources is so strong that even after the collapse of the station, some of the clips from newspapers and internal reports that accompany the closing credits mention: "clean-up and rebuilding to commence ASAP… *Tian Industries* to resume drilling" (Eubank 1.30.20). This suggests the human colonization of the threatening oceanic depth will remain as well as its dangerous consequences. Similarly, from the very moment we turned to rivers and seas to satisfy our excessive need for natural resources, our presence on and under the water has permanently left marks of erosion and pollutants that have become much more evident in the last two centuries. In fact, the human tendency to leave marks of its presence all around is illustrated in the film when the group of survivors finds traces of human trash floating in a flooded tunnel (46.33).

Throughout the story, Emily experiences a gradual understanding of the fact that the damage suffered by the station and its crew is not an earthquake, but the attack from creatures of the depths that reacted to humanity's irruption in their habitat. In "The Call of Cthulhu," the academic mind of the narrator is the one realizing that the advance of sciences "will open up such terrifying vistas of reality, and our frightful position therein that we shall either go mad from the revelation or flee from the deadly light into the peace and safety of a new dark age" (Lovecraft *The New Annotated* 124). Similarly, it is Emily, the biologist, who realizes the disaster in *Kepler Station* is the result of the abuse of technology used to take the human greed for minerals to a dangerous stage. She contemplates a mural evoking the interaction between merfolk and humans, right before the team starts their escape route (Eubank 23.24). This moment marks the beginning of her progressive comprehension of the fact that oceanic waters have always been an alien realm belonging to nonhumans. Some minutes later, after one of the survivors died due to a technical failure and another has just been killed by the unstoppable force of an aquatic creature, she claims:

> We did this.
> We drilled the bottom of the ocean.
> We took too much, and now she's taking back.
> We're not supposed to be down here.
> (53.00)

I propose to understand the "she" Emily refers to as Nature—the whole set of nonhuman forces we have insisted on considering as separate from us for many centuries. She has comprehended that there are no unexplainable attacks from the creatures. There are no records of previous encounters with them before the establishment of *Tian Industries'* facilities on the oceanic floor. Their recent and continuous violence against humans and their installations is their mere response to the irruption into their own habitat. Moreover, it is only from a human perspective that their bodies are monstrous. Cthulhu's tentacular head reminds us we are part of the network formed by the multiple connections among lifeforms, each of them, having its own perspective and understanding of life. From the creature's standing position at the depths of the oceanic trench, *Tian Industries'* employees are the intruders who have altered the sea bottom. In the end, *Underwater* is a Nautical Horror film that engages with aquatic monsters adapted from the Lovecraftian ones in order to shatter our assumptions of human dominion over oceanic waters. The presence of these creatures in the film extends the view of humanity as insignificant left by Lovecraft in his stories. When encountered by Emily and her companions, Eubank's monsters undermine our faith in technology as the way to grant our claimed supremacy on the planet. Having analyzed the devastating portrayal of humanity's extractionism of Nature in Eubank's film, this chapter is intended to encourage others to explore similar manifestations of Nautical Horror experiences that can be scrutinized as reflections upon the consequences and dangers of our Anthropocenic attempts to appropriate the Earth for our exclusive purposes and benefit, especially in times like the present when a mere virus has proven we are not in absolute control, not even on the mainland.

Notes

1 In films that receive elements from preceding literature, the literary text becomes "only one element of the film's intertextuality, an element of varying importance to viewers depending on how well or little they know or care about the precursor text" (McFarlane 26–27). For this reason, film adaptations are independent works no matter how many or few elements they incorporate into the cinematic product.
2 The Anthropocene is the name that thinkers from different areas have used in recent decades to refer to the fact that, at least form the Industrial Revolution, the mark left on the planet surface by human activity shows permanent effects of environmental consequences. Timothy Morton describes it as "a geological period in which human-made stuff has created a layer in Earth's crust: all kinds of plastics, concretes, and nucleotides, for example, have formed a discrete and obvious stratum" (2018, 5). Like others. Morton identifies the existence, since 1945, of a "*Great Acceleration* of the Anthropocene, marked by a huge data spike in the graph of human involvement in Earth systems" (*Dark Ecology* 8).
3 Emily Alder identifies an early use of the term "Nautical Gothic" in 1986 when "Dennis Berthold used the term to distinguish between the fantastic and the realistic in sea writing" (1).
4 All references to the three stories by Lovecraft considered in this text correspond to *The New Annotated H. P. Lovecraft*, edited by Leslie S. Klinger.
5 David Punter and Glennis Byron identify the root of the term "monster" as "something that serves to demonstrate (Latin, *monstrare*: to demonstrate) and to warn (Latin, *monere*: to warn)" (Punter and Byron 263).
6 Because of the similarity in their description as humanoid creatures with traces of batrachian and fish, and despite their difference in size, I propose to consider the gigantic creature that appears in "Dagon" as a taller member of the ones that threaten the narrator in "The Shadow over Innsmouth." In the final lines of his story, he confirms their name is the Deep Ones.
7 In an interview with John Squires, released on the site *bloody-disgusting.com*, William Eubank indicates that the creature design for *Underwater* changed during the two years of the post-production stage. Neither the humanoid smaller creatures that chase Emily and her companions, nor the huge Cthulhian one that appears at the end are properly named in the film as connected to Cthulhu. The intention, claims Eubank, was to make the audience find the connection by themselves.
8 Morton defines *hyperobjects* as "things that are massively distributed in time and space relative to humans" (1). They challenge our understanding of time and space. As an example, both the Deep Ones and Cthulhu live almost eternal lives since their bodies are not subject to natural deaths. Such life spans challenge human perspective since we are used to considering biological lives as finite. Besides, Cthulhu's body, as well as the immensity of the oceanic depths where the Deep Ones live, challenge the measures and spaces we are familiar with on mainland.

Works Cited

Alder, Emily. "Through Oceans Darkly: Sea Literature and the Nautical Gothic." *Gothic Studies*. 19 (2), 2017, pp. 1–15.

Cohen, M. *The Novel and the Sea*. Princeton, NJ: Princeton University Press, 2013.

Connelly, Frances S. *The Grotesque in Western Art and Culture: The Image at Play*. Cambridge: Cambridge University Press, 2014.

Edwards, Justin D. and Rune Graulund. *Grotesque*. New York: Routledge, 2013.
Hamilton, Clive. *Defiant Earth: The Faith of Humans in the Anthropocene*. Crows Nest, New South Wales: Allen & Unwin, 2017.
Hamilton, Clive, Bonneuil, Christophe, and Gemenne, François. "Thinking the Anthropocene." *The Anthropocene and the Global Environmental Crisis: Rethinking Modernity in a New Epoch*, edited by Clive Hamilton, Christophe Bonneuil, and Francoise Gemenne. Routledge, 2015, pp. 1–14.
Haraway, Donna J. *Staying with the Trouble: Making Kin in the Cthulucene*. Durham, NC: Duke University Press, 2016.
Hutcheon, Linda. *A Theory of Adaptation*. New York: Routledge, 2006.
Lovecraft, H. P. *Lord of a Visible World: An Autobiography in Letters*, edited by S.T. Joshi and David E. Schultz. Athens, OH: Ohio University Press, 2000.
———. *The New Annotated H. P. Lovecraft*, edited by Leslie S. Klinger. New York: W.W. Norton & Company, 2014.
McFarlane, Brian. "Reading Film and Literature." *The Cambridge Companion to Literature on Screen*, edited by Deborah Cartmell and Imelda Whelehan. Cambridge: Cambridge University Press, 2007, pp. 15–29.
Morton, Timothy. *Being Ecological*. Cambridge, MA: MIT Press, 2018.
———. *Dark Ecology*. Columbia: Columbia University Press, 2016.
———. *The Ecological Thought*. Cambridge, MA: Harvard University Press, 2010.
———. *Hyperobjects: Philosophy and Ecology After the End of the World*. Minneapolis, MI: University of Minnesota Press, 2013.
Packham, Jimmy and David Punter. "Oceanic Studies and the Gothic Deep." *Gothic Studies*. 19 (2), 2017, pp. 17–29.
Punter, David and Glennis Byron. *The Gothic*. Hoboken, NJ: Blackwell Publishing, 2004.
Rust, Stephen A. and Carter Soles. "Ecohorror Special Cluster: Living in Fear, Living in Dread, Pretty Soon We'll All Be Dead." *Interdisciplinary Studies in Literature and Environment*. 21(3), 2014, pp. 509–512.
Salomon, Roger B. *Mazes of the Serpent: An Anatomy of Horror Narrative*. Cornell: Cornell University Press, 2002.
Squires, John. "*Underwater* Director Shares Creature Concept Art and Talks about how He Gotthat Monster in the Movie." Accessed April 15, 2020. https://bloody-disgusting.com/interviews/3613015/underwater-director-shares-creature-concept-art-talks-got-monster-movie-exclusive/. Accessed July 19 2021.
Thacker, Eugene. *Tentacles Longer than Night: Horror of Philosophy Vol. 3*. Winchester: Zero Books, 2014.
Tidwell, Christy "Ecohorror." *Posthuman Glossary*, edited by Rosi Braidotti, and Maria Hlavajova. New York: Bloomsbury, 2018, pp. 115–117.

Film and Video

Eubank, William. *Underwater*. 20th Century Fox, 2020.
Mr H Reviews. "Underwater-Interview with Director William Eubank." YouTube, uploaded by Mr. H, 16 Jan. 2020, https://www.youtube.com/c/MrHReviews/search?query=underwater. Accessed July 19, 2021.

13 Racial (In)Visibility, Cosmic Indifference

Reimagining H.P. Lovecraft's Legacy in Victor LaValle's *The Ballad of Black Tom* (2016)

Kathleen Hudson

Any critical or cultural conversation on reading H.P. Lovecraft in the twenty-first century must at some point address his pervasive racist ideologies, for they are foundational to his construction of a "weird" universe and noteworthy in our contemporary reevaluations of his work. His impact on Weird Fiction – a speculative mode which examines the "impotence and insignificance of human beings" in a universe shaped by "malign powers and forces that greatly exceed the human capacities to understand or control them" – cannot be overstated, as his works explore the feelings of dread that arise when one faces an unknowable, indifferent universe (Weinstock 183). The rise of "New Weird" fiction and the recent commercial success of Lovecraftian adaptations, reproductions, and material offerings signal a wider acceptance of Lovecraft which sometimes results in the erasure or severe editing of the more racist aspects of his individual texts. And yet, even as contemporary author Victor LaValle identifies him as "one of the four foundational writers probably of my youth" (NPR), his own Lovecraftian novella, *The Ballad of Black Tom* (2016), begins with an unusual dedication: the work is "For H. P. Lovecraft, with all my conflicted feelings" (5).

Since *Ballad* is in direct conversation with one of Lovecraft's most overtly racist short stories, "The Horror at Red Hook" (1925), this attitude is not wholly unexpected, and LaValle is certainly not alone in his ambiguous feelings. It is true that Lovecraft has undoubtedly shaped horror and Weird Fiction up to the present day and that his work is imaginative and terror-inducing in ways that sometimes overshadow evidence of his personal beliefs. However, "Monstrous embodiment" for Lovecraft, as Jay McRoy argues, is either an "unspeakable… challenge to the 'humanocentric' philosophies," as evidenced in descriptions of the famous Cthulhu and other eldritch creatures, or manifests problematically as "a swarming, undisciplined, racially diverse social body" (335). While "The Horror at Red Hook" is a transitional piece in Lovecraft's oeuvre written before his better-known Cthulhu Mythos stories were published, one could argue that his entire creative universe is anchored, as Anthony Camara suggests, in the "belief that individuals are enslaved

DOI: 10.4324/9780367713065-14

to their biological constitutions" and are therefore complicit in the degeneration of humanity (27). Throughout his work, he thus firmly links the rise of the destructive monsters with the transgressive actions of the racial "other."

In spite of this ideology clearly underpinning the mythos, numerous cultural interpretations, including toys, games, films, TV shows, graphic novels, etc., tend to gloss over problematic aspects of Lovecraft in order to increase marketability. One might consider such examples as the TV show *South Park*'s incorporation of the mythos in some episodes, the unauthorized musical parodies of Lovecraft's work available online, or the numerous variations of toy elder gods and Lovecraft-themed video games marketed to children and teenagers. While it is hardly necessary or practical to attach warning labels to collectable Cthulhu figurines, a strategic erasure of Lovecraft's racist elements in adaptations, like selective ignorance of the broader impact of racism in contemporary society, is increasingly critically and morally untenable, stymying deeper, and more complex readings of significant texts. If anything, the retroactive editing of racism in interpretations of Lovecraft's work suggests the viewpoint of those who claim that they do not "see race," and who therein exacerbate instances of racial bias and social injustice by denying the discourses that illuminate them. It is moreover inescapably evident that contemporary American race relations are at least partially defined by a fundamentally "weird" disparity within mainstream narratives, echoing the dialectics of Weird Fiction in that processes that "make society legible/visible" hinge on what Charles Mills identifies as a racially informed "agreement to misinterpret the world" and therein undermine concepts of the "known," "unknown," and "unknowable" universe (Jungkunz and White 441, Mills 18). Nowhere is this more evident than in the development of racial performativity as it pertains to the disproportional use of deadly force employed by law enforcement officials against minority communities, an issue that serves as the topical focus of LaValle's *The Ballad of Black Tom*. This violence is symptomatic of institutional racism within law enforcement and related systems, and moreover openly challenges the "officially sanctioned realities" articulated through a social narrative which wrongfully categorizes this use of force as just, necessary, and acceptable (Jungkunz and White 442).

The resulting contradiction has grown significantly more apparent in recent social and political discourse. Evidence contesting the narratives set forth in police reports is now easily accessible, thanks to the increased availability of amateur video recording technology, and the emerging uncertainties complicate the dialogues which shape perceptions of race and criminality. While some officials vowed police reform in the wake of widespread national protests and particularly the Ferguson Uprising in 2014, since 2015 police officers across America have shot and killed 5,400 people, roughly 1,000 per year, and many more have been killed or injured due to the use of excessive physical force (Berman). Some such deaths have been recorded on camera, and the frequent discrepancies between police reports and video evidence have further eroded public confidence in the justice system and suggest a "post-truth" conceptualization of reality in which formerly objective facts are made secondary to subjective interpretations. In just one of many examples, on March 13th, 2020, a 26-year-old African American emergency medical technician named Breonna Taylor was shot and killed in her home while plainclothes police officers executed a "no-knock" search warrant. On June 11th, 2020, the breakdown of empirical reality was confirmed when Louisville authorities released the incident report on Taylor's death, a four-page document that was nearly blank and directly contradicted eyewitness accounts and material evidence. Indicative of a widespread practice in which minority narratives are erased in favor of those which both validate and are validated by white authority, such official accounts impose readings of criminality on black bodies while negating law enforcement's responsibility to the community. They moreover suggest an empirical violation, a "weirded" reality in which what is seen and understood is not accepted as "known" or even "knowable." Indeed, officials were forced to release this scant report to the public primarily due to national attention garnered by the brutal killing of George Floyd in May 2020; more often than not such incidents are followed by crippling delays and systemic coverups rather than swift public exposure, creating a narrative of absence and silence as well as one of violence.

Lovecraft's work ostensibly clashes with the aforementioned issues regarding race as many of his texts could be read as ringing endorsements of the now widely condemned practice of racial profiling in policing. However, authors such as LaValle posit that the most efficient way to approach Lovecraft creatively is rather by exploring the ways in which "writing within the mythos itself can be deployed as a subversive strategy of rewriting that addresses Lovecraft's racism" (Camara 24). Indeed, Lovecraft's stories are particularly important to modern engagements with "post-truth" politics since within Weird Fiction identities "cannot be reductively interpreted, translated, or returned" (Luckhurst 1052). Lovecraft and LaValle's works position this complex negotiation of identity within racist structures which both encompass and undermine attempts to impose material legibility on individual bodies, and which within that contradiction ultimately push those bodies into the realm of the "abhuman" and the "abcanny." Distinct from the uncanny, which suggests the return of the familiar and repressed, the abcanny eschews history and "simply disintegrates" the known universe into one "evasive of meaning" and "othered" beyond understanding (Witzel 564). Applied to these texts, the term suggests that attempts to ascribe behaviors based on race destabilize the sanctity of the "human" by erasing individuality and instead facilitate the development of undefinable alternative identities in response. Even as

Lovecraft insists on racist readings that equate minority bodies with criminality and position them as monstrous, the recurring specters of unreadable texts and the symbiotic relationship between minority groups and cosmic forces beyond human understanding subvert authoritative interpretations. Faced with what Rosemary Jackson identifies as "the impossibility of naming the unnamable presence" only evident as "absence and shadow" (39), Lovecraft depicts racialized bodies whose hybridity and the resulting "disorienting sense of unease" inspired by the mutability of the "conventional boundaries of the human body" suggest a surprisingly potent abcanny resistance to prescribed and policed identity (Hughes 90).

LaValle explores this ambiguity further in *The Ballad of Black Tom* by demonstrating that reductive, racist interpretations of identity negate the individuality of the "human" in favor of an artificial performance and facilitate the creation of the abhuman, the "nominally human bodies whose existence can no longer be satisfactorily explained or contained by conventional definitions of that species" (Hughes 15). The intervention of the "weird" occurs in both Lovecraft and LaValle's work through challenges to bodily legibility and in recurring textual indeterminacy, and LaValle reveals contemporary racial engagements to furthermore be a form of man-made horror, the widespread acceptance of a "post-truth" misinterpretation of identity which ostensibly supports a racist status quo while delegitimizing and violating individual human selfhood. The resulting "weirding" of reality and subversion of the "human" in favor of the abnormal, powerful, and undefinable "other" reframes race as a subjective and ultimately unsustainable social performance, an exchange between dominant and subjugated groups which both horrifically erases human identity and reframes the rise of the "abhuman" as a potentially constructive, if troubling, response. Since racial identity and racism are significantly informed by national and social histories, this transition from human to abhuman therein suggests that identity is effectively beyond history and the limitations of racial coding, and indeed that it is something that evolves rather than devolves as Lovecraft feared. Such arguments are both groundbreaking and critical to our current socio-political moment, and through these texts we not only gain further insight into Lovecraft's significance in a contemporary landscape but also the potential future of Lovecraftian writing in creative adaptations, such as LaValle's.

Brooks E. Hefner notes Lovecraft's preoccupation "with criminal bodies marked by racialized degeneracy," identifying a "cultural phenomenon" in early Weird Fiction "in which bodies are seen as legible texts where corporeal difference and criminal degeneracy go hand in hand" (653, 654). Lovecraft's "The Horror at Red Hook," set in New York City in the 1920s is certainly an example of this, and like many of his other texts it is constructed through the ongoing interpretation and recontextualization of subjective and incomplete narratives within broader discourses on legibility. Lovecraft echoes Edgar Allan Poe's "The Man of the Crowd" (1840), another tale about the practice and impossibility of successfully "reading" others, in stating that his story "does not permit itself to be read" due to the gaps therein, suggesting a consistent textual indeterminacy as well as the looming threat of cosmic indifference and "unknowability" that permeated his mythos (Lovecraft "Red Hook" 483). However, for Lovecraft "criminality and evil is immanently legible" in racialized bodies, conforming to John Fiske's definition of racism as "the paradigmatic instance of abnormalization by visible and thus surveillable category" (Hefner 660, Fiske 84). Red Hook and its inhabitants are described in the most xenophobic terms as "a babel of sound and filth," and "a hopeless tangle and enigma" of human trafficking and illegal immigration (Lovecraft "Red Hook" 484). By contrast, the protagonist-reader charged with negotiating the legible and illegible universe is Thomas F. Malone, a "normal-featured" New York police detective and an ideal combination of "logician" and mystical "Celt" (481, 482). His amateur obsession with the occult and the "thrill" he feels when faced with "imputations of evil," characteristics which suggest the problematic moral corruption of even this idealized figure, are challenged when the diverse neighborhood he polices joins forces with a figure of degenerative white masculinity, Robert Suydam, to undertake a series of kidnappings and murders cumulating in a black mass ritual which exposes an interdimensional void (483). Malone views the "lowly cults" of Red Hook with "an anthropologist's shudder," emerging as a voyeuristic tourist as he studies local graffiti promising destruction at the hands of mysterious forces (483, 485). While both people and texts in Red Hook have academic and entertainment value for him – they are not individualized entities but rather form "a phantasmagoria of macabre shadow-studies" – he also sees "some monstrous thread of secret continuity" therein, presupposing the ultimate legibility of material bodies and their adherence to a narrative performance (483, 485).

In spite of this dubious legibility, which pointedly suggests the Lombrosian theories of physiognomy which underscore contemporary instances of racial profiling, the population of Red Hook and the signs and texts they produce resist productive readings that might curtail criminal behavior. This phenomenon is a profound threat to the status quo, as Vincent Jungkunz and Julie White argue that "the making and maintenance of white privilege… requires that subjects be made legible, that is visible, as racialized subjects" (436). Far from effectively enforcing their authority and privilege in Red Hook and despite keeping records with "conscientious technical care," local "policemen despaired of order and reform" and the successful imposition of laws and regulations upon legible social bodies (Lovecraft "Red Hook" 485, 484). Instead, authorities "seek rather to erect barriers protecting the outside world from contagion," choosing segregation in order to maintain the homogeneity of white neighborhoods (484). Minority and immigrant communities in this instance occupy a liminal space between the subhuman (according to Malone) and abhuman; the individuality and humanity of the subjects are erased by those who police identity, transforming an entire subsection of people into a kind of force of nature which can only be contained, not understood. Ironically, however, attempts to reduce members of this population to the status of subhuman accidentally result in their partial empowerment in that their persistent illegibility and the moniker of "otherness" bestowed upon them puts them beyond the reach of social control. Malone, exceptional in his willingness to transgress the boundaries of acceptable knowledge, attempts to interpret a "fiendish, cryptical, and ancient pattern" present in the events, people, and signs seen during his "unostentatious rambles, casual conversations...and judicious dialogues with frightened prisoners" (485, 489). The kidnappings and murders are described as significant yet the motives behind them are elusive for much of the story, and no clear links are explicitly identified by Malone until it is too late. Wedded to the concept of racial profiling, authorities fail to fully appreciate the abcanny nature of the situation and the mysterious cult continues to operate relatively unhindered, rendering the policing of racialized identity ineffectual.

Moreover, the cultists resist comprehensive surveillance, undercutting the "criminalized visibility... necessary to constructions of superiority and inferiority" and meant to "stabilize racist practices and institutions" (Jungkunz and White 441). Police arrive at crime scenes to find them empty except for "paintings and rough inscriptions" of "the most terrible daemon-evocations" celebrating "Gorgo, Mormo, thousand-faced moon," written in complicated alphabets that suggest a linguistic as well as racial hybridity (Lovecraft "Red Hook" 493, 494). Suydam marries a young woman only for both of them to be killed in mysterious circumstances with the "fearsome Chaldee letters of the word 'LILITH'" written in blood in their honeymoon suite (495). Moreover, police are unable to prevent a contingent from Red Hook from taking possession – literally and figuratively – of Suydam's soon-to-be-resurrected corpse in an explicit display of ownership of a white body. Lovecraft's racial coding is painfully evident throughout this text, yet even in this reading the cult's intentions and actions remain essentially invisible to the police, suggesting the abcanny unknown. Faced with dialects "obscure and puzzling to exact philology," as well as incidents increasingly sinister in nature, Malone is tasked with translating a fundamentally illegible body – the narrative body of events, the textual body of rumors and graffiti, and the racial body of Red Hook's population – but only manages to roughly equate racial otherness with criminal intent (490).

Author and theorist China Miéville states that Weird Fiction's "monsters of the abcanny are teratological expressions of that unrepresentable and unknowable, the evasive of meaning" (381). This suggests a tension in Lovecraft's work in that his racist assumptions clash with his depictions of the undefinable and essentially link racialized, and thus "readable," criminality with cosmic otherworldliness, therein denying the social histories that inform racial identity and instead framing black bodies as abhuman and resistant to policing. The climax of the story – the resurrection ceremony of the "gangrenous corpse of a corpulent" Suydam, which takes place as the police raid a number of Red Hook tenement buildings – exposes this marriage of racist legibility and cosmic illegibility (500). During the black mass, which Malone witnesses, "strange dark men" and a "nightmare horde" open a "bottomless pit" comprised of "shapeless elemental things" and "limitless night" (500, 498, 499). A Lovecraftian depiction of the sweeping cosmic unknown includes, too, an echo of his earlier description of Red Hook, as the pit contains the "root of a contagion destined to sicken and swallow cities, and engulf nations in the foeter [sic] of hybrid pestilence," suggesting that a racially informed "cosmic sin" is destined "to rot us all to fungus abnormalities" (499). The process of devolution Lovecraft claimed was rife in urban landscapes reduces the morally corrupted Suydam to a state of "jellyfish dissolution" lost in a kind of primordial ooze, and, in an ironic twist, the racial legibility Lovecraft embraced is essentially subsumed within a broader erasure of human individualism (502).

Moreover, while the black mass and police raid end with the temporary destruction of the cult, the loss of significant material evidence and the lack of any comprehensive explanation for the events depicted suggest lingering illegible narratives outside of socially acceptable readings. Though he survives, Malone is ostracized and silenced by doctors who dismiss his recollection of events as fantasy and by fellow policemen who force him to leave future detective work to those with "a sadly limited perspective in their lack of wonder" (504). Most critically, the horror in Red Hook remains undefeated: in the final scene, set after the ill-fated raid, a police officer witnesses "a swarthy squinting hag" teaching a small child in "whispered patois" the invocation of "Gorgo, Mormo, thousand-faced moon" (505). The cult not only still exists but also continues to transmit its "unreadable" language while avoiding police interference, and characters of color remain unnamed, unknowable, and abhuman enemies of the ineffectual white authority.

LaValle's work enters into conversation with Lovecraft by similarly complicating the legibility of racial identity and examining the performativity necessary to its social maintenance. *The Ballad of Black Tom* reimagines the events of Lovecraft's original text and prioritizes the perspective of a young black man, the very subject upon whom Lovecraft applies many of his racist readings. Using the same general setting and also incorporating elements from Lovecraft's "The Call of Cthulhu" (1928) and "He" (1926), the novella is broken into two sections and the overlapping, doubled stories of two Thomas's: Charles Thomas "Tommy" Tester, the protagonist, and Thomas Malone, the same detective from Lovecraft's text, whose biases as a policeman and an occult dabbler are brought into sharp relief. Dividing the story using two subjective viewpoints echoes Lovecraft's use of incomplete narratives and moreover offers divergent negotiations of race. Tommy Tester, who later transforms into the abhuman Black Tom, shares with Malone an interest in the arcane and an ambiguous understanding of the social reality which "weirds" their universe and facilitates the development of abcanny identity. Tommy, in the earliest pages of the novel, embraces what Lovecraft rejected: while "people who move to New York… can't see the place," Tommy reads potential instead of danger in the urban streets and makes a living exploiting racial misreadings (9). Based in Harlem, New York, where he shares an apartment with his beloved father, Otis, he interrogates and embodies certain ideologies of the Harlem Renaissance and the New Negro Movement by taking advantage of racial illegibility and subjective reading practices in a constant process of self-creation.

Though he can barely sing or play the guitar, Tommy cultivates the image of "the dazzling, down-and-out musician," carrying around an empty guitar case and growing deliberately "conspicuous" in white crowds that view him as a novelty (11, 12). Using racial identity as a form of entertainment allows him to move freely in white-dominated spaces and attracts the interest of Suydam, who wishes to co-opt Tommy's skills in order to gain the loyalty of his racially diverse followers and set himself up as a post-apocalyptic messiah (18). Alternatively, the ability to be inconspicuous also proves convenient: "becoming unremarkable, invisible, compliant – these were useful tricks for a black man in an all-white neighborhood. Survival techniques" (12–13). Tommy moves between the role of entertainer, which serves as a cover for his real occupation as a trafficker in occult items, and a mask of invisibility which renders him ostensibly nonthreatening to a white audience; the other alternative is to be a threatening abnormality, a role which would provoke an immediate reaction from authorities.

These "survival techniques" are particularly important in a surveillance-dominated state designed to enforce compliance to a set of racial roles. The need for the successful performance of certain codes of conduct by racialized bodies was noted recently in PBS's article "10 rules of survival if stopped by police," a list of strategies long exercised by minority communities attempting to stem the violence disproportionally inflicted upon them by law enforcement (PBS). This discourse is furthermore echoed back by the authorities themselves, as evidenced in aggressive policing tactics, numerous recorded instances of bias, and in a controversial op-ed written by veteran policeman: to avoid getting hurt, he says, "Don't argue with me, don't call me names, don't tell me that I can't stop you, don't say I'm a racist pig, don't threaten that you'll sue me and take away my badge…don't even think of aggressively walking towards me" (Dutta). The assumption that the onus is on minorities to behave appropriately, primarily by suspending their right to freely express "words, body language, and emotions," and that the police are thus not responsible for any resulting violence renders individualized human self-expression antithetical to one's social and literal existence within the state (PBS). Moreover, this fundamentally "weird" process of dehumanization via contradictory perceptions of reality is enshrined in the national narrative, one further complicated by videos showing police shooting fleeing suspects in the back or kneeling for extended periods of time on a handcuffed individual's neck.

Tommy initially accepts that racial identity is a superficial performance upon which his safety depends, even when it supports a white supremacist ideology and undermines his human individuality: he consciously decides when "to play a role that always worked on whites. The Clueless Negro" or appear "feebleminded, and thus unthreatening, and thus invisible" (25, 58). He takes advantage of "white misunderstanding, misrepresentation, evasion, and self-deception on matters related to race" and authoritarian narratives that Black individuals must be entertaining, invisible, or submissive lest they be defined as a threat, social mores that constitute "a cognitive and moral economy psychically required for conquest, colonization, and enslavement" (Mills 19). Tommy learns to perform racial roles but not internalize them, and, in keeping with the strategy he employs while peddling occult objects, to "skirt the rules but don't break them" (20), echoing the phenomenon described in Ralph Ellison's *Invisible Man* (1952) in which "invisibility ironically stems from his material visibility" and conformity to the status quo means embracing performative "otherness" (Gallego 185). He also avoids interrogating the boundaries of his universe when possible: regarding a spell book, he "didn't know what the words meant, nor did he care to know" (14). Indeed, Tommy "didn't have to read through [a text] to be aware of its power," suggesting a self-conscious, parallel understanding of his own tenuous manipulation of racial identity as well as his relative powerlessness within the system (19). However, even as Tommy "followed the exact wording" of his contracts yet still runs afoul of supernatural forces, his performance of race does not prevent profound disruptions (64). He is still abused by policemen – Malone and his associate, Howard – and is recruited by Suydam, who emerges as a Lovecraft stand-in by parroting racist descriptions from the original story.

Tommy's interactions with the white community, and more specifically his attempt to preserve a sense of morality and individuality in his dealings with them, center the source of "weird" dread on racist systems rather than fears that racial hybridity will lead to humanity's marginalization on the cosmic stage. After Tommy hides the last page of an occult manuscript from one of his clients – a moment where Tommy "skirts the rules" in order to keep the client from abusing her power – Malone and Howard, hired to retrieve the page, raid Tommy's house and murder his father under the guise of a routine police investigation. A not-quite-sympathetic Malone acknowledges, when Tommy confronts him, that "you hadn't broken any rules," yet like other Lovecraftian heroes Tommy only partially understands this "weird" universe, and the consequences of misreading the "rules" are devastating (64). His invisibility is weaponized against him and the resulting horror is, as in Ellison's work, "not that people cannot see him but that people choose not to recognize him as an equal and fully human being" (Gallego 185). Howard informs him of his father's death while echoing contemporary examples of police shootings: he claims to have mistaken the elder Tester's guitar for a rifle, mocks Tommy's grief as evidence of the "scientifically proven" animalistic insensibility of "these people," and, when asked how many times he shot Otis, smugly replies, "I felt in danger for my life… I emptied my revolver. Then I reloaded and did it again" (62, 65). In this, as in real-life instances of police brutality, the narrative of "the black body in white space as threat, the white body in black space as threatened" is used to articulate a disingenuous "post-truth" narrative and justify the use of fatal force (Jungkunz and White 436). Faced with this blatant rejection of empirical facts and human sympathy in an instance where figures of "law and order" offer only injustice without the possibility of recourse, the reader experiences a Lovecraftian form of upheaval, a horrified reaction to this "weirded" world. As modern video evidence contradicts official police reports, so too do narratives clash in this instance, exposing a monstrously twisted reality.

Malone's own indifference to the moral or existential implications of this situation parallels Howard's more overt racism and demonstrates how racist ideologies thrive through deliberate, selective blindness: Malone "vouched for Mr Howard's character" when questioned by his superiors but also "made sure not to ask" for any further details regarding Otis's death (81). Though he knows that the official story is untrue, his adherence to the so-called "blue wall of silence" and refusal to pursue justice in this instance allow further slippages into a "weird" universe which accepts nihilistic and destructive falsehoods as truth. Coupled with his interactions with Suydam, this dehumanizing restructuring of reality forces Tommy Tester to move beyond socially prescribed boundaries as he rejects the roles of "entertainer" and "invisible man" which failed to protect him and decides to rather embrace the role of "threat" to a system of white oppression. It also reframes Lovecraft's fear of racialized impotence and cosmic indifference as secondary to the existential threat of "malice" felt by communities upon which racialized identities are violently imposed. Confronted with the death of his father, "fear of cosmic indifference suddenly seemed comical, or downright naïve" and Tommy instead asks himself the real question: "What was indifference compared to malice?" (66). Social indifference and true invisibility would rather allow for freedom from oppression and for a man subject to authoritarian surveillance which brutalizes and dehumanizes individuals within the boundaries of a racialized narrative "indifference would be such a relief" (66).

LaValle exposes Lovecraft's concept of cosmic indifference as primarily the concern of the white and powerful and moreover suggests that in their attempts to manage identity and defend their own supremacy white authorities in fact become the agents of their own destruction. After Otis Tester's death there is nothing to prevent Tommy from rejecting humanity – he reaches the conclusion that "Mankind didn't make messes; mankind was the mess" – and embracing the destructive potential of the Lovecraftian abhuman (76). Without fully explaining Tommy's transformation into an abcanny "other," thus leaving him as a narrative gap existing outside the boundaries of the "knowable," the novella then refocuses its attention on Malone, a "seeker of secrets" bearing "witness to clues in a greater mystery" who is nevertheless also vulnerable to abcanny revisions (91, 83). Echoing Tommy's performance of race, Malone "became invisible" in the areas he polices by turning a blind eye to petty crime, his "notepad filled with…lore" which he overhears from immigrants and fetishizes but does not fully understand (92). Despite his privileged position, however, Malone's suffers a series of reversals after Otis's murder which undermine seemingly static identities and parallel Tommy's own experiences. When he investigates Suydam, he is treated as a criminal by his fellow policemen and when he returns to Red Hook "a curtain of silence fell between him and the residents," circumstances alienating him from the communities in which he is reluctantly invested (99).

Most troublingly, Malone is haunted by tales of a new figure, Black Tom, who is soon revealed to be Tommy Tester reborn as Suydam's abhuman acolyte. Malone confronts Black Tom while in Red Hook and attempts to define and negate the other man's power: "'Charles Thomas Tester', he said. 'That's your name. And you belong in Harlem, not Red Hook… I told you where you're allowed to be'" (105). He applies a racially coded identity in order to make Tommy readable and therefore manageable, but surveillance is instead turned back upon him and Black Tom's answering look renders Malone uber-visible and thus vulnerable, forcing him to look "back to his notebook to escape that gaze" (104). Malone, unable to respond with physical force, verbally rejects the new, threatening identity Black Tom embodies – "You expect me to call you that?" he asks when informed of Tommy's new name – and Black Tom responds by declaring Red Hook off-limits to Malone and "humming a drone note" that disorients and temporarily cripples the policeman (105, 106). Even when Malone regains mobility, he does not then regain mastery of the area he polices and his selective blindness transforms into dangerous ignorance: he cannot understand what the citizens of Red Hook are saying to him and he asks himself "Why hadn't he ever learned how to speak to these people?" (107).

The novella's climax, as in "The Horror at Red Hook," occurs during a raid on a Red Hook tenement building. Malone enters the building's basement in time to see Tommy writing out the "Supreme Alphabet," a temporarily incomplete source of mystical power and a nod to the indecipherable graffiti in the original story and performing a black mass ritual while Suydam looks on (124). Taking control of the situation and deviating from Lovecraft's narrative, Black Tom then unexpectedly kills Suydam, who even as he is dying "can't imagine he won't triumph" in his arrogant attempt to harness cosmic power (128). He also reveals the mutilated corpse of Howard, whose blood he used to paint the Alphabet (128). Black Tom turns Howard and Suydam – both characters who verbally echoed Lovecraft's original characterizations of racial minorities as subhuman and thus manageable and "readable" – into monstrous texts, essentially reversing similar attempts by literal and figurative white "authors" to impose legibility within racist narratives.

Moreover, Black Tom's own form both exemplifies a racist understanding of "black body as threat" to whiteness and denies white attempts at policing, invoking bigoted readings before undermining their efficacy. Touting his identity as an "officer of the law" yet failing to scare Black Tom into compliance, Malone's frantic questions again suggest a continued lack of narrative comprehension and control in the face of the violent abcanny: "how...why...If not for power, then what could be the point?" (129). In answer to this Black Tom reveals his transition into the abhuman, stating that because he is "unsympathized with" – echoing Mary Shelley's *Frankenstein* (1818) – he rejected humanity and evolved into an abcanny being outside of human understanding (130). Responding to a system of identity-policing that fails to see him as a human individual, Tommy "consciously removes himself from normalizing forces and fully assumes the role of the abject, plunging out of constructions of race" and embracing a transformative potential that finds power in "unknowability" (Jarenski 101). He essentially becomes the very monster white authorities fear and one which, most critically, they cannot defeat with their own self-limited knowledge. Tommy is willing to embrace a social as well as a literal death by aligning himself with the monstrous non-human, creating a new narrative in which he prioritizes his own "words and music" over Malone's, invokes his parents' hitherto marginalized identities and sings Son House's classic Blues piece "Grinnin' in Your Face," a song which highlights the ambiguity of physical performativity (130).

Malone, whom Black Tom mockingly identifies as a "seeker," attempts to reject this narrative and the chaotic dissolution it promises, screaming "I don't want to see!" and embodying the contradictions of his own identity, his fascination with and fear of the abject, his "misreadings" of racial identity (131). As in Lovecraft's original work, the white protagonist's failure to "see" and read effectively further subverts an authoritative narrative. Malone survives this final conformation but, in Tom's final act of revenge, the option to return to selective blindness is violently denied: "Black Tom had cut off Malone's eyelids. 'Try to shut them now,' Black Tom said. 'You can't choose blindness when it suits you. Not anymore'" (133). Continuing, after the incident, to exist within a human community but no longer "of" that community, Malone is "othered" through his new knowledge and his horrifying disfigurement and, later, is further degraded by a pair of medical goggles that make him rather reminiscent of one of Lovecraft's Innsmouth crowd. It is a punishment that redefines the conscious refusal to "see race" and white adherence to performative racial identity, especially in policing, as Malone is transformed into a highly visible monster and moreover proves instrumental to his own dehumanization.

Black Tom also survives the final showdown in the basement, which ends when six officers fire 57 rounds at him, the high number echoing instances such as Amandou Diallo's 1999 murder in New York and a 2011 incident during which Miami police fired over 100 rounds at a reckless driver and nearby civilians. Once again invoking and then escaping the "matricies of dominance" which formerly rendered him hyper-visible racially yet also invisible as a human individual, Black Tom embraces an abhuman identity which twists white assumptions and places him beyond human definitions, freeing him from racist structures by recreating him metaphysically (Jarenski 101). He essentially evolves into a kind of post-human entity, using his new powers to move through time and space and create his own "weird" mirror "universe in which all the powers of the NYPD could not defeat a single Negro with a razor blade" (139). The existence of such a world – a new reality in which the familiar tale of police violence no longer ends with the destruction of the Black body – is "Impossible," yet Black Tom still hijacks the narrative, advances beyond the "human," and exposes the fragile structures that support a racist status quo (139). Black Tom vanishes from the basement and leaves Malone behind with a final verbal dismissal that further elevates abhuman potentiality over a limited, racist, self-destructive world: "I'll take Cthulhu over you devils any day" (143).

Lovecraft states in his story "The Shunned House" that "[f]rom even the greatest of horrors irony is seldom absent" (451). It is fitting, as it is ironic, that during a time of complex socio-political reevaluations of racial identities LaValle would co-opt one of the most famously racist authors of the last century to best contextualize a waking nightmare that dominates our contemporary landscape. Echoing Lovecraft's own patterns, a conclusive explanation is fittingly elusive in *The Ballad of Black Tom*. Black Tom reappears in the final pages of LaValle's novella as a pseudo-prophet to inform his friend that the rise of Cthulhu is coming in "maybe a month? Maybe a hundred years?" and that "Black Tom did it" (148). However, Tommy's rejection of humanity and absorption into the Cthulhu Mythos as an abhuman legend remains ambiguous, the implications opaque as his friend attempts to reaffirm his identity: "Your name is Tommy Tester… you're my best friend, and the worst singer I've ever heard" (148). Tommy admits that in the course of his revenge tragedy he has "lost his soul" (148) yet retains some hope of reclaiming the "human," though it is certainly implied that Black Tom has essentially moved beyond society in its current state, and his body, which served as a canvas for racial readings up to this point, ultimately "does not permit itself to be read" (Lovecraft "Red Hook" 483) and disappears completely with a final "Zig zag zig," the missing letter of the Supreme Alphabet (LaValle 149). Both Lovecraft and LaValle's work posit that humanity's failures will bring about humanity's end and that these failures are centered around the anxieties and uncertainties we feel regarding our human identity – an identity that is social, biological, existential, and moral – though LaValle's novella ends with the hopeful possibility that we might evolve beyond the historical limitations of race. In both tales, the soul of America and all humankind hangs in the balance, and their successful application of "weird" elements to national narratives, particularly those addressing racial identities, solidifies Weird Fiction's continued significance in a contemporary discourse, speaking to the fears of dispossession, displacement, and erasure which haunt us all.

Works Cited

"10 Rules of Survival If Stopped by the Police." *PBS*, Public Broadcasting Service, 2019. www.pbs.org/black-culture/connect/talk-back/10_rules_of_survival_if_stopped_by_police/.

Berman, Mark, John Sullivan, Julie Tate, and Jennifer Jenkins. "Protests Spread over Police Shootings. Police Promised Reforms. Every Year, they still Shoot and Kill nearly 1,000 People." *The Washington Post*, WP Company, 8 June 2020.

Camara, Anthony. "How to Hack Lovecraft, make Friends with his Monsters, and Hijack his Mythos: Reading biology and racism in Elizabeth Bear's 'Shoggoths in Bloom.'" *Studies in the Fantastic*, Vol. 4, Winter 2016/Spring 2017, pp. 24–47.

Dutta, Sunil. "I'm a Cop. If You Don't Want to Get Hurt, Don't Challenge Me." *The Washington Post*, WP Company, 19 August 2014, www.washingtonpost.com/posteverything/wp/2014/08/19/im-a-cop-if-you-dont-want-to-get-hurt-dont-challenge-me/.

Fiske, John. "Surveilling the City: Whiteness, the Black Man and Democratic Totalitarianism." *Theory, Culture and Society*, 1998, Vol. 15, No. 2, pp. 67–88.

Gallego, Carlos. "The Gothic in North American 'subcultures.'" *Modern Gothic*, edited by Jerrold E. Hogle. Cambridge: Cambridge University Press. 2014, pp. 174–190.

Gross, Terry and Sam Briger. "'The Ballad Of Black Tom' Offers A Tribute To And Critique Of Lovecraft." *NPR*, NPR, 29 February 2016, www.npr.org/2016/02/29/468558238/the-ballad-of-black-tom-offers-a-tribute-and-critique-of-lovecraft.

Hefner, Brooks E. "Weird Investigations and Nativist Semiotics in H.P. Lovecraft and Dashiell Hammett." *Modern Fiction Studies*, Vol. 60, No. 4, Winter 2014, pp. 651–676.

Hughes, William. *Key Concepts in the Gothic*. Edinburgh: Edinburgh University Press, 2018.

Jackson, Rosemary. *Fantasy: The Literature of Subversion*. London: Routledge, 1981.

Jarenski, Shelly. "Invisibility Embraced: The Abject as a Site of Agency in Ellison's *Invisible Man*." *Melus*, Vol. 35, No. 4 The Bodies of Black Folk (Winter 2010), pp. 85–109.

Jungkunz, Vincent and Julie White. "Ignorance, Innocence, and Democratic Responsibility: Seeing Race, Hearing Racism." *The Journal of Politics*, Vol. 75, No. 2 (April 9, 2013), pp. 436–50.

LaValle, Victor. *The Ballad of Black Tom*. New York: Tom Doherty Associates, LLC, 2016.

Lovecraft, H. P. "The Shunned House." *H. P. Lovecraft Collected Fiction, A Variorum Edition, Volume 3*, edited by S.T. Joshi. New York: Hippocampus Press, 2017, pp. 451–479.

———. "The Horror at Red Hook." *H. P. Lovecraft Collected Fiction, A Variorum Edition, Volume 3*, edited by S.T. Joshi. New York: Hippocampus Press, 2017, pp. 480–505.

———. "The Call of Cthulhu." *H. P. Lovecraft Collected Fiction, A Variorum Edition, Volume 2*, edited by S.T. Joshi. New York: Hippocampus Press, 2017, pp. 21–55.

———. "He." *H. P. Lovecraft Collected Fiction, A Variorum Edition, Volume 1*, edited by S.T. Joshi. New York: Hippocampus Press, 2017, pp. 506–517.

Luckhurst, Roger. "The Weird: A D is/Orientation," *Textual Practice*, Vol. 31, No. 6, (2017), pp. 1041–1061.

McRoy, Jay. "There Goes the Neighborhood: Chaotic Apocalypse and Monstrous Genesis in H.P. Lovecraft's 'The Street', 'The Horror at Red Hook', and 'He.'" *Journal of the Fantastic in the Arts*, Vol 13, No. 4 (2003), pp. 335–351.

Miéville, China. "On Monsters: Or, Nine or More (Monstrous) Not Cannies." *Journal of the Fantastic in the Arts*, Vol. 23, No. 3 (2012), pp. 378–392.

Mills, Charles. *The Racial Contract*. Ithaca: Cornell University Press, 1997.

Weinstock, Jeffrey Andrew. "The New Weird." *New directions in popular fiction: genre, reproduction, distribution*, edited by Ken Gelder. Basingstoke: Palgrave Macmillan, 2016, pp. 177–200.

Witzel, Guy. "Abcanny Waters: Victor LaValle, John Lagan, and the Weird Horror of Climate Change." *Science Fiction Studies*, Vol. 45, No. 3, (November 2018), pp. 560–574.

14 Finding "Something and Not Nothing"

Women of Color Repurposing Lovecraft in the Posthuman 21st Century

Loren Barbour

In his editor's note to the *People of Colo(u)r Destroy Horror!* special issue of *Nightmare* magazine, Maurice Broaddus quotes the horror historian Darrell Schweitzer: "[H.P.] Lovecraft is a defining writer. ... The whole field either reflects him or rejects him. Your whole idea about what horror is or should be probably pivots on your ideas about Lovecraft, pro or con" (16). An especially salient point of contention among readers is Lovecraft's racial rhetoric, which continues to lurk beneath discussions of his legacy and, as Schweitzer reminds us, the horror genre itself. While some fans have the privilege to dismiss or downplay this aspect of his fiction (Miller), others have no choice but to confront it. Broaddus makes clear the complex relationship readers and writers of color hold with horror fiction, any cursory review of which should identify its disproportionate valorization of white male authors whose racialized, gendered fears become co-constitutive with the ongoing construction of marginalized people as real embodiments of horrific difference. Definitively, this is the case with Lovecraft, a pillar of the genre whose racism must be understood as pivotal to both his own work and his lasting influence on the field.[1] China Miéville, one author working directly within the Weird tradition, states that we must move beyond a simple "diagnosis" of this fact to active "judgement" (qtd. in Weinstock 242), even and especially if we are to admit that some things about Lovecraft's ideas remain generative. This is a complex task to take up but a necessary one; this chapter does so through close attention to works by women of color that repurpose Lovecraftian themes, treating them as one window into the evolutions responsible for his continued relevance and even popularity in the 21st century.

Currently, women and people of color are being increasingly recognized for their part in rejecting horror's inherited racist, xenophobic, and misogynistic traditions and giving shape to a generic lexicon that surpasses its white, Western, masculine bias.[2] Broaddus argues that horror "ought to be a point of connection between people" that treats fear and pain as "universal" emotions that reveal "the same human condition" (16). Simultaneously, some authors are uniquely situated to express

DOI: 10.4324/9780367713065-15

specific fears and pains—the "very real horrors that come with existing in hostile spaces" fueled by racism, sexism, homophobia, and other forms of oppression (Wong 315). For creators of color, horror becomes a "mode of entertainment and exorcism, a space where fear can be manipulated and conquered, where terror and play, the real and the imaginary, can exist side by side" (316). To take the cheeky title *People of Colo(u)r Destroy Horror!* seriously, I see women and nonwhite authors engaged in a simultaneous process of destruction and creation; they "reflect and then subvert" (315) traditional language, themes, and tropes in favor of not only a more inclusive genre but "a better future" informed by new understandings of where horror truly lies (Broaddus 19). To explore this cycle in relation to Lovecraft, this chapter focuses on how women of color rework his philosophy of cosmic indifferentism through their positions in a heteronormative, misogynistic, white-centric culture.

This chapter analyzes two short stories from collections meant to address some of the shortcomings of the horror genre as it currently stands. In addition to the aforementioned *People of Colo(u)r Destroy Horror!* issue, the all-women fiction anthology *She Walks in Shadows* reworks the Lovecraftian legacy in light of his misogyny. The work of nonwhite women in both collections makes explicit the issues of race and gender under the more common theme of existential dread. In the first collection, "None of This Ever Happened" (2016) by Gabriela Santiago uses the threat of consumption/subsumption to suggest that the narrator's dwindling grasp on reality is linked to her marginalization in whitestream culture.[3] In a world already poised to denigrate or altogether erase their subjectivity, women and people of color do not necessarily require an encounter with the cold, uncaring cosmos to feel their insignificance, although when it happens here, Santiago reacts with an expected amount of despair and denial. This premise is not only reiterated by Valerie Valdes in "Shub-Niggurath's Witnesses" (2015) (included in *She Walks in Shadows*) but also expanded when she goes on to suggest that realizing the inconsequentiality of humanity *as a whole* might be a liberation. These different reactions are ultimately structured around a willingness to "look" at the danger embedded in the everyday and the potentially maddening freedom of life on a cosmic scale.

My analysis is based on feminist posthumanist and materialist discourse, which works to decenter the human by situating us in a larger network of matter but crucially does not disregard our individual and collective accountability in the "more-than-human" world (Nelson 393). Past posthumanist engagements with Lovecraft find common ground in a shared "anti-anthropocentrism" (Sederholm and Weinstock 7); his philosophy appealingly diminishes the significance of humans in light of grander cosmic forces of space and time that remain indifferent to whatever miniscule accomplishments we might carve out in comparison. Carl H. Sederholm and Jeffrey Andrew Weinstock succinctly state,

"Lovecraft's cosmicism is found to be congruent with philosophical outlooks that emphasize that the universe is not built for human exploitation, that people are things among other things, and that there is more to things than meets the eye" (7). These tenets are drawn from Lovecraft's staunch belief that only a "primitive myopia" fixates on the earth and its people while "ignor[ing] the background" (qtd. in Wisker 50). To a person of color, however, this disinterest should read as sheer hypocrisy from someone who also expressed great concern about the status of the human race (its evolutionary status in particular). After all, in the face of inevitable civilizational decline spurred by beings whose powers we could not hope to fathom, condemning an interracial relationship is what seems myopic. S.T. Joshi sidesteps this looming contradiction by distancing it from his writing: "[Lovecraft's racial views] may well enter into a significant proportion of his fiction ... but I cannot see that they affect his metaphysical, ethical, aesthetic, or even his late political views in any meaningful way" ("Caring About the Civilization" 360). On the contrary, a feminist posthumanism maintains that the question of race must have a profound impact on the foundations of his philosophy and how he would see "humanity" conceptualized. While I cannot resolve the tensions in his original writing, I do argue that those of us grappling with this inheritance can complicate our thinking with the reminder that the "human" itself remains an unstable category.

Unlike the world of Lovecraft's fiction, difference is not actually the result of some monstrous inheritance, introduced from outside into the family tree. That people are irreducible to one, unified, identity prompts us to change the terms of our engagement with the label "human." Setting aside Lovecraft himself, the paradoxical legacy his favored themes have left behind is, if not resolved, at least altered in the hands of new authors. The very inclusion of women and people of color into "humanity" has been historically contingent (King 163), which necessarily and fundamentally affects the ways they are able to view themselves in relation to the rest of the universe, whether from the perspective of writer or character. The entrance of these new subjectivities into Lovecraft's schema of cosmic indifferentism provides a key departure from the assumptions of a monolithic "us" against the universe and generates more nuanced possibilities for relating to the other-than-human world, including with a sense of "awe and wonder" that Lovecraft was also capable of evoking (Joshi "From the Cosmic to the Human" 115). Shifting focus from fears of difference (whether racial, gendered, or otherwise) to the conditions that foster those fears, omnipresent anxiety and danger are relocated to every level of life, not only the universal. This leaves women of color less likely to seek refuge in conventional society and makes the more-than-human world an equally viable avenue of escape or provider of comfort. Ultimately, the vastness of the cosmos in Lovecraft's imagination can be a reprieve from the stifling existence otherwise delineated by whitestream culture and, rather than instilling a sense of impotence, this larger network becomes a potential source of freedom for otherwise marginalized people.

"None of This Ever Happened": What If the Real Horror Was Inside Us All Along?

In *Nightmare*'s short story "None of This Ever Happened," Gabriela Santiago is pushed toward the maddening realization of her own insignificance as a queer woman of color. In addition to picking up Lovecraft's favored theme of dangerous knowledge, she also follows the tenet "that there is more to things than meets the eye" (Sederholm and Weinstock 7) by staging its confrontation through a creepy rock first found in her apartment dumpster. Santiago herself is both author and narrator of the story, using the first person to describe her discovery of the rock and beginning to brainstorm how she might use it as a plot device. Although she starts off asserting herself as a writer, someone with a grasp on the flow and direction of a story, her control slips as she outlines a potential character. Santiago tells us that she is "genre-savvy enough to know that you do not take a rock with the word EAT scratched into it in jagged letters into your apartment and expect anything good to happen" (65), but the mere act of thinking is enough for it to arrest her world. While the pervasive influence of the rock is similar to that of the meteorite in "The Colour Out of Space," its invasion is entirely mental. Santiago's imagination functions more similarly to dreams for Lovecraft, which serve as "gateway[s] into both knowledge and horror" that nevertheless reveal "a truer vision of reality" (Matthews 169–170). As she begins to project onto her character—blending her use of "I" versus "she"—Santiago is forced to recognize that she falls short of the autonomy she once thought she'd possessed. In the rock's temptations to face this truth, she senses the boundless possibility of something other than the human, seeming confident that "something will happen" (84) to her if she lets the knowledge in, although what that "something" is remains to be seen.

Santiago's choice of a rock to channel the reality she has so far tried to avoid aligns with an object-oriented ontology that "recovers the wonder and fear of objects" (Olivier 13) and affords them the same causal significance as any sentient being. Adapting the eco-erotic framework of Indigenous feminist Melissa K. Nelson, when this stony character intersects with Santiago, the "contact zone of human and more-than-human" (395) becomes the stage for an encounter that leaves her taken aback by "the beauty, or sometimes the horror" of the world beyond herself (393). As representative of this realm, Santiago's rock "has something to do with the lies we tell ourselves, and the truths, and the way they build up inside you" until they are forced to reemerge in a form that cannot be ignored (76). One of these lies is the sanctity of the home, which in turn unravels the illusion of safety from whitestream culture. Under its mandates, Santiago is, rather than a writer herself, no different from a character like the one she imagines, vulnerable to being apprehended by other creators (such as Lovecraft) for use in their own narratives. In the wake of this realization, Santiago is brought to the brink of mental collapse at the same time she is offered a way out. Coinciding with the height of her hysteria, the rock urges Santiago to "EAT," eat everything up to and including herself before she is eaten by others. If we read this rock as a gate to unlocking Santiago's "cosmological self" (Nelson 393), the implications of its message expand exponentially to a scale of cosmic potential that does justice to the rest of Lovecraft's mythos.

The rock demands that Santiago acknowledge the impossibility of safety as a fundamental truth of the universe. At first, danger is positioned as exterior, something that can be recovered from within her apartment. Santiago describes lying on "the cold wooden floor and star[ing] at the white, white, white ceiling" until the world is "easier to carry" again (70). However, the character she outlines (who is not meant to be a writer but here the distinctions already begin to unravel) views "the white, white, white of a blank Word document" with "a paralysis like a deer looking into the eyes of a wolf" and her "white, white, white ceiling" as a "great white mouth closing over her mind, erasing her" (70). Contrary to her words but following Lovecraft's privileging of the imagination (Bogiaris 35), Santiago's thoughts reveal an existence under siege, with the threat of consumption literally hanging above her head; significantly, this threat is coded as "white" and it is seemingly inescapable. The feminist ecocritic Stacy Alaimo comments on how the concept of home has served as "the defining container for the Western 'human,' a bounded space, wrought by delusions of safety" (336). She breaks down the dream of domestic security in which "the house erects boundaries between nature and culture, wild and civilized, imperiled and supposedly 'safe'" (415), to the would-be horror of Lovecraftian protagonists, whose only hope for salvation often lies in a retreat behind familiar walls (Bogiaris 37). For example, consider the appeal of a "placid island of ignorance" (Lovecraft qtd. in Murray and Corstorphine 159) protecting us from "an infinitely vast and complex universe" we were not meant to explore (158). Alaimo, however, points out that what is outside is always already within: "electricity, media, advertising, and consumer goods stream in along with water, air, particulate matter, human inhabitants, guests, microbes, and nonhuman pests" (418). Metaphorically, she refers to the inability of power structures like patriarchy to shut out the "chaos" imagined as nonwhite, as improperly feminine, as queer (415); however, Santiago is forced to recognize that the inverse is also true. We also cannot insulate ourselves against the regulatory apparatuses of whitestream culture. They extend into our most intimate spaces, meaning that a queer woman of color like her is in constant danger, whether she remains inside or not.

The forced identification between Santiago and fictional characters cements her sense of precarity (and alludes to the extratextual reality that nonwhite women are not often afforded creative autonomy, furthering pressure on those trying to "make it" in the industry). As she rushes to fill the blank Word document in front of her, Santiago's thoughts spiral toward Uhura from *Star Trek*, whose existence is just as tenuous. She believes that "someone has to write Uhura looking out the window and dreaming of home… [because] without the anchoring words she may be forgotten, may go drifting off into the blank whiteness of the pages without typewritten words…" (81). Without someone willing to write the words that will "anchor" her to her identity, she disappears into "blank whiteness," reduced to another flat rendition of a nonwhite character for white audiences to consume. She becomes someone with no home and no depth to dream of one. Santiago insists, "You have to write Uhura over and over again because she was there and she was real, and you're here and you're real, you're real, you're real!" (81). The repetition emphasizes her desperation, simultaneously mimicking the echoing response that comes from shouting into the void—not that of space but of the blank page, of a society that is incapable of recognizing, never mind representing, the interiority of women and people of color. In this slippage between herself and Uhura, Santiago also capitulates to the feelings of her imaginary protagonist, acknowledging the personal stakes of creation and consumption in whitestream culture. Writing becomes not only a way of saving Uhura but of saving herself because if she cannot write, she will be written about, captured by a narrative she has no control over. She invokes Lovecraft as an exemplar of this crime, accusing him of taking a Black cleaning woman and "abduct[ing] her in words" as a way of asserting his own existence in the wake of his own fears (83). In a small act of comeuppance, Santiago briefly considers putting him into *her* story, suggesting that "then an explanation emerges about the thing that lived under the streets of Providence and shifted and stretched and looked for the true and untrue spoken words" (82). Like the rock, the thing under Providence is transformed into a forced confrontation with the truths that are already inside, even if they are as yet unspoken.

For Lovecraft, these truths might have dealt with his insecurity in a world that was progressing smoothly without him—but with, in fact, a growing population of the people he so feared. In his discussion of Lovecraft's racism, David Simmons suggests that his "immensely nihilistic worldview may have led him to fear any group of people he saw as possessing *jouissance*, stolen or not," which only just happened to include people of color (17). If we take Simmons's words to be the case, Lovecraft's anxiety is not so much proprietary as it is existential—he does not feel he has been stolen from but fears that he never possessed this liveliness in the first place. Santiago displays similar insight into the source of his anxieties, imagining that even as he wrote about people of color, he had to be careful never to look them in the eye because if the source of his irrelevance was not there then "it might be somewhere else, might be close by, might be inside," might have been inside all along (83). However, as Santiago has already been forced to recognize, the barriers between inside and outside are more porous than we would often like to believe. That Lovecraft chose to displace his fears onto people of color means something, just as his externalization of malevolence onto eldritch beings from outer space means something.

Santiago does an admirable job of expressing a Lovecraftian anxiety if we were to redirect his fears away from an exterior other and remain fixated on the structures that actually profit from such discourse. She is well aware that she is not safe, that there are things that cannot be blocked by walls or doors the way they could a single body but for her, this danger finds its origin in the very real culture we reside in. The rock does not leave Santiago this single difficult truth to process. Instead, once she has awakened to this knowledge, it offers the message "EAT," channeled into her urge to eat up space on the page as she types, as she continues writing to save herself from oblivion.

When every excursion outside has the potential to violently impinge on her subjectivity, madness is always already around the corner for Santiago. Exposure to the intricacies and cold reality of the universe—no matter how overwhelming—might simply be a refreshing change of pace. The rock beckons her to "come closer and see" (84) what she might find on the other side of her feeding/writing frenzy. Significantly, Santiago does not automatically approach this thought with a sense of dread. Rather, she posits that "maybe you will go mad or maybe you will die or maybe you will go to a secondary school with a curse on the position of Defense Against the Dark Arts professor,[4] but something will happen, you will see something and not nothing" (84). Whether the outcome is maddening or magical, the only way she can find out is to look. For Lovecraft's protagonists, this act of looking has never ended well; his fiction is rife with "species of knowledge only by ignorance of which humankind can maintain even the semblance of well-being" (Burleson qtd. in Murray and Corstorphine 159). However, for women of color there remains a chance that even this brand of madness is a better alternative to the quiet, oppressive illogic of whitestream culture. Ultimately, Santiago chooses to turn away, reasserting her control over her environment and negating her brush with the truths embodied by the rock. She writes, "I will commit to one version of reality, the real one, the one where I did not take the rock with the word EAT scratched into it in jagged letters into my apartment" (89). But even this ending is not set in stone. Unlike *The Dream-Quest of Unknown Kadath*, in which Lovecraft thwarts the literal personification of chaos and allows his protagonist to awaken safely at home (Bogiaris 36), Santiago only states "what will happen" but not what does happen; we have no way of knowing whether the rock can truly be expunged from her consciousness.

"Shub-Niggurath's Witnesses": Cavorting with Chaos

If ignorance is not automatically bliss for the marginalized, what alternatives do they have? What new forms of knowledge and ways of being might be glimpsed if we refused to turn away? I look to Valerie Valdes's "Shub-Niggurath's Witnesses" from *She Walks in Shadows* for one answer. Compared to Santiago, who orchestrates an ontological reckoning as both author and protagonist, Valdes keeps a greater distance by unfolding any world-shattering revelations unto the fictional Yourladies Benitez. Perhaps because of this added layer of psychological security, Valdes ventures further into the ramifications of such "dangerous" knowledge, allowing Yourladies to actively embrace the wider, weirder universe beyond her dead-end theater job. Under the guidance of two Sisters, she dedicates herself to the will of Shub-Niggurath, one of the goddesses in Lovecraft's Cthulhu mythos; her initiation into a larger cosmic network simultaneously decenters the human without removing it from a meaningful place in the world, minor as it might be. What Lovecraft's protagonists might have sought to eradicate for the sake of their society, Valdes constructs as a form of salvation through a new relationality that positions her characters beyond what is made available by whitestream culture.

Also narrating in the first person, Valdes's protagonist is a follower of Shub-Niggurath, "the Black Goat of the Woods with a Thousand Young" (271), one of the few feminine members of Lovecraft's pantheon. In a parody of Jehovah's Witnesses-style proselytizing, the narrator and her companion Sister Honoria arrive at the door of Yourladies and attempt to convert her to Shub-Niggurath's, following with a pitch that seems perfectly coded to appeal to women of color. This includes such questions as, "Have you ever felt that no benevolent god watches over you?"; "Do you feel your life is insignificant?"; and, "Do you feel you have no real control and could be wiped out at any time by unknown forces more powerful than you can comprehend?" (272). Echoing Santiago's revelation that nowhere is safe for women of color in whitestream culture, Yourladies answers in the affirmative. Our narrator quickly assures her that there are answers to her questions "if you dare to look" (272). Although Yourladies turns them away in the moment, the Sisters sense her susceptibility and follow her to work, resolving to "continue [their] ministry until she joins [them] or goes mad" (273). Under the influence of the Sisters, Yourladies does indeed capitulate and "brutally murder[s] her supervisor with a conveniently placed umbrella" before joining the cult of Shub-Niggurath to "cavort naked … in the glorious darkness" (273), freed of earthly burdens like jobs or clothes.

Possibly keeping to the more explicitly Lovecraftian tone of the anthology, the secrets of the universe Valdes hints at are more abstract. Through the efforts of the Sisters—which include "making bloodcurdling noises, casting eldritch shadows into empty theater houses, revealing … the true forms of the Twin Blasphemies and the untranslatable Sign" from the projection booth—Yourladies comes to understand the "vast, ineffable horrors of reality" (273). However, given her decisive actions to free herself of her boss (a not uncommon fantasy for anyone who has worked for minimum wage), we can at least rest assured that capitalism is not an integral part of the picture. Alternatively, Valdes chooses to skim over what exactly Yourladies is learning in favor of what she does with the knowledge afterward.

Unlike Santiago, Yourladies does not turn away from the knowledge revealed to her but instead finds a more meaningful place within the cosmic web. This is not an unprecedented move, even among Lovecraft's fiction. Joyce Carol Oates reads the ending of "The Shadow Over Innsmouth" as a similar "if you can't beat them…join them" resolution wherein "the young hero ironically turns into one of them, and comes to rejoice in his subhumanity" (qtd. in Wisker 48). Notable, however, is the relative benignity of one man (and his cousin) versus Lovecraft's perception of the far more threatening capacity of female characters to plunge the world into chaos. Their affinity with the subhuman and inhuman embodiments of fear is made more ominous by the access granted to their reproductive sexuality, which becomes the vehicle through which humanity is infected by malevolent influence. Through the eldritch relations of women as mothers, grandmothers, and ancestors even further back, "lineage is tainted and the monstrous moves to infiltrate and eventually take over the world" (Wisker 51). This is not limited to the literally monstrous; "Lovecraft's unique contribution to the depiction of women who elicit terror and disgust is through the figure of those who are capable of miscegenation, interbreeding with the alien Other, creatures from the seas, from Hell, from other dimensions, and, controversially for contemporary readers, in Lovecraft's view, the 'racially inferior'" (31). Shub-Niggurath's title, "the Black Goat of the Woods with a Thousand Young," also associates the threat of femininity with its reproductive capacities; but in Valdes's formulation, this fertility is repurposed and provided as a form of salvation and rebirth for her followers.

After facing the maddening truth of her smallness in comparison to the cosmos, Yourladies is not necessarily rendered meaningless. She relocates herself within a new network of responsibility and finds meaning by dedicating herself to Shub-Niggurath. As the narrator tells her, "The Magna Mater grants her worshippers the knowledge and power to ensure the propagation of her seed across the cosmos. Her children are the chapters of her ongoing revelation" (272). Gaining "knowledge and power," Shub-Niggurath's followers are literally reborn (after being regurgitated by her) and find a place as part of an "ongoing revelation" much more expansive than the confines of human-only culture—case in point, Yourladies is able to abandon the drudgeries of her theater job in favor of dancing, something she truly "loves" (274). This is not an achievement of complete autonomy, but such a concept is difficult to imagine in the first place. Judith Butler argues that we are inevitably and inextricably constituted through our relations with others. Like the porous boundaries between interior and exterior, the "I" is always called into existence "by its relation to the one whom I address myself" (19), making bodily autonomy nothing more than a "lively paradox" that we can only assert situationally (21). This being the case, no one can be completely free from the influence of another; that Yourladies resituates herself in relation to Shub-Niggurath and her new sister worshippers is at least more empowering than the indignities of her former life. The freedom of the more-than-human world for women of color might always be tempered by this inescapable relationality, or perhaps this was simply the case this time. As Santiago would urge, marginalized people must first look in order to find out.

Conclusion

Although only a preliminary investigation into some of the alternative avenues paved by women of color, this chapter should be a necessary reminder that the human cannot yet be forgotten by Lovecraft's cosmic aesthetics. Given his sustained popularity in the 21st century, it seems obvious that something about his themes continues to resonate within the shifting terrain of the horror genre. We must interrogate the appeal of forces larger and stronger than our individual wills, especially as a scapegoat for fear and anxiety because in the hands of women of color, we are reminded that these powers are located much closer to home than we might like to admit: in the foundations of whitestream culture. Rather than destroy our sense of escapism, nonwhite women give readers a glimpse of the potential comfort brought by the apathetic vastness of time and space. In light of the revelation that safety is an illusion, Valdes demonstrates that entry into the cosmos as a transcendence of systemic violence—even at the cost of one's sanity—can become infinitely more appealing for marginalized people who find themselves in vulnerable positions. Although there are also others, like Santiago, who step away from the brink in order to preserve their existing sense of reality, even they are no longer guaranteed a smooth reassimilation into the status quo. These authors present us with new reactions to the truths we'd rather avoid based on an interpretation of cosmicism that does not prematurely abandon the human in favor of the other-than-human.

Incorporating the perspectives of women and people of color encourages a rereading of Lovecraft that seeks the liberatory sentiment in what he brushes off as merely horrifying—what dangerous insights his protagonists turn away from but which we might still use to expand our self-awareness. The repurposing of Lovecraft investigated here skims the surface of this potentiality, but there are surely depths to his philosophy that remain unplumbed for future creative and academic engagement.

Notes

1 For example, the quality and content of their writing aside, it seems indicative that the authors named in the introduction to *Lovecraft and Influence: His Predecessors and Successors* are overwhelmingly white English or American men (Waugh).
2 The documentary *Horror Noire*, for example, traces the history of Black people in film with attention to the contemporary critical acclaim of actors such as John Boyega and directors like Jordan Peele. Peele and Misha Green have also produced *Lovecraft Country* (2020), a television series exploring the intersections of the Jim Crow United States and Lovecraftian horror, giving rise to new expectations of what horror fiction can look like.
3 This term is adapted from Maile Arvin, Eve Tuck, and Angie Morrill's usage of "whitestream feminism" to name the primacy of whiteness in popular culture without capitulating to the idea that the "mainstream" is not or cannot ever be anything but. To do so would erase the work of women and people of color who have had a hand in horror from its inception and who continue to assert their presence in the genre, as evidenced by the work I draw on here.
4 Although beyond the scope of this chapter, this reference to the Harry Potter universe might bridge a conversation about what has quickly become a cornerstone of the contemporary Western fantasy genre and its own problematic traditions. For example, further engagement with J.K. Rowling's own racism could shed light on the limits enforced by even the most "magical" possible outcomes when they are authored by a white woman.

Works Cited

Alaimo, Stacy. *Exposed: Environmental Politics and Pleasures in Posthuman Times*. Minneapolis, MI: University of Minnesota Press, 2016.

Arvin, Maile, et al. "Decolonizing Feminism: Challenging Connections between Settler Colonialism and Heteropatriarchy." *Feminist Formations*, vol. 25, no. 1, 2013, pp. 8–34.

Bogiaris, Guillaume. "'Love of Knowledge is a Kind of Madness': Competing Platonisms in the Universes of C.S. Lewis and H.P. Lovecraft." *Mythlore: A Journal of J.R.R. Tolkien, C.S. Lewis, Charles Williams, and Mythopoeic Literature*, vol. 36, no. 2, 2018, pp. 23–41.

Broaddus, Maurice. "On the Destruction of Horror: Notes from Your People of Colo(u)r Editors." *Nightmare*, Oct. 2016, pp. 9–20.

Butler, Judith. "Beside Oneself: On the Limits of Sexual Autonomy." *Undoing Gender*. New York: Routledge, 2004, pp. 17–39.

Horror Noire: A Black History of Horror. Directed by Xavier Burgin, Shudder, 2019.

Joshi, S.T. "Caring About the Civilization." *A Dreamer and a Visionary: H.P. Lovecraft in his Time*. Liverpool: Liverpool University Press, 2001, pp. 346–388.

———. "From the Cosmic to the Human." *Lovecraft and Influence: His Predecessors and Successors*, edited by Robert H. Waugh. Lanham, MD: Scarecrow Press, 2013, pp. 105–118.

King, Tiffany Lethabo. "Humans Involved: Lurking in the Lines of Posthumanist Flight." *Critical Ethnic Studies*, vol. 3, no. 1, 2017, pp. 162–185.

Matthews, Carol S. "Letting Sleeping Abnormalities Lie: Lovecraft and the Futility of Divination." *Mythlore: A Journal of J.R.R. Tolkien, C.S. Lewis, Charles Williams, and Mythopoeic Literature*, vol. 36, no. 2, 2018, pp. 165–184.

Miller, Laura. "It's OK to Admit that H.P. Lovecraft Was Racist." *Salon*, 12 Sept. 2014, www.salon.com/2014/09/11/its_ok_to_admit_that_h_p_lovecraft_was_racist/.

Murray, Chris, and Kevin Corstorphine. "Co(s)mic Horror." *New Critical Essays on H.P. Lovecraft*, edited by D. Simmons. New York: Palgrave, 2013, pp. 157–191.

Nelson, Melissa K. "Getting Dirty: The Eco-Eroticism of Women in Indigenous Oral Literatures." *Critically Sovereign: Indigenous Gender, Sexuality, and Feminist Studies*, edited by Joanne Barker. Durham, NC: Duke University Press, 2017, pp. 391–444.

Olivier, Marc. Introduction. *Household Horror: Cinematic Fear and the Secret Life of Everyday Objects*. Bloomington, IN: Indiana University Press, 2020, pp. 12–24.

Santiago, Gabriela. "None of This Ever Happened." *Nightmare*, Oct. 2016, pp. 64–90.

Sederholm, Carl H., and Jeffrey Andrew Weinstock. "Lovecraft Rising." *The Age of Lovecraft*, edited by Sederholm, Carl H., and Jeffrey Andrew Weinstock. Minneapolis, MI: University of Minnesota Press, 2016, pp. 1–42.

Simmons, David. "'A Certain Resemblance': Abject Hybridity in H.P. Lovecraft's Short Fiction." *New Critical Essays on H.P. Lovecraft*, edited by D. Simmons. New York: Palgrave, 2013a, pp. 13–30.

Simmons, David, editor. *New Critical Essays on H.P. Lovecraft*. New York: Palgrave, 2013b.

Valdes, Valerie. "Shub-Niggurath's Witnesses." *She Walks in Shadows*, edited by Silvia Moreno-Garcia and Paula R. Stiles. Vancouver, BC: Innsmouth Free Press, 2015, pp. 271–274.

Waugh, Robert H. "Introduction." *Lovecraft and Influence: His Predecessors and Successors*, edited by Robert H. Waugh. Lanham, MD: Scarecrow Press, 2013, pp. 7–8.

Weinstock, Jeffrey Andrew. "Afterword: Interview with China Miéville." *The Age of Lovecraft*, edited by Carl H. Sederholm and Jeffrey Andrew Weinstock. Minneapolis, MI: University of Minnesota Press, 2016, pp. 231–243.

Wisker, Gina. "'Spawn of the Pit': Lavinia, Marceline, Medusa, and All Things Foul: H.P. Lovecraft's Liminal Women." *New Critical Essays on H.P. Lovecraft*, edited by D. Simmons. New York: Palgrave, 2013, pp. 31–54.

Wong, Alyssa. "The H Word: The Darkest, Truest Mirrors." *Nightmare*, Oct. 2016, pp. 310–316.

15 The Crawling Chaos

H.P. Lovecraft, Closed Gothic Spaces and "Dungeon Crawler" Videogames

Kevin Corstorphine and Matthew Crofts

H.P. Lovecraft is a highly visible influence on the modern gaming landscape; games signalling a debt to Lovecraft are produced at a rapid pace, despite increasing criticism of the writer's personal and racial views. Lovecraft's presiding influence has been recognised as lying in the "mythos" he established and the linguistic and aesthetic style that supported it rather than any single text itself, with Roger Luckhurst tracing the propagation of the "Cthulhu Mythos" by August Derleth and others after Lovecraft's death, through the critical appreciation of commentators such as Colin Wilson and Maurice Lévy, to "the mass market paperbacks of the stories published in the late 1960s [which] finally brought Lovecraft to a mass readership" (Luckhurst xiii). This chapter will continue to trace this influence by showing how distinctly Lovecraftian elements have become encoded into "dungeon crawler" video games by examining two modern examples, *Darkest Dungeon* (2016) and *Crawl* (2017) and by demonstrating that this influence extends more deeply than just a few overt references or superficial trappings. These games operate on the principle of creating the reaction of horror in the player and, through a combination of aesthetics and gameplay elements, are also capable of invoking the sense of the "weird," or the awareness of outer forces, that Lovecraft emphasises. In demonstrating this, we will also show that by embodying the player in the world of the Lovecraftian dungeon crawl and by opening up the dungeons and monster-filled mazes as a space for play, the experience is extended into forms of affect that are exemplary of both horror and the weird and that are undeniably Lovecraftian in their origins, but are not bound to, or limited by, this legacy.

Any discussion of Lovecraftian videogames must acknowledge the direct line of influence from pen-and-paper roleplaying games that extended the diffusion of Lovecraft's style popularised by mass market paperbacks. Chaosium's role-playing game *Call of Cthulhu* (1981–present) marks a further point of departure of the "Lovecraftian" from Lovecraft's work by asking players to create their own adventures in the heterocosm.[1] Indeed, Chaosium's role-playing game may have done more to extend Lovecraft's influence than is often realised, with Jones locating the game "as the most

DOI: 10.4324/9780367713065-16

essentially faithful of Lovecraftian derivations in popular culture" and Daniel Harms identifying it as "one of the most important factors" for the resurgent popularity of Lovecraft (Jones 230; Harms xv). Putting aside the question of whether "faithfulness" is the goal (or is even possible) in an adaptation of this nature, it is worthwhile to look at where it draws these supposedly faithful elements from. The game is a composite creation, less indebted to Lovecraft's 1928 short story "Call of Cthulhu" than to Lovecraft's imaginative world as a whole, and one that draws on a wide range of other authors. As Harms states: "Its creator, Sandy Petersen, combined the lore from many different Cthulhu Mythos authors to assemble the monsters and books to create the background for his game" (xv). In turn, these pen-and-paper roleplaying games have influenced the subsequent generation of videogames.

The process of dissemination of the Cthulhu Mythos texts continued with the rise of video games, as Perron notes, and "it was *Alone in the Dark* (1992) that obtained the greatest notoriety" (5). The title itself is an apt description of Lovecraft's fiction: the imagined experience of being "alone in the dark," and crucially for the similarly-influenced works that followed the game proclaimed its influence heavily, with the box art proudly displaying the tagline "A virtual adventure game inspired by the work of H.P. Lovecraft." Taylor notes that designers "drew from H. P. Lovecraft's horror writing, elements of horror and Gothic fiction and film, and added an unusual gameplay format" (47), showing that the influence was wider than just Lovecraft's fiction. This unusual gameplay focused on exploration, slow traversal of space, puzzle-solving, and searching for clues to expose the underlying mystery.[2] Horror games, particularly Lovecraftian horror, were becoming associated with slow speeds, claustrophobic settings, and unsettling story elements.

Reviewers and critics do not always look upon Lovecraftian videogame adaptations favourably; perhaps because they sit so uneasily as "adaptations." Matthew Gault, in a 2018 *Vice* review of *The Call of Cthulhu* videogame calls the mythos "played out garbage" (Gault 2018) and notes that the racism and misogyny of Lovecraft's personal life are not easily separated from the fiction. Sam Greer, in the 2018 *Eurogamer* article "Games Really Need to Fall Out of Love with Lovecraft," raises similar objections but points out that "for decades video games have been regurgitating the themes, plots and aesthetics of his stories with not one ounce of scrutiny" (Greer 2018). This surface-level engagement with the mythos has already been criticised in fiction by writers like Ramsey Campbell, D.M. Mitchell, Robert M. Price, and S.T. Joshi. As Mark Jones summarises: "the potential for ossification in these homages and pastiches has been identified by many commentators, and yet they continue unabated" (228). Victor LaValle, whose novel *The Ballad of Black Tom* (2016) is a direct response to Lovecraft's racism, writes that "you can love something, love someone, and criticize them" (LaValle

2019 xiv).[3] Linda Hutcheon in *A Theory of Adaptation* writes that a work need not be reliant on the original story if it offers "extended intertextual engagement with the adapted work" (Hutcheon and O'Flynn 8, 9). "Lovecraftian" games may be frustratingly silent on the topic of race, but they excel in engaging other themes that made the writer's stories a compelling reading.

Hutcheon seemingly identifies a broader pattern of adaptation within videogames, realising that "it was less the story itself than the story world, or what I called the "heterocosm" (literally, an other cosmos), that was being adapted" (Hutcheon and O'Flynn xxiv). Lovecraftian videogames, then, are not alone in quietly distancing themselves from the original work; they recreate the appealing aspects of Lovecraft's heterocosm without calling for a direct engagement with his written texts. Cthulhu, and even the theme of cosmic horror itself, has become another entry in the pantheon of popular culture. Hutcheon claims that adaptation "is more likely to target different audiences through different media" (Hutcheon and O'Flynn 2013 xxiii), which is indeed the case for a willing audience in gaming. In the move to gaming, the dungeon crawler expands what Hutcheon calls the "modes of engagement" (Hutcheon and O'Flynn 2013 22), from the "telling" mode (Lovecraft's written work), to both the "showing."[4] and "participatory/interactive" modes in the videogame medium. In this move, however, there is a distinct possibility of a dilution of the original work and themes. The examples we have chosen are ones that understand something deeper about Lovecraft's fiction and retain crucial elements, at the same time as taking full advantage of their shift in the modes of engagement to produce new meaning.

One videogame genre that remains critically underexplored, but that engages closely with the preceding discussion, is the dungeon crawler. These role-playing games, often combining fantasy and horror themes, again situate the player as "alone in the dark," traversing ruins or subterranean caverns like Lovecraft's characters, with fading torches, dwindling rations, and fear of encountering a monster. Subterranean passages, labyrinths stalked by monsters and hidden basements therefore act as connecting devices between Lovecraft's fiction and videogames inspired by his work. This chapter will first explore the use of space in Lovecraft, and the mental conditions encountered by his characters, which will later be relevant in thinking about the player experience of dungeon-crawler games. It will then directly compare these games to a selection of Lovecraft's short fiction, demonstrating their engagement with the same "primal" causes of fear (as associated with Lovecraft and the Cthulhu Mythos). The intention is to show the shared core themes between dungeon crawlers and Lovecraft's writing, and how core elements of this horror are recognisable as gameplay mechanics, proving a direct line of influence that goes beyond the lip service to Lovecraft's name seen in advertising material.

Lovecraft's Writing: Closed Spaces, Mental Instability

Lovecraft produced a body of fiction that reaches imaginative heights but spends a lot of time in thematic depths that continue to resonate with readers and authors. Partly this is because Lovecraft's weird fiction has become entangled with the tradition of the "weird tale" generally, even to the neglect of other important authors in the genre. Lovecraft's own construction of a weird fiction canon in his essay *Supernatural Horror in Literature* (1927) identifies the authors he admires in this mode, many of them British and Irish. As James Machin writes, his definition has become a well-recognised "formula from which most if not all discussions of weird fiction ensue" (2). Lovecraft distinguishes the weird from horror of "mere physical fear and the mundanely gruesome" and goes on to suggest that "an unexplainable dread of outer forces must be present" for the weird to function properly (Lovecraft *Supernatural* 1043). It seems appropriate to begin with how confined spaces become entangled with mental instability within the short story that gives its name to the development studio behind *Darkest Dungeon*: "The Horror at Red Hook" (1927).

"The Horror at Red Hook" is the tale of a New York detective, Thomas Malone, who uncovers a subterranean cult under the city. Investigating illegal immigration and the exploitation of a seemingly senile old Dutchman called Robert Suydam, Malone discovers that Suydam has been a willing participant in occult rites that eventually see him killed and resurrected in monstrous fashion. Having confronted a scene which oscillates between Sudyam's apartment and another dimension of horror, Malone finds himself in a subterranean basement, filled with monsters, as the roof is brought down around him. He is left with a fear of urban spaces and brick buildings. "The Horror at Red Hook" has been extensively discussed for its hysterical racial paranoia, which portrays urban areas where different people mix as inherently corrupt. As Joshi notes, the story suggests that, "a city whose urbanism has gotten out of control actually *generates* decadence" (Joshi 223). Lovecraft describes Red Hook as an area of "hybrid squalor" (Lovecraft "Red Hook" 484), where, "Syrian, Spanish, Italian, and negro elements" (Lovecraft 2017, 482) intermingle. It is even suggested that Suydam's accomplices are Yazidis, lazily demonised in the story as devil-worshippers. Malone himself is Irish, which is enough racial otherness to give him "the Celt's far vision of weird and hidden things" (482) but otherwise he is "normal-featured" (481). In this fictional world, he fulfils the role of a default protagonist, whose assumptions and world view are not so far from Lovecraft's own, and his presumed readership. The story documents the descent of this protagonist into a monstrously hybrid environment, which is strange and threatening to him. Malone survives at the expense of his peace of mind: an exchange familiar to players of *Darkest Dungeon*, but recognisable throughout closed spaces in horror literature.

Manuel Aguirre's *The Closed Space: Horror Literature and Western Symbolism* (1990) draws critical focus to the importance of enclosed spaces and Gothic literature; caverns, catacombs and labyrinths. For Aguirre "the world is defined in horror literature as *space* and, furthermore, as a *closed space*" (2). There are few writers whose work better reflects this than H.P. Lovecraft, whose weird tales frequently turn on terrible secrets uncovered in secret, subterranean tunnels. Aguirre's words, however, seem equally applicable to "dungeon crawlers," as a genre of videogame that sees adventurers charting forgotten castles, underground networks, and monster-filled mazes. Often punishingly difficult, these are equally recognisable for their atmosphere and tension as players move from room to room dreading their next encounter, as Aguirre states, "behind the many doors and walls of horror fiction lurks an Adversary" (3). In the example of "The Horror at Red Hook" above, the reader is invited to vicariously experience the fearful events happening to Malone. In the videogame, this relationship with the protagonist is even more direct. Diane Carr notes that in games, "the avatars are our emissaries in the game world and thus each is (to some degree) our double" (68). This doubling, a Gothic trope, means that avatars "are capable of generating forms of uncanny resonance" (68).

Exploring underground spaces is a theme across Lovecraft's fiction, with key examples, including "The Beast in the Cave" and "The Shunned House." Games studies often stress distinctions between kinds of spaces that are crucial in design terms. Both *Darkest Dungeon* and *Crawl* are largely procedurally generated, with *Crawl* putting other players in charge of the monsters. This means that each instance of play is unique, with tension created through design.[5] This creates structural descent, noted by Oakes as a feature of weird fiction: "whether it be into a tunnel, dungeon, tomb, cavern or labyrinth" (Oakes 2000: 4). Aguirre also focuses on this descent and claims that the world of horror symbolism is defined in terms of walls and boundaries put in place specifically to exclude a malevolent Other, which he refers to as the *numinous*. This chaotic presence can be detected in the earliest Celtic myths where other worlds leak into this one at several points, for example in the mythological structure of the Quest narrative:

> The Quest involves a journey from the Court to the Other, from Here to There, and back; and through this pattern it impressed upon us the notion that the world is the world *and* what lies beyond, that the self is the self *and* what lies within; and that wholeness and harmony reside only in this understanding.
>
> (19)

This achievement of harmony is what is most distinctively lacking in Lovecraft's fiction, and the encounter between self and Other is often a shattering revelation. In the "Horror at Red Hook" the area serves as an urban dungeon, as Lovecraft writes: "was not his very act of plunging into the polyglot abyss of New York's underworld a freak beyond sensible explanation?" (Lovecraft "Red Hook" 482) Malone's encounter with the true reality of this world is one that breaks him, and it is knowledge he is then compelled to keep secret for fear of being thought mad: "To hint to unimaginative people of a horror beyond all human conception—[...]would be merely to invite a padded cell instead of restful rustication" (482).

A descent below brings revelations to the surface in many, if not most, of Lovecraft's stories. Oakes claims that "Novels and stories in this genre also often deal with hidden secrets or revelations that come to the surface and change the lives of the characters" (Oakes 2000: 4). Notable examples might include "The Rats in the Walls" (1924) where the narrator discovers a subterranean lair beneath his ancestral home, where his predecessors indulged in slavery and cannibalism, and "The Shunned House" (1937) where the narrator discovers the elbow of a titanic monster buried beneath his basement. In each case there is the physical descent that is representative of a plunge into a version of the self that is inseparably entwined with genetic ancestry. Purity of ancestry is important for Lovecraft, as seen in his separatist racial thinking which holds hybridity and miscegenation as true horrors, but it is actually recognition of the self that makes this doubling truly uncanny.

Lovecraft's earlier work revels in this Freudian doubling that is characteristic of Victorian Gothic, as can be seen in his piece of juvenilia "The Beast in the Cave" (1918). Already using his characteristic first-person narration, Lovecraft sketches out the story of an explorer in the Mammoth Cave in Kentucky, which he had researched in the Providence Public Library (Jones 1). The narrator becomes "hopelessly lost" (Lovecraft "Beast" 17) and increasingly fearful of an unseen beast in the darkness. Here, parallels with the dungeon crawler game genre are clear. He arms himself with a rock, without hope that he can overpower the creature. This lack of power often distinguishes games that aim for a horror affect from those that seek to empower the player with over-the-top weaponry (the *Doom* series is one of few examples that do both). Using hearing to locate the creature, he manages to mortally wound it with the rock. Approaching the figure, he sees that its skin and hair are pure white, the eyes blind, and the limbs adapted to moving on all fours. The moment of horrific revelation is when he realises that this "was, or had at one time been, a MAN!!!" (25). This moment of uncanny kinship is the ultimate horror, and shades of Lovecraft's dungeon-crawling narrator can be seen in the protagonists of the dungeon crawler games we discuss, alone in the dark against hybrid horrors. In *Darkest Dungeon* the player must face the horrors unleashed by a mysterious ancestor, and in *Crawl* defeat actually means that the hero player actually becomes the monster, turning against the next player to be put in control. In the case of *Darkest Dungeon*, specifically, this results in madness.

Madness and Difficulty: *Darkest Dungeon*

Lovecraft's stories frequently employ the recurring trope of madness within, maintaining a consistent link between inner and outer forces, and the ways that the latter can impact the human mind. As S.T. Joshi notes in *The Weird Tale*: "An unusually large number of Lovecraft's characters go mad at some point or other, and many others have madness imputed to them" (212). This serves several purposes within the text, not least in the ways the destabilising of the narrator's sanity allows the reader's imagination to run riot: just *what* was so sublimely horrible that even a sight of it can send someone mad? More significantly, this is presented not just as a reaction to trauma, but to *revelation*: it is not the "horrors" that are harmful, but the confrontation with truths, even, perhaps especially, long-buried yet familiar ones. As Joshi notes: "These characters end up not dead but psychologically shattered, and the suggestion is that their impure approach to intellection has brought this about" (205). This lack of understanding as a character trait is a feature that continues in gaming, including *The Call of Cthulhu* roleplaying game and its spiritual successors. Dave Alexander points out that "early versions of the game often resulted in the characters going insane, and even with modifications of the game play this still remains a possibility, makes it an even closer reflection of Lovecraft's invariable plotting" (qtd. in Jones 229). Lovecraftian video games, then, tend to engage with madness not just as a feeling or affect afflicting the reader but as a tangible mechanic that changes how the player's avatar operates.

Darkest Dungeon is instantly recognisable to any genre aficionado as a Lovecraftian game. It shows the influence very clearly from the name of the developer (Redhook Games) to the inclusion of a dramatic narration by voice actor Wayne June, who has previously recorded audio versions of Lovecraft's short stories.[6]) *Darkest Dungeon* draws on a wealth of Lovecraft's short stories to present an innovatively told, disturbing narrative of ancestral corruption, otherworldly powers and crumbling mansions. The game allows, even forces, players and their team of heroic avatars to confront this; risking madness, death and other afflictions as they penetrate deeper into the subterranean passages created by their sinister ancestor. What makes the game stand apart is its mechanics that, like Lovecraft's prose, indoctrinate the player into this narrative of cosmic horror by placing emphasis on the psychological aspects of their mission.

This includes an "affliction system" that invites the player to, "battle not only monsters, but stress! Contend with paranoia, masochism, fear, irrationality, and a host of gameplay-meaningful quirks!" (*Darkest Dungeon* Website, https://www.darkestdungeon.com/game-overview/ accessed 1st October 2021). By making these negative character traits a game mechanic, *Darkest Dungeon* introduces an element of pessimism that is usually absent from games but very much present in Lovecraft's fiction. The game is also incredibly challenging, and the "permadeath" system means that a carefully levelled-up and equipped party of adventurers can be wiped out in any given confrontation with monsters in the dungeons of the title. Should they live, they may be changed by their encounters with horror and must be sent to an asylum to recover, or else continue to suffer negative gameplay affects due to post-traumatic stress.

"The Horror at Red Hook" provides parallels in content that go beyond the general Lovecraftian mood of the game. Malone has been so affected by the collapse of Sudyam's residence and the sights he has borne witness to that he fears the city itself. Lovecraft describes him as "staring queerly for a second at the tallest of the buildings before him, and then, with a series of terrified, hysterical shrieks, breaking into a frantic" (Lovecraft "Red Hook" 480). This has immediate and grounded consequences for his ability to perform his job. He has been compelled to take a leave of absence and move to the small village of Chepachet to undertake his "psychological convalescence" (481). Lovecraft's recurring motif of forbidden knowledge suggests that there is a terrible truth at the heart of the universe that humans are not meant to know. Malone may be seen as "insane" but actually he knows something that others do not. Malone has not been locked up for his recovery, but Joshi's point about asylums fits well: "madhouses in Lovecraft are habitually places housing those who have glimpsed some truth about existence too horrible to bear [...] It is not necessarily the case that the inmates of asylums are actually mad" (Joshi 213). In *Darkest Dungeon*, characters can go to the abbey to pray, meditate, or even self-flagellate as penance; they can also go to the tavern to drown their sorrows. Like Lovecraft's "mad" characters, it is more appropriate to think of their being victims of traumatic, but truthful, experiences.

Darkest Dungeon's gameplay is "roguelike," with turn-based combat, procedurally generated dungeons and the aforementioned permanent death of characters. The player, then, is not empowered as such, as every encounter may end in a death which is only made worse by the bleakly mocking comments of the narrator. Lovecraft's fiction, too, is characterised by selfish and flawed protagonists who very pointedly do not rise up to the occasion in some kind of heroic fashion, as in Aguirre's characterisation of the quest narrative. Oakes notes that, "a few basic guidelines shape the majority of his human characters. One is that they cannot suddenly become capable of performing extraordinary feats" (Oakes

2000: 31). Although storytelling in videogames is evolving away from it, the on-screen avatar still tends to be a vehicle of empowerment—not human frailty. If anything, Lovecraft's fiction shows a trajectory from being potential heroic to cowardice. In "The Horror at Red Hook" he asks, "what could reduce a dauntless fighter to a quivering neurotic; what could make old brick slums and seas of dark, subtle faces a thing of nightmare and eldritch portent" (482). This is the horror of *Darkest Dungeon*: the cast of hired warriors can be broken and afflicted with gameplay-altering traits that might see them run from a battle, or even turn on their companions as the crazed, cannibalistic narrator of "The Rats in the Walls" does.

Darkest Dungeon's plot revolves around the player inheriting a mansion owned by a relative in ways that clearly point to "The Rats in the Walls." He has uncovered the otherworldly monstrosities by excavating the land he possessed and has now passed down through the family. Like Lovecraft's fiction, more generally, the player is faced by a threat coming uncannily from their own lineage, and this is a threat that is greater than anything human. The human nature of the characters is emphasised by their reliance on basic needs such as food and light. Light, in particular, serves a specific gameplay function, as torches fade and monsters become stronger in the dark. Absence of light is key to "The Beast in the Cave," which emphasises the challenges faced in such dark and hidden places. The narrator's lack of supplies leads him to think that "starving would prove my ultimate fate; of this I was certain" (Lovecraft "Beast" 18). Starvation is no less horrific because it is mundane compared to unnatural monstrosity. Similarly, his dwindling torch brings its own fears, in a line that could be lifted from *Darkest Dungeon*: "already my torch had begun to expire; soon I would be enveloped by the total and almost palpable blackness of the bowels of the earth" (18). Redhook Games' use of overt references to Lovecraft's fiction as a marketing tool is only the beginning of a relationship between the game and Lovecraft's Mythos; there are also important structural and tangible parallels. We could even go so far as to characterise much of Lovecraft's fiction as comprising a "dungeon crawl" in literary form, and the legacy of this fiction is evident in its adaptability to the videogame format.

Monsters and Disorientation: *Crawl*

Crawl is in many ways the opposite of *Darkest Dungeon*. It is fast paced, requires frantic button pressing, and is, most significantly, multiplayer. Whereas *Darkest Dungeon* uses difficulty, character permadeath, mechanics of disease, and mental instability to recreate the atmosphere of a literary dungeon crawl, *Crawl* places characters directly in the chaos. *Crawl* turns the dungeon crawl into a 30-minute competitive multiplayer session: one player is the living hero while the others try to kill them by setting traps and unleashing monsters. When the hero dies, the "ghost" that killed him takes his place and the crawl continues. The hero who levels up can buy equipment and spells while the ghosts can increase the power of their monster forms. The session culminates in fighting a boss fight to return to the surface. Once the boss is defeated, the hero that was in control at the time makes it to the surface and the other characters remain trapped in a true cosmic horror ending. In focusing on the dungeon crawl as an experience, then, *Crawl* is able to turn it into a fun, multiplayer experience rather than an emotive, narrative one. Whereas *Darkest Dungeon* adds on sub-systems to the dungeon crawl to better recreate the oppression of Lovecraft's fiction, *Crawl* positions players so that they generate their own frustration. This in turn puts the focus on two distinct elements of cosmic horror: monsters and disorientation.

Crawl's presentation is less overtly "Lovecraftian" than *Darkest Dungeon*, but the game's marketing overtly re-uses the language of the Cthulhu mythos, particularly to describe the dungeon and its inhabitants. *Crawl*'s "Greenlight" trailer, for instance, refers to "the dark gods" being "pleased with the living blood I had spilt" (*Crawl* Greenlight Trailer Y). That this recognisable language is directed at the *monsters* accords with Joshi's assertion that "the most distinctive feature of Lovecraft's fiction is its elaborate system of imaginary gods, places, and other paraphernalia" (Joshi 190). The trailer's voice-over also replicates the panicked, unravelling tone of Lovecraft's own narrators. In the "Lurking Fear" the narrator describes a shadow as: "a blasphemous abnormality from hell's nethermost craters; a nameless, shapeless abomination which no mind could fully grasp and no pen even partly describe" (Lovecraft "Lurking" 355). *Crawl*'s trailer is similarly nebulous about its own monsters, describing them as "Long dead things with tentacles and blades" (*Crawl* Greenlight Trailer). A later trailer concludes with: "And I'll not think at all of the soul who took my place, shrieking in those caverns beneath our feet, cursed to drift the halls forever. Dead. And alone." (*Crawl* early access trailer) The tone here matches the basement full of monsters in "The Horror at Red Hook": "nothing can ever efface the memory of those nighted crypts, those titan arcades, and those half-formed shapes of hell that strode gigantically in silence" (Lovecraft "Red Hook" 498). Monsters in *Crawl* then are not just the familiar tentacled creatures inspired by the Cthulhu mythos: they are positioned as unknowable, indescribable horrors from below.

Crawl's mechanic of becoming the monster yourself is also an articulation of Lovecraft's fears. In "The Beast in the Cave" the narrator realises with hysteria, emphasised through punctuation that the "creature" he killed was once human (Lovecraft "Beast" 25). Equally, in the "The Lurking Fear" there comes a similar revelation about the "creatures" underground: "the frightful outcome of isolated spawning, multiplication, and cannibal nutrition above and below the ground; the embodiment of all the snarling chaos and grinning fear that lurk behind life." (Lovecraft "Lurking" 373) Not only are the creatures degenerate human beings, but their classification is indivisible from their subterranean existence and their chaotic nature. *Crawl* players may not be the products of cannibalistic incest but their requirement to act the role of monsters, "as a creature of the old gods," through the use of "arcane symbols" marks this same embodiment of "snarling chaos" (*Crawl*, Greenlight). Oakes writes that Lovecraft believed "that the universe is an amoral place where there is neither good nor evil" (33), a sentiment recognisable across his oeuvre. By pitting players against each other, *Crawl* skilfully enacts this aspect of Lovecraft's fiction.

Crawl's other distinct element is its use of disorientation: through its title and gameplay it emphasises that the dungeon is something labyrinthine that needs to be escaped. Not only are the dungeon layouts randomly generated, but players must descend into multiple floors until they are able to challenge the boss. One of the later *Crawl* trailers, the Nintendo Switch version, advertises its key gameplay in a sentence, "Crawl the dungeon while your friends possess the traps, beasts, and bosses against you" before later adopting the phrase "Lose yourself to the darkness of the void" (*Crawl* Switch trailer). Giving players only limited details of the scenario has been recognised as in keeping with horror fiction, as Rouse III notes: "A popular game design device is to give players some information about their surroundings, while leaving a lot out. This again is a natural fit for the horror genre" (III 18). In situating the game not as a voyage *into* the dungeon, as is common in the genre (even in *Darkest Dungeon*), but as a flight from it this effect is heightened. This echoes a section from "The Beast in the Cave":

> I was lost, completely, hopelessly lost in the vast and labyrinthine recesses of the Mammoth Cave [...] That nevermore should I behold the blessed light of day [...] my reason could no longer entertain the slightest unbelief. Hope had departed.
>
> (Lovecraft "Beast" 17)

This story "is an example of the futile – and as it turns out, dangerous - attempt to control wild nature; but nature has the last laugh" (Joshi 221). This too reflects a wider trend within Lovecraft's writing: "One disturbing tenet of Lovecraft's cosmicism is that the human race is at the mercy of its environment and subject to forces it cannot control" (Oakes 32). As players race from room to room, beset by foes, alternating between hero and monster the disorientation of the gameplay inadvertently emulates this sensation of being subject to an uncontrollable environment. Players are at the mercy of forces they cannot comprehend, let alone stop, which is all part of the crawl.

Conclusion: "In that gaping abyss we will find our redemption"

The Dungeon Crawl, whether represented in literary fiction or in a videogame, is an *experience*. It is something that readers or players must encounter by degrees. For the weird tale this is accomplished through language; we are told about the loss of light in "The Beast in the Cave," we experience Malone's quest alongside him in "The Horror at Red Hook." That Lovecraft was able to accomplish this so effectively is a feat; as he writes in "The Lurking Fear": "What language can describe the spectacle of a man lost in infinitely abysmal earth; pawing, twisting, wheezing; scrambling madly through sunken convolutions of immemorial blackness without an idea of time, safety, direction, or definite object?" (Lovecraft "Lurking" 366). Videogames like *Crawl* and *Darkest Dungeon* bring us into a similar experience into abysmal earth with them. Their mechanics of mental instability and difficulty send us "scrambling madly" just as Lovecraft's prose seeks to do. Their procedurally generated maps and disorientating gameplay puts us in the position of "twisting" through the "immemorial blackness" with the same loss of safety or direction. It is undoubtedly the case that elements of Lovecraft's world view and perhaps even themes belong firmly in the past. These games differ from the stories which have inspired them by introducing a playfulness that is not only inherent to the medium but also one that allows for a revision of Lovecraft's presentation of the fear of the Other, in particular. *Darkest Dungeon* does this through engaging single-player gameplay that at least raises the possibility of redemption over ancestral evil, and *Crawl* takes this further by its rapid and light-hearted switching of adventurer and adversary in a multiplayer setting. The history of gaming may have deep ancestral roots that intertwine with fiction but the innovation and forward-thinking approach of dungeon crawlers may potentially point to a way out, even if the hope of victory remains an illusion designed to pull the player back into the depths for another try.

Notes

1 A term used by Linda Hutcheon (as discussed in detail later) to denote the idea of multiple versions of a fictional "cosmos" created through the process of adaptation.

2 Following *Alone in the Dark*, Infogrames would go on to collaborate with Chaosium, publisher of *The Call of Cthulhu* roleplaying game to produce two traditional adventure games: *Shadow of the Comet* and *Prisoner of Ice* [...] both inspired by the Cthulhu mythology created by H.P. Lovecraft (Therrien, 2009: 33–34).

3 As LaValle points out, there is a potentially delightful, if not entirely redeeming, irony in that Lovecraft has attracted "such a diverse cast of readers that Howard himself would probably never believe it possible" (xiv). In this context, then, works can potentially engage with the Cthulhu mythos and its cycle of shared themes, moods, fictional gods, and monsters without replicating racial hatred, even if encoded into the originals.

4 It should of course be noted that Lovecraft's fiction has a long history of visual companion artwork from the pulp magazines and paperbacks to comic books that interweave the "showing" mode with his words.
5 A full-blown analysis of the differences between these and more linear Lovecraftian game experiences, such as *Eternal Darkness: Sanity's Requiem* (2002) and *Amnesia: The Dark Descent* (2010), is a matter for another study.
6 An overt example is the downloadable expansion called *The Color of Madness* (2018) which is clearly based on Lovecraft's "The Colour Out of Space" (1927).

Works Cited

Aguirre, Manuel. *The Closed Space: Horror Literature and Western Symbolism*. Manchester: Manchester University Press, 1990.

Alone in the Dark. Infogrames, 1992.

Amnesia: The Dark Descent. Frictional Games, 2010.

Campbell, Ramsey. "Introduction." *New Tales of the Cthulhu Mythos*, edited by Ramsey Campbell. Wisconsin: Arkham House, 1980, pp. ix–xi.

Carr, Diane. "Space, Navigation and Affect." *Computer Games: Text, Narrative and Play*, edited by Diane Carr, David Buckingham, Andrew Burn and Gareth Schott. Cambridge: Polity, 2006, pp. 59–71 (68).

Crawl. Powerhoof Games, 2017.

Crawl early access trailer, Youtube. Available at: https://www.youtube.com/watch?v=WY0N12w3csI

Crawl Greenlight Trailer, Youtube. Available at: https://www.youtube.com/watch?v=2_3xrqjTyes

Crawl Switch trailer, Youtube. Available at: https://www.youtube.com/watch?v=QZE8Nibvsw0

Darkest Dungeon. Red Hook Studios, 2016.

Darkest Dungeon Website. Available at: https://www.darkestdungeon.com/

Eternal Darkness: Sanity's Requiem. Silicon Knights, 2002.

Gault, Matthew. "Call of Cthulhu' Shows We Need to Move Past H.P. Lovecraft Once and for All." *Vice.com*, 2018. Available at: https://www.vice.com/en_us/article/zm9jyx/call-of-cthulhu-shows-we-need-to-move-past-hp-lovecraft-once-and-for-all

Greer, Sam. "Games Really Need to Fall Out of Love with Lovecraft." *Eurogamer*, 2018. Available at: https://www.eurogamer.net/articles/2018-10-09-games-really-need-to-fall-out-of-love-with-lovecraft

Harms, Daniel. *The Cthulhu Mythos Encyclopedia*. Michigan: Elder Signs Press, 2008.

Hutcheon, Linda and Siobhan O'Flynn. *A Theory of Adaptation* (second edition). Abingdon, Oxon: Routledge, 2013.

Jones, Mark. "Tentacles and Teeth: The Lovecraftian Being in Popular Culture" in *New Critical Essays on H.P. Lovecraft*, edited by David Simmons. New York: Palgrave, 2013, pp. 227–248.

Joshi, S. T. *The Weird Tale*. Pennsylvania: Wildside Press, 1990.

LaValle, Victor. *The Ballad of Black Tom*. New York: Tom Docherty Associates, 2016.

LaValle, Victor. "Introduction." *The New Annotated H.P. Lovecraft: Beyond Arkham*, edited by Leslie S. Klinger. New York: Liveright, 2019, pp. ix–xiv.

Lovecraft, H. P. "The Beast in the Cave" in *H. P. Lovecraft Collected Fiction, A Variorum Edition, Volume 1: 1905–1925*, edited by S. T. Joshi, New York: Hippocampus, 2017, pp. 17–25.

———. "The Colour out of Space." in *H. P. Lovecraft Collected Fiction, A Variorum Edition, Volume 2: 1926–1930*, edited by S. T. Joshi, New York: Hippocampus Press, 2017, pp. 367–399. Lovecraft, H. P. "The Lurking Fear," pp. 223–239.

———. "The Lurking Fear." in *H. P. Lovecraft Collected Fiction, A Variorum Edition, Volume 1: 1905–1925*, edited by S. T. Joshi, New York: Hippocampus, 2017, pp. 349–373.

———. "The Horror at Red Hook." in *H. P. Lovecraft Collected Fiction, A Variorum Edition, Volume 1: 1905–1925*, edited by S. T. Joshi. New York: Hippocampus, 2017, pp. 480–505.

———. "The Rats in The Walls." In *H. P. Lovecraft Collected Fiction, A Variorum Edition, Volume 1: 1905–1925*, edited by S. T. Joshi. New York: Hippocampus, 2017, pp. 374–396.

———. "The Shunned House." In *H. P. Lovecraft Collected Fiction, A Variorum Edition, Volume 1: 1905–1925*, edited by S. T. Joshi. New York: Hippocampus, 2017, pp. 451–479.

———. *Supernatural Horror in Literature. Collected Essays Volume 2, Literary Criticism*, edited by S.T. Joshi. New York: Hippocampus Press, 2004, pp. 82–135.

Luckhurst, Roger. "Introduction." *H.P. Lovecraft: The Classic Horror Stories*, edited by Roger Luckhurst. Oxford: Oxford University Press, 2013, pp. vii–xxviii.

Machin, James. *Weird Fiction in Britain 1880–1939*, Basingstoke: Palgrave, 2018.

Oakes, David A. *Science and Destabilization in the Modern American Gothic: Lovecraft, Matheson and King*. London: Greenwood Press, 2000.

Perron, Bernard. "Introduction: Gaming After Dark." *Horror Video Games*, edited by Bernard Perron. Jefferson, NC: McFarland, 2009.

Prisoner of Ice. Infogrames. 1995.

Rouse III, Richard. "Match Made in Hell: The Inevitable Success of the Horror Genre in Video Games." *Horror Video Games*, edited by Bernard Perron. Jefferson, NC: McFarland, 2009.

Simmons, David. "'A Certain Resemblance': Abject Hybridity in H.P. Lovecraft's Short Fiction." *New Critical Essays on H.P. Lovecraft*, edited by David Simmons, Basingstoke: Palgrave Macmillan, 2013, pp. 13–30.

Shadow of the Comet. Infogrames. 1993.

Taylor, Laurie N. "Gothic Bloodlines in Survival Horror Gaming" in *Horror Video Games*, edited by Bernard Perron. Jefferson, NC: McFarland, 2009.

Therrien, Carl. "Games of Fear: A Multi-Faceted Historical Account of the Horror Genre in Video Games." *Horror Video Games*, edited by Bernard Perron. Jefferson, NC: McFarland, 2009, pp. 15–25.

16 Dreaming in Layers

Lovecraftian Storyworlds in Interactive Media

Eoin Murray

H.P. Lovecraft's narratives and wider storyworlds have seen a surge in adaptation and production by large video companies in the last five years. Players now have the chance to do battle with Cthulhu (e.g. *Call of Cthulhu* [2018]), investigate the lives of Innsmouthers (e.g. *The Sinking City* [2019]), and traverse Nightmare planes conjured by the powers of The Great Ones (e.g. *Bloodborne* [2015]). These recent incarnations of Lovecraft's world demand academic inquiry to examine how successful video game media is able to conjure the spirit of the writer's work in the early 21st century age. Video games, though, still struggle to be seen as "art" by many in mainstream culture and are often faced with a "lack of respect" in comparison to older forms of media (Martin 201). Linda Hutcheon notes that adaptation to a perceived lower art form can often generate immediate negative criticism (3). However, Hutcheon's definition of adaptation as a transposition that is both creative and interpretive in the manner in which it appropriates an original piece highlights the potential of video games to not only engage with Lovecraft's work, but also to "repeat and change" original narrative aspects for the benefit of both a new and a pre-existing audience (9). In the strictest sense, *Bloodborne* is not "faithful" to any one of Lovecraft's stories, but it does evoke his storyworld in ways that are both adaptive and insightful. *Bloodborne* manages to "substantiate that which we most appreciated in the source novels" and is, in this regard, faithful; the environmental ambiance and tension towards an encounter with an Eldritch Horror are central to the *Bloodborne* experience (Stam 54). This essay seeks to analyse how video games can be so well suited to presenting Lovecraftian narratives and how traversing these storyworlds can impact a player's experience. In particular, my analysis focuses on how *Bloodborne* makes use of impossible storyworlds and the interactive nature of its medium to craft a chilling horror experience that resonates with Lovecraft's own style by creating an "estrangement of our sense of reality" (Noys and Murphy 117).

DOI: 10.4324/9780367713065-17

In order to answer these questions and thoroughly analyse my chosen case study, I have drawn on a variety of scholars on Lovecraft (Janicker; Kneale; Petley; Sederholm and Weinstock) and horror in gaming (Krzywinska; Taylor; Rouse III) with some reference to environmental storytelling and emotions in gamers. Given the depth of Lovecraft's own storyworlds, their high place of cultural importance to society, and generations of readers who have become entranced with notions of eldritch horror, it is vital to assess the successful ways his work translates to video games. On average, 75% of American households have at least one video gamer (Entertainment Software Association) in them and such an enormous audience presents the opportunity to introduce thousands of people to Lovecraft's work; analysing particularly successful examples of this could be helpful to both scholars and gaming companies alike. This essay will add to knowledge on adaptation, emotions in video games, and on Lovecraft's work; gaming companies will also find insight into how to employ successful ludic techniques useful for later horror genre video games. This essay will begin by examining Lovecraft's style of writing and ways in which it lends (or does not lend) itself to adaptation by differing media. Following that, the chapter will move to examine video games in more depth, including significant attention to *Bloodborne*. The chapter will include examinations of the game's storyworld and environments for the ways they impact a player's experience as well as generate a terrifying atmosphere. The chapter will conclude by arguing that the power of games to forge emotional connections with players and video game's interactive nature makes them a prime media to adapt Lovecraft's work.

Lovecraftian Adaptation

One of the most difficult elements of Lovecraft's works to adapt is their complex and often-unseen visuals. James Kneale has noted the trend in Lovecraft's short stories to leave the majority of his creatures unseen. Kneale references the "trend" in many tales that begin with a narrator apologizing for their lack of clear memory or the use of journals from long-dead authors to avoid directly "witnessing" cosmic horrors (112). The technique of rendering the monster "unseen" is not new to many styles of horror texts and is in fact crucial to making something terrifying. Dani Cavallaro goes into great detail to examine exactly what it means to apply the word "terror" to an experience or creature. She discusses the word together with horror to ensure that the difference between the two is understood: "If horror makes people shiver, terror undermines the foundations of their worlds. The Latin root of terror, *terrere*, indeed means "to shake up"" (2–3). Horror lends itself to the experience of witnessing; a person sees and understands a horrific creature but is repulsed by the sight. Whereas a terrifying creature is defined so due to its indeterminate nature and serves to unnerve in a way that cannot be accurately described

(2). In this essay, I follow Cavallaro's definition as a means of capturing elements of both horror and terror in video game media. A reader's mind or imagination will serve to conjure their own specific form of the terrifying creature that is entirely their own; every reader may have a different incarnation which makes any adaptation of an author's descriptions highly challenging. Terror more easily lends itself to Lovecraft's style of writing yet by relying so heavily on the experience of visual terror any adaptation becomes a great deal more difficult.

Rebecca Janicker talks directly about Lovecraft's fluid style of writing and his in-depth descriptive passages which are full of dense architectural references and completely devoid of action (472). This is not to say that any and all narratives must include action (to argue such a point would be far beyond the scope of this chapter) but Ari Hiltunen succinctly notes that narrative functions well as a goal-oriented structure and that such a structure naturally involves the struggle for, and attainment of, a goal (8). He writes, "fear is connected to goal-oriented action. When a man is afraid, he seeks safety and directs his actions towards this goal" to highlight how easily understandable and relatable goal-oriented structures are (Hiltunen 8). Suffice to say, traditional quest narratives provide a suitable and adaptable structure that can cross to differing media with little major issues. Lovecraft's works, however, rely on lengthy descriptive passages rather than on more goal-driven high-action tales which present yet another stumbling block to any form of "easy" adaptation.

Continuing on from Lovecraft's lack of action in his stories, Julian Petley has discussed Lovecraft's lack of notable characters. Petley draws attention to the use of characters who, by Lovecraft's own admission, are lacking; he goes on to say that the lack of distinct and fleshed out characters is a primary reason Lovecraft's works resist direct adaptation (38). In his own words, Petley notes Lovecraft's stories are "short on "characters" (especially female ones) and "action" as conventionally understood" (43). When adapting a work to a different media "there cannot be absolute compatibility between the adapted text and its adaptation" (Loannidou 231) but a touchstone of adapting works can be found in memorable characters. The use of characters as recognizable figures to an audience in a new adaptation is an option Lovecraft's works could not employ; for just as he was resistant to grand action narratives, so too was he resistant to notable characters to the point that "even ardent Lovecraft aficionados agree that his work is not easy to adapt" (Petley 43). A more useful touchstone to this effect could be found in Lovecraft's more popular creatures (Cthulhu, Nyarlathotep, etc.), yet these figures are difficult to translate to a visual media due to their classification as overwhelming or even indescribable creatures.

However, this essay is not arguing that the adaptation of Lovecraft's work should not occur, but in fact, quite the opposite. Both Rebecca Janicker as well as Carl Sederholm and Jeffrey Andrew Weinstock have argued that comics are successful for adapting Lovecraft's work and even serve to shed new light on the process of adapting his tales. As Sederholm and Weinstock suggest, "The turn to other media may shed light not only on the process of adaptation but also on the way the Lovecraftian weird functions" (Sederholm and Weinstock 4). Janicker analyses Lovecraftian comic adaptations in great depth and notes that "taking Lovecraft as their putative inspiration, comics nonetheless can—and do—succeed in engaging with the hellish scenarios invoked by his prose" (476). The success of comics is important to note since a comic relies so heavily on visuals. Janicker builds on Scott McCloud's work and states "he designates comics as a kind of halfway house between literature and cinema" (475). Janicker's deduction on the success of Lovecraftian adaptations in a media that finds itself treading the borders between film and book is highly useful to this essay, as it will focus on another media that sits between the two: video games.

Lovecraft in Video Games

Video games have successfully brought some of Lovecraft's narratives to the fore in recent years, including Cyanide's *Call of Cthulhu*, Frogwares' *The Sinking City* and, the main topic of this essay, FromSoftware's *Bloodborne*. However, it is prudent to first establish why video games have successfully adapted Lovecraft's works and how the media is suited to the task. Imagine Games Network (IGN), an independent game media website, reviewed all three of the above video games: *The Sinking City* scoring 7.8/10 "Good," *Call of Cthulhu* scoring 8.6/10 "Great," and *Bloodborne* scoring 9.1/10 "Amazing" (Borba; Schmeyer; Tyrrel). Therefore, a valid deduction would be to say that all three of these games, despite requiring a visual manifestation of inherently "unseeable" Eldritch Horrors, were successful. The key reason for the success of these adaptations lies in the player's active role. A player functions on a more interactive level than a reader or a viewer and must be satisfied in different ways; specifically, their engagement with and immersion into the game's ludic challenges and diegesis. Jane Yellowlees Douglas and Andrew Hargadon term this investment "The Pleasure Principle" and should a player lack either engagement or immersion in the game, they'll lose interest and cease playing (153). Therefore, the "repeat and change" aspects adaptations hinge upon must incorporate a balance of engagement and immersion in a way specific to gaming media. Richard Rouse III argues that upon their inception horror video games place players in a new situation with an original brand of horror in the responsibility they have and feel for the figure on the screen (15). Unlike less interactive media such as books or films, players must take an active level of responsibility for characters in video games. The "death is no longer something happening to someone else" and therefore the player is pulled deeper into the experience and emotionally affected (Rouse III 15). Rouse III sums up this point well by stating, "the goals of video games and the goals of horror fiction directly overlap" since both seek to unnerve and repulse those who engage with them (15).

Video games and emotions have a complex relationship, one that is beyond the scope of this essay. However, a brief analysis into the scholarship on the subject serves to demonstrate how emotions in players can conjure the same visceral response that Lovecraft's terrifying descriptions seek to evoke. Jonathan Frome syntheses the complexity of emotions felt by gamers by discussing how there cannot be a single word to describe sensations such as ""having fun by being frustrated" or "being uncertain of the reason your avatar's movements don't correspond to your button presses"" (859). Frome goes on to give a very broad definition of emotions as "bodily changes that are prompted by appraisals of situations based on one's goals and concerns" (859). There is a clear physical reaction involved in an emotional process. Several scholars have made note of the power of video games to create a deep emotional connection with a player (Domsch; Douglas and Hargadon; Hefner et al.; Isbister; Jerčić; Murray) and such a deep emotional connection conjures a physical reaction when presented with specific situations over the course of the gameplay.

As players are drawn further into the gaming experience, they begin to suspend disbelief and are no longer sitting on a chair with a controller in their hands guiding an avatar through a game level. Instead, players identify with and project onto the character they are controlling; they may even feel anxious at the prospect of failure or death, exhilarated when they are successful, proud when they achieve a victory, or even sympathetic for losses of their avatar (255). This personal connection increases the amount of emotional investment players have in the experience and therefore makes an impact on the emotions they feel. It becomes easier to see how effective video games are at portraying the horror genre when examined in this way. Players are pushed to the edge of their ability to remain calm while experiencing the "shaking" effects of terror or the revulsion of horror. The experience then becomes a struggle to remain successful at besting ludological trials (enemies, environmental hazards, puzzles, etc.) while being emotionally gripped by fear. For many players, this is where the fun of the experience is found, and the greater the fear produced, the sweeter the success of victory becomes.

A player moving through a Lovecraftian storyworld may not be literally terrified to madness by witnessing an Eldritch Horror in the same way a character in one of Lovecraft's short stories may have been. But the experience of the said horror existing as a very real threat to their success of ludological victory makes it compellingly frightening. Such a simple form of antagonism is a boon to video games as Rouse III notes, "game storytelling works best when the plot is fairly simple" (16). While several video game examples go against Rouse III's point, having shown the ability to build themselves around complex narrative experiences (Telltale Games for example), the point is useful insomuch as justifying simple motivations work well. A player does not need to understand why an Eldritch Horror desires them harm. In fact, the creature may be so utterly inhuman that its motivations cannot be understood. But a player is aware that this creature will attack and kill them and could emerge at any time. This creates a constant tension in the player's emotional state that is compounded by the additional semiotic systems a video game can make use of such as the aural, the tactile (controllers vibrating for example), and the interactive (Elferen 30). All combine as one to provide a media experience that has been shown to adapt Lovecraft's stories both directly and indirectly successfully and introduced his works to countless new players.

Bloodborne

Bloodborne has received critical acclaim since its release, including PlayStation Game of the Year (2015) and a BAFTA for Game Design in the same year and therefore can be justifiably called a successful commercial release. However, the game's style and presentation also stand out for the ways it matches Lovecraft's own style of narrative by focusing on strong environmental ambiance, building tension, and creating a deep anticipation for Eldritch Horrors. Both *The Sinking City* and *Call of Cthulhu* made use of named protagonists with deep backstories that worked to evoke sympathy for their plights (both protagonists are white, middle-aged men who are veterans of the first world war and who suffer from forms of PTSD). *Bloodborne* follows suit with the kind of adaptations that Petley described, such as being short on characters and action as conventionally understood. The game's protagonist serves more as a vehicle to move through the detailed environments and face the horrors of the storyworld. Despite this, the players will still naturally form a bond with them and may even project themselves onto the "blank-slate" character. In this way, *Bloodborne* follows Lovecraft's penchant for environmental ambiance over character development and action.

This is not to say that the character serves little narrative function and is wholly unknown. The protagonist of *Bloodborne* (henceforth referred to as the Hunter) is from a foreign land and travelled to the city of Yharnam (where the game takes place) to receive healing via the "Old Blood." The "Old Blood" is a miracle cure that will heal any injury and has made Yharnman famous in the past. While the city of Yharnam does a great deal to evoke a sense of the "Gothic Victorian" in its landscape through the use of tall spires, grand cathedrals, and obscuring fog, it never directly pulls from Lovecraft's works, save to use the term "Great One" to refer to the Eldritch Horrors of the game. Instead, *Bloodborne* provides the original city of Yharnam and other locations (notably Dreams and

Nightmares) for the Hunter to explore; the Dream and Nightmare locations having been created through the power of Great Ones at the desperate behest of humans. The motivation for this exploration is formed by The Hunter's status as a stranger; as they explore and learn small nuggets of information about Yharnam, so too does the player. Both the player and the protagonist are learning at the same time in an organic fashion showing *Bloodborne's* strong storytelling mechanics.

The storytelling of *Bloodborne* is done through the game's environments that serve as both ludological levels testing player skill and in-depth narrative locations that must be explored to fully interpret the story. The game does its best to avoid ever giving the player any form of direct narrative exposition and often leaves the truth ambiguous or past stories unfinished. This form of ambiguous storytelling fits well with Lovecraft's own style mentioned at the beginning of this section as some of his short stories end abruptly with the fate of those involved left unclear, as "The Haunter of the Dark" and "Dagon" illustrate. Environmental storytelling, as a sphere for academic inquiry, was first used in the analysis of theme park rides (Fernandez-Vara 2). Don Carson, a designer for theme parks, computer games, and software, states regarding environmental storytelling: "it is the physical space that does much of the work of conveying the story the designers are trying to tell. Color, lighting and even the texture of a place can fill an audience with excitement or dread" (2). Henry Jenkins also mentions the power of environmental storytelling but adds that the most successful examples of the feat all make use of pre-existing narrative or genre conventions an audience will recognize (118). In a similar vein, Tanya Krzywinska notes the allure of a "pre-branded product" when discussing *Call of Cthulhu: Dark Corners of The Earth* (267). Even while not directly referencing Lovecraft's works, *Bloodborne* remains a Lovecraftian game tightly focused on environmental ambiance and tension building towards the witnessing of an unspeakable terror. The game offers players the experience of exploring levels and landscapes to see what elements of the inspirational work they may find while attempting to unravel the game's own narrative.

Dreaming in Layers

The storyworld of *Bloodborne* is separated into two distinct planes; the "real world" where the city of Yharnam exists (termed the "Waking World" by characters in-game), and the Dream/Nightmare planes which were created by the Great Ones. A separation into "Waking" and "Dream" space links to Lovecraft's own works such as *The Dream-Quest of Unknown Kadath* where Randolph Carter learns to navigate both spaces. The duality of human desire and Great One creation immediately forms a sense of Otherness about that place that toes the line of terrifying and horrific (Said). The Hunter will not directly feel this sense of Otherness but it will transfer over to the human player, affecting their emotions and impeding their ability to play at a skilful level. Thus, the link between environmental design and player experience is formed. Beyond this though, is the main crux of this chapter, the player's experience with exploring Lovecraftian environments. The Dream/Nightmare planes are the most rewarding to analyse for their design, since each of them is, upon close inspection, connected to one another. From the peaceful Hunter's Dream to the ghastly Nightmare Frontier and Hunter's Nightmare, all locations make use of subtle environmental designs that not only evoke a Lovecraftian sense of terror, but also serve to offer insidious insight into their connections to the observant player.

The Hunter's Dream is the first Dream/Nightmare location the player will come across in *Bloodborne*. The area consists of a workshop surrounded by a field of flowers that appears to be isolated from all other spaces but, naturally, a player will be inclined to test the barriers of the space and explore it. Mark J.P. Wolf discusses this predilection gamers have towards exploring in *The Medium of the Video Game* where he notes the crucial difference between video games and other visual media: a player will not remain idle as they absorb an understanding of the space around them through static images, but rather through a self-motivated and directed method of exploration (Wolf). Fraser further analyses the use of space in video games and notes the complexity of the relationship a player will build with a video game space as their own understanding consistently evolves the more time spent gaming in that space (94). The necessity gamers have to explore unknown spaces suits aspects of horror and Lovecraft's own works well. In several of Lovecraft's narratives, the characters he wrote of, all had their desires to explore and learn, leading them to encounter their doom. The Hunter's Dream though serves as an antithesis to this notion as it presents a safe space for the player to become more accustomed to the gameplay. Soft, soothing music is heard, a friendly Non-Player Character (NPC) serves as a level-up point to increase the player's power, and (with the exception of the game's finale) no enemy creatures appear there.

However, The Hunter's Dream is far from unconnected to the more monstrous spaces in the game. Looking into the distance of The Hunter's Dream, a player will be able to make out several tall pillar-like structures jutting up from the foggy ground (see Figure 16.1).

These pillars may appear innocuous at first glance yet could be connected with the darkest areas of later Nightmare locations. They could be ship masts that are jutting up from wreckage located in a space known as The Hunter's Nightmare. Such a statement may seem at first to make rational sense; however, as the player traverses more of the Nightmare planes, the more the geography begins to seem impossible (see Figure 16.2 and Figure 16.3).

Figure 16.1 The "pillars-like structures" in The Hunter's Dream.
Source: (FromSoftware)

Figure 16.2 A ship mast all but hidden in the Nightmare Frontier.
Source:(FromSoftware)

The appearance of the masts is eventually traced back to the final area of The Hunter's Nightmare. As Figure 16.3 shows, the ship masts seem to stand tall but not stretch endlessly into the sky. Yet in the Nightmare

Figure 16.3 The ships found at the end of The Hunter's Nightmare.
Source: (FromSoftware)

Frontier, should the player angle the camera down and focus, the same ship masts are in fact visible though heavily obscured through the fog. Looking at both figures, it seems impossible for the Nightmare Frontier to exist above The Hunter's Nightmare and the ship masts to reach The Hunter's Dream; yet this is workably the case. What makes this point particularly valuable is that it relies upon the player's exploring. A more experienced player would likely possess a schema that encourages them to assess the environment around them. In the same way, a seasoned Lovecraft admirer would note that the author naming the protagonist of "Haunter of the Dark" Robert Blake was a nod to Robert Bloch, author of "The Shambler from the Stars" that Lovecraft's short story was a sequel to.

By demanding a player investigate the world around them to establish these twisted geographical connections, the game at once rewards those observant enough to find them and forces a confrontation with an impossible world. Marie-Laure Ryan states one of the characteristics of the impossible fictional storyworld is contradictions (130). These contradictions can exist at varying levels of literature but for the case of an interactive storyworld, it is not the words on the page that cannot be reconciled but a physical location. By the laws of physics presented in the game, the three Dream and Nightmare planes should not exist as they currently do and the impossibility of the world that the player can witness, catalogue, and be stumped by breeches "the outer contours of human understanding and rationality, where the imagination can easily locate monstrous terrors" (Krzywinska 278). The theory behind this experience pulls from Slavoj Zizek's description of The Real as something that defies understanding and halts logic (1992). Krzywinska goes on to describe the impact encountering the Real has had in Lovecraftian fiction, stating, "in the yawning maw of

Cthulhean, all certainties and comforting correspondences become merely the blown dust of illusion" (278). The shattering revelation that the worlds they are traversing through are in fact connected could serve to freeze a player for a few moments and change their understanding of the space around them. While the player is in no danger from these uncomfortable questions, they move through the storyworld as The Hunter and adopt the concerns, goals, and worries this character may have (Isbister 11). So, the world at once coming together (and apart) from their observations blurs boundaries and serves to make safe spaces feel unsafe.

Laurie N. Taylor notes that transgressing boundaries is a key feature to the gothic story; she puts forward the term "ludic-gothic" to discuss how the act of boundary transgression forms horror in video game media (47). *Bloodborne* certainly makes use of the gothic in its environments and thus Taylor's focus on boundaries is particularly apt when analysing how the player explores the game's Lovecraftian Dream and Nightmare worlds, especially following the revelation that all are impossibly connected. Crossing these boundaries is a process that generates fear since the player will be exploring the unknown that is presented to them in an impossible fashion. It appears as though anything could happen or any form of obstacle come forward to halt progress. While this is an illusion to a degree (as the amount of processes a finished media artefact could put forward is finite), the potential given over by the player's own emotions makes the prospect much more powerful. *Bloodborne*, having shown its Dreams and Nightmares to be impossibly connected, opens the player's mind to countless other possible events, each of which may be more frightening to them than the last. In this way, exploring the game becomes a fearful process that constantly puts a player on edge, forever waiting for one of their imagined scenarios to be realised.

Conclusion

Overall, the strength of *Bloodborne*'s adaptation of Lovecraft's storyworld lies in its ability to kindle emotional investment and responsibility in a player for The Hunter moving through the storyworld. Unlike media such as comics and films, video games ensured that death was now something that happened to the player as punishment for their failure and this serves to escalate the tension of the experience, adding a level of responsibility designed to heighten emotional tension. Not only does this suit the horror genre of gaming in general but is also particularly effective when combined with the elements of madness and Otherness Lovecraft's work is known for. *Bloodborne* forces a player to stop and wonder what else the game's impossible worlds may do that they cannot predict. The threat of what could come to assault them keeps the players at a high state of tension, affecting their ludic performance and drawing them deeper into the experience. A player cannot help but project onto the player character of a game, tying their emotions to the fate of the avatar on-screen and experiencing fear on their behalf. This emotional connection ties with *Bloodborne's* Lovecraftian style in its environmental ambiance and building terror to affect players on a visceral level. The power of Lovecraft often lies in the unseen and video games can make use of this by turning a player's own mind and emotions against them. This ability makes video games one of the best media through which to introduce a vast new audience to the terrifying world of H.P. Lovecraft.

Works Cited

Bigben Interactive. *The Sinking City*. Frogwares, 2019.

Bloch, Robert. "The Shambler from the Stars." *Weird Tales*, vol. 26, no. 3, 1935, p. 132.

Borba, John. "The Sinking City Review – IGN." *IGN*, 2020, https://uk.ign.com/articles/2019/06/25/the-sinking-city-review.

Carson, Don. "Environmental Storytelling: Creating Immersive 3D Worlds Using Lessons Learned from the Theme Park Industry." *Gamasutra*, 2000, p. 7.

Cavallaro, Dani. *The Gothic Vision: Three Centuries of Horror, Terror, and Fear*. New York: Continuum, 2002.

Domsch, Sebastian. *Storyplaying: Agency and Narrative in Video Games*. Berlin: De Gruyter, Inc., 2013. *ProQuest Ebook Central*, http://ebookcentral.proquest.com/lib/bangor/detail.action?docID=1000613.

Douglas, Jane Yellowlees, and Andrew Hargadon. "*The Pleasure Principle*." *Proceedings of the Eleventh ACM on Hypertext and Hypermedia – HYPERTEXT '00*, May 2000, pp. 153–160, doi:10.1145/336296.336354.

Elferen, Isabella Van. "¡Un Forastero! Issues of Virtuality and Diegesis in Videogame Music." *Musica and the Moving Image*, vol. 4, no. 2, 2011, pp. 30–39, doi:10.5406/musimoviimag.4.2.0030.

Entertainment Software Association. 2019 Essential Facts about the Computer and Video Game Industry. *Entertaiment Software Association*, 2019, p. 24.

Fernandez-Vara, Clara. "Game Spaces Speak Volumes: Indexical Storytelling." *MIT Web Domain*, January 2011. *dspace.mit.edu*, http://dspace.mit.edu/handle/1721.1/100274.

Focus Home Interactive. *Call of Cthulhu*. Cyanide, 2018.

Fraser, Benjamin. "Why the Spatial Epistemology of the Video Game Matters: Metis, Video Game Space and Interdisciplinary Theory." *Journal of Gaming & Virtual Worlds*, vol. 3, no. 2, July 2011, pp. 93–106. *IngentaConnect*, doi:10.1386/jgvw.3.2.93_1.

Frome, Jonathan. "Interactive Works and Gameplay Emotions." *Games and Culture*, vol. 14, no. 7–8, SAGE Publications, November 2019, pp. 856–874. *SAGE Journals*, doi:10.1177/1555412019847907.

FromSoftware. *Bloodborne*. 2015, https://www.google.co.uk/#safe=off&q=bloodborne.

Hefner, Dorothée, et al. "*Identification with the Player Character as Determinant of Video Game Enjoyment*." *Entertainment Computing – ICEC 2007*, edited by Lizhuang Ma et al., Springer Berlin Heidelberg, 2007, pp. 39–48.

Hiltunen, Ari. "The Anatomy of the 'Proper Pleasure'." *Aristotle in Hollywood: Visual Stories That Work, Intellect Books Ltd*, 2001, pp. 123–131. *ProQuest Ebook Central*, http://ebookcentral.proquest.com/lib/bangor/detail.action?docID=283022.

Hutcheon, Linda. *A Theory of Adaptation*. Taylor & Francis Group, 2012. *ProQuest Ebook Central*, http://ebookcentral.proquest.com/lib/bangor/detail.action?docID=1016075.

Isbister, Katherine. *How Games Move Us: Emotion by Design*. Cambridge, MA: MIT Press, 2016.

Janicker, Rebecca. "Visions of Monstrosity: Lovecraft, Adaptation and the Comics Arts." *Journal of the Fantastic in the Arts*, vol. 26, no. 3, 2015, pp. 469–488.

Jenkins, Henry. "Game Design as Narrative Architecture." *First Person: New Media as Story, Performance, and Game*, 1st ed., Cambridge, MA: MIT Press, 2004, https://whel-primo.hosted.exlibrisgroup.com/primo-explore/openurl?sid=google&auinit=H&aulast=Jenkins&atitle=Game%20design%20as%20narrative&title=Computer&volume=44&issue=53&date=2004&spage=118&issn=0018-9162&vid=44WHELF_BANG_VU4&institution=44WHELF_BANG&url_ctx_val=&url_ctx_fmt=null&isServicesPage=true.

Jerčić, Petar. *The Effects of Emotions and Their Regulation on Decision – Making Performance in Affective Serious Games. Blekinge Tekniska Högskola*, 2019, http://www.diva-portal.org/smash/get/diva2:1284122/FULLTEXT02.pdf.

Kneale, James. "From beyond: H. P. Lovecraft and the Place of Horror." *Cultural Geographies*, vol. 13, no. 1, SAGE Publications Ltd, January 2006, pp. 106–26. *SAGE Journals*, doi:10.1191/1474474005eu353oa.

Krzywinska, Tanya. "Reanimating Lovecraft: The Ludic Paradox of Call of Cthulhu: Dark Corners of the Earth." *Horror Video Games*, McFarland & Company, Inc., 2009, p. 22.

Loannidou, Elisavet. "Adapting Superhero Comics for the Big Screen: Subculture for the Masses." *Adaptation*, vol. 6, no. 2, 2013, pp. 230–238, doi: 10.1093/adaptation/apt004.

Murray, Janet Horowitz. *Hamlet on the Holodeck: The Future of Narrative in Cyberspace*. New York: Simon and Schuster, 1997, https://books.google.co.uk/books/about/Hamlet_on_the_Holodeck.html?id=bzmSLtnMZJsC&pgis=1.

Noys, Benjamin, and Timothy S. Murphy. "Introduction: Old and New Weird." *Genre*, vol. 49, no. 2, Duke University Press, July 2016, pp. 117–134. *read.dukeupress.edu*, doi:10.1215/00166928-3512285.

Petley, Julian. "The Unfilmable? H. P. Lovecraft and The Cinema." *Monstrous Adaptations Generic and Thematic Mutations in Horror Film*. Manchester: Manchester University Press, 2017, pp. 35–47.

Rouse III, Richard. "Match Made in Hell: The Inevitable Success of the Horror Genre in Video Games." *Horror Video Games: Essays on the Fusion of Fear and Play*. Lanham, MD: McFarland & Company, Inc., 2009, p. 11.

Ryan, Marie-Laure. "Impossible Worlds and Aesthetic Illusion." *Immersion and Distance*. Leiden: Brill Rodopi, January 2013, pp. 131–148. *brill.com*, doi:10.1163/9789401209243_006.

Said, Edward W. *Orientalism*. New York: Pantheon Books, 1978.

Schmeyer, D. M. "Call of Cthulhu Review – IGN." *IGN*, 2020, https://uk.ign.com/articles/2018/10/30/call-of-cthulhu-review.

Sederholm, Carl, and Jeffrey Andrew Weinstock. "Introduction: Lovecraft Now." *Journal of the Fantastic in the Arts*, vol. 26, no. 3, 2015, pp. 444–449.

Stam, Robert. *Beyond Fidelity: The Dialogics of Adaptation*. Rutgers, NJ: Rutgers University Press, 2000, p. 22.

Taylor, Laurie N. "Gothic Bloodlines in Survival Horror Gaming." *Horror Video Games*. Lanham, MD: McFarland & Company, Inc., 2009, p. 16.

Tronstad, Ragnhild. "Character Identification in World of Warcraft: The Relationship between Capacity and Appearance." *Digital Culture, Play, Identity: A World of Warcraft Reader*. Cambridge, MA: MIT Press, 2008, p. 15.

Tyrrel, Brandin. "Bloodborne Review – IGN." *IGN*, 2017, https://uk.ign.com/articles/2015/03/24/bloodborne-review.

Wolf, Mark J. P. "The Video Game as a Medium." *The Medium of the Video Games*, edited by Mark J. P. Wolf, University of Texas Press, 2001, pp. 13–34.

Žižek, Slavoj. *Looking Awry: An Introduction to Jacques Lacan Through Popular Culture*. Cambridge, MA: MIT Press, 1992.

17 "Bringing … Uncertain Geographies Under … Control"?

Exploring the Lovecraftian 'Walking Simulator'

David Simmons

The last ten years have witnessed a spate of critically revered videogames that focus on exploration, object collection, and simple puzzle solving. Sometimes referred to as 'walking simulators,' examples of such games include *Gone Home* (2013), *Everybody's Gone to the Rapture* (2015), *Firewatch* (2016), and *What Remains of Edith Finch* (2017). Often made by smaller, independent studios, these games intentionally shun many of the usual mechanics involved in big-budget, mainstream videogames (such as an emphasis upon combat and fast-paced action) in favour of something more cerebral. Indeed, if, as videogame scholar James Newman claims "space is key to videogames," (31) then 'walking simulators' take this centrality to its logical extreme by making the exploration of virtual space the only significant ludic task that the player needs to achieve. One of the earliest examples of the 'walking simulator,' *Dear Esther* (2008), involves the negotiation of an uninhabited Hebridean island, during which the player is unable to do anything other than perambulating the virtual landscape; "By removing other stimuli," Dylan Holmes suggests "*Dear Esther* foregrounds the space itself" (Holmes 165). Indeed, the game ends when the player makes their way to the elevated center of the island and then seems to gain the ability to fly, in effect freeing them from their previous physical constraints. The critically lauded *Gone Home* also places an emphasis on the exploration of a virtual space; in this case, the player is confined to their character-avatar's childhood home, with the 'pleasures' of the gaming experience coming from the traversal of, and interaction with, the minutiae of this emotionally resonant, domestic environment.

At first glance, this apparent emphasis on the "mastery of space" (Newman 115) makes it all the odder that an increasing number of contemporary 'walking simulator' games have drawn upon elements taken from the fiction of H.P. Lovecraft in their narratives. While Lovecraft's fiction is surprisingly varied in approach, one of the common themes in the author's work is the undermining of a sense of ontological mastery or control, with the narrator of one of the writer's perhaps best-known stories famously exclaiming that "The most merciful thing in the world, I

DOI: 10.4324/9780367713065-18

think, is the inability of the human mind to correlate all its contents. We live on a placid island of ignorance in the midst of black seas of infinity, *and it was not meant that we should voyage far*" [my italics] (Lovecraft "Call" 21). Similarly, scholar Tanya Krzywinska, in one of the few academic pieces on Lovecraftian videogames to date, notes of the author's inert protagonists: "the stories are marked by inaction and characters are frozen in terror; rather than act on their situation in an attempt to master it, they are more likely to be consumed by dread" (277).

Despite this apparent contradiction between the stasis of Lovecraft's protagonists and the agency of the videogame form, a growing number of 'walking simulators,' including *The Vanishing of Ethan Carter* (2014), *Conarium* (2017), *Call of Cthulhu* (2018), *The Sinking City* (2019), and *Moons of Madness* (2019), employ recognisably Lovecraftian elements. Such games represent a significant part of a larger resurgence of Lovecraft-influenced videogames that include such diverse fare as *Sundered* (a 2D platform exploration game) *Darkest Dungeon* (a side-scrolling dungeon crawler), *Sea Salt* (a top-down action strategy game), *Cultist Simulator* (a card-based simulation), and *Gibbous: A Cthulhu Adventure* (a point-and-click adventure) to name but a few. Indeed, such is the growth of Lovecraft-influenced videogames being released at the moment that several specialist websites have felt the need to publish articles on the subject, with many critiquing this current glut (see "Games Really Need to Fall Out of Love with Lovecraft" and "I Think We're All Set on Lovecraft Games for a While").

Taking as its genesis the criticisms that 'walking simulators' deviate too far from the standard conventions of the videogame, this chapter will explore the reasons why and the ways in which selected examples of the form paradoxically seek to fuse the ontological uncertainty of Lovecraft's writing with the videogame format's conventional "eradication of the unknown and … bringing of uncertain geographies under the control and influence of the player" (Newman 115). It will chart the historical precedents for the contemporary spate of Lovecraftian 'walking simulators,' examine the formal characteristics of recent key examples of the form and explore what the ludic and narrative benefits of such ideologically incongruous cross-medial appropriation might be.

Krzywinska's chapter "Reanimating Lovecraft: The Ludic Paradox of *Call of Cthulhu: Dark Corners of the Earth*" is instructive in examining this paradox. Functioning as a sort of template for many of the contemporary Lovecraftian 'walking simulators,' Krzywinska notes that *Call of Cthulhu: Dark Corners of the Earth* (2005) is "played in first-person, yet it can hardly be described as a first-person shooter. In fact, much of the early part of the game is spent without any form of weapon" (279). There are two points to note here. Firstly, that the use of the first-person perspective – the player views the game as though they are looking through the eyes of the character they control – has become fundamental to the 'walking simulator' subgenre. While a few outliers exist (*To the Moon*, *Oxenfree*, *Death Stranding*), the vast majority of 'walking simulators' use a first-person viewpoint. There is a neat correlation here with Lovecraft's stories, most of which are told through first-person narration. Mark Fisher writes in his exploration of Weird fiction:

> That is one reason why [Lovecraft's stories] are so often written in the first person: if the outside gradually encroaches upon a human subject, its alien contours can be appreciated; whereas to attempt to capture "the boundless and hideous unknown" without any reference to the human world is to risk banality.
>
> (20)

Similarly, the 'walking simulator' frequently uses the first-person perspective to aid immersion in a verisimilitudinous virtual space before introducing more abstract, fantastical elements that gain emphasis through their incongruity with the otherwise quotidian environment. This can be seen in the way that *Dark Corners of the Earth* begins with the player exploring the Holt family mansion before introducing more esoteric elements (snatches of narrative found in documents and drawings) that suggest the cultists holed up there may have communicated with a higher power. Secondly, rather than empowering the player, *Dark Corners of the Earth* tends to present them with "many boundaries" (Krzywinska 280), both physical and psychological, such as the "insanity effects" that disempower the player and that significantly work "against the rhetorics of mastery that are intrinsic to … games" (283). In this manner, *Dark Corners of the Earth* follows many of the conventions of the subgenre known as survival horror. As many scholars have noted, survival horror involves "the subversion of gameplay norms" (Taylor 50). In contrast to the typical "imperialistic impetus" and "macho militaristic masculinity" of many action-orientated, big-budget videogames, Ewan Kirkland proposes that survival horror videogames are "much more strategic, driven by resource management, stealth, and the comparatively meek tactics of hiding and running away" (26). Perhaps more importantly, given the frequent contemporary adoption of Lovecraftian elements by 'walking simulators,' long-running survival horror videogame series such as *Silent Hill*, *Fatal Frame*, and, most famously, *Resident Evil*, have long embodied the deterministic sentiment that "the ultimate horror … is … that, despite our strongest feelings to the contrary, we are not the masters of our own fate" (Kirkland 2009: 77).

In many of his more effective stories, Lovecraft espouses the philosophy of "cosmic indifferentism"; writing in a letter about this concept that "all my tales are based on the fundamental premise that common human laws and interests have no validity or significance in the vast cosmos-at-large." (*Selected Letters* 150). The 'walking simulator,' as a form that tends to subvert many videogame conventions seems to echo, in ludic form, this anti-humanocentric pose. The disempowering of the player-avatar in the 'walking simulator' – the player can often only move forwards through a preordained narrative, interacting in a simplistic fashion with a limited range of objects in the environment – reflects the loss of agency inherent in the fatalism that forms a recurrent part of Lovecraft's cosmic narratives. If, as Krzywinska proposes, horror-based videogames tend to offer the player "a complex interaction between bounded choice and determinism" ("Hands-On" 221) then the Lovecraftian 'walking simulator' seems to err towards determinism. Interestingly, these limitations have led some critics to decry 'walking simulators' as sufficiently interactive enough to be categorised as videogames, and, while the details of this debate lie outside the scope of this chapter, such criticisms do suggest that 'walking simulators' might well be suitable vehicles to convey "the most radical and full-fledged form of determinism" (Joshi 45) frequently espoused in Lovecraft's fiction.

The 2010 videogame *Amnesia: The Dark Descent* forms a bridge between *Dark Corners of the Earth* and the examples being considered in this chapter. The player controls Daniel, from a first-person perspective, as he attempts to escape from the horrors of Brennenburg Castle. The game's narrative is "heavily influenced by the writings of H.P. Lovecraft" (Perron 235), involving an uncovered otherworldly item that exerts a malign influence on those who come into contact with it. Yet, *Amnesia*'s most significant impact on later examples of the Lovecraftian 'walking simulator' is in just how much it goes out of its way to disempower the player. Right from its opening screen, *Amnesia* foregrounds its deviation from standard videogame tropes and ludic conventions, informing the player that "*Amnesia* should not be played to win. Instead focus on immersing yourself in the game's world and story." As Bernard Perron notes, disempowerment is central to *Amnesia's* structure: "Nothing much is given to put a gamer at ease" (236). The player must navigate the darkness of the castle while desperately searching for oil to fill their lamp lest they be plunged into darkness and go 'mad.' The player must also run and hide from the monsters that inhabit the castle as they are given no weapon to use to confront them. Both features contribute to a constant sense of dread on the part of the player as they must push on through the shadow-shrouded castle knowing that they are seriously ill-equipped to deal with what they may face.

The inability of the player to exert mastery over the gameworld is a significant element of the several recent examples of the Lovecraftian 'walking simulator.' *Conarium*, which is based most directly upon Lovecraft's novella *At the Mountains of Madness*, exemplifies this approach right from its opening sequence. *Conarium* begins with protagonist Frank Gilman negotiating a linear path along a bizarre alien landscape before meeting a mysterious non-player character called Dr. Faust who intones

"I believe no more we can harbour ourselves on the safest shores for there are things that cannot be undone." Not only does this preamble point towards the deterministic nature of the game and its narrative, suggesting that whatever the player does they will inevitably find themselves returning to a version of this horrifying moment with Faust, but the *in medias res* framing immediately puts the player off balance, foregrounding their lack of understanding and demanding that they frantically search out story fragments (littered throughout the gameworld) in order to have any idea of what is happening. These snippets of narrative usually come in the form of written documents, scientific records and diary entries distributed throughout the environment, as well as flashback sequences that Gilman experiences first hand. The retrospective nature of these story fragments further emphasises the impression that the player, as Gilman, is unwittingly moving towards the realisation of a fate that has already been decided for them by forces out of their control. On a more ludic level, Gilman lacks the special abilities frequently afforded to other videogame protagonists. He cannot "perform acts that [the average person] could not perform in real life" (Salmond 87). Instead, in contrast to the typical videogame character, Gilman is "quite helpless" (Eker). The character is unable even to run for more than a few seconds, a fact that severely hampers him, and the player, in several chase sequences that can be found in the second half of the game. At times, *Conarium* almost seems to delight in confusing the player. It lacks any of the 'handholding' elements that feature in many contemporary videogames and, to make matters worse, repeatedly transports the player into new environments with little sense, initially, of what they should be doing. Numerous reviewers commented upon the "frustrating" (Eker) nature of play and at least a few of those writing about *Conarium* suggested that the lack of faculties afforded the player meant that it was "pushing at the limits of what constitutes being called a game" (Bolt).

Yet, these elements, while potentially frustrating, do successfully replicate, in ludological form, the sense of confusion that Lovecraft's protagonists frequently experience in his writing. In forcing the player to grapple with its often counter-intuitive mechanics, *Conarium* might be seen as an instance of cross-medial adaptation, or what Bolter and Grusin (2000) might call "remediation," a refashioning of an older media form (Lovecraft's fiction) by a new media form (videogames). In this process of remediation, the idiomatic characteristics of the older form must be adapted and transformed so that they work for the new form. Therefore, *Conarium* takes the epistemological and ontological collapses of Lovecraft's stories and refashions them into disempowering game mechanics which emphasise the player's inability to master their environment. Furthermore, the circular nature of the game's narrative, with Gilman's abnormal fate being foretold by Dr. Faust effectively evokes the determinist, cosmicist ideology underpinning stories such as *At the*

Mountains of Madness and *The Shadow Over Innsmouth* in which the narrator characters eventually realise "that every event in the cosmos is caused by the action of antecedent and circumjacent forces, so that whatever we do is unconsciously the inevitable product of [external forces] rather than our own volition" (Lovecraft qtd in Joshi *Weird* 171).

While those playing *Conarium* may be denied the empowering levels of agency that are typically found in many videogames, what is evident are the lengths the game's designers have gone to incorporate the "atmosphere of breathless and unexplainable dread" (Lovecraft "Introduction" 23) which permeates much of Lovecraft's writing. This ambiance is incorporated into both the narrative and ludic elements of the game. Noticeably, over the six to seven hours that it takes to finish *Conarium*, the player is almost continually isolated. Firstly, on an Antarctic base from which all the other scientists have disappeared, then in a dilapidated and deserted stately home (through a series of disturbing and disorientating visions), followed by a claustrophobic stint in a one-man submarine, and finally in the various tombs, subterranean caves, and desert ruins which house the remains of the story's extra-terrestrial entities. Significantly, one of the earliest tasks that the player is faced with, in the game is trying to ascertain whether there is anyone that Gilman can contact to come and rescue him. This involves the player interacting with the Antarctic base's broken radio equipment and exploring the surface level of the base itself. The size and scale of the deserted base quickly serve to accentuate the character's insignificance in the virtual space and it rapidly becomes clear that no one is coming to find them. A further sense of dread is created through the lack of lighting, as Stobart suggests:

> For videogames ... the use of darkness serves to heighten tension, as the player does not know what is in the gloom beyond the flashlight, leading to feelings of apprehension and an acute awareness of noise and movement on the screen.
>
> (79)

The poor and inconsistent lighting of many of the game's virtual environments – through the eerie luminescent glow of strange alien fauna, the underpowered headlamp of a submersible – also helps to unnerve the player by highlighting their weakness in navigating the gameworld. Without a torch or other similar lighting device, the player is frequently forced to explore scantly lit environments in which their vision is severely limited. Effective use of diegetic sound effects also adds to the sense of mounting anxiety, with judicious use of echoes underscoring the loneliness of the player-avatar.

The sense of remoteness that *Conarium* relies upon to create a recognisably Lovecraftian atmosphere may also be a direct result of its creation by Zoetrope Interactive, a mid-tier videogame studio based in

Turkey. Many of the structural elements of the game such as the relatively small number of environments, their often-poor lighting, and the notable absence of multiple non-player characters allow for a reduced, and more manageable production budget for a smaller videogame company. While in his 2011 article, Kirkland notes that survival horror is a "genre ... in decline" due to an increasing demand for elements such as "expansive visual effects" and "non-linearity" (29), these self-same 'limitations' seem an apposite fit for the Lovecraftian 'walking simulator,' in which feelings of claustrophobia, isolation, and sense of unjust linearity are a perfect fit for the author's oppressively indifferent vision.

Significantly, since Krzywinska's pioneering work on Lovecraftian videogames (and the initial release of *Call of Cthulhu: Dark Corners of the Earth*), changes in the industry have seen fundamental developments regarding the sale of videogames. The popularisation of online delivery platforms (most prominently Steam, Xbox Live, and PlayStation Network) have created a viable space for the production and distribution of so-called 'indie' and mid-tier budgeted videogames, made by smaller studios who often lack the finances available to larger 'triple A' development companies (who are often themselves part of larger multinational media companies). As these larger studios have become increasingly focused on reiterating upon commercially proven formulas (such as the Call of Duty or FIFA franchises) it has been suggested that smaller studios such as Zoetrope Interactive (with reduced overheads) can take more artistic risks, including releasing videogames that do not adhere to mainstream expectations of the form: "The indie creed is one of experimentation and innovation" (Pearce 274). It is no coincidence that all the contemporary 'walking simulators' under discussion in this chapter were created and published by 'indie' or mid-tier studios. The recognisability of Lovecraft's iconography functions as an attractive means of pulling in a specialist but still sizeable audience eager to engage with a beloved narrative universe. Tellingly, on Zoetrope Interactive's official website for *Conarium*, the game is described in terms that position it as a niche product ("Lovecraftian," "Danse Macabre," "suspense filled") targeted at a specific audience of horror-genre fans rather than everyone who might play videogames.

Like *Conarium*, the designers of *The Vanishing of Ethan Carter* (hereafter *Ethan Carter*) evidently recognise the importance of "setting and landscapes in videogames" (Stobart 96). The game effectively depicts a near photorealistic recreation of rural Wisconsin. Though *Ethan Carter* is perhaps the least directly Lovecraftian of the 'walking simulators' discussed in this chapter (with the narrative also drawing from writers including Edgar Allan Poe, Stephen King, August Derleth, and, most prominently, Ambrose Bierce), the game is still indebted to trends that have been identified as key to Lovecraft's fiction. This means that while the game's designers stated, "You cannot do a direct translation of Lovecraft to a movie or a videogame. You need to try to make your own equivalent" (Chmielarz qtd in Herbers) *Ethan Carter* still shares Lovecraft's "entangling of times and spaces" into what James Kneale calls his "weird geography" (45). Fisher notes that "Lovecraft's stories are obsessively fixated on the question of the outside" (16) and *Ethan Carter* exemplifies this fascination in its opening sequence. The sequence mirrors that of *Conarium*, in so much as it entails the player controlling the protagonist, in this case, the occult detective Paul Prospero, as he walks down a narrow and linear virtual corridor. However, whereas Gilman emerges from his oppressive corridor only to be confronted by the machinations of Dr. Faust, Prospero exits a murky (disused) train tunnel into the beauty of Red Creek Valley – a stunningly realised depiction of a small, bucolic area in the Great Lakes region. Waning sunlight pokes through the autumnal forest canopy while dilapidated bridges span expansive lakes in a pastoral environment that stretches as far as the player-avatar can see. The contrast is profound and immediately highlights the emphasis the game's designers have placed upon constructing a credible recreation of the natural environment.

The significance of achieving this level of verisimilitude is discussed in an online interview with game developer, Adrian Chmielarz. Chmielarz suggests that "believability of the environment [was] important" to the making of *Ethan Carter* to the extent that a new technique called photogrammetry was invented for the game: "in short, you photograph the real world, and then special software spits out a 3-D game-ready asset that looks exactly like the real thing."

Significantly, *Ethan Carter* differs from other Lovecraftian 'walking simulators' in offering the player a near photorealistic environment to explore that is also structured as an open world. An open-world videogame is one in which "a player and their character are free to roam the created landscape" (Salmond and Salmond 154) Yet, notoriously, the nonlinear nature of most open-world videogames can pose major problems for storytelling; as Steve Poole writes in *Trigger Happy: Videogames and the Entertainment Revolution*: "[a game] cannot simply leave the whole story up to the player" (101). While the freedom of the open world might empower the player to explore what they want to, when they want to, this structure also risks the player getting 'lost' as they are not forced to follow a prescriptive path, causing frustration and eventually, disengagement. Consequently, *Ethan Carter* opens with the warning "*The Vanishing of Ethan Carter* is a narrative game that doesn't hold your hand," yet the risks taken with the open-world structure of *Ethan Carter* could be considered necessary given how essential "irruption" (Fisher 20) is to the game's recreation of Lovecraft's fiction in ludic form. Fisher proposes that the centrality of irruption "accounts for the supreme significance of Lovecraft setting so many of his stories in New England." (19). Having established a sense of verisimilitude, Lovecraft's stories then depict an "irruption into *this* world of something from outside" (20), which gains its imaginative and ideological power from the heightened sense of a transgression of the Real. In Lovecraft's fiction, this transgression is frequently a catalyst for a broader cosmicist horror, with stories such as *The Call of Cthulhu* and *At the Mountains of Madness*, suggesting that there are indifferent forces beyond humanity's comprehension which have the potential to govern and shape what happens to mankind. The cognitive dissonance caused by the nascent realisation of this situation leads to the protagonist of many Lovecraft stories going mad – a process that *Ethan Carter*, and the other 'walking simulators' discussed in this chapter, attempt to replicate.

Despite its opening warning, *Ethan Carter* does attempt to guide the player through visual cues, most notably a set of train tracks that act as a sort of ongoing waypoint, helping to orientate the player should they lose their bearings at any point. Indeed, these train tracks quickly become a vital tool for the player as Prospero is soon experiencing several ghostly visions, in which he is repeatedly and abruptly teleported to other parts of the game-world as a means of revealing aspects of the titular character's backstory. These visions constitute one of the game's key devices for depicting an irruption into the Real. Prospero's supernatural abilities enable him to see into the past of other characters, positioning him as an interloper into other's memories. The player must then use this skill to piece together clues that tell the story of Ethan's tragic demise. *Ethan Carter* juxtaposes its photorealistic recreation of rural Wisconsin with such incongruous irruptions as a faceless astronaut who you chase through the forest, an interstellar journey to an unknown point in outer space, a house with teleporting rooms, and a brief sojourn into an underwater setting with a gigantic, tentacled 'Sea Thing.'

The narrative of the game gains its power from the irruption of these fantastical elements into what is, by contemporary standards, a very convincingly realised virtual environment. Ironically, this process is also key to the frustration many players felt concerning the vagueness of the game's plot. Because the 'meaning' of the story is never definitively explained, players have interpreted it in wildly differing ways. One interpretation of what is happening is that the memories that Prospero witnesses tell the story of Ethan's family who irresponsibly summon 'The Sleeper,' a dormant entity whose malevolent power is such that, once summoned, it proceeds to their violent deaths. Such a reading adheres to many of the narrative tropes of Lovecraft's writing, including the idea of "a monstrous race ... [that] constantly threaten[s] to return through various fissures in our own world, bringing with them eternal chaos" (Wisker 66). However, a second and equally valid interpretation supported by the closing scene of the game, suggests that the narrative outlined in the first interpretation is in fact nothing more than a story written by Ethan to try and cope with a set of 'real-life' issues caused by family discord.

The last example that I wish to discuss is both the most recent and the most traditionally game-like of the 'walking simulators' covered in this chapter. Funcom's 2019 release, *Moons of Madness*, tries to combine the Lovecraftian elements evident in *Conarium* and *Ethan Carter* with many of the ludological conventions of mainstream videogames to mixed success. Thus, in *Moons of Madness*, the player-avatar Shane Newehart is gifted with such standard videogame items as a crowbar and a spacesuit, tools which they can use to interact with and exert control over the virtual environment. Perhaps, most importantly, early in the game, Newehart finds a working 'biogage,' a wristwatch-type device that enables them to interact with electronic equipment, scan the environment for points of interest, and display waypoints indicating where to go to next. This device is significant because it marks a substantial deviation from the disorientating techniques of *Conarium* and *Ethan Carter*. While the biogage has undoubtedly been included to ease the player's journey through the game, to shift the balance back to what Krzywinska calls "bounded choice" ("Hands-On" 221), the result is that the device strips *Moons of Madness* of much of its tension. The ease with which the player can refer to the biogage's inbuilt compass whenever they want, works against the sense of disorientation and disempowerment so central to the appeal of other Lovecraftian 'walking simulators.'

One area where *Moons of Madness* does have more success is in constructing an interesting visual aesthetic. The game is set on a remote, isolated outpost on Mars (with hallucinatory flashbacks set in environments related to Newehart's childhood). The extra-terrestrial setting proves both original and effective in conjuring up an existential sense of loneliness. The game manages to evoke a sense of Lovecraftian irruption by visually contrasting the clinical sterility of the Martian station with the viscosity of the tentacular horrors that are revealed as the narrative progresses. The game's look borrows liberally from cinematic science fiction tropes (most prominently the *Alien* series) that are themselves indebted to Lovecraft's stories. Newehart's mother's experiments for the malevolent Orochi corporation are revealed to have involved genetic manipulation of human and extra-terrestrial plant material creating biological mutations that are decidedly Giger-esque in appearance. Newehart eventually must blow up Mars' twin moons in a bombastic ending to the game that epitomises its cinematic leanings. *Moons of Madness*'s visuals create a sense of interest in the player, spurring them on to explore further in a manner that parallels Lovecraft's writing; as Fisher notes, "it is not horror but fascination – albeit a fascination usually mixed with a certain trepidation – that is integral to Lovecraft's rendition of the weird" (Fisher 17).

In many ways, *Moons of Madness* speaks to the limitations of the commercial videogame to effectively remediate a Lovecraftian aesthetic. *Moons of Madness* is the most game-like of the examples looked at in this chapter, the videogame targeting the widest audience, yet it was also the least successful in most reviewer's opinions. Called a "cosmic mess" (Hile) and "boring" (Peterson) *Moons of Madness* falls between two stools in its attempts to fuse Lovecraft's "profound sense of dread"

("Introduction" 25) with videogame conventions like forced stealth segments and boss fights; as one reviewer noted, "What transpires is an unsatisfactory blend of the two" (Eker).

In conclusion, with titles like *Old Gods Rising* (2020), *Cthulhu: Book of Ancients* (2020), and *Call of the Sea* (2020) recently released, the Lovecraftian videogame seems to be in rude health; whether the same can be said about the Lovecraftian 'walking simulator' seems less certain. In this chapter, I have shown that while the Lovecraftian 'walking simulator' shares elements in common with other videogames, notably their rendering of visually impressive, verisimilitudinous digital environments, and the use of a first-person perspective to relate events, many of the more-effective Lovecraftian 'walking simulators' work in a manner that runs counter to the mainstream conventions of the form (which promote the empowerment of the player and encourage the concomitant mastery of virtual space). Whether by serendipity or conscious design, the modest production budgets of examples such as *Conarium* and *Ethan Carter* change the player's expectations of what they might offer and, consequently, enable them to more closely emulate the formal and ideological elements of Lovecraft's fiction. Both *Conarium* and *Ethan Carter* (and *Moons of Madness*, albeit less successfully) seek to remediate the cosmicist determinism of Lovecraft's stories into the ludological mechanics underpinning the player's experience. The indifference of the cosmos towards humankind, embodied in so much of Lovecraft's fiction, is manifested in each game's deliberate disempowering of the player and their avatar. Each of the three examples uses advances in computer graphics to effectively present the irruption of something monstrous into a verisimilitudinous virtual environment, confronting the player with something "entirely foreign" (Fisher 20) and disorientating to their experience. In debilitating the player to such an extent, the 'walking simulator' pushes the "suitably Cthulhean comment" (Krzywinska "Reanimating" 286) to its extreme, bringing Lovecraft's ideas to a genre-savvy audience eager to experience the horror of disempowerment.

Works Cited

Bolt, Neil. "[Review] 'Conarium' is a Respectable Take on a Classic Lovecraft Tale, But Lacks a Sense of Danger." *www.Bloody-Disgusting.com*. 12 March 2019. Available at: https://bloody-disgusting.com/reviews/3546365/conarium-review/

Chmielarz, Adrian. "5 Weird Tales from the Development of The Vanishing of Ethan Carter, out next week on PS4." *Blog.eu.playstation.com*. 09 July 2015. Available at: https://blog.eu.playstation.com/2015/07/09/5-weird-tales-from-the-development-of-the-vanishing-of-ethan-carter-out-next-week-on-ps4/

Eker, Nathanial. "Conarium Review." *www.PushSquare.Com*. 13 February 2019. Available at: http://www.pushsquare.com/reviews/ps4/conarium

———. "Mini-Review: Moons of Madness – A Lovecraftian Snooze Fest." *www.PushSquare.com*. 27 March 2020. Available at: http://www.pushsquare.com/reviews/ps4/moons_of_madness

Fisher, Mark. *The Weird and the Eerie*. London: Repeater, 2017.
Herbers, Barry. "Exclusive Interview with The Vanishing of Ethan Carter Developer." *Gamenesia.nintendoenthusiast.com*. 25 July 2013. Available at: https://gamnesia.nintendoenthusiast.com/articles-exclusive-interview-with-the-vanishing-of-ethan-carter-developer/
Hile, Bryson. "Moons of Madness Review: A Cosmic Mess." *Fansided.com*. 13 April 2020. Available at: https://apptrigger.com/2020/04/09/moons-of-madness-review/
Holmes, Dylan. *A Mind Forever Voyaging: A History of Storytelling in Videogames*. CreateSpace Independent Publishing. 2012.
Joshi, S.T. *H.P. Lovecraft: The Decline of the West*. Cabin John, Maryland: Wildside Press, 1990a.
———. *The Weird Tale*. Holicong, PA: Wildside Press, 1990b.
Kirkland, Ewan. "Survival Horrorality: Analysis of Videogame Genre." *The Irish Journal of Gothic and Horror Studies*. Vol 10, 2011. 22–32.
Kneale, James. "Ghoulish Dialogues: H.P. Lovecraft's Weird Geographies." In *The Age of Lovecraft*. Eds. Carl Sederholm and Jeffrey Andrew Weinstock. Minneapolis, MN: University of Minneapolis Press, 2016. 43–61.
Krzywinska, Tanya. "Reanimating H.P. Lovecraft: The Ludic Paradox of *Call of Cthulhu: Dark Corners of the Earth*." In *Horror Video Games: Essays on the Fusion of Fear and Play*, edited by Bernard Perron. Jefferson, North Carolina and London: McFarland & Company Inc, 2009. 267–288.
———. "Hands-On Horror." *ScreenPlay. Cinema/Videogames/Interfaces*, edited by Geoff King and Tanya Krzywinska. London: Wallflower, 2002. 206–223.
Lovecraft, H.P. "The Call of Cthulhu." *H. P. Lovecraft Collected Fiction, A Variorum Edition, Volume 2: 1926–1930*, edited by S. T. Joshi. New York: Hippocampus Press, 2017. 21–55.
———. *Selected Letters, Volume II 1925–1929*, edited by August Derleth and Donald Wandrei. Sauk City, WI: Arkham House, 1968.
———. "Introduction." *The Annotated Supernatural Horror in Literature*, edited by S.T. Joshi. New York: Hippocampus Press, 2000. 25–33.
Newman, James. *Videogames*. 2nd ed. London: Routledge, 2013.
Pearce, Celia. "Independent and Art Games." *The John Hopkins Guide to Digital Media*, edited by Marie-Laure Ryan, Lori Emerson and Benjamin J. Robertson. Baltimore, Maryland: John Hopkins University Press, 2014. 273–277.
Perron, Bernard. *The World of Scary Videogames: A Study in Ludic Horror*. New York: Bloomsbury, 2018.
Peterson, Cody. "*Moons of Madness* Review: Mars is Boring." *Screenrant.com*. 30 March, 2020. Available at: https://screenrant.com/moons-of-madness-review/
Salmond, Michael. *Video Game Design: Principles and Practices from the Ground Up*. London and New York: Bloomsbury, 2016a.
——— and Jacqueline Salmond. "The Gamer as Tourist: The Simulated Environments and Impossible Georgraphies of Videogames." *Tourism and the Creative Industries: Theories, Policies and Practice*, edited by Philip Long and Nigel D. Morpeth. Oxon and New York: Routledge, 2016b. 151–163.
Stobart, Dawn. *Videogames and Horror: From Amnesia to Zombies, Run!* Cardiff: University of Wales Press, 2019.
Wisker, Gina. *Horror Fiction: An Introduction*. New York and London: Continuum, 2005.

18 Queering Cthulhu

Reclaiming Lovecraft's Monstrous Others

Nowell Marshall

In their introduction to *The Age of Lovecraft*, Carl Sederholm and Jeffrey Weinstock suggest that scholarship on H.P. Lovecraft's work has coalesced in three particular areas: critiques of his racism and xenophobia (25–26), discussions of his "antihumanist orientation" in the fields of new materialism, posthumanism, speculative realism, and object-oriented ontology (4), and analyses of his influence on popular culture and contemporary speculative writers (12–23).[9] In contrast, readings of gender and sexuality in Lovecraft's work are relatively sparse. Victoria Nelson argues that "sex is *the* major unaddressed issue of Lovecraft's work" (115) and traces his aversion to sexuality to his father's death from syphilis. For Nelson, Lovecraft's avoidance of sexuality is a reaction to images of sexually transmitted infections he may have seen as a child. Taking an intertextual approach to gender and sexuality, Gavin Callaghan argues that "women are not absent from his weird fiction," but that "it is merely the traditional romantic structure of desire, pursuit, and bonding that he eschewed" (160–161). Callaghan traces Lovecraft's shifting use of bee imagery from his early works where bees represent fertility (61) through later "'lecherous' and 'libidinous' sexual associations" (63). Writing around the same time as Callaghan, Gina Wisker explores Lovecraft's use of witches, hags, and femme fatales, arguing that Lovecraft's work relies on "various constructions of the monstrous feminine," particularly miscegenational women (31).

Building on these arguments, Carl Sederholm shows that Lovecraft defined himself against sexuality: "In some correspondence, Lovecraft suggests directly that sex was beneath him, something that should be associated with animals and not intellectually inclined men" (135). As Sederholm notes, Lovecraft wrote about his disinterest in sexuality, confessing in a letter to Reinhold Kleiner that "About romance & affection I never have felt the slightest interest; whereas the sky, with its tale of eternities past & to come, & its glorious panoply of whirling universes, has always held me enthralled" (qtd in Sederholm 136). Sederholm combines these two previous lines of inquiry—Lovecraft's refusal of sexuality (his asexuality)[10] and his depiction of women as monstrous—to develop

DOI: 10.4324/9780367713065-19

a reading of "The Dunwich Horror" that positions Lavinia Whateley as abject, a figure who "stands in for Lovecraft's general fear of women and sexuality" and his fear of the body (141). As thoughtful as these readings are, the promise/threat of queerness that lies at the heart of the Cthulhu mythos has gone unexamined. Throughout "The Call of Cthulhu," Lovecraft's heroes define themselves not only against nonwhite bodies but also against hyperwhite bodies and the queerness perceived to be inherent in those bodies—a threat that extends to Cthulhu himself.[11]

Since the mid-1990s, queer and trans theorists have built on feminists' attempts to analyze and reclaim monsters as metaphors for marginalized people. In "My Words to Victor Frankenstein above the Village of Chamounix," Susan Stryker writes, "I find a deep affinity between myself as a transsexual woman and the monster in Mary Shelley's *Frankenstein*. Like the monster, I am too often perceived as less than fully human due to the means of my embodiment" (245). Stryker advocates reclaiming the monster and using its power for activism "without using it as a weapon against others or being wounded by it myself" (246). For Stryker, like angels, monsters are harbingers of change; historically, they have "functioned as messengers and heralds of the extraordinary" (247). In *Skin Shows*, Jack Halberstam takes a slightly different approach to reclaiming the monster, arguing that "Gothic fiction is a technology is subjectivity. One which produces the deviant subjectivities opposite which the normal, the healthy, and the pure can be known" (2).[12] In this sense, racialized and sexualized monsters not only "make strange the categories of beauty, humanity, and identity," as Halberstam suggests (6), but also actively produce those categories and the normative white male hero in many narratives. This is particularly true of H.P. Lovecraft's 1928 short story "The Call of Cthulhu," a text whose white male heroes define themselves against and are overcome by the queer monstrosity that Cthulhu represents.

Often discussed as a weird tale, as an American gothic, or as a science fiction story (Smith 830), "The Call of Cthulhu" can also be discussed within what Sara Wasson and Emily Alder have recently termed gothic science fiction, "a hybrid category that can be deployed in the service of a wide range of ideologies, world-views and strategic investments" (16) and a narrative mode that links these seemingly disparate styles through its focus on hybrid forms and monstrosity (4–5).[13] Framed using the gothic trope of the recovered manuscript (24) and featuring several nested narratives presented as found manuscripts, "The Call of Cthulhu" is notable for how it produces its white male heroes by presenting artists, eccentrics, and people of color as harboring secrets that the narrator, Francis Wayland Thurston, must uncover.

Rather than retread common ground regarding Lovecraft's xenophobia and racism,[14] this chapter reads against the grain of the story, looking at the cultists and those most affected by (or sympathetic to) Cthulhu's emergence in the story. Drawing on Victorian understandings of aestheticism, eccentricity, and "the artist," the early twentieth-century definitional conflation of *queer* as both odd and homosexual, and theorizations of queer space and futurity, this chapter argues for a queer reading of Cthulhu through attention to his minions and the horror he generates in the (presumably) straight white men who encounter his totems, his cultists, and Cthulhu himself.

"The Call of Cthulhu" is broken into three main parts. In part one, "The Horror in Clay," readers are introduced to the story through a posthumous manuscript "Found Among the Paper of the Late Francis Wayland Thurston, of Boston" (21). Lovecraft's choice to reveal the narrative through a recovered manuscript immediately establishes the stakes. Thurston has died. All that remains are his papers and the files on Cthulhu that he has compiled. Through his posthumous manuscript, Thurston relates his initial encounter with an image of Cthulhu while sorting the papers of his great uncle, George Gemmell Angell, a professor at Brown University, who died at ninety-two while also attempting to uncover the truth of Cthulhu (22). Thus, early in the story, the mystery of Cthulhu takes on great power, and that power is directly opposed to the white patriarchal family: Angell has died "childless" (23) while pursuing the secret of Cthulhu, and the headnote suggests that the same fate awaits Thurston. In this sense, Cthulhu and his cult embody a threat to what Lee Edelman has termed reproductive futurity, a system that "remains, at its core, conservative insofar as it works to *affirm* a structure, to *authenticate* social order, which it then intends to transmit to the future in the form of its inner Child" (2–3). The death of heterosexual white men and the subsequent loss of their potential to create families (and thus reproductive futurity) features prominently throughout the rest of the story. Thurston recounts how Angell

> had been stricken whilst returning from the Newport boat; falling suddenly, as witnesses said, after having been jostled by a nautical-looking negro who had come from one of the queer dark courts on the precipitous hillside which formed a short cut from the waterfront to the deceased's home in Williams Street. Physicians were unable to find any visible disorder, but concluded after perplexed debate that some obscure lesion of the heart, induced by brisk ascent of so steep a hill by so elderly a man, was responsible.
>
> (23)

Angell's death is officially ruled the result of natural causes, but Thurston doubts this. Key to this passage is the "nautical-looking negro" and the "queer dark" court from which he emerges. A professor at Brown, an Ivy-League university that in 1926 was coeducational, but remained a primarily white, male space, Angell is jostled by a working-class black man and literally dies from this confrontation with class and racial difference.

Thurston's suspicions about Angell's death begin to mount when he unpacks a locked box in Angell's effects and finds a "queer clay bas-relief" and Angell's "disjointed jottings, ramblings, and cuttings" (23). This bas-relief is the first of three images of Cthulhu Thurston encounters in the story and offers the first glimpse of Cthulhu, "a sort of monster, or symbol representing a monster, of a form which only a diseased fancy could conceive" (23). Thurston reads a document titled "Cthulhu Cult" and learns about the other two sections of the story chronicling the clay tablet's creator, Henry Anthony Wilcox, and Inspector John Raymond Legrasse's narrative. Among these papers, Thurston also finds references to people having "queer dreams" (24). The *Oxford English Dictionary* notes that the word *queer* was used to reference homosexuals as early as 1914. Consequently, the word *queer* functions as a double entendre throughout this 1928 story, implying both sexual orientation and the earlier, but overlapping definition of queer meaning "strange, odd, peculiar, eccentric. Also: of questionable character; suspicious, dubious."[15] Only a few pages into the story, Cthulhu and his cult are firmly associated with a diseased mind[16] and queer dreams.

This consolidation of the black and the queer initiated with the "queer dark" court continues when Thurston discovers the creator of the clay bas-relief: Henry Anthony Wilcox, "a thin, dark young man of neurotic and excited aspect" (24), "a precocious youth of known genius but great eccentricity," who "had from childhood excited attention through the strange stories and odd dreams he was in the habit of relating. He called himself 'psychically hypersensitive', but the staid folk of the ancient commercial city dismissed him as merely 'queer'" (25). In this passage, Wilcox is depicted as black and coded as queer in both senses of the word.[17] In *Romantic Genius*, Andrew Elfenbein traces "the intimate connection between homosexuality and genius" through the eighteenth and nineteenth centuries" (1), and H.L. Malchow observes that as early as the 1880s, aestheticism was associated with "gender ambiguity and homosexuality" (147). For his neighbors, Wilcox's "neurotic and excited aspect," his "known genius," and his "great eccentricity" confirm his queerness ("Call of Cthulhu" 24–25). Yet, as Anne McClintock has demonstrated in *Imperial Leather*, Wilcox is also perceived as queer because of his blackness: "By the nineteenth century, popular lore had firmly established Africa as the quintessential zone of sexual aberration and anomaly—'the very picture,' as W.D. Jordan put it, 'of perverse negation'" (428). Thus, these early descriptions work together to position Wilcox as a threat that is simultaneously black and queer.

Wilcox's bas-relief depicting the famously unnatural image of Cthulhu[18] as incorporating features of "an octopus, a dragon, and a human caricature" ("Call of Cthulhu" 23) is an unconscious production: "the youth had found himself working, chilled and clad only in his nightclothes, when waking had stolen bewilderingly over him" (26). During his interviews with Angell, Wilcox confesses "fragments of nocturnal imagery," "terrible Cyclopean visits of dark and dripping stone," and an intelligence shouting "gibberish" (26). Like the dreams that fuel Wilcox's sculpting, Wilcox's unconscious production of the Cthulhu bas-relief expresses wish fulfillment and manifests his unconscious black queer desire[19] to reclaim the monstrosity thrust upon him by society and fashion it into a symbol of monstrous power. As the rest of this chapter will show, this coupling of queerness with nonwhiteness and occasional hyperwhiteness is presented as a threat that pervades "The Call of Cthulhu."

After speaking with Wilcox, Angell begins logging friends' dreams and notices a pattern: "Average people in society and business—New England's traditional salt of the earth'—gave an almost completely negative result" (28). In her discussion of AIDS rhetoric, Jan Zita Grover critiques the use of the phrase "general population," arguing that it becomes a metaphor for unspoken heterosexuality: "As a term, it bespeaks neither sex nor revolution. Its very amorphousness guarantees widespread identification. Who, after all, would not regard him- or herself as part of the general population? The answer, of course, is that no self-respecting queer can or should" (23). A similar slippage appears in Angell's observations where "New England's traditional 'salt of the earth'" (with its emphasis on *traditional*) becomes a metaphor for heterosexuals. Likewise, Angell's notes reveal that "Scientific men were little more affected" ("Call of Cthulhu" 28) and that "These responses from aesthetes told a disturbing tale" (28), suggesting that the dreamers were not only aesthetes but also emotional—the traditionally gendered opposite of the rational and the scientific. Perhaps unsurprisingly, Angell confirms that "It was from the artists and poets that the pertinent answers came" (28). Coupled together, these passages suggest that the men affected (strangely enough, Angell reports nothing about women) were all emotionally sensitive and coded as queer via their aestheticism and genius.

Thurston recounts one exception to this phenomenon from Angell's records:

> One case, which the note describes with emphasis, was very sad. The subject, a widely known architect with leanings towards theosophy and occultism, went violently insane on the date of young Wilcox's seizure, and expired several months later after incessant screamings to be saved from some escaped denizens of hell.
>
> (29)

Notable about this case is that neither Angell nor Thurston in his recounting specify the race of the man or hint at his sexuality. Like the other dreamers, he is creative, but he is otherwise unremarkable. Critical race scholar George Yancy defines whiteness as that which positions itself as the cultural center, an unmarked, invisible universal system of "privileges, norms, rights" and "sites of power and hegemony that benefits whites individually and institutionally" (7–8). Within this framework (and given Lovecraft's routine specificity of the races and ethnicities of his nonwhite characters), this architect appears to be white and, as an architect concerned with mathematics, measurements, and angles, he also belongs to the category of "traditional," rational men discussed above. It is no surprise, then, that when confronted with dreams that appeal to nonwhite, queer characters, this architect is driven mad and dies. Throughout the story, Cthulhu's emergence and those who dream of and represent him in their art threaten the dominant establishment. In 1928, that Western establishment is predominantly straight, white, and patriarchal.

Part two of the story relates Inspector Legrasse's investigation of Cthulhu's cultists and reinforces Lovecraft's pattern of defining the straight white hero against black, queer adversaries. In 1908, at the American Achaelogical Association conference, Angell encounters Inspector John Raymond Legrasse, who displays an idol of African origin taken in a raid on "a dark cult totally unknown to them, and infinitely more diabolic than even the blackest of the African voodoo circles" in "the wooded swamps south of New Orleans" ("Call of Cthulhu" 30–31). Angell reveals how the white professors gathered at the conference react to the Cthulhu idol: Upon "one sight of the thing," the men collectively experience "a state of tense excitement" as they all "gaze" intently on the "diminutive figure" (31). They are fascinated by its "utter strangeness," pass it "slowly from man to man," and carefully study its "eight inches in height" (31). The men are simultaneously compelled to touch the idol and repelled by its alien composition, which "belonged to something horribly remote and distinct from mankind as we know it; something frightfully suggestive of old and unhallowed cycles of life in which our world and our conceptions have no part" (32).

The phallic description of the idol and the obsessive way the white men pass it among themselves both doubles and inverts the erotic space where the idol was found. Instead of being an exclusively white male space, the swamps where the cultists perform their rites are comprised of "black haunted woods" (34) with "malformed" trees; these "black arcades of horror" are a nonwhite space "unknown and untraversed by white men" (35). The only whiteness in the swamp is something quite different from the white police who accompany Legrasse. Instead of the unmarked, invisible universal whiteness that Yancy describes, Legrasse's men hear tales of "a huge, formless white polypous thing with luminous eyes...It was nightmare itself, and to see it was to die. But it made men dream, and so they knew enough to keep away" (35). This creature embodies *gothic whiteness*, a monstrous whiteness that gothic authors use to define normative whiteness against. In *White*, Gary Dyer observes that "the extreme, very white white image is functional in relation to the ordinary, is even perhaps a condition of establishing whiteness as ordinary" (222). Likewise, in discussing the perpetuation of white supremacy, Yancy notes that whites often define themselves as normatively white "through a process of juxtaposing the 'good white' with the 'bad white'" (4).[20] "The Call of Cthulhu" builds on this design, defining Legrasse's white lawmen as "good" and "normative" by juxtaposing them against monstrous hyperwhiteness and the queer blackness present at the cultists' orgy. Notably, Legrasse's men find the cultists near the land the gothic white monster inhabits: "The present voodoo orgy was, indeed, on the merest fringe of this abhorred area" (35). Legrasse speculates that the black cultists worked in conjunction with the hyperwhite monster based on one of his men's claim that

> he heard antiphonal responses to the ritual from some far and unillumined spot deeper within the wood of ancient legendry and horror. This man, Joseph D. Galvez, I latter met and questioned; and he proved distractingly imaginative. He indeed went so far as to hint of the faint beating of great wings, and of a glimpse of shining eyes and the mountainous white bulk beyond the remotest trees.
>
> (36)

Thus, gothic whiteness becomes aligned with queer blackness, and both are represented as a threat to normative white masculinity.

Legrasse's men are confronted with the cultists' orgy and experience the attraction and repulsion characteristic of abjection:[21]

> Then the men, having reached a spot where the trees were thinner, came suddenly in sight of the spectacle itself. Four of them reeled, one fainted, and two were shaken into a frantic cry which the mad cacophony of the orgy fortunately deadened. Legrasse dashed swamp water on the face of the fainting man, and all stood trembling and nearly hypnotized with horror.
>
> (36)

As the men approach the orgy, they are simultaneously enthralled ("hypnotized with horror") and repelled (as noted by their fainting and frantic crying), and these reactions stem from the sight not only of nonwhite sexuality, but—as the narrative makes clear—sexuality among working-class, nonwhite, and mixed-race men.

Legrasse's men arrest the cultists, who "all proved to be men of a very low, mixed-blooded, and mentally aberrant type. Most were seamen, and a sprinkling of negroes and mulattos, largely West Indians or Brava Portuguese from the Cape Verde Islands, gave a colouring of voodooism to the heterogeneous cult" (37). Both the West Indies and the Cape Verde Islands lie in the tropics, what were once called torrid zones. As Felicity Nussbaum discusses in *Torrid Zones*, since the mid-eighteenth century, Europeans have debated the effects of climate on sexuality and generally attributed sexual excess to people from warmer climates (8-10). Long-standing associations of sexual excess with people of color, people of mixed heritage, and seamen inform Legrasse's encounter with the cultists and shape the men's response to the orgy. The men's reaction parallels that of the professors at the American Archeological Association conference when Professor Webb tells them about the "nameless rites" and "queer hereditary rituals" that he encountered on a trip to West Greenland in 1860 among a "cult of degenerate Esquimaux" [sic] who possessed a similar idol (32–33). In both situations, the white men define themselves against queer sexualities of color, which they perceive as inferior and a threat to "civilization."

This need for the white hero to define himself against the monstrous racial and sexual other escalates in the final section of the story when Thurston stumbles across a 1925 copy of the Australian journal *Sydney Bulletin* and learns of Gustaf Johansen's encounter with cultists in the South Seas. Thrown off course by a storm in March 1925, the crew of the *Emma* is attacked by the *Alert*, a pirate ship "manned by a queer and evil-looking crew of Kanakes and half-castes" (46) and kills the invaders. Roger Luckhurst's notes to his edition of the story unpack the racial dimensions of this encounter, noting that Kanakas is a "generic racial term used for native islanders in British colonies in the Pacific; acquired a pejorative, racist usage in Australia" (457). Reading Johansen's account, Thurston notes that the attacking islanders are not only killed, but they are also blatantly dehumanized:

> Of the swarthy cult-fiends on the *Alert* he speaks with significant horror. There was some peculiarly abominable quality about them which made their destruction seem almost a duty, and Johansen shows ingenious wonder at the charge of ruthlessness brought against his party during the proceedings of the court of inquiry.
>
> ("Call of Cthulhu" 50)

In *Precarious Life*, Judith Butler writes, "The question that preoccupies me in the light of recent global violence is, Who counts as human? Whose lives count as lives? And, finally, What *makes for a grievable life*?" (20). For Butler, those who are not recognized as human are derealized and subjected to violence: "If violence is done against those who are unreal, then, from the perspective of violence, it fails to injure or negate those lives since those lives are already negated" (33).[22] Johansen's incredulity at being charged with ruthlessness during the inquiry demonstrates this problem. Trained to see nonwhite people as *in*human, Johansen and his fellow seamen brutally murder their attackers. Schooled in colonialist rhetoric, their actions seem justified to them because of the nonwhite, queer threat to white "civilization" that they encounter. Unlike their supervisors who charge them with unnecessary ruthlessness, they are unable to recognize their violence *as* violence when perpetrated against men of color because those men *are* men of color and perceived as queer.

Having captured the *Alert*, the sailors continue until they encounter the "monstrous acropolis" of R'lyeh (51) where they are accosted by a "blackness almost material" (52). Of the men eight men who disembark onto R'lyeh, "two perished of pure fright" (53), Cthulhu devours Donovan, Guerrera, and Angstrom (53), Parker is swallowed by the city's emerging architecture (53), and Briden looks at Cthulhu, goes mad, and is found dead when the *Vigilant* discovers the *Alert* and rescues Johansen (53). Names in Lovecraft's fiction are often significant, and the last names of these sailors are no exception.[23] According to immigration records compiled by William Filby and Mary Meyer, all of these last names are of Western European descent: Donovan (Irish), Guerrera (Spanish or Italian), Angstrom (Swedish), Parker (English or Irish), and Briden (French). Perhaps most interesting in this last part of the tale are Johansen's "brave Norwegian" (54) actions. Sensing that he cannot outrun Cthulhu, he swiftly turns the *Alert*, rams Cthulhu, and splits him apart—only to see his monstrous body immediately reform behind him. Like the island pirates who are positioned as a queer threat, Cthulhu is also represented as a monstrous threat to white, Western European superiority, but unlike those pirates who are easily killed, Cthulhu reforms and pursues Johansen, ultimately driving him insane and causing his death.

Like the two previous sections, this last part of the story defines its white hero against the onslaught of queer assailants of color, but here, Johansen must also survive the onslaught of Cthulhu's hybrid, alien body. In his foundational study of race and colonialism, *Black Skin, White Masks*, Frantz Fanon discusses a form of scapegoating that he terms collective catharsis, "a channel, an outlet through which the forces accumulated in the form of aggression can be released" (464). Fanon argues that, historically, literature has provided collective catharsis by associating nonwhite bodies with monstrosity:

> In the magazines the Wolf, the Devil, the Evil Spirit, the Bad Man, the Savage are always symbolized by Negroes or Indians; since there is always identification with the victor, the little Negro, quite as easily as the little white boy, becomes an explorer, an adventurer, a missionary "who faces the danger of being eaten by the wicked Negroes."
>
> (464)

"The Call of Cthulhu" takes the very shape of the narratives that Fanon critiques. In the first part of the story, Professor Angell, a white man, encounters and literally dies from the horror of making brief contact with a black man of lower social class; in the second part of the story, Legrasse and his men are terrified by the all-male orgy involving working-class men, men from Caribbean and African islands, and men of mixed heritage and by the hyperwhite monster nearby; in the last part of the story, Johansen's fellow Western European crewmen battle and kill island pirates, and he goes mad from seeing Cthulhu, the pirates' patron saint, emerge (53). Like the little white boy that Fanon discusses, throughout the story, readers are expected to identify and sympathize with the white male heroes' struggle against the nonwhite, the hyperwhite, and the queer.

Near the end of the story, Thurston visits Wilcox to confirm Angell's interview notes, and Wilcox describes

> his dreams in a strangely poetic fashion; making me see with terrible vividness the damp Cyclopean city of slimy green stone—whose *geometry*, he oddly said, was *all wrong*—and hear with frightened expectancy the ceaseless half-mental calling from underground.
>
> (43)

By portraying R'lyeh's geometry as "*all wrong*" and emphasizing that point, Wilcox offers a startling vision of queer space. For Halberstam, queer spaces develop "in opposition to the institutions of family, heterosexuality, and reproduction. They also develop according to other logics of location, movement, and identification" (1). R'lyeh's wrong geometry suggests the queer space it embodies and extends—at least conceptually—to those whose dreams it influences. If Thurston finds this vision terrifying, that is because he inhabits a subject position diametrically opposed to Wilcox's. Thurston benefits from the social systems in place that oppress blacks, queers, and queers of color, but as an artist and visionary, Wilcox imagines a different world where the coming of Cthulhu wipes away those systems.[24] Through his dreams, Wilcox has perceived "the thoughts that spread fear to the dreams of the sensitive and called imperiously to the faithful to come on a pilgrimage of liberation and restoration" (50). The horror of R'lyeh lies in this contrast between the world as it is and the city's symbolism of a repressed queer space always threatening to rise again and liberate the oppressed.

Several passages suggest Cthulhu and the lost city of R'lyeh as repressed presences waiting to resurface. During the discussion of the "diabolist Esquimaux" [sic] (33), Legrasse translates the cultists' chants as "In his house at R'lyeh dead Cthulhu waits dreaming" (34). Later, R'lyeh is depicted as something repressed that threatens to return to challenge dominant power systems:

> The great stone R'lyeh, with its monuments and sepulchres, had sunk beneath the waves, and the deep waters, full of the one primal mystery through which not even thought can pass, had cut off the spectral intercourse. But memory never died, and high priests said that city would rise again when the stars were right.
>
> (39)

And again, near the end of the story, R'lyeh is termed "the nightmare corpse-city" (50). These images posit R'lyeh as a city both dead and not dead, something undead and uncanny, waiting to resurface. In *Cruising Utopia*, José Muñoz argues that "queerness is always in the horizon" (11), a hope that offers "a backward glance that enacts a future vision" (4). For Wilcox, as for the cultists and those of us who come to Lovecraft's work as queer readers, R'lyeh becomes a form of monstrous queer futurity, a lost queer space that can only be imagined through dreams and lore. Its return forever looms on the horizon, promising and threatening to overturn the world of the present. Thurston and Angell mythologize Cthulhu and the disruptive queer potential he anticipates by glancing back to and drawing on the combined stories of Wilcox and Legrasse. In the process, Cthulhu emerges into the world as the passionate product of two men.

Notes

1 In addition to Halberstam discussed here, see Stryker.
2 Halberstam, *Skin Shows*, 2.
3 Halberstam, *Skin Shows*, 6.
4 See Sara Wasson and Emily Alder, "Introduction."
5 H.P. Lovecraft, "The Call of Cthulhu," 24.
6 Lovecraft, "The Call of Cthulhu," 27.
7 Lovecraft, "The Call of Cthulhu," 37, 33.
8 Lovecraft, "The Call of Cthulhu," 41.
9 Lee Herrmann observes that Lovecraft's settings are settler-colonial and colonial, often working as plot devices in themselves such that trade, exploration, and settlement induce dysgenia, degeneration, or potential apocalypse" (305). For an in-depth look at Lovecraft's use of eugenics and a surprising reading of his work as utopian, see Timothy Murphy's "Physiology Is Destiny." While some authors like Jeff VanderMeer have argued for the need to move away from Lovecraft's influence, more recent critics like Timothy Jarvis and Anthony Camara have shown how contemporary authors have appropriated Lovecraft's mythos to subvert his racism and biological determinism. Jarvis draws on Gilles Deleuze and Felix Guattari's concept of "becoming-Other" to argue that Laird Barron and Caitlín R. Kiernan have succeeded not by overcoming Lovecraft's influence but by "taking on and transforming his tropes" (1135). Camara reads Elizabeth Bear's novelette "Shoggoths in Bloom" to illustrate how the text resists Lovecraft's master-slave narrative and instead "stages a mutually transformative, symbiotic cross-species encounter between its protagonist and a Shoggoth" (26).
10 Karli June Cerankowski and Megan Milks cite the Asexual Visibility and Education Network's definition of asexuality as "A person who does not experience sexual attraction." However, they are careful to note that asexuality can take many forms and can coexist with people simultaneously identifying as "romantic and aromantic, monogamous and polyamorous, gay, straight, bisexual, and lesbian" (651). Lovecraft did eventually marry Sonia Davis, so he might also be considered *demisexual*, someone who needs to develop a relationship with another person before feeling comfortable enough to have sex.
11 All references to "The Call of Cthulhu" in this essay are drawn from the *Variorum Edition*.

12 For a discussion of how the monster is socially constructed as a threat to society through popular culture, see Edward Ingebretsen's *At Stake: Monsters and the Rhetoric of Fear in Public Culture*.
13 Reading Lovecraft as a gothic-science-fiction author makes sense given his definition of "the true weird tale" as an offshoot of classic gothic narratives. For Lovecraft, "the true weird tale has something more than secret murder, bloody bones, or a sheeted form clanking chains according to rule. A certain atmosphere of breathless and unexplainable dread of outer, unknown forces must be present" (*Supernatural Horror* 84).
14 For thoughtful discussions of racism in Lovecraft's writing, see Carl Sederholm and Jeffrey Weinstock, "Introduction: Lovecraft Rising"; Jed Mayer, "Race Species, and Others: H.P. Lovecraft and the Animal"; and Jeffrey Weinstock, "Afterword: Interview with China Miéville," all in *The Age of Lovecraft*. Sederholm and Weinstock review Lovecraft's racist and xenophobic comments in his letters (25-28). Mayer argues Lovecraft's racist classification of "negroes" with animals does more than dehumanize people of color. By lumping humans with animals, Lovecraft "offers an implicit challenge to human exceptionalism" (117). Miéville argues that Lovecraft's racism can't be "divorced from the writing" because "the antihumanism one finds so bracing in him is an antihumanism predicated on murderous race hatred" (241).
15 Eve Sedgwick discusses the potential uses of queer in depth in *Tendencies* and updates this discussion in her posthumous *The Weather in Proust* where she defines queer as referring to "the open mesh of possibilities, gaps, overlaps, dissonances and resonances, lapses, and excesses of meaning when the constituent meanings of anyone's gender, or anyone's sexuality, aren't made (or can't be made) to signify monolithically" (198–200).
16 Victorian sexology viewed homosexuality (inversion) as a form of mental illness. For Richard von Krafft-Ebing, inversion could be congenital or acquired (239) and was often accompanied by "psychic hermaphrodism" (290).
17 Although Wilcox is ultimately revealed to have no relation to the Cthulhu cult beyond his dreams, both Angell and Thurston initially assume that he is in league with the cultists. In this sense, he is also perceived as dark because, as white men, Angell and Thurston associate paganism with darkness.
18 Although Cthulhu has often been read as a symbol of cosmic horror, Callaghan asserts a "basically caricatural relationship of Cthulhu to the human form" (4). For Callaghan, Cthulhu is less a representation of cosmic horror than a parody of the human.
19 Sigmund Freud argues that dreams are manifestations of wish fulfillment. See *The Interpretation of Dreams*.
20 Even theorists openly opposed to whiteness studies have acknowledged that normative whiteness defines itself against extreme forms of whiteness. For instance, in her critique of whiteness studies, Robyn Wiegman argues that "the hegemonic formation of white identity today must be understood as taking shape in the rhetorical, if not always political, register of disaffiliation from white supremacist practices and discourses" (119).
21 In *Powers of Horror*, Julia Kristeva defines abjection as being "drawn toward an elsewhere as tempting as it is condemned. Unflaggingly, like an inescapable boomerang, a vortex of summons and repulsion places the one haunted by it literally beside himself" (1).
22 Butler initially introduced these questions as ways of accounting for violence against people of Arabic and Palestinian descent in the wake of 9/11 and ongoing global conflicts before applying the idea to Black Lives Matter in an interview with critical-race theorist George Yancy.

23 That said, Callaghan observes that in his correspondence, Lovecraft sometimes "humorously" combined Irish first names with Jewish last names (6). For Callaghan, this is emblematic of "Lovecraft's collectivized view of America's various ethnicities, and their shoggoth-like hybridization, within the corridors of his own mind, into a single, loathsome mass" (6–7). Since the early 1990s, scholars working in whiteness studies have shown that people of some Western European origins were not perceived as white until the late-nineteenth through mid-twentieth centuries. See, for example, Noel Ignatiev's *How the Irish Became White* and Karen Brodkin's *How Jews Became White Folks*. Given these arguments, Lovecraft's combining these names from these ethnic groups may have been him joking about the "newly and emerging white."

24 Victor LaValle explores this desire to overthrow an oppressive system in *The Ballad of Black Tom*, his radical black retelling of Lovecraft's "The Horror at Red Hook." The novel follows Black Tom, a black man whose unarmed father is violently murdered by a private detective who is assisted and goes unpunished by police. Black Tom retaliates by waking Cthulhu to destroy his unjust society. This essay expands this idea to address not only racial injustice, but also oppression experienced by queers and queer people of color.

Works Cited

Brodkin, Karen. *How Jews Became White Folks and What That Says about Race in America*. New Brunswick, NJ: Rutgers University Press, 1998.

Butler, Judith. *Precarious Life: The Powers of Mourning and Violence*. New York: Verso, 2004.

Callaghan, Gavin. *H.P. Lovecraft's Dark Arcadia: The Satire, Symbolism and Contradiction*. Jefferson, NC: McFarland, 2013.

Camara, Anthony. "How to Hack Lovecraft, Make Friends with His Monsters, and Hijack His Mythos: Reading Biology and Racism in Elizabeth Bear's 'Shoggoths in Bloom.'" *Studies in the Fantastic* Vol. 4 (2016–2017): 24–47.

Cerankowski, Karli June and Megan Milk. "New Orientations: Asexuality and Its Implications for Theory and Practice." *Feminist Studies* Vol. 36, No. 3 (2010): 650–664.

Dyer, Gary. *White*. New York: Routledge, 1997.

Edelman, Lee. *No Future: Queer Theory and the Death Drive*. Durham, NC: Duke University Press, 2006.

Elfenbein, Andrew. *Romantic Genius: The Prehistory of a Homosexual Role*. New York: Columbia University Press, 1999.

Fanon, Frantz. "The Negro and Psychopathology." *Literary Theory: An Anthology*, edited by Julie Rivkin and Michael Ryan. Malden, MA: Blackwell, 2004, pp. 462–469.

Filby, William and Mary Meyer, *Passenger and Immigration Lists Index: A Guide to Published Arrival Records of about 500,000 passengers Who Came to the United States and Canada in the Seventeenth, Eighteenth, and Nineteenth Centuries. 1982–1985 Cumulated Supplements in Four Volumes*. Detroit: Gale, 1985.

Freud, Sigmund. *The Interpretation of Dreams*, edited and translated by James Strachey. New York: Avon, 1965.

Grover, Jan Zita. "AIDS: Keywords." *AIDS: Cultural Analysis, Cultural Activism*, edited by Douglas Crimp. Cambridge, MA: MIT Press, 1988, pp. 17–30.

Halberstam, Jack. *In a Queer Time and Place: Transgender Bodies, Subcultural Lives*. New York: New York University Press, 2005.

———. *Skin Shows: Gothic Horror and the Technology of Monsters*. Durham, NC: Duke University Press, 1995.

Herrmann, Lee. "'Bothersome Forms, of Course, Were Mechanically Exterminated': Colonialism, Science, Racial Dysgenia, and Extermination in the Works of H.P. Lovecraft, Intertextually and Beyond." *Comparative Studies in Modernism* Vol. 14 (2019): 303–328.

Ignatiev, Noel. *How the Irish Became White*. New York: Routledge, 1995.

Ingebretsen, Edward. *At Stake: Monsters and the Rhetoric of Fear in Public Culture*. Chicago: University of Chicago Press, 2001.

Jarvis, Timothy. "The Weird, the Posthuman, and the Abjected World-in-Itself: Fidelity to the 'Lovecraftian Event' in the Work of Caitlín R. Kiernan and Laird Barron." *Textual Practice* Vol. 31, No. 6 (2017): 133–1148.

von Krafft-Ebing, Richard. *Psychopathia Sexualis with Especial Reference to Contrary Sexual Instinct: A Forensic Study*, edited by Brian King. Burbank, CA: Bloat, 1999.

Kristeva, Julia. *Powers of Horror: An Essay on Abjection*. Translated by Leon Roudiez. New York: Columbia University Press, 1982.

LaValle, Victor. *The Ballad of Black Tom*. New York: Tor, 2016.

Lovecraft, H.P. "The Call of Cthulhu." *H. P. Lovecraft Collected Fiction, A Variorum Edition, Volume 2: 1926–1930*, edited by S. T. Joshi. New York: Hippocampus Press, 2017, pp. 21–55.

———. "The Call of Cthulhu." *The Classic Horror Stories*, edited by Roger Luckhurst, Oxford University Press, 2013, pp. 24–52.

———. *Supernatural Horror in Literature. H. P. Lovecraft, Collected Essays Volume 2: Literary Criticism*, edited by S. T. Joshi. New York: Hippocampus Press, 2004, pp. 82–135.

Malchow, H.L. *Gothic Images of Race in Nineteenth-Century Britain*. Stanford, CA: Stanford University Press, 1996.

Mayer, Jed, "Race Species, and Others: H.P. Lovecraft and the Animal." *The Age of Lovecraft*, edited by Carl Sederholm and Jeffrey Weinstock. Minneapolis, MN: University of Minnesota Press, 2016, pp. 117–132.

McClintock, Anne. "Imperial Leather: Race, Gender, and Sexuality in the Colonial Context." *Feminist Literary Theory: A Reader*, edited by Mary Eagleton. Malden, MA: Blackwell-Wiley, 2011, pp. 428–432.

Muñoz, José. *Cruising Utopia: The Then and There of Queer Futurity*. New York: New York University Press, 2009.

Murphy, Timothy. "Physiology Is Destiny: The Fate of Eugenic Utopia in the Fiction of H.P. Lovecraft and Olaf Stapleton." *Utopian Studies* Vol. 29, No. 1 (2018): 21–43.

Nelson, Victoria. *The Secret Life of Puppets*. Cambridge, MA: Harvard University Press, 2001.

Nussbaum, Felicity. *Torrid Zones: Maternity, Sexuality, and Empire in Eighteenth-Century English Narratives*. Baltimore: John's Hopkins University Press, 1995.

Sederholm, Carl. "Lovecraft's Reluctant Sexuality: Abjection and the Monstrous Feminine in "The Dunwich Horror." *The Age of Lovecraft*, edited by Carl Sederholm and Jeffrey Weinstock. Minneapolis, MN: University of Minnesota Press, 2016, pp. 133–148.

Sederholm, Carl and Jeffrey Weinstock. "Introduction: Lovecraft Rising," *The Age of Lovecraft*, edited by Carl Sederholm and Jeffrey Weinstock. Minneapolis, MN: University of Minnesota Press, 2016, pp. 1–42.

Sedgwick, Eve. *The Weather in Proust*, edited by Jonathan Goldberg. Durham: Duke University Press, 2011.

Smith, Philip. "Re-visioning Romantic-Era Gothicism: An Introduction to Key Works and Themes in the Study of H.P. Lovecraft." *Literature Compass* Vol. 8, No. 11 (2011): 830–839.

Stryker, Susan. "My Words to Victor Frankenstein above the Village of Chamounix." *The Transgender Studies Reader*, edited by Susan Stryker and Stephen Whittle. New York: Routledge, 2006, pp. 244–256.

VanderMeer, Jeff. "Moving Past Lovecraft." *WeirdFictionReview.com* (2012). September 1, 2012. https://weirdfictionreview.com/2012/09/moving-past-lovecraft/. Accessed June 28, 2020.

Wasson, Sara and Emily Alder. "Introduction." *Gothic Science Fiction 1980–2010*, edited by Sara Wasson and Emily Alder. Liverpool: Liverpool University Press, 2011, pp. 1–18.

Weinstock, Jeffrey. "Afterword: Interview with China Miéville." *The Age of Lovecraft*, edited by Carl Sederholm and Jeffrey Weinstock. Minneapolis, MN: University of Minnesota Press, 2016, pp. 231–243.

Wisker, Gina. "'Spawn of the Pit': Lavinia, Marceline, Medusa, and All Things Foul: H.P. Lovecraft's Liminal Women." *New Critical Essays on H.P. Lovecraft*, edited by David Simmons. New York: Palgrave Macmillan, 2013, pp. 31–54.

Wiegman, Robyn. "Whiteness Studies and the Paradox of Particularity." *Boundary 2* Vol. 26, No. 3 (1999), pp. 115–150.

Yancy, George. "Introduction: Fragments of a Social Ontology of Whiteness." *What White Looks Like: African-American Philosophers on the Whiteness Question*, edited by George Yancy. New York: Routledge, 2004. 1–23.

Yancy, George and Judith Butler. "What's Wrong With 'All Lives Matter'?" *The New York Times*. January 12, 2015. https://opinionator.blogs.nytimes.com/2015/01/12/whats-wrong-with-all-lives-matter/. Accessed June 28, 2020.

19 Weird Bedfellows

H. P. Lovecraft, m/m Romance, and the New Queer Families of Jordan L. Hawk's *Whyborne & Griffin* Series[1]

Brian Johnson

The attractiveness of H. P. Lovecraft's fiction to queer readers and contemporary Mythos authors is no secret.[2] As the emergence of a robust "queer weird" attests, Lovecraft's personal distaste for "the greater & grosser offenses" of Oscar Wilde (Lovecraft to August Derleth 64) has in no way deterred modern readers and cultural producers from imaginatively appropriating the author's work and making it resonate with the exigencies of their own queer visions. Quite the contrary, the very ubiquity of such revisions attests to the queer implications of Lovecraft's stories—implications that have been central to the vexed mythology of Lovecraft's own supposed "closetedness." To many readers, Lovecraft's well-documented homophobia and imputed asexuality have seemed like strategies of disavowal, and his writing's infamous prolixity and lexical excess like the inscriptions of a compensatory, barely sublimated literary eroticism.[3] It is little wonder, then, that Lovecraft's oeuvre now operates so conspicuously as an attractor for queer world-making. Recent fictions like Paul La Farge's *The Night Ocean* (2017) and critical-biographical works like Scott Poole's *In the Mountains of Madness* (2016) explore this territory, as do numerous queerly inflected weird tales and short works of Lovecraftian homoerotica and fanfic by W. H. Pugmire, Laird Barron, Stanley C. Sargent, Johnny Murdoc, Lula Lisbon (D. P. Lustcraft), and David Holly, among others.[4]

My focus in this chapter is how the ever-expanding subgenre of queer weird revisionings of Lovecraft has recently hybridized with another newly consolidated popular subgenre: male/male (m/m) romance. Despite its superficial resemblance to gay romantic fiction written by gay men, m/m romance actually emerged in the 1990s out of slash and digital fanfic archives before taking on a life of its own in the independent epublishing/Amazon/Goodreads ecosystem, where it currently thrives alongside the (heterosexual) popular romance novel as a genre, like slash, "written almost exclusively by and for women" (Salmon and Symons qtd. in Allan 74).[5] In what follows, I begin to map the transformational poetics of this surprising marriage between Lovecraftian horror and m/m romance by examining trans writer Jordan L. Hawk's self-published

DOI: 10.4324/9780367713065-20

fifteen-volume paranormal-historical m/m romance series, Whyborne & Griffin (2012–19).[6] These episodically self-contained but serialized novels and novelettes, set in the Innsmouth-like coastal city of Widdershins and in Mythos-related sites around the world between 1897 and 1902, follow the developing romance and paranormal adventures of Dr. Percival Endicott Whyborne (a philologist-sorcerer loosely modelled on the closeted myth of Lovecraft himself) and Griffin Flaherty (an ex-Pinkerton private investigator and Whyborne's soul mate). Dr. Christine Putnam (Whyborne's feminist archaeologist colleague and sister-like best friend) and Iskander Barnett (a cosmopolitan Anglo-Egyptian ghūl-hunter they meet in the fourth volume and Christine's romantic partner) round out the series' *Buffy*-like "Scooby Gang" or "core four," whose world-saving investigations unfold in a streamlined, continuity-rich, partially modified simulacrum of the Mythos universe. Therein, the fictional New England city of Widdershins, along with a variety of frontier-like American and international locations, function as settings for elaborate conspiracy plots involving alien Gods, evil necromancers, and strange races, but also as exotic backdrops for the developing relationship between Whyborne and Griffin that anchors the series in the sexually explicit and emotionally gratifying tropes of m/m romance and its promise of HEA ("happily ever after").

Hawk's series is a dazzling pastiche of Lovecraftian Mythos elements and plots, but it is also a powerful and complex work of queer self-apprehension. Not only does Hawk give countless Mythos elements queer twist after queer twist, as I explore in more detail below, but his adaptation of Lovecraftian horror to the conventions of m/m romance intervenes in Lovecraft's universe in a way calculated to purge the Mythos of Lovecraft's own homophobia, sexism, and racism, while also radically reimagining the very object Michel Houellebecq singles out as holding for Lovecraft no interest whatsoever: the life of the "average American family" (57). At one level, Lovecraft's authorial indifference to depicting "ordinary" family life (like his travestying of the family in grotesque cosmic genealogies) is what marks his fictions as deviations from nineteenth-century bourgeois realism's tacit heteronormativity. For readers whose gender and sexuality place them at odds with the "banal and beatific happiness, adequately symbolized by the family life of an insurance agent in an American suburb" (Houellebecq 51), Lovecraft's delirious "Outsider"-like flight from the quotidian to gape at obscene mysteries willy nilly articulates what Judith Halberstam famously called "a queer art of failure"—that specifically queer structure of feeling that derives from the (often-anguished) discovery that "[u]nder certain circumstance failing, losing, forgetting, unmaking, undoing, unbecoming, not knowing may in fact offer more creative, more cooperative, more surprising ways of being in the world" (2).[7] But whereas Lovecraft never overtly refers his cosmic horrors to a queer critique of the heteronormative family, Hawk reaccentuates and transvalues the Lovecraftian melodrama of family secrets and unspeakable couplings in terms of the liberatory queer ethics of m/m romance to develop a more sociologically grounded, politically nuanced, and internally differentiated articulation of the Mythos. In Hawk's novels, as we will see, cosmic monstrosity undergoes a Manichaen splitting into a pantheon of good slaves and evil masters, the purpose of which is both to anatomize homophobia's generation of "gay shame" within the family and society and to provide a utopian articulation of what a queer "chosen family" can look like. Ultimately, I suggest, Hawk's rewriting of the Mythos to articulate not just a celebration of (monogamous) queer romantic love but a whole inclusive poetics of the queer family is significant among recent queerings of Lovecraft not only because it constitutes a substantial creative engagement with Lovecraft's own inescapably nebulous and contradictory "queerness," but because it offers an important intervention into questions of gender, voice, and sexuality that have emerged in genre debates about m/m romance and the new online "family" of m/m romance authors and readers themselves.

Queering Lovecraft's Bachelor-Heroes

On the origin of Whyborne & Griffin's "dork with a book" scholar-hero, Dr. Percival Whyborne, Hawk has noted his indebtedness to the unconventional heroism of the "posse of learned men" who "go kick the monster's butt" in "The Dunwich Horror" (Interview with Boys in Our Books). Indeed, Lovecraft's fiction abounds with non-cisgender-conforming male protagonists whose esoteric scholarly interests, physical slightness, sickliness, and preference for observation over action make them seem like archly flattering authorial self-insertions. Miskatonic University alumnus Whyborne seems birthed fully formed from the template of these observer- and victim-heroes, many of which Lovecraft even depicted in intense homosocial pairings taking fatal nighttime excursions to the graveyard. Describing himself as "too gawky, too shy, too *strange*" (1.2), "too bookish, too quiet, too awkward" (1.16), Whyborne could be taken as a biographical portrait of Lovecraft himself or at least one of the Providence author's own "nervous" alter egos—Randolph Carter, for instance, a character whose travels through the dreamlands where he encounters malign Mythos deity Nyarlathotep in *The Dream-Quest of the Unknown Kadath* are discernible influences on both Whyborne's characterization and the series metaplot. Complementing the weedy hero with unkempt hair is "dashing" former asylum inmate, dime-novel reader, and ex-Pinkerton P. I. Griffin Flaherty. Conventionally handsome, Griffin is a nod to Lovecraft's occasional use of adventure-hero types and police detectives—retired Investigator Legrasse from "The Call of Cthulhu," for example—but also a direct descendant of Lovecraft's institutionalized victim-heroes: the men who have seen too much and who are driven to madness by their encounters with the Great Old Ones and their earthly progeny.

Despite their allusion to such stock figures from the Lovecraft canon, however, Hawk's romantic protagonists transcend their prototypes when they are hybridized with the sexualized heroes of m/m romance. In keeping with popular romance's general generic tendency to link love with adventure, both characters are at once more active and more capable than the average Lovecraftian hero, triumphing book-by-book over the latest cult or bogey in a way that is rare in a traditional weird tale, where the accent usually falls more grimly on failure, horror, and existential anguish. In a review, Derie aptly compares the first volume to an *Indiana Jones* film ("Widdershins"), and this characterization remains pertinent throughout the series, whose plots and tone are also closely tied to the ambience of WB paranormal-adventure fanfic staples like *Buffy* and *Supernatural*. Moreover, within the sometimes hegemonic but still remarkably fluid gender politics of m/m romance as a genre, where embracing counterhegemonic expressions of gender and sexuality is *de rigeur*, Whyborne's "girlish" masculinity signifies differently than it does in Lovecraft's fictions, functioning not as a sexist marker of human fragility, but instead as an eroticized object.[8] Meanwhile, conventionally handsome Griffin, whose body is "a marvel, from the perfect ripple of muscle along his shoulders, to the temptation of his flat, small nipples, to the thickness of his member" (2.1), is modelled as much on the erotically idealized "spectacular masculinity" of romance generally (Allan 93) as on the paradigm of Lovecraft's tortured madmen. Most importantly, both characters' Lovecraftian afflictions—Whyborne's nervousness and insecurity, Griffin's "fits" and "madness"—are no longer confined to illustrating humanity's fundamental triviality and weakness in the face of cosmic indifference as they do in Lovecraft's chilly anti-humanist nightmares; in Hawk's more humanistic universe, insecurity and mental suffering are given robust social and familial causes and systematically exposed as psychic consequences of the (often violent and traumatic) heteronormative regulation of queer subjectivities.

The affective terrain of Hawk's Whyborne & Griffin novels is thus very different from that of most Mythos stories. Where Lovecraft's vulnerable human heroes contend primarily with fear and madness, Hawk's romantic protagonists balance the romance genre's standard quota of quips, banter, and playful innuendo with a searching examination of shame—the affect that Eve Sedgwick singles out as having exemplary salience for queer subjectivity and politics on the grounds that, in its earliest apprehension and subsequent unfolding, queerness entails a "sense of identity [that] is for some reason tuned most durably to the note of shame" (63). Hawk's reorientation of the heroes' psychology around shame rather than fear or "madness" (fear's post-rational dissipative state in Lovecraft's stories), is especially evident in the novels' treatment of obstacles to romantic love. Among these obstacles, shame and queer self-hatred are paramount, even as the social and familial causes of internalized homophobia are foregrounded and dismantled. Such a toxic convergence of identity with social censure is made painfully evident in the pejorative nickname bestowed upon Whyborne by a homophobic museum colleague (and secret evil cult member) who dubs him "old 'Why-were-you-born'" (1.9). Whyborne's biography accordingly unfolds as a genealogy of abjection and queer repression. Although the son of a wealthy Widdershins family, he remains an outsider, bullied by his older brother Stanford throughout childhood (1.22) and goaded by his father Niles who regrets that he has been unable to "cure" his strange son of his "womanish ways" (3.9). Ashamed both of his body's disjunction from the standards of hegemonic masculinity and the forbidden desire he felt as a teen for his doomed, ephebically named best friend Leander, Whyborne dreams only of escape from the prison-like family home (1.24), to him "a version of Hell" (4.1). When he does finally leave, however, his rebellion is confined to the sublimating arenas of work and education. Meanwhile, he "ruthlessly suppresses" his same-sex desires (1.5) and finds himself "cursed to be a stranger in [his] own homeland, forever cut off from sympathy and affection" (1.4). In the period that precedes the narrative and his meeting of Griffin, he had "been living inside a photograph: just a facsimile of life without either color or depth" (1.16). When Griffin first notices him, he is "like a bottle of champagne, yearning to be opened…[y]ear after year, the pressure building slowly, with no release" (1.14).

Griffin's shame is complementary; originating in the repressiveness of rural religious bigotry, it ultimately detours through institutions of social discipline that stand in for homosexuality's criminalized status during the period in which the novels are set, while also hinting at the pseudoscience of Conversion Therapy—the institutional version of Niles Whyborne's misguided attempts to "cure" his son's effeminacy. Orphaned as a child and separated from his siblings, Griffin runs afoul of his adoptive family's fundamentalist Christian beliefs following a sexual "indiscretion" with a male friend from a neighbouring Kansas farm. Promising his adoptive parents never to repeat the misadventure, he is driven out of the rural community and joins the Pinkerton Detective Agency in Chicago, visiting a female prostitute en route in a desperate attempt at sexual reprogramming. Beyond the ambit of his parents' gaze, however, he becomes a frequenter of bathhouses, "living free of such banalities of hearth and home," revelling in becoming part of a carefree but emotionally indifferent circle of "men who fucked other men" (1.5.2). Indeed, Griffin's habits of professional dissimulation, which include donning disguises and seducing female witnesses, frame his bathhouse adventuring as a form of closeted sexuality. Thus, when Griffin's Pinkerton partner is killed by a supernatural entity in a Chicago basement, Griffin's emotional breakdown feels symbolically overdetermined—as if it is a veiled shame response, obliquely imputing an emotional cost to his queer sexual promiscuity that the novel itself will not directly acknowledge. This impression is reinforced not only by the fact that it is a lover and fellow Pinkerton who signs the papers committing him to the asylum and leaves him there "like a child leaving behind a broken toy" (2. 21), but also by a telling slippage in the diagnosis that institutionalizes him: "They admitted me for 'violent delusions,' but someone added a note about 'sexual deviance.' Do you know the 'cures' they inflict on us?" (3.5). As Griffin soon discloses, these "cures" include torture and rape at the hands of sadistic asylum attendants and doctors, the trauma of which leads Griffin to repeatedly apprehend himself as "damaged" and to refer to his time in the asylum as something that "shames [him], still" (2.21). Later, after he is rescued from the asylum by his adoptive father, Griffin discovers to his relief that "the cure hadn't taken" (3.5), paving the way for his relocation to Widdershins and the beginning of his relationship with Whyborne.

In the emotional trajectory of its episodes, the relationship between Whyborne and Griffin typifies the conventions of series-based m/m romance. From the beginning, the pair's innate goodness and complementary differences—Whyborne's insecurity and sexual inexperience, Griffin's shame-based belief that he must "earn love" through acts of service—work in tandem to produce the romance genre's characteristic narrative of reciprocal growth towards sexual fulfilment and emotional flourishing. Both men initially believe themselves to be unlovable, and each helps the other "come out of shame" into self-acceptance and a readiness to love.[9] Supplementing these expected narrative developments and satisfactions, and conforming to the additional subgeneric conventions of paranormal romance more generally, is the addition of nonrealist elements that function as symbols of love's progress. Whyborne's initiation into magic use when he studies a *Necronomicon*-like grimoire called the *Liber Arcanorum*, for instance, closely parallels his growing sexual confidence and initiation into romantic love between men. As the series progresses, the correlation between magic and libido becomes more overt and explicit as Whyborne not only masters more spells, but learns of his innate connection to the "Maelstrom," a "flood of magic" underneath the town of Widdershins that is ostensibly "too dangerous and raw for anyone to touch directly" (5.26), but which Whyborne draws upon for his sorcery and which, by the climactic eleventh book of the series, he is channelling directly through his body. This hidden vortex of "raw" magic thus frequently operates as a queer libidinal metaphor, the marvellous correlate of the "fire" that "boil[s] beneath the surface" of Whyborne's skin (1.14). When Griffin, too, acquires magical senses midway through the series, the lovers' sexual sorcery fully converges in the weaving of collaborative magic that instrumentalizes the consummation of queer desire in service of the series' anti-homophobic paranormal allegory—a more complex appropriation of Lovecraft's discourse of otherness to which I will now turn.

Queering the Mythos, Loving the Monstrous

Complementing the reinvention of Lovecrafts's arcane dabblers as symbols of sexual liberation is the series' more far-reaching reimagining and allegorical grafting of the Mythos onto the central conflicts of the romantic adventure plot and its patently anti-homophobic themes. Hawk's world-building in this regard emphasizes consistency, continuity, and dualism—an approach that brings the cosmic presences and earthly monsters of the Whyborne & Griffin universe closer to the rationalized agon and moral melodrama of Derleth's revised Mythos than to Lovecraft's more improvisational, inconsistent, and generally pessimistic Yog-Sothothery.[10] Hawk's reinvention of the Mythos proceeds ambidextrously, as it were, developing the paraphernalia of cosmic alterity in two complementary directions simultaneously: towards a critical anatomy of homophobia and towards a deconstruction and transvaluation of the monster as Other.

On the one hand, then, Hawk strategically domesticates Lovecraft's personification of cosmic indifferentism in the star-families of the Elder Things, the Great Old Ones, and Outer Gods by reimagining the cosmic entities and their human worshippers as personifications of a more intimate and disciplinary "indifferentism"—ostensibly towards humanity as a species (which they plan to enslave), but, allegorically, towards the play of sexual difference and desire that distinguishes queerness from heteronormativity. Thus, for example, the Elder Thing- and Outer God-like "masters," whose apocalyptic arrival in Widdershins from "the Outside" is prophesied and feared throughout the series, ultimately do arrive in the final adventure, presaged by a medicalized process of human mental enslavement designated by the normative lingo of social hygiene: "purification" and "becoming Perfected" (11.15). After being dosed by the masters' human cultists, ordinary humans lose their individuality and become wax-skinned robotic "zealots" (11.16), subsuming their personalities and desires into an undifferentiated mass whose only wish is to serve the cosmic lawbringers. In one of the irregular chapters of the series narrated by "Widdershins" itself—that is, by the sentient and rebellious Maelstrom of wild magic that broke free of the masters to bring about Whyborne's birth—the narrative voice laments how the apparent triumph of the masters and their legions reduces "the mosaic of colour and joy" created by the town's "thousand sparks of life" to "empty grey sameness" (11.39). The psychosexual costs of this greying of the mosaic are made explicit in the tragedy of the Perfected Woman—a minor but symbolically important character who embraces the eradication of her suppressed queer longings (11.6). The masters' "gift" of "Perfectability," in other words, operates as a fantastic answer to parental wishes to "cure" a child's queer presentation, a necromantic version of the thinly veiled "Conversion Therapy" that Griffin experiences at the asylum. As the Perfected Woman's example shows, the Lovecraftian motif of body-snatching or mesmerism recurs in Hawk's depiction of heteronormative interpellation as a kind of mental rape—a cosmic evil, typically signalled by the presence of phallic medical "probes" and needles that are used to straighten out queer subjectivities that are "too rambunctious" (11.6).

Episodes like this one follow a rigorous symbolic logic that Hawk maintains with tireless consistency, inventiveness, and nuance across all the books of the series. "The Outside" itself—a realm that always threatens to (and does) erupt violently into the lives of the queer protagonists—locates ideology within a persecutory geography wherein "the veil" between realms through which it always threatens to burst connotes the membrane of an embattled queer subjectivity. Prior to the masters' arrival from the Outside (and thus for the majority of the series), their extra-dimensional shock troops prepare the ground: Nyarlathotep, the Mi-Go-like yayhos, the byakhee, the hounds of Tindalos, and others all function as ranked but symbolically interchangeable signifiers of a deadly heteronormativity with which the heroes must do battle. Within this symbolic economy, the relation between human cultists like Whyborne's father and brother and the evil cosmic Gods they worship allegorizes the lobotomizing operation of heteronormative ideology.

On the other hand, even as the masters and their progeny embody the invading forces of heteronormative coercion and homophobic violence, Lovecraftian monstrosity becomes itself the subject of a deconstructive critique writ large within Hawk's version of the Mythos' internecine conflicts. This unsettling of Lovecraft's poetics of monstrosity begins at the level of Mythos genealogy, where Hawk embraces Derleth's revised Mythos' emphasis on cosmic dualism (already present in Lovecraft, but muted), making the cosmic clash between master- and servitor races who vie for cosmic supremacy central to the series' evolving metaplot. Hawk's Mythos world is thus not only populated by the masters and their faithful servants and cultists, but by nonhuman entities that, like Lovecraft's insubordinate Shoggoths, have rebelled against their creators. As Whyborne and Griffin eventually discover, the yayhos were initially created by the masters as the genetic engineering wing of their inter-dimensional imperialist machine. Obedient slaves, but also creators in their turn, the yayhos used terrestrial species as raw material for second-order creations that would also serve the masters: from human beings, they made the amphibious ketoi (Deep Ones) and from species of eusocial insects like ants or bees, they made the umbrae—a species of abject "oily, jelly-like" beings, each with cyclopean yellow eyes housing "a tripartite pupil" that are clearly modelled on Lovecraft's "formless protoplasm[ic]" Shoggoths (Hawk 11.25; Lovecraft, *ATMM* 142).

The "fishy," "oily," and "jelly-like" qualities of these "servitor races" are treated ironically in Hawk's reinvention because whereas Lovecraft imbued the Deep Ones and the Shoggoths with the racist signifiers of his own xenophobic disgust, Hawk evokes the racist imaginary Lovecraft's monsters embody in order to invert and expose it. Thus, whereas the Deep Ones' sexual trysts with mainlanders index Lovecraft's "hysterical terror of miscegenation" and the Shoggoths evoke Lovecraft's nightmare of an ascendant "ethnically heterogeneous" underclass (Miéville xviii, xxiii),

Hawk's analogous ketoi and umbrae only appear to be "demons" from the Outside, and their rebellions align with those of the series' protagonists. In spite of some unsettling first impressions, in other words, both the ketoi and the umbrae turn out to be queer-affirming fellow travellers, and even in their malevolent forms are usually presented sympathetically. Like the queer protagonists and their feminist, cosmopolitan allies, the rebellious servitor races of the series array themselves against the heteronormative dystopia of their former masters. The ketoi, for example, are a subaquatic matriarchy of noble fish people who cannot countenance the narrowness of a culture in which "[o]nly a man and a woman can wed" (5.21). The umbrae, meanwhile, also a matriarchy, are imprisoned in the masters' alien city beneath the Alaskan ice in a polar reversal of the Elder Things' Antarctic city from *At The Mountains of Madness*; there, the umbraes' monstrous hive-mother mourns for her lost children who have been kidnapped and brainwashed by evil power-hungry necromancers (6.44).

At the level of the Mythos alone, such reversals repudiate Lovecraft's vision of the monster as other, recognizing "monster" as a strictly stigmatizing ideological figure. Hawk's fiction thus parses Lovecraftian monstrosity as a signifier of otherness into social and metaphysical usages, rejecting the former as a hegemonic form of discursive violence (against queer subjectivities—indeed, against the queerness *of* subjectivity, as Whyborne and Griffin's numerous allies and even some of their self-harming homophobic human antagonists imply) and selectively retaining the latter only as a signifier of impersonal or systemic moral evil (now associated predominantly with heteronormativity and misogyny, but also with racism and classism). Accordingly, Hawk reserves its unqualified use for ideas personified in nonrealist forms (the masters, Nyarlathotep, the yayhos, etc.) and rejects its application to individuals or sociocultural groups.

As the Stonewall-evoking `battle in the streets for Widdershins in the final book, *Deosil*, makes abundantly clear, to be "fishy," "oily," and "jelly-like" in Hawk's novels is to be counted among "the mosaic of colour and joy" that is Widdershins—there simply is no contradiction. Like the reclamation of "queer," the embrace of "monstrosity" is depicted throughout the series as a reparative act of self-valuation intrinsically responsive to the identity-constituting trauma of queer shame. Nowhere is this more evident than in the ubiquitous scenes of "true love"-affirming explicit gay sex between Whyborne and Griffin. For fans of m/m romance, the sexual explicitness of such scenes provides a generically mandated narrative and sensorial payoff that will delight rather than shock. Nevertheless, given their recurrence within Mythos fiction based on the work of a notoriously homophobic author, the gay sex scenes in Whyborne and Griffin also retain the savour of a critical transgression as political as it is erotic. Beyond their self-evidently titillating validation of queer sexualities, what such scenes perform is a generic queering of Lovecraftian body horror and its own "monstrous" and excessive figures. When Whyborne savours the feeling of Griffin's "thick cock fill[ing his] mouth," imagines variations on penetrative sexual positions, revels in "taking his spend into me," or describes "white gobs of semen splatter[ing] against the floor," Hawk rewrites the horror of the homosocial geologist victim-heroes of *At the Mountains of Madness* who recoil at "the freshly glistening and reflectively iridescent black slime which clung to those headless bodies and stank obscenely with that new unknown odour whose cause only a diseased fancy could envisage" in the Antarctic tomb (*ATMM* 142). If Lovecraft's abject fascination with slimy and sticky bodily fluids, the mental "penetration" of male bodies by other men, and the "weird" biological juxtapositions of his hybrid fauna strike some readers as evidence of homoerotic displacement, Whyborne and Griffin's explicit and lovingly rendered sex life is, among other things, a narrative exercise in riotous desublimation that unapologetically affirms and literalizes such intertextual intuitions.

Meanwhile, echoing filmmakers Grant Cogswell and Daniel Gildark's *Cthulhu* (2007) and the queer critical readings of "The Shadow over Innsmouth" suggested by Price and Derie, Whyborne's discovery that he is not only from a bloodline of sorcerers but is in fact of ketoi ancestry on his mother's side (5.19) concretizes the symbolic parallels between monsters and queer men in the biological Lovecraftian trope of "tainted" genealogy. When Griffin thoughtlessly blurts, "How could my love be one of the very monsters we've fought against?" (5.21), he immediately corrects himself, voicing the novels' queer ethic. "You are not tainted. Or corrupted, or anything else," he tells Whyborne. "If you're one of the monsters we've fought against, then—then they can't *be* monsters. No more so than humans, at any rate. Some terrible and some good, but not inherently evil" (5.21). Griffin himself repeats this deconstructive logic in his own shifting identification with monstrosity: first, fearing the malevolent umbra whose attack precipitates his institutionalization, then vertiginously experiencing another dangerous umbra's point of view through a sequence of supernatural dreams, eventually learning that these murderous umbrae had been kidnapped and corrupted by human sorcerers, and finally accepting a gift of supernatural "shadowsight" through a telepathic bond he forms with umbra Queen, the Mother of Shadows. Echoing his earlier intervention into Whyborne's lapse into self-loathing at the discovery of his ketoi blood, Griffin reflects:

> At one time, the umbrae nest would have been my greatest nightmares come true.... [But now] I was at home among the umbrae, in Widdershins, with my strange family, in a way I'd never been before. If that meant that there was something wrong with me, I had no desire at all to have it fixed.
>
> (11.19)

Through tropes like interspecies sex and telepathy, then, hybridity, impurity, corruption, and taintedness become badges of queer pride in a work that is itself proudly, generically "impure."

Queer Families, m/m Romance, and the Politics of Reading

As I have argued, Hawk's queer revisionism encompasses both a rewriting of the chaste homosociality of Lovecraft's male heroes in terms of the tropes of m/m romance and a critical rewriting of the Mythos itself, which it transforms into a dualist allegory of queer self-apprehension and striving against heteronormative coercion. It also, as I suggested at the outset, constitutes a utopian reimagining of the heteronormative nuclear family. Whyborne and Griffin's immediate families both prove to be disappointing: Whyborne's because his father and brother epitomize homophobic bullying and normative gender identity so completely that "[t]he motorcar would make a better replacement family" (4.23), and Griffin's because the warmth of his adoptive parents freezes up when faced with the early stirrings of Griffin's bisexuality and again when he comes out to them, introducing Whyborne as his husband. The rift this creates never heals, and Griffin remains estranged from his adoptive father until the latter's death. Into the gap created by these breakdowns of familial care, Hawk develops what he regards as the central theme of the series: "finding the family who loves you for yourself" (Hawk, Interview at "Joyfully Jay").

The core of the series' chosen family is constituted by Whyborne and Griffin in both their human and extra-human dimensions. Dismissing Whyborne's worry that his search for the biological brothers from whom he was separated by the orphan train signals Griffin's compensatory longing for "real" family after his relationship with Whyborne "cost[s] him" his adoptive family's love, Griffin counters: "You *are* my family. I hope to find my brothers. I hope they are happy in their lives and will be happy for me in mine. But they'll never take the place of you, or Christine, or Heliabel" (4.23). As an adopted child, Griffin is perhaps uniquely suited to teaching Whyborne about the fluid potential of family ties. Moreover, Griffin's inclusion of both Whyborne's feminist best-friend Christine (whom Whyborne regards as "more of a sister to me than the one who shared my blood") (4.21), and Heliabel (Whyborne's benevolent mother whose support of the same-sex couple is the social index of her eventually revealed ketoi heritage) in his accounting of family already indicates Hawk's interest in dramatizing the idealized chosen family as a network of variously minoritarian allies. Beyond the racializing metaphor of Heliabel's ketoi blood, the chosen family's utopian multiculturalism is explicitly signalled by the addition of Anglo-Egyptian Iskander Barnett to the group in volume four as Christine's professional and romantic partner, his mixed-race background, and mother's nomadic ancestry functioning as signs for the cosmopolitan migrancy Hawk tacitly opposes to Lovecraft's white supremacist xenophobia. Whyborne's discovery that his presumed-dead twin sister Persephone is in fact not only still alive, but is a ketoi/human hybrid who was cast back into the sea as a child, where a ketoi ritual transformed her body into one resembling the ketoi's original, unhybridized form, may also, like Whyborne's gender trouble, obliquely hint at Hawk's own trans identity, which he shared with readers in October of 2019, shortly after the publication of the final Whyborne & Griffin novel ("Cue Diana Ross: I'm Coming Out"). As the series' chosen family expands to include a greater and greater array of "human" and "nonhuman" diversity, the two major strands of Hawk's revisionism converge: the rewriting of tragic Lovecraftian homosociality into sexual queer partnership and the dualistic transvaluation of Mythos monstrosity meet in the series' culminating constitution of a chosen family that fights for Widdershins against the depredations of the crypto-heteronormative masters.

The vertiginous and voluptuous strangeness of Lovecraft's universe, especially when it finds itself hybridized by the very different ideological commitments of a reparative queer aesthetic, ironically makes it a productive bedfellow for m/m romance, a genre that directly thematizes queer love and polymorphous, heterogeneous queer families. Hawk's queer Lovecraftian romance universe, I also want to suggest, has special significance for its community of online readers whose sex, gender-identifications, and sexualities are too various and too motile to be hastily or summarily categorized by the reductive, often-repeated, and, in this instance, patently false claim that m/m romance is a genre written by and for straight women.[11] Speaking in the omniscient third-person voice of Widdershins—the town whose magical/libidinal energy vortex "gathers its own," but is also a kind of metafictional analogue for the author himself—Hawk appears to acknowledge precisely this dispersed online community of readers who gather in virtual book clubs and on Goodreads as another such chosen family by evoking a paradoxical image of connectedness that attaches even to the private scene of reading. As the masters are defeated and the lovers reunite,

> Color surges back through the mosaic I created, all the stolen pieces restored one after another, until it becomes a virtual cascade of light, hue, and joy. Chains of being spiral off in all directions, each link seeing the other, and being seen in return. *Even those few who touch no chain are restored, because even if no one else sees them, I do. I know them for all that they are, and their value is no less than any other.*
> (11.42; emphasis added)

If Lovecraft's fiction of cosmic terror was, as Houellebecq has argued, fundamentally a literature of hatred for life, the queerest intervention of Hawk's m/m Mythos romances has been to transform materialist horror into a fictional crucible whose "weird" allegorical generativity creates a structure of inclusivity in which the values of love, affirmation, and community transcend the real horrors of alienation, melancholy, and shame.[12]

Notes

1 For a superb contemporaneous study of the generic convergence of weird fiction with m/m romance in Hawk's Whyborne & Griffin series, see Weimer, who graciously shared his article with me in manuscript. The happy coincidence of our studies gives some sense, I hope, of the richness and pertinence of Hawk's extraordinary series to Lovecraftian scholarship, particularly to its queer inflections.

2 By "Mythos," I refer to the intricate fictional pantheon of alien gods, monsters, and shared story elements that Lovecraft began developing in his work through a complex accretion of allusions to his own stories and to those of contemporaneous authors whose concepts and characters he sometimes borrowed, even as he encouraged them to make use of elements from his own evolving storyworld. For the purpose of this essay, which focuses on Hawk's intertextual relationship with Lovecraft, my references to "the Lovecraft Mythos" indicate the pantheon of alien gods as Lovecraft developed them in his own writing. As we shall see, however, Hawk's complex rewriting of Lovecraft's work owes much to August Derleth's systematization of the Mythos in his own post hoc attempts to rationalize the Lovecraft "universe" along Manichean lines. For a useful overview of the history of the Mythos and its formation, see Daniel Harms's Foreword to *The Cthulhu Mythos Encyclopedia*.

3 On queer readings of Lovecraft's fiction, see Price, Derie, Pace, and Johnson. For a fuller discussion of the debates around Lovecraft's sexuality, see Pace, Sederholm, and Johnson.

4 See Derie's extensive survey of this field of cultural production in *Sex and the Cthulhu Mythos*.

5 On the debate over differences between gay male romance and m/m romance, see Brooks, Buben, and Lauture; Allan; Neville; Thornton; Foster.

6 The series consists of eleven core novels: *Widdershins* (vol. 1; 2012), *Threshold* (vol. 2; 2013), *Stormhaven* (vol. 3; 2013), *Necropolis* (vol. 4; 2014), *Bloodline* (vol. 5; 2014), *Hoarfrost* (vol. 6; 2015), *Maelstrom* (vol. 7; 2015), *Fallow* (vol. 8; 2016), *Draakenwood* (vol. 9; 2017), *Balefire* (vol. 10; 2018), and *Deosil* (vol. 11; 2019). It also includes three short stories written by Hawk—*Eidolon* (vol. 1.5; 2014), *Carousel* (vol. 3.4; 2015), and *Undertow* (vol. 8.5; 2017)—and an additional story, *Remnant* (vol. 3.5; 2014), co-written by K. J. Charles (a crossover with Charles's own occult detective series, The Secret Casebook of Simon Feximal). The co-authored story with m/m genre-compatriot Charles is itself and example of the way the production environment of Hawk's Whyborne & Griffin series mimics the collaborative atmosphere in which Lovecraft's original Mythos developed.

7 For a queer reading of "The Outsider," see Price.

8 Jonathan A. Allan has argued that m/m romance often uncritically celebrates "hybrid masculinity"—a seemingly alternative but actually hegemonic version of masculinity that still privileges the spectacular male body of popular (heterosexual) romance. He acknowledges, however, that it would be reductive to view the whole genre (which is more diverse than I have time to fully explore here) as complicit in this "remasculinization" of queer love between men (98).

9 There are some limits to the series' critique of queer shame, which is profound but not radical. As its ambivalent framing of Griffin's bathhouse adventures during his "wilder days back in Chicago" (5.19) and its corresponding privileging of the romance genre's "soul mates" trope suggests, the sexual ethics of Whyborne & Griffin remain tacitly homonormative with respect to monogamy. In the series' monogamous post-shame romantic utopia, "true love" makes monogamy's disciplinary dimension superfluous.

10 "Yog-Sothothery," an allusion to Lovecraft's cosmic "Outer God" Yog-Sothoth, was Lovecraft's own ironical term for his haphazardly accreting Mythos—what he also called, with clear bemusement, his fiction's "gradually developing hash of theogony—or daimonogeny," its "pseudo-mythology" (Lovecraft to Derleth 336).

11 Although this is not the place for a detailed consideration of the debate over "authenticity of voice" in m/m romance, I see much to recommend in Lucy Neville's refusal of the polarizing binary between a "creators and consumers of m/m erotic content who are attempting to see a reflection of their own lived queer identities," on the one hand, "and those who only 'play at queerness' whilst otherwise living a heterosexual (if not heteronormative) life," on the other. "If we take "queer"…as a word for all forms of sexuality that do not conform to the conventional heterosexual model of penetrative sex between an active cisman and a passive ciswoman," she suggests, "then, yes, women engaging with m/m sex is queer. While this definition of queerness is certainly a broad one, David Halperin warns us that 'even to [try to] define queer…is to limit its potential, its magical power to usher in a new age of sexual radicalism and fluid gender possibilities'—so broad definitions may be on safer ground" (220–221). Although I have noted the presence of a certain homonormativity in the series' generically typical preference for monogamy over other forms of sexual relationship above (n. 9), the semantically overdetermined weird allegorizing of Hawk's broadly queer Lovecraftian romances might nevertheless be read as polymorphously complicating their own structural homonormativity. In the Whyborne & Griffin novels, I hear Hawk tacitly making the case for contradictory, capacious, and fluid forms of identification, performance, and fantasy that are not exhausted by the novels' formal capitulations to generic convention. For a fuller discussion of the issues informing this debate see Foster; Thornton; and Brooks, Buben, and Lauture.

12 This essay is respectfully dedicated to the MM Romance and Gay Fiction group at Goodreads. Thank you, my friends, for sharing your experience, your knowledge, and your wisdom with me.

Works Cited

Allan, Jonathan A. *Men, Masculinities, and Popular Romance*. Routledge, 2020.

Brooks, Emily, Alex Buben, and Fender Lauture. "M/M Romance." *Unsuitable* n.d., https://sites.duke.edu/unsuitable/malemale-romance/. Accessed January 5 2021.

Derie, Bobby. *Sex and the Cthulhu Mythos*. New York: Hippocampus Press, 2014.

———. "Widdershins (2013) by Jordan L. Hawk." *Deep Cuts* 3 August 2019, https://deepcuts.blog/2019/08/03/widdershins-2013-by-jordan-l-hawk/. Accessed January 5 2021.

Foster, Claire Rudy. "Why Are So Many Gay Romances Written by Straight Women?" *Electric Literature* 20 March 2018, https://electricliterature.com/why-are-so-many-gay-romance-novels-written-by-straight-women/. Accessed January 5 2021.

Halberstam, Judith. *The Queer Art of Failure*. Duke University Press, 2011.
Harms, Daniel. Foreword. *The Cthulhu Mythos Encyclopedia*, Elder Signs Press, 2008.
Hawk, Jordan L. "Cue Diana Ross: I'm Coming Out." *Jordan L. Hawk* 23 October 2019a, http://www.jordanlhawk.com/2019/10/23/cue-diana-ross-im-coming-out/. Accessed January 5 2021.
———. *Balefire*. Whyborne & Griffin, Book 10. 2018.
———. *Bloodline*. Whyborne & Griffin, Book 5. 2014a.
———. *Carousel*. Whyborne & Griffin, Book 3.4. 2014b.
———. *Deosil*. Whyborne & Griffin, Book 11. 2019b.
———. *Eidolon*. Whyborne & Griffin, Book 1.5. 2014c.
———. *Draakenwood*. Whyborne & Griffin, Book 9. 2017a.
———. *Fallow*. Whyborne & Griffin, Book 8. 2016.
———. *Hoarfrost*. Whyborne & Griffin, Book 6. 2015a.
———. *Maelstrom*. Whyborne & Griffin, Book 7. 2015b.
———. *Necropolis*. Whyborne & Griffin, Book 4. 2014d.
———. *Stormhaven*. Whyborne & Griffin, Book 3. 2013a.
———. *Threshold*. Whyborne & Griffin, Book 2. 2013b.
———. *Undertow*. Whyborne & Griffin, Book 8.5. 2017b.
———. *Widdershins*. Whyborne & Griffin, Book 1. 2012.
———. "Interview." *Boys in Our Books* 3 December 2013c, https://boysinourbooks.com/2013/12/03/author-interview-jordan-l-hawk/. Accessed January 5 2021.
———. "Interview." *Joyfully Jay* 8 October 2019c, https://joyfullyjay.com/2019/10/interview-deosil-by-jordan-l-hawk/. Accessed January 5 2021.
Hawk, Jordan and KJ Charles. *Remnant*. Whyborne & Griffin, Book 3.5. 2014.
Houellebecq, Michel. *H. P. Lovecraft: Against the World, Against Life*, translated by Dorna Khazeni, Orion, 2005.
Johnson, Brian. "Paranoia, Panic, and the Queer Weird." *New Directions in Supernatural Horror Literature: The Critical Influence of H. P. Lovecraft*, edited by Sean Moreland, Palgrave, 2018, pp. 253–278.
La Farge, Paul. *The Night Ocean*. Penguin, 2017.
Lovecraft, H. P. *At the Mountains of Madness. H. P. Lovecraft Collected Fiction, A Variorum Edition, Volume 3: 1931–1936*, edited by S. T. Joshi. New York: Hippocampus Press, 2017a, pp. 11–157.
———. "The Call of Cthulhu." *H. P. Lovecraft Collected Fiction, A Variorum Edition, Volume 2: 1926–1930*, edited by S. T. Joshi. New York: Hippocampus Press, 2017b, pp. 21–55.
———. "The Shadow Over Innsmouth." *H. P. Lovecraft Collected Fiction, A Variorum Edition, Volume 3: 1931–1936*, edited by S. T. Joshi. New York: Hippocampus Press, 2017c, pp. 158–230.
———. "Letter to August Derleth. 20 January 1927." *The Letters of H. P. Lovecraft to August Derleth: 1926–1931*, edited by David E. Schultz and S. T. Joshi. New York: Hippocampus Press, 2013a, pp. 63–65.
———. Letter to August Derleth. 16 May 1931. *The Letters of H. P. Lovecraft to August Derleth: 1926–1931*, edited by David E. Schultz and S. T. Joshi. New York: Hippocampus Press, 2013b, pp. 335–339.
Miéville, China. Introduction. *At the Mountains of Madness* by H. P. Lovecraft, Modern Library, 2005, pp. xi–xxv.

Neville, Lucy. *Girls Who Like Boys Who Like Boys: Women and Gay Male Pornography and Erotica*. New York: Palgrave, 2018.

Poole, W. Scott. *In the Mountains of Madness: The Life and Extraordinary Afterlife of H. P. Lovecraft*. Berkeley, CA: Soft Skull Press, 2016.

Price, Robert M. "Homosexual Panic in 'The Outsider.'" *Crypt of Cthulhu* 8, 1982, pp. 11–13.

Sederholm, Carl H. "H. P. Lovecraft's Reluctant Sexuality: Abjection and the Monstrous Feminine in 'The Dunwich Horror.'" *The Age of Lovecraft*, eds. Carl H. Sederholm and Jeffrey Andrew Weinstock. Minneapolis, MN: University of Minnesota Press, 2016, pp. 133–148.

Thornton, Marshall. "M/M Romance vs. Gay Fiction." *Marshall Thornton's Blog at Goodreads* 13 September 2011, https://www.goodreads.com/author_blog_posts/1549344-m-m-romance-vs-gay-fiction. Accessed January 5 2021.

Weimer, Christopher B. "Romancing Weird Fiction: Lovecraftian Reinscriptions in Jordan L. Hawk's *Whyborne and Griffin*." *Aeternum: The Journal of Contemporary Gothic Studies* 8(1) June 2021, 61–76.

20 Lovecraft, Hauntology, and the Rhetoric of Unthinkability

Michael Cerliano

We are living in what might be called a Lovecraftian moment. Walk into any hobby or comics store, and you will find yourself confronted with any number of comic books, graphic novels, games, toys, novelties, and other tchotchkes bearing the name or face of Cthulhu or his creator. The same rule holds true for the online world, where countless websites and discussion groups allow acolytes to hold forth on any aspect of the mythos. Lovecraft is also often invoked in discussions of the crises facing humanity, either through humorous references or through the use of his ideas as a way of reckoning with imminent—and immanent—disaster. This cultural omnipresence reveals a larger anxiety about the current state of the planet. To put things simply: it appears to many of us that the world is ending. We know it. We talk about it, both in our private lives and in public spaces, including in the numerous Lovecraftian fan communities. A cursory glance at current events appears to confirm it: the COVID-19 pandemic, uncontrolled climate change, nuclear proliferation, and a fresh natural disaster seemingly every week. It seems that when one half of the planet is drowning, the other half is on fire.

Recent decades have seen the rise in scholarly and popular discourses of a mode of talking about these approaching disasters: the hauntological. Though the term "hauntology" was originally devised by Jacques Derrida in *Spectres of Marx*, Mark Fisher developed it further in works such as *Ghosts of My Life* and in his *K-Punk* blog in ways that caused it to spread throughout a variety of fields in the humanities and arts. Fisher's work, much like that of other theorists who emerged from Warwick University's Cybernetic Culture Research Unit in the 1990s, explicitly engages to one extent or another with Lovecraft's writing, and his work opens new possibilities for understanding Lovecraft's contemporary resonance while also reflecting a deep reading of Lovecraftian texts. Just as hauntology has emerged into the cutting edge of contemporary theory, another, seemingly unconnected trend has also appeared: a rebirth of nihilism and pessimism as critical projects in the academy, whose most prominent theorist is Eugene Thacker. Thacker's work, even more than Fisher's, builds on Lovecraftian concepts and tropes to develop a new model of thinking about humanity, its place in the cosmos, and its

DOI: 10.4324/9780367713065-21

relationship thereto. Indeed, Thacker's most acclaimed work—his trilogy comprised of the volumes *In the Dust of This Planet*, *Starry Speculative Corpse*, and *Tentacles Longer Than Night*—is itself a conscious engagement with the tradition of philosophical pessimism from the perspective of horror, in which the philosopher reads horror as philosophy and philosophy as horror, drawing links both thematic and structural between continental philosophy and the tradition of weird literature.

If we are living in a Lovecraftian moment, we are also living in a hauntological moment and a neo-pessimistic moment and, as I will argue in this chapter, the two are entwined. In fact, in contemporary hauntology as developed by Fisher, we find specters of Lovecraft, who serves as a kind of prophet of disaster; in contemporary nihilism, we locate a decentering of the human and a repositioning of ourselves in the universe, and in contemporary Lovecraftianism, we find his name and writings invoked to provide a framework for speaking about the looming nightmares of our era.

It is because of this hauntological aspect of Lovecraft—and cosmic horror more generally—that his presence in our culture can be explained. Lovecraft, throughout his work, allows us to consider the possibility of a haunted humanity, and a haunted planet, through his use of the spectral presences of his various monsters, eldritch gods, and interdimensional entities. Though they appear to be intruders from the outside, Thacker's concepts allow us to see that they are an integral part of the human-centered world while at the same time acting to destabilize it—and even to destroy it. Although a reading of Lovecraft's complete works is beyond the scope of this chapter, we can find the introduction and development of these themes through a look at two of his most popular texts, "The Call of Cthulhu" (1926), and *At the Mountains of Madness* (1931). These texts reveal the extent to which his writings embody this kind of negative hauntology, serving as a model for such a philosophical or critical approach and suggesting why they may particularly resonate in our current moment: because Lovecraft's tales both mark the limits of our ability to comprehend the possibility of civilizational collapse and human annihilation while, at the same time, they give us the rhetorical matrix to do so. To understand all of this, we must first turn to the theorists who are most helpful in understanding this aspect of Lovecraft's work; after that, we will look at how these concepts are used by Lovecraft and consider what they ultimately mean for readers in our current historical moment, an aspect of both Lovecraft's writings and of these contemporary thinkers that has been overlooked in Lovecraftian scholarship.

Speaking of Horror: Fisher, Thacker, and the Possibility of a Negative Hauntology

Hauntology makes its first appearance as a term and a concept in Derrida's 1993 work *Specters of Marx*, in which Derrida reckons with the legacy of

Marxism in the then-emerging post-communist, neoliberal world. Central to Derrida's reading of Marx is the notion of "spectrality," itself a playful adaptation of Marx's concept of the "specter of communism." Spectrality, for Derrida, refers to the instability within a text or system which creates a space for a "haunting" to take place. According to Derrida, "If there is something like spectrality, there are reasons to doubt this reassuring order of presents and, especially, the border between the actual or present reality of the present, and everything that can be opposed to it: absence, non-presence, non-effectivity, inactuality, virtuality, or even the simulacrum in general, and so forth" (48). Ontology, which concerns itself with being and existence, seeks to stabilize a system and render it apparently closed; what is needed is a philosophy of traces, remnants, and apparitions, which Derrida terms a "hauntology," writing of it that

> to haunt does not mean to be present, and it is necessary to introduce haunting into the very construction of a concept. Of every concept, beginning with the concepts of being and time. That is what we would be calling here a hauntology.
>
> (202)

A haunting could be many things. This could be the unfulfilled promise of socialism, as in Derrida's text, or it could be the dream of a lost future, or an otherwise unspoken fear. These concepts are explored in the reading of hauntology presented by Mark Fisher. In his essay collection, *Ghosts of My Life: Writings on Depression, Hauntology, and Lost Futures*, Fisher takes up the idea of hauntology as a theoretical mode for exploring a particular affect in post-1970s culture, particularly as found in popular music. Fisher's earlier book, *Capitalist Realism*, describes how capitalism, particularly in its post-Cold War form, forecloses the very idea of a political and cultural alternative. In *Ghosts of My Life*, Fisher turns to those cultural threads that offer a promise of what might be. After describing his own relationship with Derrida's work, Fisher asserts that hauntology is best thought of as "the agency of the virtual," in which unseen ideas act on (and are acted out by) the participants within any system. Fisher notes that his reading is greatly influenced by that of Martin Hagglund, who sees in hauntology a grappling with the very notion of the specter itself.

Fisher, building on Hagglund's reading of Derrida, identifies two directions in hauntology: in the first, hauntology is a way of speaking of, commenting on, and conjuring with "that which is (in actuality) no longer, but which remains effective as a virtuality" while in the second, hauntology "refers to that which (in actuality) has not yet happened, but which is already effective in the virtual (an attractor, an anticipation shaping current behavior)" (19). While Fisher does engage with some of the darker implications of hauntology as a theme and a critical mode—for instance, in the article, "What is Hauntology?" where he asserts that haunting "happens when a place is stained by time, or when a particular place becomes the site for an encounter with a broken time" —much of Fisher's writing about hauntology is in a more affirmative mode, in which hauntology reveals the failed dreams and latent promises (or at least, hopes) of a better, post-capitalist world within the realms of music, literature, architecture, and other projects. But Fisher overlooks the potential of his hauntology for a negative reading: what if, instead of a dream, our culture carries within it a nightmare?

However, some suggestion of this is present in his reading of Lovecraft. In *The Weird and the Eerie*, Fisher identifies the weird as "a particular kind of perturbation" in which the weird entity produces "a sensation of wrongness" and is something that, to the observer, "should not exist, or at least it should not exist here" (15). Lovecraft's stories, according to Fisher, "are obsessively fixated on the question of the outside: an outside that breaks through in encounters with anomalous entities from the deep past, in altered states of consciousness, in bizarre twists in the structure of time" (16). Lovecraft's weird tales feature an "interplay" between our observed, human world, and the world of his cosmic entities (19). Fisher's reading of the weird is in opposition to his concept of "the eerie." For Fisher, eeriness lies in a horror derived from an unexpected absence or presence in a space, rather than the intrusion of something horrific into a space. If an observer witnesses or detects the movement of something horrific into his or her presence, the horror can be conceived as "weird"; however, if the observer arrives in a place only to find something unexpected—or, conversely, to not find something that was expected—the horror, in Fisher's text, is characterized as "eerie." In other words, Fisher's differentiation of these two modes relies on whether the act of arrival or departure is present within the story itself. A weird being shows up; an eerie being is already there, waiting for us. While Fisher's reading of Lovecraft is insightful, as is his general approach to the concepts of the weird and the eerie, it appears to circle around the fact that Lovecraft's work operates within both of these modes and, moreover, that this unity could be read in terms of a negative hauntology.

This idea of a negative hauntology makes sense when Fisher's insights are read alongside those of Thacker. In his book *In the Dust of This Planet*, the first in his trilogy confronting what he calls, in the subtitle, the "horror of philosophy," Thacker enumerates three ideas about the world that relate to cosmicism and weird literature. First, there is the "world-for-us," which is the world of human beings, human civilization, and all the activities that constitute human relations, and also the world as we experience it through our own, human eyes when we engage with it. Everything we do, see, or think about, according to Thacker, falls into this category. The second concept is the "world-in-itself," which is everything outside the world-for-us: it is the world of animals, of nature, of that which neither exists for us nor concerns itself much with us unless our paths cross. According to Thacker, we are unable to actually experience the world-in-itself because every time we engage with it, it enters into the world-for-us.

Our philosophy is fundamentally anthropocentric, and our experience of the world is, as well. We cannot—indeed, can never—actually experience the world-in-itself. For Thacker, this problem is mitigated by a third concept: the "world-without-us," which "allows us to think the world-in-itself, without getting caught up in a vicious circle of logical paradox" (5). Each of these three categories is associated with a particular conception of the world, too: the world-for-us is the "World," the world-in-itself is "Earth," and the world-without-us is "Planet." Thacker uses these terms as shorthand for each of his concepts and also as a way of capturing something of their essence: "World" calls to minds Heidegger's "worlding," the creation of a context to give human actions meaning; "Earth" suggests a sphere unto itself that does not require human activity to exist; and "Planet" emphasizes the apocalypticism of cosmic horror, which so often depicts a dying or devastated planet devoid—or very nearly so—of all life, yet still participating in the movements of the spheres, still maintaining a never ending place in the cosmos. If Planet and the world-without-us seem frightening, it is because, for Thacker, these ideas have not typically been explored in western philosophy, but rather in supernatural horror, which he argues can "be understood as being about the limits of the human as it confronts a world that is not just a World, and not just the Earth, but also a Planet" (8). Horror picks up at the limits of philosophy and is "about the paradoxical thought of the unthinkable," a "non-philosophical attempt to think about the world-without-us philosophically" (9). Thacker's approach is continued across the rest of his trilogy: in the second volume, *Starry Speculative Corpse*, Thacker reorients himself from reading horror as philosophy to reading philosophy as horror; and the third and final volume, *Tentacles Longer Than Night*, is composed of a series of loosely connected meditations on the themes Thacker develops in the previous two volumes. In this text, Thacker returns again and again to Lovecraft as a central figure, particularly in regard to "the limit of thought" (120), which for Thacker (and Lovecraft) is best represented by horror—particularly cosmic horror—as the revelation of the limits of the human capacity for categorizing the universe and speaking about it. Cosmic horror in particular is well suited for this, because it is "against both anthropomorphism and anthropocentrism" (124).

With these concepts in mind, we now turn to a close reading of two tales central to both the Lovecraftian mythos itself and to the negative hauntological reading provided for us via the work of Fisher and Thacker. Though this reading could apply to much of Lovecraft's mature fiction, I have selected these two stories due to their importance for Lovecraft's development as a writer and for their cultural influence and preeminence. Both "The Call of Cthulhu" and *At the Mountains of Madness* are well-known, even beyond dedicated fans of Lovecraft, and their plots, imagery, and themes are prime examples of the spectral quality of Lovecraft's creations.

Horror Within and Without: Lovecraft's Spectral Monsters

"The Call of Cthulhu" is perhaps Lovecraft's most famous story, and its central entity, the titular Cthulhu, is arguably his most influential creation. Additionally, "The Call of Cthulhu" serves as a representative work for exploring the concept of negative hauntology, the reason for which is the presence of the nightmare of Cthulhu—his presence is as an idea or generalized fear of the overtaking of "civilization" by primal forces, which Lovecraft presents in terms very similar to Fisher's concept of the eerie. Indeed, the central drama of the text is not so much the awakening of Cthulhu, but rather the revelation of the hidden knowledge of the deity's presence on—and within—Earth. Throughout the story, Lovecraft plays with the ideas of occultation and revelation, presence and absence, the horror of which is rooted in a gradual realization that the entity is already here, within the earth and within human history. The theme is introduced in the opening sections, in which the narrator, Francis Wayland Thurston, begins the tale with what has become one of Lovecraft's most celebrated passages:

> The most merciful thing in the world, I think, is the inability of the human mind to correlate all its contents. We live on a placid island of ignorance in the midst of black seas of infinity, and it was not meant that we should voyage far. The sciences, each straining in its own direction, have hitherto harmed us little; but some day the piecing together of dissociated knowledge will open up such terrifying vistas of reality, and of our frightful position therein, that we shall either go mad from the revelation or flee from the deadly light into the peace and safety of a new dark age.
>
> (21–22)

While this might seem like an overwrought reworking of the old adage, "ignorance is bliss," this paragraph is vitally important to both this story and to Lovecraft's work in his later, "cosmic" period. While Thurston, narrator and protagonist of the story, speaks of scientific investigation as a form of "piecing together dissociated knowledge," and therefore as a potential source of horror, it feels unrelated to his initial assertion: that the horror explored in the story is ultimately already present within the human mind itself, and only in its "correlation" are we able to tap into it, to feel it, and to be transformed by it, presumably for the worse. The word, "correlate," is interesting, as a few paragraphs later, Thurston speaks of his "correlation" of the papers of his late great-uncle, George Gammell Angell (23). Later, he further describes "correlating the theosophical and anthropological notes" collected by his uncle during the latter's association with Henry Anthony Wilcox, the young sculptor whose dreams and premonitions of Cthulhu initiate Angell's investigations and set the story in motion (41). These later uses of the term reveal the full meaning of this opening paragraph: the horror of Cthulhu is not so much "discovered" as it is remembered through correlation. As Thurston elaborates, following his opening statement,

> Theosophists have guessed at the awesome grandeur or the cosmic cycle wherein our world and human race form transient incidents ... but it is not from them that there came the single glimpse of forbidden aeons which chills me when I think of it and maddens me when I dream of it. (22)

Thurston asserts that it is not through human systems of knowledge (be they occult or otherwise) that we glean these truths, but rather through our engagement with something beyond them, something that they can only serve to elaborate on or put into words or concepts that may be expressible by humans of an overwhelming, but unseen, presence. Cthulhu's slumber beneath the sea cannot be thought of as an intrusion, but rather as an example of the deity's spectrality. Cthulhu's literal, physical presence within the earth—and, as we see later in the story, his presence in the belief systems of numerous religious traditions, from indigenous faiths to folk witchcraft to hermetic and theosophical movements—creates the conditions for the unease, malaise, and existential fear that run through the tale.

These fears are manifested in a variety of ways throughout the text. One of the most significant forms this awakening knowledge takes is in the prophetic dreams of Wilcox, a "psychically hypersensitive" artist who carves a bas-relief inscribed with hieroglyphs spelling out "Cthulhu fhtagn," which he has transcribed from his uneasy dreams (25–26). Dreams, of course, according to Wilcox, "are older than brooding Tyre, or the contemplative Sphinx, or the garden-girdled Babylon (25). This is not merely poetry on Wilcox's part: as we see in the tale, dreams, much like Cthulhu itself, are portrayed as something primal and deep, dwelling within human consciousness much as the great sleeper itself, as seen in the spontaneous outbreaks of ecstatic worship by the long-repressed Cthulhu cult in various locations throughout the world (40). Cthulhu himself, "not dead but dreaming," is a literal embodiment of the unconscious fear of destruction. In other words, the entity is a materialization of the literally unthinkable, and the process of his awakening is manifest in a series of rituals that express the drive-toward-the-unthinkable that is the culmination of this dream. This is in many ways consistent with Lovecraft's literary corpus: throughout Lovecraft's writings, dreams are a source of hidden knowledge, access to arcane worlds, and other apparently occult endeavors. A notable early example can be found in his story, "Hypnos," written in 1922 and published in 1923, in which another sculptor (this time, unnamed) and his newly acquired only friend explore a dreamworld under the influence of narcotics, only to experience disturbing, indescribable nightmares that culminate in the apparent death of his friend who, the narrator ultimately learns, did not exist, and may have been an incarnation or manifestation of the god Hypnos or another cosmic entity. As with "The Call of Cthulhu" and other works, the dreams of the narrator remain ambiguous, embodying in their indescribability the concept of the unthinkable. This concept, in turn, finds a literal representation in his associate, whose disappearance and replacement with a statue bearing the name, Hypnos, prefigures the spectrality and further indescribability of unthinkable creatures like Cthulhu.

The unthinkable, of course, takes a variety of forms, depending on who it is that is gripped by fear or dread. Thurston and the protagonists of the stories he pieces together reflect Lovecraft's own fears of degeneration and social collapse, particularly regarding what they conceive of as "civilization." The places and peoples who first feel the stirrings of Cthulhu, and who are excited into ecstasy—or derangement—are certainly those on the margins of society: colonized and post-colonial peoples (Haitians, Latin Americans, Indians, Filipinos, Africans, and the Irish), immigrants (the "hysterical Levantines" in New York), and those involved with avant-garde art (in Paris) and alternative spiritualities (in California). Lovecraft makes much of this, as Thurston describes the "voodoo orgy" that alerts police in Louisiana to the presence of the Cthulhu cult in the area (35). Despite Lovecraft's display of his own racial hangups in this and other texts, "The Call of Cthulhu" does leave open the possibility of something more profound and troubling than the author's racism. In the subsequent interview with one of the worshippers, he explains the mythology of their religion, stating that the Great Old Ones, such as Cthulhu "lived ages before there were any men" and that "their dead bodies had told their secrets in dreams to the first men" (37–38). Cthulhu, then, is not described as a human invention, nor can Cthulhu be thought of as an intrusion into human life civilization; instead, Cthulhu and the Great Old Ones have always been a part of human existence, and civilization has grown up through the millennia with this entity and the faith devoted to it. This idea differentiates the story from the tradition of invasion literature by locating the source of—and knowledge and fear of—civilizational destruction within civilization itself, rather than in an intrusion from the outside. We fear our doom because we carry it with us. The specter of annihilation is always present.

If "The Call of Cthulhu" introduces this idea into the Lovecraftian mythos, *At the Mountains of Madness*, continues and develops this idea, presenting readers with Lovecraft's most notable meditation on both the immanence of annihilation and the effect of this knowledge on humanity itself. While the story may appear to readers to be a simple lost civilization tale, *At the Mountains of Madness* expands the theme of the unthinkable dream. Besides, it encompasses not only a fear of the destruction of the current world order but also the fear brought about by a total decentering of humanity itself, on what humanity believes to be its own planet.

In the story, the geologist William Dyer relates the events of a disastrous expedition to Antarctica that discovers the ruins of a lost city built by an early civilization of "Elder Things," or Old Ones, who Dyer and his colleagues learn found themselves in conflict with other species that made their way to Earth, including the spawn of Cthulhu. Over time, the Old Ones bred the shoggoths, creatures who possess such abilities as shape-shifting and being able to perform any task needed. Toward the end, the Old Ones reawaken from their place of refuge and attack the party, leaving only Dyer and his assistant to return.

Obviously, the tale contains the cosmic indifference that is a hallmark of Lovecraft's writing, but there are a number of elements that tie it to the concept of negative hauntology of "The Call of Cthulhu." One such element is the use throughout the text of dream imagery in the descriptions of the story's setting. Though the tale lacks the prophetic dreams of the earlier text, one cannot help but notice the numerous invocations and suggestions of the concept. The Antarctic landscape is compared to a "land of Dunsanian dreams" (23); the ruins are described as "dream-like" (50); and, most intriguingly of all, Dyer's description of his and Danforth's memories of their escape as "dream-fragments involving no memory of volition, details, or physical exertion" (151). By invoking Lord Dunsany, Lovecraft calls to mind the Anglo-Irish writer's own pantheon of otherworldly and occasionally malevolent gods, and the wider use of dream imagery not only emphasizes the strangeness of the events and places in the text, but their spectrality as well. Like the literal dreams in "The Call of Cthulhu," the dream-imagery of *At the Mountains of Madness* prepares Lovecraft's readers for his exploration of the notion of spectrality itself as embodied in the monsters of this story. In doing so, he sets up an interesting parallel with the earlier work, in which premonitions of disaster are followed by an awakening to the disaster as, in a way, already unfolding throughout human history.

This theme is perhaps the most readily apparent in the descriptions of the ancient city itself and of the relationship of the Old Ones to Earthly biology. Much is said about how utterly alien the ruins are: the "Cyclopean" city is described as possessing "no architecture known to man or to human imagination," composed of "febrile structures" of various conic, cubical, and cylindrical shapes (52), and, later, as a "mountainside tangle of regular cubes, ramparts, and cave-mouths" that "seem identical in substance with the surrounding rock surface" (67). Of course, the Old Ones and shoggoths would make use of the materials they had at hand to construct the settlement; but when read in concert with "The Call of Cthulhu," which makes much of Cthulhu's innate connection to Earth itself (particularly as it is experienced by human life), perhaps we are invited to consider the possibility that these creatures are an essential part of this planet and of life on it. Like Cthulhu and other creations by Lovecraft, the Old Ones and shoggoths are a spectral presence, both of and not of the earth, whose interplay of presence and absence serve to raise questions about humanity's place of primacy on the Earth and its relationship with the wider cosmos. This is especially evident when one considers the intimate role the Old Ones played in the development of life on Earth: Dyer relates at one point the idea that the Old Ones, after engineering the shoggoths, "allowed other cell groups to develop into other forms of animal and vegetable life" (95–96), one form of which appears to be "a shambling primitive mammal … whose vaguely simian and human foreshadowings were unmistakable" (100). As with the presence of Cthulhu, the Old Ones are an essential aspect of humanity's existence and our experience of life. The shoggoths they create are the embodiment of our fears of displacement and finitude, written into our very DNA.

Speaking of Monsters: The Nature of Our Lovecraftian Moment

And so we find ourselves where we started, speaking of Lovecraft while considering what might be our deepest and most intimate fear. Though this chapter began with a glance at the current state of Lovecraft within our wider culture, one finds echoes in other, perhaps unexpected places. Lovecraft, the most materialist of the weird fiction writers of his generation, is paradoxically one of the best-served by a hauntological reading that engages with the inherent spectrality of his monsters, a reading that takes into account not only the post-1990s developments in hauntology but also the cosmic pessimism provided by Fisher and Thacker. Lovecraft's work lends itself to this negative hauntological reading in which the fear of destruction—of civilization, humanity, and life itself—manifests in a number of distinct ways: premonitions of disaster encountered in dreams and expressed through art, ritual, and speculation on humanity's place in the universe; disturbance, and indeed outright madness, brought about by the revelation of dark knowledge; and finally, an attempt to share these feelings and this knowledge with a hopefully sympathetic audience. Perhaps it is this quality that best explains Lovecraft's continued presence in our culture, and his prominence at this particular historical moment. We are haunted by Lovecraft's creations, and we find in them the imagery and the vocabulary we need to articulate our awareness of our own displacement within the very philosophical and linguistic world which we have built for ourselves. Our world, it seems, is filled with hidden monsters and terrifying secrets, the most menacing of which is our repressed, occulted, or uncorrelated knowledge of the possibility of our annihilation. To speak of monsters is to speak of death.

Works Cited

Derrida, Jacques. *Specters of Marx: The State of the Debt, the Work of Mourning, and the New International*. Trans. Peggy Kamuf. London: Routledge, 1994.

Fisher, Mark. *Ghosts of My Life: Writings on Depression, Hauntology, and Lost Futures*. Winchester, UK: Zero Books, 2014.

———. *The Weird and the Eerie*. London: Repeater, 2017.
———. "What is Hauntology?" *Film Quarterly*, vol. 66, no. 1, 2012, pp. 16–24.
Lovecraft, H. P. *At the Mountains of Madness. H. P. Lovecraft Collected Fiction, A Variorum Edition, Volume 3, 1931–1936*, edited by S.T. Joshi. New York: Hippocampus Press, 2017, pp. 11–157.
———. "The Call of Cthulhu." *H. P. Lovecraft Collected Fiction, A Variorum Edition, Volume 2, 1926–1930*, edited by S. T. Joshi. New York: Hippocampus Press, 2017, pp. 21–55.
———. "Hypnos." *H. P. Lovecraft Collected Fiction, A Variorum Edition, Volume 1, 1905–1925*, edited by S. T. Joshi. New York: Hippocampus Press, 2017, pp. 325–333.
Thacker, Eugene. *In the Dust of This Planet*. Winchester, UK: Zero Books, 2011.
———. *Starry Speculative Corpse*. Winchester, UK: Zero Books, 2015.
———. *Tentacles Longer Than Night*. Winchester, UK: Zero Books, 2015.

21 Falling into the Void

"Nyarlathotep"

Carl H. Sederholm

In his book, *In The Dust of This Planet*, Eugene Thacker argues that life in the twenty-first century is "increasingly unthinkable" (1).[1] To illustrate, Thacker focuses on the kinds of disasters one increasingly expects to see addressed on the evening news: floods, fires, pandemics, hurricanes, and earthquakes, not to mention the wide variety of equally destructive forces waiting in the wings to reveal themselves to an already frightened audience. All these things, Thacker suggests, stretch the limits of human thought, not because they are individually hard to understand, but because, collectively, they raise eschatological questions concerning the possible end of human life, the earth, and perhaps even the universe. Although there is nothing particularly new about eschatological questions, they seem to have taken on greater urgency in this new millennium as things like environmental threats, global pandemics, natural disasters, and civil unrest all appear to be increasing. Death, disease, and destruction do not rest, and they never wait for convenient times to strike.

No less gloomy is Timothy Morton's urgent sense of how much damage the earth has already sustained since at least the late eighteenth century. In one of his most striking claims, Morton suggests that "the end of the world has already occurred" and that it can be dated back to "April 1784, when James Watt patented the steam engine, an act that commenced the depositing of carbon in the Earth's crust" (*Hyperobjects* 7). From that time forward, human beings have operated as "a geophysical force on a planetary scale," the kind that is difficult to measure, let alone understand (7). To put it simply, some actions have overwhelming consequences. Like Thacker, Morton believes that human beings are quickly approaching an unthinkable set of conditions. To underscore the point, Morton introduces the concept of "hyperobjects," or objects that "exist on almost unthinkable timescales" (*Ecological Thought* 19). Hyperobjects come in all shapes and sizes and range from naturally existing things (e.g. black holes) to things created by human hands (e.g. plastics, Styrofoam, fast food containers). For Morton, the concern over hyperobjects grows when seemingly harmless individual objects take on a distinctly frightening aspect in the aggregate. Plastics, for example, are rapidly changing

DOI: 10.4324/9780367713065-22

the face of the earth by cluttering the landscape, clogging the seas, and polluting the air. As Morton writes, "Alongside global warming, 'hyperobjects' will be our lasting legacy" (130).[2] Ironically, that legacy will ultimately outlast all talk of innovation, financial success, or independence. Like barnacles encrusting themselves to other things, hyperobjects are capable of infinite patience and slow destruction. But hyperobjects do not cling to surfaces; instead, they change how we attempt to process an overwhelming world. According to Morton, "Hyperobjects don't just burn a hole in the world; they burn a hole in your mind" (130).

But Thacker and Morton are not solely thinking about contemporary human predicaments, as bad as those are; they are also anticipating what can happen when the impact of current predicaments shifts to a future without human beings. According to Thacker, this means addressing both "the limits of the human," and the real implications of a "world-without-us," or a world that is ultimately indifferent to human flourishing (*In the Dust* 8).

This kind of thinking has broad appeal for approaching H.P. Lovecraft because Lovecraft is also interested in the kinds of overwhelming experiences that challenge human perception, press beyond human limits, and leave human concerns far in the background. Such questions lie at the heart of the weird experience. As described by Mark Fisher,

> [T]he weird is a particular kind of perturbation. It involves a sensation of *wrongness*: a weird entity or object is so strange that it makes us feel that it should not exist, or at least it should not exist here. Yet if the entity or object *is* here, then the categories which we have up until now used to make sense of the world cannot be valid. The weird thing is not wrong, after all: it is our conceptions that must be inadequate.
>
> (15)

Like Fisher, other scholars are increasingly exploring the ways Lovecraft's sense of the weird helps confront challenging questions relative to the nature of reality, life, thought, language, and perception, making his work that much more relevant in a world that is increasingly unthinkable.[3]

Even a cursory glance at some of Lovecraft's stories demonstrate how often his narrators suffer extreme anxiety when they learn that their expected perceptions of the world can fail, and that human life is not necessarily at the center of everything. In "The Shadow Over Innsmouth," for example, Robert Olmstead discovers that antiquarian research does not lead to a blithe sense of family pride, but to the uncovering of seemingly impossible points of origin. Similarly, in "Pickman's Model," the narrator discovers the strange secret behind his friend's extraordinary talent for realism. To warn against obtaining such earth-shattering knowledge, Lovecraft sometimes extolls the small mercy of human limitations.

His most famous passage about this comes from the opening lines to "The Call of Cthulhu" in which he states:

> The most merciful thing in the world, I think, is the inability of the human mind to correlate all its contents. We live on a placid island of ignorance in the midst of black seas of infinity, and it was not meant that we should voyage far. The sciences, each straining in its own direction, have hitherto harmed us little; but some day the piecing together of dissociated knowledge will open up such terrifying vistas of reality, and of our frightful position therein, that we shall either go mad from the revelation or flee from the deadly light into the peace and safety of a new dark age.
>
> (21–22)

Because our bodies and brains are limited and finite, we cannot process all that we experience as clearly as we hope. This is especially true when confronted with traumatic or frightening or life-threatening experiences. There are simply no obvious means of experiencing all the ways we might be broken, wounded, maimed, killed, or destroyed. Rather than witness it all firsthand, we might simply black out, shift into denial, or claim that everything was simply meant to be that way. The implications of these reactions are fascinating; not only do they help illustrate the limits of human perception, but they also point to the ways some circumstances can occur without being fully experienced or understood.

A Lovecraftian Eschatology

Much of Lovecraft's fiction nevertheless resonates with the overall idea of exploring cognitive limits. His purpose, however, was not simply to overwhelm the mind but to raise even broader, more eschatological, questions about the overall purpose of life, nature, and the universe. These are necessarily broad questions that raise multiple perspectives from a variety of religions, traditions, cultures, and beliefs. For example, in the Classical Christian sense, eschatology refers to the end of worldly desires and interests and the establishing of the Kingdom of God on the earth. In other faith traditions, it also brings to mind a longed-for paradise, a state of renewal, change, or long-lasting human flourishing. On a more individual level, eschatology has to do with the end or *telos* of a human life, or what Frank Kermode described as "a need in the moment of existence to belong, to be related to a beginning and an end" (4). This need is more than just finding one's general sense of purpose; it also has to do with exploring where we are and why we think we are here.[4]

It is not difficult to find evidence of such thinking in Lovecraft. As Benjamin E. Zeller points out, Lovecraft frequently introduced elements of millennialism (a classic example of eschatological thinking) into some of his best-known tales such as "The Call of Cthulhu," "The Dunwich Horror," and "The Shadow Over Innsmouth." Given Lovecraft's explicit atheism, his interest in millennial ideas or images might seem surprising at first. But as Zeller explains, Lovecraft's millennialism does not necessarily constitute a specifically religious position. As Jewett and Shelton also argue, many eschatologically themed texts in popular culture "embody secularized versions of biblical paradigms." This is certainly true of Lovecraft, especially since he was so interested in demonstrating just how little human beings really understand about their own experience.

Not surprisingly, Lovecraft also brought a distinctively weird perspective to his millennial ideas, one that appears more like nihilism than hope. To capture this darker, more pessimistic, mood Zeller suggests calling Lovecraft's approach "anti-millennialism" because it routinely presents the world as subject to imminent destruction and transformation without offering any chance of everlasting peace, hope, or salvation. In Zeller's words, "For Lovecraft, there is no hope in a collective salvation, but rather expectation that the imminent future would bring a transition to something far worse. From Lovecraft's perspective, and especially in light of his political views during the interwar period, the world faced a future of disunity, social collapse, war, decline, and even destruction." Zeller's point cannot be stressed enough. Lovecraft imagined the prospect of a looming collapse, one that would bring destruction without any lingering sense of hope. And yet, Lovecraft's interest in collapse was more than just an expression of gleeful nihilism. Rather, he was interested in taking readers to the limits of thought and experience so he could imagine the cosmic implications of human limits and speculate about how those limits might change our overall sense of things. Put another way, Lovecraft's fiction imagined collapse not only in terms of shifting ideological or political winds but also as a means of increasing that all-important sense of cosmic fear or dread that was central to his work. As he famously argued in *Supernatural Horror in Fiction*,

> The one test of the really weird is simply this—whether or not there be excited in the reader a profound sense of dread, and of contact with unknown spheres and powers; a subtle attitude of awed listening, as if for the beating of black wings or the scratching of outside shapes and entities on the known universe's utmost rim. And of course, the more completely and unifiedly a story conveys this atmosphere, the better it is as a work of art in the given medium.
>
> (84)

It is this combined sense of dread and the prospect of "contact with unknown spheres and powers" that lies at the heart of Lovecraft's overall project (84). His anti-millennialism, as Zeller suggests, is directly tied to this larger sense that there is something terrible lurking beyond what everyday life presents to our senses.

Approaching "Nyarlathotep"

"Nyarlathotep" (1920) describes a world in commotion and the ways it can slip into a rapid decline. Promising to show everyone sights beyond their wildest expectations, Nyarlathotep draws people to him with his frightful displays of power and his awful prophetic promises. Though the story never explains Nyarlathotep's motives, there is enough suspicion around him to suggest that he is a disruptive and frightening figure, someone far outside of normal human experience. When Lovecraft's narrator and main character dares to confront Nyarlathotep during one his presentations, he is cast out from and left to wander the streets with the rest of the population. As everyone wanders into stranger and stranger places, the narrator discovers that the world he knew is transforming into something he could never have predicted.

In his interpretation of "Nyarlathotep," S.T. Joshi describes its shift from civilization to ruin as "an allegory on the downfall of civilization—the first of many such ruminations in the length and breadth of Lovecraft's fiction and his philosophical thought" (240). Although my own reading will ultimately differ from Joshi's, there are nevertheless at least two reasons to consider the story this way: First, the story takes place at an undisclosed time of great social and cultural unease, a time so unstable and so contentious that it is already teeming on the brink of decay and downfall. Though Lovecraft never clarifies the exact context, there is enough internal information in the text to suggest an early twentieth century setting. As Lovecraft describes the cultural mood, there was a nagging and "brooding apprehension of hideous physical danger," not to mention a vague but growing "sense of monstrous guilt" ("Nyarlathotep" 202). Not surprisingly, all those who felt that way began to speculate about the future, but even such seemingly idle talk sparked feelings that "no one dared consciously repeat or acknowledge" what they heard lest they lead to real results (202). Following these dark human moods, the weather also began to behave in unpredictable patterns; instead of the expected cooling off for the autumn, an unusual heat "lingered fearsomely" in the area, leading to the general conclusion "that the world and perhaps the universe had passed from the control of known gods or forces to that of gods or forces which were unknown" (202).

Second, Lovecraft broadly hints that the general state of loss, decay, and decline immediately led to Nyarlathotep entering, unwelcomed, into "the lands of civilisation" with his demonstrations, displays, and prophecies about an even darker future (203). In this sense, Nyarlathotep clearly represents the monstrous Other, the kind that wanders in unbidden when communities or cultures are going through a significant transition, the kind that highlights deep cultural divides. According to Jeffrey Jerome Cohen, the monster must appear in such contexts because it "is difference made flesh, come to dwell among us" (7). Like other monsters before him,

Nyarlathotep also arouses feelings of attraction and repulsion. People were drawn to his exhibitions in part because they needed to know just what he was showing. But they attended even though they led to sleepless nights and anxious feelings about the future. As Lovecraft's narrator explains, "where Nyarlathotep went, rest vanished" ("Nyarlathotep" 203).

Although Lovecraft explores even more of Nyarlathotep's monstrous qualities in later tales, he initially describes him in terms that evoke a stereotypical exotic other or foreign threat, a figure that is not only "swarthy, slender, and sinister," but also "out of Egypt," and characterized by "old native blood" (203). Given that Nyarlathotep's "exhibitions of power" also feature images of "hooded forms amidst ruins, and yellow evil faces peering from behind fallen monuments," it has often been suggested that he is gesturing toward the larger "yellow peril," or the fears attributed to stereotyped images of Asians that were spread in the late nineteenth and early twentieth century (204).[5] Lovecraft expressed some of his own fears about Japanese and Chinese persons overtaking "Caucasian civilization" in a 1919 letter to some of his friends. In his words,

> Orientals must be kept in their native East till the fall of the white race. Sooner or later a great Japanese war will take place, during which I think the virtual destruction of Japan will have to be effected in the interests of European safety. The more numerous Chinese are a menace of the still more distant future. They will probably be the exterminators of Caucasian civilization, for their numbers are amazing.
>
> (qtd. in Klinger 34)

Given that this letter was written only a few months before Lovecraft wrote "Nyarlathotep," it is reasonable to believe he still held similar racist views and that he drew upon them to hint at significant points of decline of his projected ideals of what a civilized community should look like. Lovecraft also surely understood that exploiting those fears, even with a passing reference, would be enough to provoke similar fears in sympathetic readers. Considering Nyarlathotep's own outsider status, it would also make sense to read this story as an example of Lovecraft's larger thematic reflections on the loss of certain social or cultural ideals—ideals that frequently included ignorant and loathsome fears of other human beings.

Even though Lovecraft is certainly gesturing toward racist fears in "Nyarlathotep," I do not agree with Joshi's suggestion that the story is best understood as an allegory of the author's specific fears about broad societal or racial collapse. The story is much too elliptical and dreamlike to function as an obvious allegory. Moreover, "Nyarlathotep" is typically held to be a prose-poem, a genre that generally thrives on the enigmatic, and not necessarily on the transparently allegorical. As Mary Ann Caws explains, "In the prose poem a field of vision is represented, sometimes mimetically and often pictorially, only to be on occasion, cut off abruptly; emotion is contracted under the force of ellipsis, so deepened and made dense" (977–978). Although there is no single definition of a prose poem, "Nyarlathotep" certainly has some of the features Caws describes. As I will discuss in more detail below, the story presents one very specific field of vision only to turn from it abruptly as the story builds toward its climactic and strange finish. If "Nyarlathotep" were solely an allegorical reflection on the decline of civilization, it would presumably play up the inciting factors leading to that decline rather than dancing around them in such vague and uncertain ways. Even if there are strong hints about general social or racial decay, Lovecraft does little to develop them explicitly. Instead, Lovecraft bobs and weaves around his opponent, never taking the opportunity to throw a punch.

Rather than read "Nyarlathotep" as a broad allegory of the downfall of civilization, I suggest that we read it more narrowly as a reflection on the decline and fall of a particular kind of perception, perhaps even of a specific narrative point of view. That decline and fall, as I discuss in more detail below, is central to understanding "Nyarlathotep" because that is what connects it to the larger themes of a Lovecraftian eschatology. Put another way, any fictional recital of imminent social decay, no matter how interesting or expertly crafted, does not necessarily make something weird—and "Nyarlathotep" is definitely a weird tale. To ignore the qualities that make "Nyarlathotep" weird is to ignore what makes the story so interesting—and potentially so frightening.

A Narrator's End

One of the biggest challenges of reading "Nyarlathotep" is understanding what happens to the narrator's voice somewhere between the penultimate and the concluding paragraphs. This is particularly important because the narrative chiefly relies on the first-person perspective and experiences of an unnamed narrator who claims to be "colder and more scientific than the rest," someone who can presumably be counted on to tell his tale clearly and reasonably (204). And yet, there are at least two key moments when the narrator's voice seems to disappear from the narrative altogether, thereby allowing some other voice and perspective to potentially enter into the tale. This is not to say that the narrative voice simply becomes vague or unreliable or distant. Instead, I am arguing that the dominant narrative voice is lost in ways that suggest Lovecraft is formally introducing a cosmic perspective into his narrative in ways that confront the narrator's own perceptions.

The first instance of this shift comes in the short opening paragraph which features just a few loosely connected phrases joined together by ellipses. Although the paragraph does little to advance the story's plot, it nevertheless introduces some useful ideas relative to understanding at least some aspects of Nyarlathotep's character. The paragraph opens by stating Nyarlathotep's name and continues by introducing three loosely connected phrases— "the crawling chaos," "I am the last," and "I will tell the audient void" (202). Although Lovecraft never develops (or explains) any of these ideas as explicitly as he might have, his short paragraph nevertheless provides a small glimpse into the larger cosmic horrors that will soon shatter his narrator's sense of place, purpose, and logic. These phrases also suggest something of Nyarlathotep's role in the narrative. He is not only a destructive force, but he is also the voice that can fathom the depths, the voice that can tell out to the "audient void" and confidently expect a response (202).

The second instance of a meaningful shift in narrative voice occurs somewhere between the penultimate and the ultimate paragraph. As I discuss in the next section, a careful reading of the final paragraph may shed light on Lovecraft's decision to leave his narrator's voice behind, effectively suspending it in the nightmarish events he experienced in the moments leading up to the end of the penultimate paragraph. This is a rather surprising move to make, especially considering that the narrator appears to be writing while looking back on events from a position of relative peace and calm. As he states, "I do not recall distinctly when it began, but it was months ago" (202). As the narrator continues, he guides readers through the main events with a calm, confident, and rational tone, one that appears confident the world as he knows it can be grasped, understood, and explained. For example, while attending one of Nyarlathotep's mysterious exhibitions, the narrator explains that he frankly refused to be moved by what he saw, primarily on the grounds that he is "colder and more scientific than the rest" and therefore cannot see any reason to fall for Nyarlathotep's claims (204). He also explains that, unlike those around him, he was decidedly "*not* afraid" of Nyarlathotep and "never could be afraid" of anything Nyarlathotep said, predicted, or presented (204). After the narrator speaks out against Nyarlathotep's exhibitions, he finds himself cast out from Nyarlathotep's presence and is left to wander the streets alongside everyone else. Ironically, he quickly drops his bold and confident position as the world he once knew begins to change before his eyes. Now (presumably) describing himself as "quivering and afraid," the narrator walks toward what he calls "the sightless vortex of the unimaginable" (205). Whereas he once could appeal strictly to empirical thought, he can now only gesture to realities he can neither describe nor explain. As he disappears, so does his ability to perceive things rationally.

If that were all that happened to him, the narrator in "Nyarlathotep" would not require much attention. Many of Lovecraft's narrators rhetorically falter in the face of the inexplicable or the impossible. For Lovecraft, calling attention to the ways human perception weakens and falls, particularly when faced with a cosmic perspective, is of paramount importance. As Graham Harman describes this point, Lovecraft was so fascinated by the "fission" between observer and observed that he frequently uses fictional means to highlight it (258). He was especially interested in exploring moments in which his characters faced problems that were "unintelligible but real" (259). As Harman explains, to understand just how limited our commonplace perceptions really are, "we need to endure a breakdown of the usual situation in which perceptions and meanings simply lie before us as obvious facts" (258). It is precisely this kind of breakdown that Lovecraft articulates at this point in "Nyarlathotep"; it is also the primary reason why the narrator disappears in his own narrative. He is no longer the confident and rational being he once was. His thinking is becoming weird.

Between the Paragraphs

In *Supernatural Horror in Literature*, Lovecraft mentions that readers need "a certain degree of imagination and a capacity for detachment from everyday life" if they want to discover the power of the weird (83). In particular, people need to free themselves "from the spell of the daily routine to respond to rappings from outside" (83). Put another way, human beings are easily caught unawares, partly because of our easy familiarity with our surroundings and partly because of our willingness to accept what we experience as real. As Bert O. States argues, "[t]he world gets past us inconspicuously at face value. We are tranquilized by the parade of recurrent contexts" (1). To overcome this complacency, States continues, we need to pay greater attention to our experiences, including our dreams; such attention can help us understand more about our experiences, and our stories about them (1–2).

In "Nyarlathotep," the narrator's own experiences follow a similar pattern. He is initially complacent, confident in his perceptual position and unwilling to see the world outside of what he expects. His disappearance marks his taking a step—willingly or not is unclear—into a state outside of the everyday. When he disappears into "the sightless vortex of the unimaginable," he also begins to realize that his perceptual field now includes things far beyond his experience and his expectations (205). What makes his disappearance especially strange is that it appears to happen somewhere between the penultimate and the ultimate paragraphs, as if he fell into the margins. Stranger still, there is no return to the opening frame and there is no resolution to all the story's loose narrative strands. Instead, Lovecraft appears to follow the narrator into the impossible by expanding the context and pushing it into something more cosmic than quotidian. The result is a paragraph that does not know quite how to begin. It opens with a sentence that is as enigmatic as it is impersonal: "Screamingly sentient, dumbly delirious, only the gods that were can tell"

(205). In context, the sentence's first two clauses could refer to the narrator's physical and mental state after his disappearance, but there is no way to be sure. He would certainly be frightened and disoriented, but why would he not discuss himself in the first person, as if he were no longer the subject of the story? Lovecraft never addresses these questions. What does seem clear, however, is that the narrative voice, once so confident and rational, is now impersonal, distant, and lost. To underscore the point, Lovecraft turns from the narrative "I" that he has used in the story so far. This deliberate turn from the "I" is an odd thing for him to do; as Fisher argues, Lovecraft typically relied on the first person in his tales "to provide a sense of scale" between his human subjects and nonhuman entities (20). In Fisher's words,

> That is one reason why they are written in the first person: if the outside gradually encroaches upon a human subject, its alien contours can be appreciated; whereas to attempt to capture 'the boundless and hideous unknown' without any reference to the human world at all is to risk banality.
>
> (20)

But Lovecraft risked such banality in "Nyarlathotep" to highlight just how poorly equipped the narrator's powers of perception really were. In Lovecraft, human perception is nearly always insufficient and untrustworthy anyway.

Having dispensed with the first-person voice, Lovecraft can turn to a glimpse of the horrific cosmicism characteristic of his best work. In this case, he takes readers on a sweeping, but necessarily brief, visionary journey into a nightmarish and surrealistic space where everything is rotten, ruined, abject, and terrible. Even though Lovecraft refers to this space as the "graveyard of the universe," he is not likely referring to a physical destination so much as to an environment where all creative forces sputter and fail (205). To help readers see what he sees, Lovecraft imagines a scene in which everything is covered in death and decay. Readers take a panoramic journey "past ghastly midnights of rotting creation," where they see "corpses of dead worlds with sores that were cities" and feel the "charnel winds that brush the pallid stars and make them flicker low" (205). But it is not enough for Lovecraft to show readers a place in which planets fester and rot, human creations fail, and nothing is stable. He also wants readers to see beyond the general wreck and ruin into those surreal spaces where readers may peer just beyond the "half-seen columns of unsanctified temples" so they can hear the "muffled, maddening beating of drums, and [the] thin, monotonous whine of blasphemous flutes" (205). Looking further, readers may also see the strange, ungraceful dancing of the "gigantic, tenebrous ultimate gods" (205).

If Lovecraft were merely taking readers sightseeing, they might find these descriptions mildly interesting or just completely baffling. But instead of tying everything together, Lovecraft gathers his narrative threads and places them into Nyarlathotep's hands in ways that remain both inexplicable and uncanny (205). He then takes his panoramic view of things and stretches it to even stranger new limits. In his closing sentence, Lovecraft writes,

> And through this revolting graveyard of the universe, the muffled, maddening beating of drums, and thin, monotonous whine of blasphemous flutes from inconceivable, unlighted chambers beyond Time; the detestable pounding and piping whereunto dance slowly, awkwardly, and absurdly the gigantic tenebrous ultimate gods—the blind, voiceless mindless gargoyles whose soul is Nyarlathotep.
> (205)

What are we to understand by all this? In some ways, the scene is more surreal than meaningful, especially since it suggests such an expansive new context without offering any real explanation or purpose. Perhaps Lovecraft is simply attempting to frighten readers by bringing them to what Julia Kristeva has elsewhere described as "the ultimate edge of belief … [and] the threshold of nonmeaning" (135). Although the scene does suggest some threat of nullity or nonmeaning, Lovecraft is not simply dangling his readers over a fictional void. Instead, he is playing alongside the void just enough to suggest the possibility of meaning and purpose and intention outside of human perception. As Graham Harman explains, Lovecraft is drawn to the idea of the "unintelligible but real," or objects and experiences that are present but impossible to account for (235).

In the story that bears his name, Nyarlathotep could be described as the dominant metaphor of this new cosmic perspective. After all, he is the one that challenges all meanings, reverses all expectations, and reduces reason to fear. As one of his names suggests, he is also "the crawling chaos," the one who spreads nightmares, shows off terrible power, and challenges human confidence. He is also the being who "will tell the audient void," the one who can fathom its depths in ways few others can (202). When Nyarlathotep shouts into the void, he knows he will get a response. But most importantly, Nyarlathotep represents the beginning of not only something new, something real and purposeful, but also something outside of human understanding. If he were only a metaphor of human destruction of that moment when civilization slips its moorings and everything descends into chaos, the emphasis on experiencing the "unintelligible but real" would be lost (235). More than a racist stereotype or a simple traveling showman, Nyarlathotep is a sign of human limitations and a harbinger of weird experience. He is the one that holds everything together, not an empirically minded human convinced that his limited powers are infinite.

Notes

1 Although I am drawing primarily on Thacker's *In the Dust of this Planet* here, I am also indebted to Dylan Trigg's discussion of similar problems in *The Thing*. See also Timothy Morton's *The Ecological Thought* for additional commentary on how the changing world impacts our thinking (4).
2 For Morton's initial discussion of "Hyperobjects," see *The Ecological Thought*, pp. 130–135. Morton developed the idea further in *Hyperobjects*.
3 There are several examples of scholarship addressing these and other topics. I am primarily thinking of Graham Harman's *Weird Realism*, Benjamin E. Zeller's article, "The Altar Call of Cthulhu," and several of the essays in Carl H. Sederholm and Jeffrey Andrew Weinstock, eds, *The Age of Lovecraft*. It is also important to note that even though Timothy Morton's work is not about Lovecraft specifically, he is quick to point to Lovecraft as an example of thinking beyond the scale of the human.
4 Save for the passage by Kermode, I am chiefly drawing on Jerry Walls's "Introduction" to *The Oxford Handbook of Eschatology* in this paragraph.
5 The point has not been developed at length specifically regarding "Nyarlathotep," but Joshi calls attention to it in his notes on the story in *The Call of Cthulhu and Other Weird Stories*, p. 370. Leslie S. Klinger's *The New Annotated H. P. Lovecraft* also provides some helpful commentary and pointed me to the letter I cite in this paragraph. See note 9, pp. 33–34, in Klinger. For a general discussion, see William F. Wu, *The Yellow Peril: Chinese Americans in American Fiction, 1850-1940*.

Works Cited

Caws, Mary Ann. "Prose Poem," *The New Princeton Encyclopedia of Poetry and Poetics*, Alex Preminger and T. V. F. Brogan, eds. Princeton, New Jersey: Princeton University Press, 1993, pp. 977–978.

Cohen, Jeffrey Jerome. "Monster Culture (Seven Theses)," *Monster Theory: Reading Culture*, edited by Jeffrey Jerome Cohen. University of Minnesota Press, 1996, pp. 3–25.

Fisher, Mark. *The Weird and the Eerie*. London: Repeater, 2016.

Harman, Graham. *Weird Realism: Lovecraft and Philosophy*. Zero Books, 2012.

Jewett, Robert and John Shelton Lawrence. "Eschatology in Popular Culture," *The Oxford Handbook of Eschatology*. Oxford University Press, 2007. Web. http://doi.org/10.1093/oxfordhb/9780195170498.013.0039.

Joshi, S. T. *H. P. Lovecraft: A Life*. New York: Hippocampus Press, 1996.

Kermode, Frank. *The Sense of an Ending: Studies in the Theory of Fiction*. Oxford University Press, 1966.

Klinger, Leslie, ed. *The New Annotated H. P. Lovecraft*. W. W. Norton, 2014.

Kristeva, Julia. *Black Sun: Depression and Melancholia*. Trans. Leon S. Roudiez. Columbia University Press, 1989.

Lovecraft, H. P. "The Call of Cthulhu." *H. P. Lovecraft Collected Fiction, A Variorum Edition, Volume 2: 1926–1930*, edited by S. T. Joshi. New York: Hippocampus Press, 2017, pp. 21–55.

———. *Supernatural Horror in Fiction. Collected Essays Volume 2: Literary Criticism*, edited by S. T. Joshi. New York: Hippocampus Press, 2004, pp. 82–135.

———. "Nyarlathotep." *H. P. Lovecraft Collected Fiction, A Variorum Edition, Volume 1: 1905–1925*, edited by S. T. Joshi. New York: Hippocampus Press, 2017, pp. 202–205.

Morton, Timothy. *The Ecological Thought*. Harvard University Press, 2010.

———. *Hyperobjects: Philosophy and Ecology after the End of the World*. University of Minnesota Press, 2013.

States, Bert O. *Dreaming and Storytelling*. Cornell University Press, 1993.

Thacker, Eugene. *In the Dust of this Planet: Horror of Philosophy, Vol. 1*. Zero Books, 2011.

Trigg, Dylan. *The Thing: A Phenomenology of Horror*. Zero Books, 2014.

Walls, Jerry L. "Introduction." *The Oxford Handbook of Eschatology*. Oxford University Press, 2007. Web. http://doi.org/10.1093/oxfordhb/9780195170498.013.1

Wu, William F. *The Yellow Peril: Chinese Americans in American Fiction, 1850–1940*. Archon Books, 1982.

Zeller, Benjamin E. "Altar Call of Cthulhu: Religion and Millennialism in H. P. Lovecraft's Cthulhu Mythos." *Religions* 11.1 (2019): 18. *Crossref*. Web. doi: 10.3390/rel11010018.

Index

Page numbers followed by 'n' refers to notes numbers

abcanny 8, 188–189, 191, 193, 196–197
abhuman 188–189, 191–192, 196, 198
abject 150, 197, 254, 259, 275, 277, 304
abjection 259, 272
Abraham, Nicholas 72–74, 76–77
adaptation 3–4, 6, 12, 18, 19–25, 43, 46–52, 72, 74, 99, 111, 152, 162, 172, 186–187, 189, 214–215, 224n1, 227, 228–230, 232, 237, 269, 286
aesthetics 5, 31, 39, 210, 213–214
The Age of Lovecraft (2016) 3, 158, 253, 264n14, 306n3
Alfredo, A Tragedy (1918) 17
Alhazred, Abdul 13
Allen, Zadock 178
All God's Chillun Got Wings (1924) 15
Alt-right 84
Alves, Franciso 45
American Gothic 168, 254
Amnesia: The Dark Descent (2010) 225n5, 244
Anthropocene 2–3, 8, 11n2, 29, 158, 172, 174–175, 184n2
antidetective 132, 133–134, 136
anti-millennialism 298
anti-Pastoral 164, 166
Aragão, Rodrigo 53–54
Arkham House 44, 58, 61
artworks 103–111, 113–115, 225n4
"Astrophobos" (1918) 18
Atomic Robo and the Shadow from Beyond Time (2016) 96, 100
At the Mountains of Madness (1936) 10, 19, 24, 79, 103–105, 111, 244, 249, 276–277, 285, 288, 291–292
Baiestorf, Petter 49–50
The Ballad of Black Tom (2016) 8, 186–187, 189, 192, 198, 214
Bianchi, Dan 20
biographical approaches to Lovecraft 57–60, 63, 65, 71–72, 82, 86n1, 90, 92–93, 95
Bloodborne (2015) 9, 227–228, 230, 232–234, 237–238
Brazilian culture 6, 47
Brazilian horror cinema 6, 43–44, 46, 48, 54
Brown, Bruce 86n1, 99
Burrows, Jacen 7, 71–72, 84, 93–94

"The Call of Cthulhu" 7, 9–10, 22, 31–33, 37, 39, 39n3, 44, 47–48, 50, 103–104, 106–107, 111–112, 132–135, 140, 173, 177, 179, 182, 192, 214, 254, 255–259, 270, 285, 288–289, 291–292, 297
Call of Cthulhu (Role Playing Game) 12, 213–214, 219, 224n2
Call of Cthulhu (Focus Entertainment 2018) 214, 227, 232, 242
Call of Cthulhu, Dark Corners of the Earth (2005) 233, 242, 247
Campbell, Ramsey 17, 25n3, 62, 214
The Case of Charles Dexter Ward 21, 46, 90, 100
The Cats of Ulthar (2007) 21
The Cats of Ulthar (Section of *Lovecraft: Nightmare Suite* 2003, 2013) 21–22
Caws, Mary Ann 300–301
Chambers, Robert W. 17
chosen family 270, 278–279
Christensen, Carlos Hugo 46

Cinema Novo 46
cognitive dissonance 249
Cohen, Margaret 176
Coleridge, Samuel Taylor 176
colonialism 95, 261
"The Colour out of Space" 7–8, 18, 36–37, 40n11, 40n12, 118–119, 124, 126, 128–130, 130n3, 135, 145, 146–149, 153, 159, 165–167, 169, 204
comics 3, 6–7, 12, 59, 71–72, 74–82, 84–86, 86n1, 90, 97–98, 230, 237
Comics Studies 71
Conarium (2017) 242, 244–248, 250–251
contamination 119–130, 131n9, 144–147, 149–152, 164, 167–168, 180
"Cool Air" 21
A Cor que Caiu do Espaço [*The Colour out of Space*, 2016] 43, 49
Corman, Roger 46–47, 49, 54n9
correspondence, correspondents 6, 8, 58, 61–65, 67, 68n1, 68n5, 253, 265n23
cosmic horror 5, 7–8, 12, 28–35, 37–39, 103–106, 108–111, 113–114, 119, 130, 136, 143, 145, 153, 158–159, 215, 219, 222, 228, 264n18, 269, 285, 288, 302
cosmic indifferentism 30, 35, 202–203, 243, 274
cosmicism 8, 31, 35, 203, 210, 223, 287, 304
"The Courtyard" (2014) 74–75, 78–79, 81, 85, 93, 95
COVID-19 6, 10, 172, 174, 284
criminal, criminality 29–31, 35, 38, 187–189, 190–192, 196, 272
cryptomimesis 7, 72, 74, 83
Cthulhu 2–3, 9, 19–20, 22, 33–34, 37, 68n3, 85, 96, 98–99, 106–107, 109, 111–112, 132, 134–136, 138–140, 172, 177–179, 180–181, 183, 184n7, 184n8, 186, 198, 215, 227, 229, 254–258, 261–263, 264n17, 264n18, 265n24, 284, 289–293
Cthulhu (2007) [film] 277
Cthulhu Mythos 40n14, 62–63, 65, 71, 135–136, 140–141, 151–152, 186, 198, 208, 213–215, 222, 224n2, 254, 280n2
Cunha, Fausto 45
Cymbeline 12–13

"Dagon" 173, 177, 179–180, 182, 184n6, 233
dangerous knowledge 204, 208
Dawkins, David 23–24
de Camp, L. Sprague 60–62, 67
degeneration 122, 124–125, 162, 169, 187, 263n9, 291
Derie, Bobby 92, 95, 271, 277, 280n3, 280n4
Derleth, August 44, 58, 61, 116n1, 213, 247, 268, 280n2
Derrida, Jacques 73–74, 82–84, 154n8, 284–286
determinism 244, 251, 263n9
disempowerment 244, 250–251
"The Doom that Came to Sarnath" 21
Dórea, Gumercindo Rocha 44–45
downwind, downwinders 124–126, 129, 130n7
dread 9–10, 20, 23, 25, 30–31, 53, 113, 124–126, 127–129, 158, 166–167, 186, 194, 202, 207, 216–217, 233, 242, 244, 246, 250, 264n13, 291, 298
The Dream-Quest of Unknown Kadath 24, 108, 207, 233, 270
dreams 22, 31–32, 39n3, 47, 76–77, 86n3, 93, 152, 177, 181, 204, 232–233, 237, 256–258, 262–263, 264n17, 264n19, 272, 277, 287, 289–291, 292–293, 303
"The Dreams in the Witch House" 16, 20–21, 74–77
Dunsany, Lord, Dunsanian 14, 62, 82, 93, 138, 292
"The Dunwich Horror" 18, 79, 254, 270, 298

Echhardt, Jason C. 92–93
ecocriticism 57, 159, 165
ecoGothic 159, 166
ecohorror 166, 176
ecophobia 159–161
Edições GRD (GRD Editions) 44
eerie 32, 35, 122, 126, 138–139, 141, 246, 287, 289
Elder Things 106, 109, 113, 274, 276, 292
Ellis, Warren 95–96
epublishing 268

eschatology 10, 297, 301
Estrela Radiante [*Shining Star*, 2013] 43, 49
Ethics/Post-Anthropocentric Ethics/ Posthuman Ethics 144–145, 147–149, 150–151, 153, 270, 281n9
Eubank, William 8, 172–175, 179–180, 182–183, 184n7

Farnese, Harold S. 16, 19
feminist posthumanism 203
first person (narration) 10, 104, 112, 135, 204, 208, 301, 304
first person (gaming) 242–244, 251
Fisher, Mark 1, 130n1, 132, 134, 137, 159, 169, 243, 284, 286, 296
A Força dos Sentidos [*Force of the Senses*, 1978] 46–47
"From Beyond" 23, 143, 146
From Beyond (1986) 52

Gafford, Sam 92–93
Garret, Jean 46–48
gender 2, 9–10, 22, 24, 48, 202, 253, 256–257, 264n15, 269–271, 278–279, 281n11
Goodreads 268, 279, 281n12
Gorey, Edward 21
gothic 22, 35–36, 46–47, 159–160, 168, 214, 217–218, 237, 254, 258–259, 264n13
Great Old Ones 78, 97, 270, 274, 291
grotesque (the) 8, 36, 39n2, 51, 53, 107, 112, 121, 159, 162–165, 168, 172, 178–180, 269
Gurjan, George 44

Hamlet 13
Haraway, Donna 145, 150, 175
The Haunted Palace 46–47, 49, 54n8
hauntology, hauntological 10, 284–289, 292–293
Hawk, Jordan L. 9, 268–269
Hearthstone, Heroes of Warcraft 7, 103, 105, 108–110
Herald, Lovecraft & Tesla 98
"Herbert West, Reanimator" 18, 24
heteronormativity 8, 269, 274–276
homophobia 9, 202, 268–271, 274
homosociality 278–279
Horror (genre) 1, 12–13, 17, 20, 23, 25, 33, 36, 43–44, 46, 48–49, 51–54, 59, 67, 71, 74, 84, 86, 90, 92, 97, 103–105, 106–107, 111–112, 115, 152, 159, 161, 174, 176–178, 201–202, 205, 210, 211n2, 211n3, 213–215, 216–218, 222–223, 228, 231, 234, 237, 247, 255, 269, 271, 285, 287–288
"The Horror at Red Hook" 8, 79, 186, 189, 197, 216–218, 220–222, 224
The Horror in the Theater, An H. P. Lovecraft Triptych of Terror 21
"The Hound" 23
Howard Lovecraft and the Three Kingdoms 7, 99
H. P. Lovecraft, He Who Wrote in the Darkness 91–92, 97, 100
The H. P. Lovecraft Historical Society 19, 21
Hutcheon, Linda 4, 173–174, 215, 224n1, 227
Hyperobject(s) 2–3, 7, 11n1, 119, 130n2, 133, 136, 181, 184n8, 295–296, 306n2

Ibsen, Henrik 15
Illegible/illegibility 190–193
Impossible Worlds 237
Indie (videogames) 247
inhuman agency(s) 118, 120–123, 128–129, 130n4
In the Dust of this Planet (2011) 285, 287, 295, 306n1
irruption 97, 174, 177, 182–183, 248–251

Janicker, Rebecca 147–148, 165–166, 228–230, 245
Jimenez, Phil 95–96
Joshi, S. T. 25n2, 46, 49, 57, 60–61, 68n2, 68n7, 83, 86, 86n4, 87n5, 91–92, 143, 203, 214, 216, 219–220, 222–223, 244, 246, 299, 306n5

Kermode, Frank 297, 306n4
Khouri, Walter Hugo 46, 48
The King in Yellow 17, 37, 40n13
Kleiner, Reinhart 13, 17, 62, 253
Kneale, James 36, 59, 164, 228, 248
Kristeva, Julia 264n21, 305
Krzywinska, Tanya 4, 228, 233, 236, 242–244, 250–251
Kuhn, T. S. 132–133, 135, 139

landscape 29–30, 33–37, 40n11, 76, 78, 127, 148–149, 159–161, 162–165, 169, 189, 198, 292, 296
LaValle, Victor 8, 186, 214, 265n24
legible/legibility 187–190, 192, 197
Lenihan, Zack 21
London Horror Festival 23
Lovecraft Circle 59–61, 63, 68n6
Lovecraft, H. P. 1, 6, 28–29, 31, 33, 36, 45, 51, 79, 90, 92, 95, 138, 186, 213–214, 217, 238, 241, 244, 268, 296
Lovecraftian hero (bachelor-hero, victim-hero, adventure-hero) 195, 270, 277
Lovecraft revival 45
Lovecraft's Follies 18
Lovecraft, Winfield Scott 84–85
Ludic/ludology 228, 230, 237, 241–242, 244–246, 248
"The Lurking Fear" 8, 23, 159, 161–162, 164–166, 169, 222, 224

MacCormack, Patricia 144
Magic, The Gathering (MTG) (Wizards of the Coast) 7, 103, 105
Mariana Trench 174, 178
Mar Negro [*Black Sea*, 2013] 43
masculinity (hegemonic masculinity, non-cisgender-conforming, effeminacy, "spectacular masculinity") 9, 190, 243, 259, 270–272, 280n8
Mayer, Jed 144, 264n14
The Merchant of Venice 13
mesh 29, 38, 175
Mestres do Horror e da Fantasia 45
Miéville, China 151, 153, 191, 201, 264n14, 275
misogyny 8, 153, 202, 214, 276
m/m romance, male/male romance 10, 268–271, 273, 276, 278–279, 280n1, 280n5, 280n8, 281n11
Modernist 66, 79
Monster, monstrosity 2–3, 9, 33–35, 37–39, 50–53, 95–96, 98, 106, 111, 114, 147, 167, 173–174, 178–179, 184n5, 197–198, 213, 215, 217–219, 221–223, 228, 254, 256–257, 259, 261–262, 264n12, 270, 274–277, 279, 299
Monstrous Feminine 253
Moons of Madness 242, 249–251
Moore, Alan 7, 71, 75, 78, 84, 93, 100
Morton, Timothy 11n1, 29, 130n2, 139, 159, 175, 184n2, 295–296, 306n1, 306n3
"My Favorite Character" 90

Narrative 4, 7, 9, 12, 20, 22, 29–31, 33–35, 38, 46–47, 52, 60, 71, 74, 76–77, 79–82, 86, 86n3, 91–92, 104, 112, 114, 124, 133, 141, 159, 161–162, 164–166, 167–168, 172–173, 176, 178–179, 187–188, 190–191, 194–196, 197–198, 206, 217, 219–220, 222, 227, 229, 232–233, 242–244, 245–250, 254–256, 259, 263n9, 272–274, 276–277, 301–303, 304–305
Nature, nature 2–3, 8, 11n1, 16, 19, 29, 35, 37, 39, 40n11, 103, 105, 113, 137, 141, 142n2, 153, 158–160, 161–163, 165–167, 168–169, 172–174, 175–177, 181, 183, 191, 205, 223, 287, 297
Nautical Horror 8, 172, 176–178, 183
Neonomicon 7, 71–72, 75, 79, 81, 85, 93, 95
Neoreaction A Basilisk, Essays on or Around the Alt-Right 84–85
Nervo Craniano Zero [*Cranial Nerve Zero*, 2012] 43, 52
network 62, 64, 68n5, 68n7, 121, 149, 158, 162, 164, 172, 175, 183, 202, 204, 208–209, 278
New Weird 28, 186
Night Gaunts, An Entertainment Based on the Life and Work of H. P. Lovecraft 18, 24
nihilism 6, 10, 153, 284–285, 298
Nikolavitch, Alex 91
Nua por Dentro do Couro [*Naked Under the Leather*, 2014] 43, 49, 51
nuclear 7, 50–51, 118–120, 121, 124–125, 127–129, 130, 130n1, 130n2, 284
nuclear weird 7, 119–120, 124, 127, 129–130, 130n2, 131n9
"Nyarlathotep" 10, 21, 299–300, 302–304, 306n5

Olmstead, Robert 17, 178, 180–182, 296
Open Circle Theatre 20–21, 24

other, otherness Other 36, 85, 113–114, 143–145, 148–150, 151–153, 167–169, 187–191, 194, 196, 198, 204, 209, 216–218, 224, 233–234, 237, 260, 263n9, 273–274, 276, 299–300
other-than-human 159, 163, 169, 203, 210
Outer Gods 108, 274
"The Outsider" 18, 21, 39n5, 94, 101n2, 280n7

paradigm 7, 132, 135–137, 139–142, 190, 271, 298
paranormal romance 273
pastoral 160, 164–166, 169, 248
People of color 201–203, 206–207, 210, 211n3, 254, 260, 264n14, 265n24
Pessimism 10, 220, 284–285, 293
Petley, Julian 228–229, 232
Philips, Whipple Van Buren 83–84
"Pickman's Model" 7, 18, 21, 24, 39n5, 103–104, 106, 112–113, 296
"The Picture in the House" 21
Planetary/The Authority, Ruling the World 95–97, 100
Plant Horror 167
Podesta, Renzo 99
Poe, Edgar Allan 46, 48, 176, 189, 247
police, policing, policeman, policemen 23, 30, 35, 39n7, 78, 187–198, 258, 265n24, 270, 291
posthumanism 8, 28, 85, 143–145, 147, 150–151, 153, 154n1, 202–203, 253
prejudice 6, 65, 68n2
prose poem 10, 300–301
Providence 7, 71–72, 75, 76–86, 86n2, 86n3, 86n4, 87n5, 93–95, 99–100

queer family 270, 279
queer, queerness, queering, queer world-making 204–205, 254–256, 257–259, 260–262, 263, 264n15, 265n24, 268–270, 271–273, 274–276, 277–279, 280n1, 280n3, 280n7, 281n9, 281n11
queer shame 276, 281n9
queer subjectivity 271, 274–276

race, racism, racist 2, 6, 8, 15, 19, 29, 36, 40n10, 43, 48, 50, 53, 62, 65, 71–72, 82–85, 86n4, 93–95, 97, 101n3, 151–153, 161, 186–188, 189–191, 192–194, 195–197, 198–199, 201–203, 206, 209, 213–215, 216, 218, 223, 249, 253–255, 257, 259–261, 263n9, 264n14, 265n24, 269, 275–276, 278, 291, 300–301, 305
radiation, radioactive 50, 118–119, 120–129, 130n2
Radiotheatre Series 19, 21
Randolph Carter 17, 97, 233, 270
"The Rats in the Walls" 18–19, 73, 86n4, 218, 221
Real Person Fiction (RFP) 71–72, 86n2
Real, the 33, 37–38, 105, 202, 236, 249
Reanimator, The Musical 21, 24–25
Reilly, John 98
Remediation 59, 245
"The Repairer of Reputations" 80
"The Rhyme of the Ancient Mariner" 176
Richard II 13
Romantic Gothic 159
Rouse, Richard III 223, 228, 231–232
Rust, Stephen A. 176
Rutherford, Brett 18

Sandifer, Elizabeth 72, 85
Schevill, James 18
science fiction 12, 45, 50, 68n3, 84, 97, 100, 118, 250, 254, 264n13
Sederholm, Carl H. 3, 10, 28, 49, 65, 151–152, 158, 202, 204, 228–230, 253, 264n14, 306n3
Sedgwick, Eve 264n15, 271
Selected Letters 6, 59, 69
Sevilha, Fabiana 49
Sexism 6, 202, 269
Sexuality 9–10, 209, 253–254, 257, 259, 264n15, 269–271, 272, 281n11
"The Shadow Over Innsmouth" 20–21, 24, 39n7, 47, 65, 116n1, 135–136, 173, 177–178, 180–181, 184n6, 209, 246, 277, 296, 298
Shakespeare, William 12–15, 17, 59
Shaw, George Bernard 15
Shea, J. Vernon 1, 83

The Shell and the Kernel 72
Sherman, Charley 20
Shoggoths 108, 275, 292–293
"The Shunned House" 8, 18, 21, 146, 148–149, 152, 154n7, 159, 167, 169, 198, 217–218
Simmons, David 9, 71–72, 86n1, 86n2, 90, 100, 151, 206
social reality 46, 54, 193
Soles, Carter 176
Some Notes on a Nonentity, The Life of H. P. Lovecraft 92, 100
Southern Gothic 29–31, 39n2
space (virtual) 241, 243, 246, 251
spectrality 36, 286, 290–293
"The Statement of Randolph Carter" 21–22
Storytelling 81, 221, 228, 231, 233, 248
Storyworlds 227–228
The Strange Adventures of H. P. Lovecraft 7, 86n1, 98
Strange Interlude 15
Supernatural Horror in Literature 10, 17, 66, 103, 160, 216, 303
survival horror 243, 247

tentacular thinking 175
terror 9, 31, 93, 135, 186, 202, 209, 228–229, 231, 233–234, 236, 238, 242, 275, 279
Thacker, Eugene 2, 28–29, 176, 284–285, 287–288, 293, 295–296
"The Thing on the Doorstep" 18, 21, 46
1001 Arabian Nights 13
Thurston, Francis Wayland 22, 104, 112, 133, 135, 177, 179–180, 182, 254–257, 260, 262–263, 264n17, 289–291
Tidwell, Christy 176
Torok, Maria 72, 74, 76
trans identity 279
Transsexual 254
True Detective 6, 29–31, 34–38, 40n10, 40n14, 40n15

Unbound Productions / Wicket Lit 21–22
Underwater (2020) 8, 172–76, 178, 180–183, 184n7
"The Unnamable" 23
Unthinkable 28–29, 138, 288, 290–291, 295–296

The Vanishing of Ethan Carter 242, 247–248
video games 4–5, 8–9, 12, 99, 187, 213–214, 219, 227–228, 230–231, 234, 237–238
virus/viral 8, 144–145, 147–148, 151–152, 154n3, 154n6, 172, 174, 183
Visceral Theatre Company 21

walking simulator 241–244, 247–251
waste 7, 119, 124, 126–129, 131n8
Weimer, Christopher B. 280n1
Weinstock, Jeffrey Andrew 3, 28, 49, 65, 151, 158, 186, 201–202, 204, 228–230, 253, 264n14, 306n3
Weird Tales 44, 59, 62, 130n1, 143
weird, weird fiction, weird story, weird tale, *weirding* 4, 6–7, 9, 11, 11n2, 12, 14, 16, 25, 29–30, 32, 35, 38, 58, 63, 65–67, 71, 76, 81–82, 115, 119–120, 123–124, 127, 129, 132–135, 138–141, 146, 153, 158–160, 161–162, 164, 166, 169, 186–189, 191, 194–195, 198–199, 201, 213, 216–217, 224, 230, 243, 248, 250, 253–254, 264n13, 268, 271, 277, 280, 280n1, 281n11, 285, 287, 293, 296, 298, 301, 303, 305
white male heroes 254, 262
Whyborn and Griffin 9, 269–271, 274, 280n1
Wilde, Oscar 15, 268
Wilderness 37–38, 160–162, 163–164, 166, 169, 174
Willer, Claudio 45
Wiswell, T. L. 22, 24–25
women of color 8, 201–203, 207–208, 210
A Mulher do Desejo-A Casa das Sombras [*The Woman of Desire-The House of Shadows*, 1975] 46–47

xenophobia 65, 68n2, 71–72, 145, 151, 161, 253–254, 279

Zeller, Benjamin E. 297–298, 306n3
Zombie Joe's Underground 21–22

Taylor & Francis Group
an informa business

Taylor & Francis eBooks

www.taylorfrancis.com

A single destination for eBooks from Taylor & Francis with increased functionality and an improved user experience to meet the needs of our customers.

90,000+ eBooks of award-winning academic content in Humanities, Social Science, Science, Technology, Engineering, and Medical written by a global network of editors and authors.

TAYLOR & FRANCIS EBOOKS OFFERS:

- A streamlined experience for our library customers
- A single point of discovery for all of our eBook content
- Improved search and discovery of content at both book and chapter level

REQUEST A FREE TRIAL

support@taylorfrancis.com

Routledge
Taylor & Francis Group

CRC Press
Taylor & Francis Group

Made in the USA
Las Vegas, NV
29 October 2024

284283de-81bf-4376-9cf6-32f1b72444d9R01